# A DREAM
# of DARING

## GEN LAGRECA

*To Cassandra,*
*all the best,*

*Gen La Greca*

Winged Victory Press, Chicago
www.wingedvictorypress.com

Available in ebook and print formats from Amazon and other booksellers.

*A Dream of Daring*
ISBN paperback: 978-0-97445796-3
Library of Congress Control Number: 2012952967

Published by Winged Victory Press
www.wingedvictorypress.com

Cover by Elizabeth Watson, graphic designer
emwatson@earthlink.net

Clothing on the cover courtesy of the Gentleman's Emporium
www.gentlemansemporium.com

Edited by Katharine O'Moore-Klopf of KOK Edit
www.kokedit.com

Printed in the United States of America
First edition 2013

Quality discounts are available for bulk purchases of this book. For information, please contact Winged Victory Press.
Email: service@wingedvictorypress.com

Also available in hardcover, paperback, and ebook editions
**NOBLE VISION**
a novel by Gen LaGreca

# ADVANCE PRAISE FOR *A DREAM OF DARING*

"I thoroughly enjoyed the plot twists and turns, the passionate inter-racial romance, the delicious rebellion against convention, and the challenge to subjugation of all kinds."
—Marsha Familaro Enright, President, Reason, Individualism and Freedom Institute

"Grab your seat for a tumbling ride back to the high-stakes, hoop-flying, tumultuous time when cotton was king. Gen LaGreca takes you for a jaunt in her carriage through fields of fragrant words, luscious descriptions, and panoramic views. Hang on as the road gets bumpy, with zesty characters stirring up the dirt and sudden plot twists swerving you onto uncharted paths. Wait, the hooves have left the ground and you're airborne till the end. You'll come back excited, enchanted, and enlightened."
—Barry Farber, host of *The Barry Farber Show* and author of *Cocktails with Molotov*

"This is a heroic and inspiring novel that's also packed with rich insights, lessons—and warnings—for today. It is a highly potent cocktail of psychology, philosophy, and politics with a generous pour of economic history, not to mention romance, violence, and money shaken into the mix."
—John Blundell, author of *Margaret Thatcher: A Portrait of the Iron Lady* and *Ladies for Liberty: Women Who Made a Difference in American History*

# PRAISE FOR THE AUTHOR'S FIRST NOVEL, *NOBLE VISION*

"The novel deals with some of the most serious issues of the day, lending the story an immediacy and vibrancy. The author's prose is polished and professional."
—*Writer's Digest* magazine

". . . A well-researched . . . sensitively written . . . inherently captivating novel of suspense, *Noble Vision* is very highly recommended reading."
—*Midwest Book Review*

"This is a beautifully written book! . . . For a first novel, this is a marvelous achievement."
—Midwest Book Awards

"The mounting conflicts of this lovingly sculpted first novel will keep you turning pages late into the night."
—Laissez Faire Books

# AWARDS FOR *NOBLE VISION*

*ForeWord* Magazine
Book of the Year Finalist in General Fiction

*Writer's Digest* 13th Annual International Book Awards
Honorable Mention in Mainstream Fiction

Midwest Book Awards
Finalist in General Fiction

Illinois Women's Press Association Fiction Contest
Second Place

# ACKNOWLEDGMENTS

The research for this novel began as a daunting task but became one of the most exciting intellectual adventures I've ever had. The books, websites, and institutions that made every aspect of the antebellum period and the early industrial age come alive for me are too numerous to list. I'll settle for mentioning just a few noteworthy moments in my study.

In Dearborn, Michigan, the kind people at the Henry Ford Museum and Greenfield Village were most helpful. At Louisiana State University's Hill Memorial Library, I will always remember holding in my white-gloved hands the crisp pages of the actual plantation journals of a cotton planter in the 1850s. I was also aided by the rich array of artifacts and documents, as well as the friendly, knowledgeable staffs at the Cabildo, the Historic New Orleans Collection, the Rural Life Museum, and the various Louisiana plantations that are preserving history—the Cottage, Rosedown, Butler Greenwood, Oakley, Frogmore, Laura, and others. I'm especially grateful to Helen Williams, the director of the West Feliciana Historical Society Museum, for patiently answering my questions and directing me to many useful resources.

The following people read the manuscript and offered valuable suggestions: Steve Radow, James Peron, Bradley Norwood, Marsha Enright, and Sara Pentz. My superb editor, Katharine O'Moore-Klopf of KOK Edit, was indispensable in giving the manuscript its final polish.

My enduring gratitude goes to Edith Packer for being the first person to suggest to me that I could—and should—write fiction. It has since become the passion of my life.

The Meddler
But do you dream of daring—

Cyrano
I do dream of daring . . .

From Act 1
*Cyrano de Bergerac*
Edmond Rostand

# CHAPTER 1

Thomas Edmunton was out of step with the world around him.

He sat in an open carriage, observing the fields just off the road. In his mind he was upturning the dormant winter soil and cultivating the land in ways never before imagined. His body tensed with a nervous energy, as if he were ready to jump out of the carriage and prepare the earth for a spring unlike any other. There were new methods to explore, discoveries to make, changes to transform this countryside . . . and the world. The vision of what could be—and one day *would* be—didn't give him a moment's peace.

But his tailcoat and top hat told of a different purpose that would occupy him that early February afternoon. Instead of farming the dual fertile fields of the land and his imagination, he was in a caravan of coaches climbing up a hill on a plantation to a funeral for its mistress, Polly Barnwell.

Tom saw the big house of the Crossroads Plantation shrinking in the distance as the horses trotted past an iron gate and into a clearing. When the carriage stopped, he jumped out to assist the two women traveling with him. He extended his hand to help Charlotte Barnwell descend. Then he turned to her daughter, Rachel. Before the young beauty could step down of her own accord, Tom placed his hands around her tiny waist, swung her through the air, and planted her on the ground with the lighthearted air of lifting a ballerina in a dance. The gesture seemed incongruous with the women's voluminous black dresses and long veils, the funeral attire of Louisiana's gentry in 1859.

"Why, Tom, you have the wildest eyes," said Rachel.

He had reason to have wild eyes, he thought, but he mustn't think about that now.

"It's downright indecent to look so happy at a funeral!" she whispered.

1

He realized he was smiling, almost laughing, and quickly subdued his expression. He kissed her hand and explained simply, if not completely. "I couldn't help but notice how lovely you look."

"Be mindful of the occasion, Mr. Edmunton."

Rachel lowered her head and peered up at him in the gently reproachful way that he knew well. Despite her protest, the red-haired belle he was courting smiled at his attentions. As his hand lingered on hers, their eyes locked. But her smile faded to disappointment when he suddenly dropped her hand and his attention moved to an older man approaching them. The man raised his arms to embrace Rachel.

"Hello, darlin'," said Senator Wiley Barnwell to his daughter.

Rachel kissed her father's cheek.

The senator then bowed to his wife in greeting. "Charlotte, my dear."

"Hello, Wiley." Mrs. Barnwell smiled at her husband. She was a woman whose age was difficult to guess. Her face made her look younger, while her clothing added to her forty-five years. She possessed the same smooth skin and vibrant red hair as her twenty-one-year-old daughter. But her dress, cut high to her chin, and her braid, coiled at the back of her neck like a snake ready to bite anyone who might dare unravel it, weren't only for mourning. They were typical of her normal style. "Did you take care of the things you came here to do for the sale, Wiley?" she asked her husband.

"Yes, dear. In fact, I took care of *more* than I'd hoped to."

Tom knew the senator had inherited the Crossroads and was here reviewing the plantation records with an eye to selling the place, but the pointed way in which Barnwell looked at his wife seemed to imply something more.

"My boy," the senator said, turning to Tom, "I want to thank you for accompanying the women, so I could come earlier and tend to a few matters."

"My pleasure, Senator." Tom bowed his head to Greenbriar's most distinguished citizen.

The senator's pale complexion and thinning white hair suggested a mellowness of age beyond his fifty-five years. But his eyebrows remained dark, bushy, and arching, as if warning the world that he was still strong-willed—even intimidating—when the moment called for it. His tall, solid build enhanced his air of authority. He looked like the town elder that he was.

"Senator, please forgive me for asking at a time like this, but did you—"

"Now, don't worry, Tom," Barnwell said kindly. "I got it here just fine. I took right good care of it."

"Golly, Tom, I thought you might be thinking about something else at Aunt Polly's funeral." Rachel pouted.

Tom was undeterred. "If I may ask, sir, where is it?"

The senator pointed through the trees to the big house and its dependencies down the hill. "It's in the old carriage house. Safe as anything could ever be."

Wiley Barnwell gave Tom a reassuring look, then extended his curved arm to his wife. Charlotte hooked her black-gloved hand through it, and the couple walked to the ceremony. In like fashion, Tom escorted Rachel across the grassy field drilled with headstones that was the Barnwell family cemetery.

Tom walked handsome and soldier-tall in his formal clothes, with a poise and self-confidence beyond his twenty-six years. Only his face revealed his youth in the open, innocent way he looked at people, as if he expected the world to be as forthright with him as he was with it. His blond hair and blue eyes reflected the Irish-English lineage of his ancestors, who had arrived in Louisiana sixty years ago to obtain a land grant from the Spanish colonial government and, in time, to amass three thousand acres of wilderness on the east bank of the great Mississippi River north of Baton Rouge, transforming it into one of the richest cotton plantations in the country. A fire in Tom's eyes and a tenseness in his body gave a vitality to his figure even when he was at rest.

He glanced at Rachel on his arm as she greeted some of the guests. Her ivory skin and red hair provided a bright contrast to the black mourning bonnet framing her face. Her comely features—the pursed lips, the small pointed nose, and the crystal blue eyes—reminded Tom of the serene beauties he had seen in paintings. He liked the contrast between the pristine, classical beauty to be gazed at from afar and the sensuous creature she could be in his arms.

Another eligible planter in the group was intrigued with Rachel Barnwell. Nash Nottingham, twenty-eight, walked toward the couple. His lackluster brown hair and eyes were like a sedative offered after a bracing dose of Tom's brilliant gold hair and flaming blue eyes. Nash gave a brief nod to Tom, then planted a protracted kiss on Rachel's hand.

"My, what a beautiful ring!" Rachel gaped at a large sapphire on Nash's finger.

"Oh, that? Just a trinket from André Benoir in Paris."

"How lovely to shop at such an exclusive place."

While the two chatted, Tom noted the showy gold carvings on Nash's walking cane and the large diamonds on his watch fob, also likely purchased on one of the wearer's frequent trips to Paris. These objects possessed a brilliance that the owner's face lacked. The fashion statement that was Nash Nottingham left Tom with a vivid memory of what the man wore, rather than of what he said or did. The hopeful planter followed Rachel as she walked with Tom. When the couple stopped at the black crescent of guests gathered before a closed casket, Nash positioned himself on Rachel's other side.

The preacher placed his notes on a podium. His simple black suit and string tie were humble compared with the finery of Greenbriar's most affluent citizens.

Carriages tended by black coachmen formed a caravan against the stone walls of the cemetery. On the sidelines the slaves from the Crossroads Plantation clustered in a large group; they had been given time off from their tasks to say farewell to their mistress. Tom noticed a white face among them, a stocky man with suspicious eyes, a short tangle of hair, and a frown that seemed to be his natural expression. His frontiersman's coat of buckskin with long fringes set him apart from both the aristocrats and the bondsmen. He appeared to belong to neither camp, thought Tom, figuring he must be Bret Markham, the overseer, whom he had heard the senator praise for his work at the Crossroads. But something about the man made Tom uneasy as his eyes stopped on the bulges under Markham's coat made by the whip and gun that he had brought to the funeral.

In the custom of the gentry, Polly Barnwell's body lay in a body-shaped cast-iron casket, adorned with a wreath of wrought iron to symbolize permanence. A hole had been dug for the coffin in front of a white marble tombstone. The statue carved for Polly's grave site was of a little girl holding a flower basket, commemorating the deceased's well-known love for children. This love, the townspeople had often said, was intensified by the untimely death of her husband, Henry Barnwell, twenty-four years earlier, too soon in the marriage for Polly to have borne her own offspring.

Tom restlessly turned to Senator Barnwell, standing behind him. "Excuse me, sir, but could you tell me where the old carriage house is?"

"Tom! How could you?" whispered Rachel. "The pastor's about to begin!"

Nash looked pleased at her reproach.

But the senator smiled patiently. "I forgot, my boy. You've never been here before, have you? It's the red building with the white door. That's where I put it." He pointed down the hill. "See?"

Through the tangle of oak branches on the hillside, Tom saw the sprawling big house and a cluster of smaller structures around it. His eyes stopped on the building Barnwell described.

"I see it, yes. Thank you, sir, for taking good care of it," Tom whispered.

Rachel poked him as the pastor began the service.

"My dear brethren, let us live a life of honor and fear not our final day of reckoning," said the clergyman. "And let us honor Polly Barnwell, who lived such a blessed life and to whom we must now bid farewell."

As the pastor recited a local version of an ancient prayer, Tom seemed unaware of the lowered heads around him. His head was raised, his face filled with hope.

*Lord, make me an instrument to sow good.*
*Where there is despair, let me sow hope;*
*Where there is darkness, let me sow light;*
*Where there is sadness, let me sow joy.*

*Lord, make me an instrument to sow good.*
*Where there is ignorance, let me sow wisdom;*
*Where there is strife, let me sow calm;*
*Where there is death, let me sow life.*

The words seemed to hold a special meaning for Tom. His eyes again traveled through the trees to the red building with the white door. Was the latch closed tightly? Was the item inside safely out of sight of any curious glances? What would *he* sow with it? he wondered, as Wylie Barnwell took the podium to give the eulogy.

Greenbriar's state senator and prosperous planter walked imperially. With a rich baritone voice that matched his imposing presence, he gave a moving account of Polly's kind and generous nature. He described how his sister-in-law's slaves loved her and cared for her during her long illness and ultimate passing from consumption. Tom noticed many of Polly's slaves weeping, giving truth to the senator's words. He also heard the hushed sounds of Rachel and her mother crying near him.

"My brother would have been proud to know that after his untimely death, his young wife confidently seized the reins of the plantation he had recently purchased. With not the firm hand of a man but the gentle touch of her gender, she worked the rich soil on the bluffs, the great gift from the silt deposits of the mighty Mississippi, to produce some of the finest cotton crops in the country—and the world. Now, twenty-four years later, the Crossroads Plantation that she so lovingly tended is her gift to pass on to a new owner."

The heir to the plantation looked directly at Ted Cooper, a prominent planter in the area. Tom knew that the senator hoped Cooper would purchase the place. At a youthful fifty, Cooper stood out in the crowd. He had the sun-bleached hair, lean frame, and ruddy complexion of a planter still active at his work and looking for new opportunities. With sharply intelligent brown eyes and a shrewd half-smile, he subtly nodded at Barnwell in response.

Tom noticed that Bret Markham was also looking at Cooper. The overseer appeared uneasy, as if he himself were at a crossroads, with his fate hanging on a new owner's pleasure.

Tom's thoughts again wandered down the hill: Was *he* at a crossroads too? he wondered.

The preacher ended the ceremony with the same thought he had used to start it: "Remember, my brethren, what you do today, you are judged by in eternity. Live a life of honor and fear not your final day of reckoning."

Tom wondered if he would reach the reckoning he sought: recognition and reward for his work on a dream that was the reason he lived. He so keenly yearned for such a day that he was unaware of the evasive eyes and lowered faces of others who heard the preacher's words, planters who shot somber glances at the slaves.

Four field hands gently lowered the casket into the ground. The guests gathered flowers that had been brought there and placed on a nearby table, and then they filed past the grave and dropped the blooms on the casket in a final farewell.

Rachel didn't throw all of her flowers on her aunt's coffin. She kept a few and offered some of them to her mother. "For Leanna," she said.

Charlotte shook her head. "You go ahead, dear. I'll wait for you in the carriage. The air here makes me ill."

Tom accompanied Rachel to the smallest headstone in the burial grounds. It was sculpted in the form of a winged baby kneeling with her head bent and her hands covering her face. The cherub seemed to be crying at a sad turn of fate. When Rachel placed her flowers at the statue's feet, Tom read the inscription on the stone: *Leanna. Stillborn daughter of Charlotte and Wiley Barnwell.*

"Is this the sister you told me about?" Tom asked softly.

"That's Leanna." She nodded sadly. "I often wondered what it would've been like if she had lived. It got frightfully lonely for me growing up here." She glanced at the countryside, where the plantations carved out of it were often a mile or more apart. Tom looked sympathetically at Charlotte and Wiley's only surviving child. "I had a doll I called Sis, and I would laugh with her and whisper secrets in her ear." She smiled at the recollection. "Leanna was only two years younger. If she had lived, I just know we would've been the best of friends."

Rachel bowed her head wistfully before the little angel. Tom put a comforting arm around her shoulder.

\* \* \* \* \*

The sun hung low amid the gangly oaks when guests gathered outside the big house for refreshments after the ceremony. The house stood high on a bluff outside the town of Greenbriar. A few simple planks for the entrance steps, a cypress gallery wrapping around paneled doors and windows, and a dormered roof displayed the home's modest beginnings as an English cottage. The train-like additions to the structure, the lacy wrought-iron railings, and the marble statuary around a formal front garden reflected the prosperity that the little cottage had realized through the years.

The silverware and china bore the flowery initials—*PB*—of the plantation's deceased mistress. The reception, with generous trays of food and fine spirits that were circulated among well-dressed guests who spoke in subdued voices, was a study in elegance and refinement. On the other side of the hill, out of view, were the slaves' cabins.

As life has a way of indomitably asserting itself, conversations turned from memories of the deceased to affairs of the living. Sipping punch with Rachel, her mother, and a few powdery-faced matrons with rosy cheeks, Tom looked distracted as they talked about their gardens and households.

When he felt he had conversed long enough to be courteous, he put down his punch cup and excused himself. Rachel looked disappointed as he walked away. He was heading toward the place dominating his thoughts, the old carriage house, when he heard his name called.

"Say, Tom." It was Wiley Barnwell, leaning over the gallery. "Come here, my boy."

Tom smiled, trying to hide his impatience at having his departure delayed. In two strides, he climbed the six steps to the veranda, where the senator stood with Nash Nottingham and Ted Cooper under a cloud of cigar smoke. Tom nodded in greeting to the men.

"Have you heard about Royal Cluster, the new seed that Millbank in Woodville is selling?" Barnwell asked Tom.

"The one mentioned in the *Cotton Almanac*?"

"That one, indeed. Royal Cluster's supposed to come off the boll easier than Sugar Loaf or Brown's Prolific."

"It's worth trying," said Tom.

"Got myself ten bushels, and while I was at it, ordered five for you."

"That's very nice of you, Senator. How much do I owe you?"

"Nothing at all, my boy. It's a gift to the son of my best friend." He put a hand over his heart. "May he rest in peace."

"Why, thank you. That's very kind of you, sir."

"'Twasn't easy for you, coming back here after the colonel's passing," said Barnwell. "You did a mighty fine job."

Tom felt pleased too with the job he had done in the past eighteen months since his father's death.

Greenbriar's scorching summers made possible the heaven-white cotton that gave planters their fortunes, but the torrid climate also brought hellish diseases that made death a palpable presence in every household. With Tom's mother and only sibling, a brother, snatched from him years ago by yellow fever, and with his father the more recent prey of typhoid, Tom became the sole heir to the two properties of Colonel Peter Edmunton. One was Indigo Springs, the family's cotton plantation with more than one hundred slaves. The other was the Edmunton Bank, a private concern in the seamy port town of Bayou Redbird, just down the bluff from Greenbriar. Tom's father had found a business opportunity in the place where the sprawling bayou met the great Mississippi River. There crops were hauled in steamboats to New Orleans for shipment to mills in New England and Europe. Ship after ship stacked thirty feet high with cotton bales brought high finance to the port town and its local bank, so Tom's father had done well. But Tom's interests lay elsewhere.

After heading to Philadelphia for school at the age of fourteen, then remaining to live and work there, Tom remembered how reluctant he had been to return home when his father died. Now, after eighteen months, two demanding cotton harvests, untold sleepless nights spent learning the intricacies of banking and farming, much faltering, and constant exhausting work, he felt pleased with the results. The plantation and bank were doing well, and he was able to resume work on an endeavor that consumed him, a project he had begun in Philadelphia and taken home with him and whose outcome now stood in a small building behind the big house. He looked out at the lush landscape of his childhood with the pride of someone who had found a challenge beyond the countryside and met it.

He smiled at the seasoned planter who had mentored him like a son. "You've been very helpful, Senator. I'm much obliged. I'll try the new seed on ten acres of my richest soil."

"Wiley, I do believe you rescued this boy from the Yankees," said Cooper.

Barnwell laughed, puffing a fresh smoke ring into the air. "I reckon he's now a fine planter." Barnwell slapped Tom on the back. "A hard worker. And smart too!"

Tom inclined his head in gratitude.

"Yup, Tom's gonna do well here, growin' cotton and runnin' our bank. He'll make a good *family* man too."

Tom wondered how many more ways the senator could show encouragement of his courtship of Rachel.

His rival apparently got the same impression, because Nash Nottingham frowned, his cigar pausing in midmotion toward his mouth. "Maybe one day Tom'll even stop soundin' like a Yankee and talk like us again," he drawled.

After a dozen years in the North, Tom had lost all trace of his Southern accent.

"And what about *you?*" Barnwell turned to Nash as if just noticing him. "Are you fixing to try the new seed too? And maybe plowing and composting this year with some vigor? Your father, rest his soul, would be shocked to see you depletin' his soil almost as fast as you're depletin' his money."

Nash bristled at the upbraid; then, like a cunning salesman responding to a skeptic, he raised his head higher and spoke louder. "I like to leave the particulars to the overseer, Senator. And with all due respect, sir, I'm fixing to raise a mighty good crop this year, as I believe you will see."

Cooper pointed to one of the fields partly visible through the oaks. "I could try the new seed on that fresh-tilled land out there." He looked at Barnwell. "That is, if we come to an agreement."

"Tom," said Barnwell, "Ted here is interested in expanding his holdings."

"The Crossroads could be a fine addition to the land I have now," said Cooper. "I say a man can never have too many fields to sow or too much money to reap. And I intend to reap a harvest fit for the good Lord himself."

"Fit for the devil, I'd say!" quipped Barnwell. "The Crossroads, added to your other holdings, would give you enough cotton-growin' land to clothe a small country!"

"Unlike virtue, an excess of money never reaches the point of pain. The more you have, the better it feels." Cooper grinned. He had the swagger of many men who had acquired heady fortunes from the fertile banks of the Mississippi at the peak of cotton's reign.

"Cooper would sell his own mother for a sack of gold," said Barnwell.

"Not just gold. Silver'd do too," replied Cooper.

Barnwell laughed heartily, then turned to Tom.

"Ted will need a little cash to make improvements. You know, get the Crossroads running just like he wants. I suggested we talk to you."

Although the New Orleans cotton factors—the brokers who sold the planters' crops to the manufacturing markets in the Northeast and Europe—often advanced money or supplies to their clients during the growing season, the Edmunton Bank also made loans to planters, as well as to shopkeepers, yeoman farmers, and other enterprising townspeople. Through the years, Colonel Edmunton had nurtured the local planters' business, developing a solid relationship with them.

"Your daddy and I did business many times," said Cooper. "He gave me good terms, and I must say, he always bet on a winner in me."

Tom considered the matter. "I'm sure we can discuss that. The land here would make excellent collateral for a loan."

"Why no," said Cooper, "this land, like all my properties, would be mortgaged to the hilt. How do you think I expand, boy?"

"Oh? Well, then you can certainly feel free to use your securities to cover the loan, Mr. Cooper."

"That's Yankee talk," said Cooper, sweeping his hand to dismiss the notion. "Here we keep our money in slaves. I've got plenty of them to put up."

Tom studied him for a long moment. "I'm afraid I don't accept people as collateral."

His words stunned the other men into an awkward silence.

Finally Cooper replied. "I didn't say *people*; I said *slaves*."

"And I said what I said."

"And you're fixing to do business here?" pressed Cooper.

"I *am* doing business here."

Cooper glared at Tom, pointing two cigar-holding fingers in the younger man's face. "Listen, boy, your daddy made loans like I'm proposing many times. Many, *many* times."

"But my father isn't here, Mr. Cooper. I am."

Barnwell broke the sudden tension in the air with a friendly laugh. "You might allow me to teach you something about the banking business too, Tom," he said with fatherly affection. "You've been gone so long that those Yankees got to you. But you learn quick. We'll discuss the matter when you get back from your travels."

"I declare, it seems you just got here. Going away already?" Nash looked hopeful.

"Only for a few weeks," Tom replied pointedly, as if to dash any romantic designs his rival might entertain in his absence.

"Tom's headed to the North," added Barnwell.

"It escapes me how anyone would want to go where the weather's cold, the folks are nasty, and the factories are smelly." Nash turned to Tom. "Can't stay away, can you?"

"Tom's got something he's bringing to Philadelphia," said Barnwell. "To a contest. That so, boy?"

"Yes."

"In fact, the thing happens to be right here at the Crossroads," Barnwell explained. "Tom was fixing to take his trip today, but when he told us he wouldn't be able to attend the funeral, and Rachel looked so gloomy, I suggested we bring it here, so he could attend the service, then board a steamer with it first thing tomorrow and get to Philadelphia in time for his engagement."

Tom was grateful to the senator for his suggestion. To please Rachel, he had arranged to postpone his departure until after the funeral. Since the Crossroads was only three miles from the steamboat docks, whereas his plantation was an additional four miles away, he had agreed to bring his cargo here, then continue down to Bayou Redbird with it in the morning.

"What exactly *is* this thing?" asked Cooper.

Tom hesitated.

"I hauled it here with me so Tom could spend some time patching things up with Rachel in the carriage, but I don't know much about it. I'm mighty curious," Barnwell said, hinting.

"Actually, I hadn't planned to say much about it yet, Senator."

"Oh, come now, Tom," Barnwell continued jovially, "if things go as you're hoping, you'll need customers, won't you?"

Tom considered the matter.

"You might be looking at your first prospects right here. And if we like it, why, we'll tell everybody else up and down the Mississippi and bring you a whole mess o' business."

Tom smiled, grateful that the senator wanted to help him. He told himself that such assistance from a prominent man should be encouraged.

"Okay, gentlemen, I'll show it to you, if you're interested."

"It's in the old carriage house." Barnwell extinguished his cigar in an ashtray. "Let's go."

The men walked the dirt path toward the back of the house. While Barnwell and Cooper moved ahead, discussing the sale of the Crossroads, Nash took Tom aside.

"Say, old boy." Nash laughed nervously. "I've been meaning to talk to you about the . . . uh . . . note that's due."

"You mean *past* due."

"Well . . . all right. It's a tad late. With you going away, I hope you won't have that nasty George Jones press me on it." Jones was Tom's bank manager.

Nash waited, but the young banker didn't reply.

"Look, Tom, I can't quite pay the loan back now. Nothing serious. I had a bad year . . . couple of bad years. That's all."

"When the rest of us had good years?" Tom asked curiously, without reproach, trying to understand the man before him who seemed so different from himself.

"I was hoping you could give me more time. And perhaps," he added tentatively, "you could extend just a little more."

Tom offered two raised eyebrows in response. He surveyed the sartorial splendor that was Nash Nottingham, from the beaver top hat to the shirt with the gemstone buttons to the shiny leather boots, all looking new and costly.

Reading Tom's thoughts, Nash laughed. "Like my outfit? After all, a man's got to buy himself a few decent threads."

"Is that what you were doing in Paris when you missed the due date on the note?"

"I might've traveled and shopped, and neglected a few bills, but that's a trifle compared to what this year's crop'll bring in." Nash grinned. "Come on, Tom, you haven't been back long enough to remember how things work here. King Cotton pays all debts."

"Does it?"

"When you're at Bayou Redbird tomorrow, do you think you could tell Jones to give me a little more time?"

The banker seemed distracted.

"Tom? . . . Say, old boy . . ."

Tom gazed at the old carriage house as if he had reached a temple. The chipped paint and worn planks of the small building showed its neglect in favor of a newer, larger structure nearby where the plantation's coaches and carriages were now kept.

"Tom?"

Tom glanced at Nash, as if suddenly remembering his existence. "Okay, I'll talk to Jones."

Barnwell summoned a servant, who swung open the wide door. A grin formed on Tom's face at the reunion with his progeny.

Nash, Cooper, and the senator walked into a space that was empty except for a dilapidated coach, an old relic apparently not meriting transfer to the new location, and a strange new device unlike anything they had ever seen. The two objects seemed to illustrate the past and the future, but nothing of interest in the present to the men, who looked curious but unexcited.

Tom watched them surveying the mechanical object that was ten feet long and five feet wide. Slowly, they walked around it, with the crunch of their steps on the dirt floor the only sound. They bent down, cocked their heads, and peered at various parts of the device.

The object was a conglomerate of iron and steel, pipes and valves, gears and belts, wheels and shafts, and levers and pedals that formed a vehicle. In the rear, it had a steering wheel, a driver's seat between two large cleated wheels, and a hitch for attaching implements behind the device. On top of the frame, spanning from the driver's seat to the front of the vehicle, was a long metal cover that seemed to encase the invention's motor. In front, two smaller wheels supported the device. Two long rods on hinges rested along either side of the body and could be pivoted forward and hitched to a horse for hauling the device.

Tom took his top hat and pointed it at the metal concoction as if he were presenting a royal coach to a king. "Gentlemen, this is a motor plow. It's actually much more than that. It's a traction vehicle for pulling various farm implements, or a *tractor* for short."

"It's what?" asked Nash.

"It's the *new age*," said Tom.

"Maybe you'd like to explain," said Barnwell.

With a flick of his wrist, Tom tossed his hat on the seat of the device and faced his audience. "This vehicle can be used for tilling and planting. But the even bigger news is the *engine*."

"Are you saying this thing can pull better than a horse?" asked Cooper.

"I'm saying the horse is *doomed*."

"Where's the furnace and boiler?" asked Nash.

"This is no steam engine."

"No horse? No steam? Impossible!" said Cooper.

"Steam takes too long to heat. The fire is too dangerous, the water tank is too heavy, and it's impractical to have to chop wood or stoke coals at every turn. Steam won't do at all for a quick-starting, fast moving, lighter-weight, easy-to-use vehicle that will transform the world." Tom spoke without boasting, as if he were just stating facts.

"Transform the world, eh?" Cooper was skeptical.

"Once it's fine-tuned, yes."

"The world's as it's always been and always will be," jibed Nash. "No contraption can change that."

Tom didn't seem to hear the remark. "This new engine is unlike any other. It's an engine that *carries its own power plant inside of it.*"

He patted the device as a proud father would stroke a newborn. He didn't notice that the others received his news with blank faces.

"The engine uses an entirely new principle of power," explained Tom. "It works on *oil,* on the exquisitely timed and orchestrated explosion of petroleum fuel within the engine." His prior boredom with the reception had vanished from his face. "This explosion is harnessed so that the energy produced from it is used to drive the wheels. Gentlemen, this is no steam engine. It's *far* more useful than steam could ever be."

"And the engine's in there?" Cooper pointed to the covered area in front of the driver's seat.

"In there." Tom nodded.

"Let's see," said Barnwell.

Tom opened a small black box by the driver's seat and reached underneath various papers to grab a few tools. He lifted the engine cover from its grooves and, with Barnwell's help, removed the bulky casement to reveal the workings.

The men stared quietly, their faces curious as the enthusiastic inventor explained his creation.

"You see the engine block here, with two cylindrical chambers in it. The explosions occur inside the chambers in a very carefully timed sequence. First, a combustible fuel—I use kerosene—flows into a chamber, then the fuel is compressed, then an electrical spark ignites it and expands it, and finally the spent fuel leaves the chamber, and the cycle begins again. These four phases that occur in each cylinder—the introduction of the fuel, its compression, its explosion, and its removal—drive a piston in the chamber to move up and down. The piston is connected to a crankshaft, which is connected to the wheels." Tom pointed to the parts as he spoke. The others came closer, stretching their necks to see.

"And that, gentlemen, is the whole of it. A lightning-quick stream of fuel combustions and exhausts in the chambers cause the changes in pressure and volume that drive the pistons up and down, which in turn move the wheels of an incredibly powerful vehicle. This is a new kind of power for a new age!"

His audience was speechless, their eyes wary. Tom didn't seem to notice or care about their reactions. He continued, engrossed in his subject.

"This is the tank that holds the kerosene." He pointed to a long cylindrical vessel with a cap. "And here's another tank." He pointed to a smaller vessel. "It holds gasoline."

"What's that?" asked Nash.

"A by-product in the petroleum mixture that's more flammable than kerosene. Some inventors have written about its superior ignition properties, which can be used for starting this type of engine, so I obtained some and tried it in my device."

The remark about a useful petroleum product called gasoline left the men's faces blank.

"And here's the ignition crank." He bent down and pointed to a handle below the engine, between the front wheels. "The crank triggers an electrical spark that ignites the gasoline and starts the engine." He sprang up and walked to the vehicle's cab. "These levers and pedals by the driver regulate the amount of fuel and air going into the engine. They also get the device in gear, control the speed and direction, and put the tractor in neutral to stop the motor. The wheel is used for steering, like the reins on a horse."

Tom finished his description and smiled proudly. "That's the basic idea of the self-propelled personal vehicle. I've plowed and harrowed fields with it on my own property." He lifted the papers in the black box by the driver. "These are diagrams and instructions that show how to start the engine and operate the vehicle," he said, waving the papers in his hand. "Anyone can do it." He flipped through the papers. "And these drawings illustrate the tractor performing field jobs with various attachments, from plowing to harrowing to seeding to cultivating. I also have calculations showing the incredible productive output of the machine over manual labor." He dropped the papers and tools back in the small compartment, then faced his puzzled audience. "This vehicle is powerful beyond imagination. With one small, inexpensive tank of fuel, a mere few gallons, a man can till acres."

Cooper cast a doubtful look at Tom, as if the young man in formal clothes seemed too refined to have created the imposing mechanical object before them. "You fabricated this thing yourself?"

"I did. I conceived the project when I studied engineering in college, and I worked on it while I had a job designing and repairing motors for a large mill company in Pennsylvania. When I was with the mill, I must've seen every kind of engine ever made."

And where'd you see this one?" asked Barnwell.

"Nowhere."

"Nowhere?"

"There are experiments going on here and in Europe, but no one's ever put a portable engine like this to wide-scale practical use before."

"And *you* will?" asked Nash in disbelief.

"I hope to."

"What's this contest you're entering?" asked Cooper.

"The North has investment money, and I need more of it than my bank can safely risk. I need it for research, design, manufacturing, sales. You see, getting *all* the engine parts to work, and work in harmony—getting the right grade of fuel, the right electrical sparking mechanism to ignite the fuel, the right mix of air with the fuel for combustion, the right valves to let the fuel in and out of the chambers, the right timing mechanism for sequencing the explosions, the right steering levers and pedals for the driver's easy use, the right cooling system to prevent overheating, the right lubricating system to keep the parts running smoothly—the right *everything*—is daunting. But it'll be done," Tom said confidently. "This is just the beginning."

The men looked astonished as the young inventor expended his own sizable energy, waving his hands, moving around the device, and pointing to parts as he made his points.

"I need to hire skilled machinists and open a factory to design and make the parts. It'll take years to develop a product that will be reliable, safe, simple, powerful, durable, and affordable. But this is the start, right here. My tractor works. It shows what can be done. With design improvements it'll be ready to manufacture and sell all over the country—and the world." Tom gazed at the conglomerate of metal as if it were gold. "The first internal-combustion tractor!"

The men exchanged questioning glances.

"The contest is for the best new invention. It's an event that draws investors from all over the country. They hover around, talk to the inventors, study the entries. I hope to find supporters."

"All this trouble for a plow? Why bother? Why not just keep using horses?" queried Nash.

"It's not just a plow. It's the *new age*."

"Has anyone actually seen this thing work?" asked Nash.

"Not I," said the senator. "I hauled it here by horse."

"I've been working on this in private, in isolated fields on my land where nobody goes, not even my field hands."

"Let's get it outside and see how it works," urged Nash. "*If* it works."

Tom shook his head. "Today's affair is hardly the right occasion. Besides, it has no brake yet, and the engine's roar scares horses and startles people that aren't used to the sound. I need to show it to you in a level field away from the house. I'll demonstrate it when I get back."

"Do you have a patent on this contraption?" asked Cooper.

"I was making changes constantly, until the final days before this trip, so I had to wait till I had some stability in the design and a workable prototype. Now, I'm ready to apply."

"Do you really think anyone will invest in this thing?" asked Barnwell.

"Absolutely. Why, the implications are tremendous! First, there's the engine. A compact, powerful, self-propelled engine that runs on cheap fuel—the perfect replacement for the horse!"

The others looked dubious.

"It could operate horseless carriages and motored wagons of every kind at a fraction of the expense and trouble we have now. It could be used not only on the farm but also in the city—for transportation, deliveries, hauling. It could eliminate the costly, time-consuming upkeep of draft animals. And farmers could redirect the acreage they use for grazing to produce cash crops instead.

"The same kind of engine could power boats and trains. It could be used wherever steam or animals are used, but far more conveniently and less expensively." Tom's eyes widened as if the vision he saw were bursting from them. "Gentlemen, the internally powered engine will completely change the way we view transportation and farming."

The men listened, their puzzled faces shifting from the device to its creator. They stared in amazement at a facet they had never seen of the quiet young man who had joined their circle eighteen months ago.

"Now, if we apply this engine to farming in the form of a tractor, like the one I have here, the possibilities are vast," said Tom. "Hitch a plow to the vehicle, and it'll turn the soil. Hitch a harrow, and it'll break up and smooth the surface. Hitch a disc that'll make a ridge in the soil for a hopper to gravity-drop seed into, followed by a roller to smooth the soil over the planting, and it'll plant seed in rows."

As he spoke, Tom moved to the rear of the device, kneeling and gesturing to show the placement of the tools he envisioned.

"If you space the wheels to rest between planting rows and keep the engine high off the ground, a tractor like this could straddle the growing plants and turn the soil. Weeding and cultivating could be done mechanically."

Tom rose. With his arms outstretched and his fingers almost touching the dilapidated old coach on one side of him and the new tractor on the other, he looked like a bridge between two worlds.

"Gentlemen, the new age is coming. That's why I aim to develop this thing."

"Does this mean you'll be moving up North?" Nash asked hopefully.

"I want to develop it here, where I can test it on cotton."

"You sure have some big plans there, Tom," said Cooper with a mocking grin. "I mean, a *new age?*"

"What's wrong with the age we have?" asked Nash.

"How can you be so sure of what you're saying?" added Cooper.

"Because my tractor works. *It works.* The rest is details—thousands of tedious details and years of laboring through them. But there's a new principle at work in this engine, and there's no denying that. There's no going back." He smiled, his eyes bright with confidence. "With the tractor, an entire field can be worked by one man in one day. All it takes is a small, maneuverable engine able to move wheels and haul farm equipment."

His thoughts were a world away as he gestured, his face pensive.

"Today we have mechanized textile mills that substantially increase production over manual methods. Just imagine that kind of machine power in a small, personal vehicle. Picture that out in the fields. I tell you, there'll be a day when one machine will perform the work of a hundred hands. It will empty the fields of men!"

"Empty the fields of men?" repeated Cooper, his curiosity now tinged with displeasure.

"We don't need to empty the fields," added Nash. "We have plenty of hands that we need to occupy. Whatever would we do with them?"

"Why, a man's lot will change with changing times," Tom replied excitedly. "Machines will work the fields, and men will no longer have to break their backs and waste their lives digging dirt and picking crops. There'll be plenty of other jobs to do. The new age will need workers to operate the machines. It'll need mechanics, inventors, engineers, architects, mathematicians, and builders to design the machines, to erect the factories, and to produce greater and greater advances to move mankind forward."

"What about the slaves?" Cooper asked accusingly. "Where do they stand in your wild scheme?"

Tom seemed to look through the men to the vision that filled his mind, making him powerless to speak to anything else. "The new age is *science*. It has no place for slaves."

A biting silence greeted his pronouncement. If Tom hadn't been consumed with his own thoughts, he might have felt as if he had been slapped.

Nash broke the awkward pause, his voice growing bolder as he spoke, as if he had suddenly found a playing field on which he could score a point. "Let me explain something to you, my friend. Slavery is completely intertwined with life here, and you're not going to change that."

"Slavery is inextricably linked with the economy worldwide," added Cooper. "Thanks to slavery, we have cotton. And thanks to cotton, men are better clothed, their comfort better promoted, their industry more highly stimulated, and civilization more rapidly advanced."

"You mean you need slavery to advance civilization?" asked Tom.

"Look here," said Cooper, "we don't rhapsodize about any new age here. We don't even *think* that humbug."

Barnwell, who had remained quiet, now squeezed Tom's shoulder affectionately. "You've been away so long, Tom, you forgot how things work here. What I mean is, they're children. We look after them. They need our help and would be completely lost without it. Why, it's right honorable of us to take care of them," he declared. "They can't do the work you're talking about. Mathematicians! Engineers! Imagine!" He roared with laughter. "It's like expectin' a baby to build a steamboat. They're like children, I tell you."

"Isn't that because you treat them that way?" asked Tom.

"Our slaves are treated better than any workers up North," said Cooper. "You want to make wage laborers out of them? We give them *much* more than that here. We don't fire them. We feed them. We house them. We care for them when they're sick. We look after their young. And we keep them comfortable in their advancin' years. I tell you, havin' our protection and security is the superior system to wage labor."

"You mean having no choice about your life is superior to having a choice?" asked Tom quietly.

"You listen, boy, and listen good," said Cooper. "You got something new, we're open-minded; we'll give it a look. But if any tractor gets developed here, it'll be by us, for us, and serving us and our ways."

"No men can make the tractor kowtow to their notions of how the world should run. The tractor will come with its own notions."

"There's a word for your talk," Cooper said sharply, his voice low, his finger pointing in Tom's face.

"Now, now, Ted," said Barnwell soothingly. "Tom needs time to adjust to life here. This new age isn't coming tonight, is it?" He laughed. "I reckon we'll have lots of time to discuss it."

He put his arm around Cooper's shoulder and steered him toward the door. "Let's get back to the guests, Ted. Tomorrow I'll take you around and show you the plantation journals. Bret Markham, the overseer, kept the books in right good order, everything recorded, every penny accounted for. He may look unscrubbed, but he's a fine man. Intelligent, I tell you."

Tom and Nash followed, with Tom swinging the door closed behind them.

\* \* \* \* \*

The fire had dwindled to embers, its flames no longer reflecting on the shiny armoire. From the triangular slit in the drapes, a gray tinge of moonlight beamed into the room. Tom sat at a table before the fireplace, writing intently, his sleeves rolled up, his vest open, his jacket flung on the bed behind him. His lamp cast a shadow of his wiry figure against the carpet of his bedroom at the Crossroads.

Before supper, Rachel Barnwell and her mother had left for home, with Charlotte commenting that the air at the Crossroads made her ill. Nash Nottingham and the other guests had left as well. Tom had remained for the night to get an early start to the docks with his invention the next morning. His host and the new owner of the Crossroads, Wiley Barnwell, had also remained, along with the prospective buyer, Ted Cooper, so that they could discuss business the next day. Tom, eager to excuse himself but fearful of appearing rude, had sat through a seemingly interminable supper followed by a smoke in the gentlemen's parlor, discussing planting schedules, tillage methods, and cotton gins with the two older men. At eleven o'clock, when Barnwell and Cooper had finally decided to retire, a servant escorted Tom to his bedroom on the upper floor. Finally, he was free.

Once relieved of social obligations, Tom jotted down a few thoughts. The discussion earlier that day about cotton seed had provoked new ideas that he wanted to pursue. The new seed was said to yield cotton that could be picked more readily. Cotton that was easy to pull off the boll. For the rest of the day, the matter of harvesting the cotton had sown its own seeds in his fertile mind.

What if one day the new engine could be made so powerful that it would be able to do more than just drive itself and haul *passive* farm tools like a plow? What if this engine could also possess enough power to run *active*—motorized—farm equipment in the field the way a steam-powered or water-powered engine runs machinery in a factory? This was an idea that had never occurred to him before. He paused to ponder the matter. What if there were a machine to pull the cotton off the boll? And what if it could be powered by a tractor's engine to do the cotton picking mechanically?

He took a fresh piece of paper from a box of stationery, dipped his pen in its inkwell, and sketched the tool he imagined on that machine. He drew an illustration of a metal object shaped like a hand, with prongs that resembled human fingers, only they were thinner and pointier. Then he sketched a cotton plant and showed how the prongs of the spindle might mechanically grasp the cotton and twist it off the boll.

Sitting there in the night, with only the fuel of his imagination, he had no way of knowing that a century later there would exist such a machine, twenty feet tall and just as long, yet delicate enough to weave between the rows of fragile, growing plants without trampling them. This factory-in-the-field would mechanically pick cotton by a method similar to the one he outlined that evening—performing work that had previously required one hundred men. Tom had no way of knowing that other harvesters, as they would come to be called, would pick a countless variety of crops throughout the world in quantities and at speeds that were unfathomable. He had no way of knowing that such mechanization would produce, with only a miniscule fraction of the labor used in his day, an unimaginable abundance of food.

His hands stiffened as he sketched, and he realized they were cold. He looked up to find that the fire had gone out. A glance at the mantel clock showed that it was a few minutes past one. Suddenly aware that he was tired, he rubbed his eyes and yawned. He decided that he had written enough to capture his thoughts. He had to rise early for his travels, so he needed a good night's sleep.

He began unbuttoning his shirt when he remembered something. He had not put the engine cover back on his tractor after removing it earlier to show the motor to the senator and his companions. He would do that now to save time in the morning.

He put on his jacket and curled his finger through the handle of his lamp; the candle flickered in its glass cylinder as he went down the stairs. In the parlor he found someone to help him with the bulky engine cover, a sole servant awake at that hour. It was Tucker, the young man who had earlier escorted him to his room and who was now placing wood in the fireplaces for the morning.

A cacophony of songs from nocturnal animals and insects that were invisible to the eyes but whose presence was indisputable to the ears greeted the two men as they left the house. Tucker took the candle and led the way to the old carriage house. Tom looked up to see a sky aglow in the moonlight. Like so many planters, he had learned to search the heavens for signs of fair weather for planting, rain for crop growth, then fair weather again for picking the cotton before the winter storms came. In the distance he detected clouds forming and wondered if it would rain the next morning when he had to go to Bayou Redbird.

As the men approached the old carriage house, they could see that the door had been swung open, to Tom's surprise. A ribbon of lantern light streamed out the door. A horse in a harness stood outside the structure. The men moved closer. Tucker was the first one to reach the entrance and look inside. He gasped. The lamp rattled precariously in his hand. Tom grabbed the light to steady it. Then he looked inside. He too gasped, and the lamp rattled again.

The tractor was missing. Near the spot where the device had stood, a man's body lay in a nightshirt and robe on the floor, his face as gray-white as his hair, his chest covered with blood, his unblinking eyes frozen in a final moment of horror. It was Senator Wiley Barnwell. Standing over the senator, his hands spotted with blood, was Ted Cooper.

# CHAPTER 2

The old carriage house was colder, darker, and emptier than it had been mere hours before when a young inventor, a new discovery, and an ardent dream had filled it with life. Now a jaundiced light flickered on Tom as he stood near the door, his features as frozen in horror as Barnwell's. Fresh blood colored the side of his mouth where Cooper had punched him.

Ted Cooper sat up against a wall in the shadows, his long legs stretched in front of him and his hands folded in his lap. A swollen bruise around one eye and blood under his nose told of a more heated moment, when he had tried to leave and had exchanged blows with Tom, who had finally knocked him down and forced him to remain.

Both men waited, glaring at each other, while the corpse stared up vacantly in the eerie silence. After discovering Barnwell, Tom had rushed to check his pulse, found none, then sent a shaken Tucker into town to summon the sheriff. Too tense to sit, too shocked to pace, Tom now stood like a sentry guarding a prisoner.

Finally, he heard the clatter of horses' hooves. He stepped outside to find Tucker returning with four others. Tom recognized the men as local citizens whom he knew casually.

A somber, light-haired man with a badge walked toward him. "Mr. Edmunton?"

"Yes, Sheriff."

"Your man, Tucker, says there's been a death here, that you two found a body on the premises."

"That's right."

Sheriff Robert Duran spoke with the calm voice of a judge. His pale blond eyebrows seemed nearly invisible on his face, making his dark, inquiring eyes more prominent. He was not tall, but he did not seem to need height. His stocky build and solemn manner gave the impression of a firmness that was both physical and mental, imparting an air of authority to him beyond his thirty-two years.

"You may know our doctor and coroner, Dr. Don Clark," the sheriff said, pointing to the gray-haired man walking toward them with a saddlebag flung over his shoulder.

"Hello, Doctor." Tom inclined his head in greeting.

"Good evening," the doctor replied.

The gravity of the occasion was softened by the doctor's half-smile, as if, even in adversity, he retained the kindness of a healer. But adversity seemed to have the opposite effect on the sheriff, who was more stoical than Tom had ever seen him.

"And these are my deputies, Jeff and Bart."

Tom nodded to the two men approaching him.

All four showed signs of hasty dress—a shirt only partially tucked into pants, a pair of suspenders twisted, pant legs caught haphazardly in boots, disheveled hair—attesting to their quick response in the emergency.

"Come this way," said Tom grimly.

The lawmen and the doctor entered the old carriage house, their steps sounding in the silence at a steady pace until they saw the shocking sight, and then they rushed toward the body, stirring dust as they ran.

"My God!" cried Dr. Clark. "It's Wiley Barnwell!"

The sheriff whirled to Tom. "Who did this?" he demanded.

Tom's face turned to the figure now standing in the darkness by the wall.

Duran followed Tom's glance. He gasped incredulously. Seconds passed before he found a whisper of his former voice.

"Uncle Ted!"

"Hello, Robbie," said Cooper.

Tom's voice was hard. "When Tucker and I walked in here earlier, we found the senator lying there as you see him. And we found Ted Cooper standing over the body with blood on his hands. Mr. Cooper tried to leave the scene. He's here now only because I blocked his departure."

"I've nothing to hide," Cooper protested.

Sheriff Duran gaped at his uncle in dismay.

"It's *not* what he's implying!" Cooper told his nephew.

"It's not?" The inventor looked as if a pressure valve inside him was blowing open. "You standing over the body? You murderer!"

"That's a lie. A lie, you scoundrel!" Cooper leaped at his accuser.

Tom lunged at him in return.

The sheriff, having recovered his presence of mind and his voice, wedged himself between the men and shouted, "Get back! Both of you!" He pushed them apart. More quietly, he added, "I'll hear you out presently, one at a time."

The deputies moved closer to ensure that the two men heeded the order.

The sheriff left his deputies with Tom and Cooper for a moment while he kneeled by the coroner. Dr. Clark was crouched over the body, already at work examining it and measuring the wound, with instruments from his saddlebag spread before him.

"Where's the murder weapon, Doctor?" asked the sheriff.

"It's not here."

"What happened?"

"The senator was stabbed on the left side of his chest. The weapon penetrated just above the heart." Dr. Clark pointed as he spoke, looking back and forth from the glassy eyes of the deceased to the intelligent eyes of the sheriff. "It appears a knife was thrust downward in one sharp blow, then was removed." He picked up the bottom of Barnwell's robe, where dark red streaks ran across the light brown fabric. "The weapon was apparently wiped here, and then it was taken away. I'll conduct a search to see if we can recover it."

The sheriff rose and walked toward Tom and Cooper.

"Did either of you see a weapon?"

"No," they each replied.

"I want to hear exactly what happened. First, Mr. Edmunton. What were you doing here, and what did you see?"

His voice heavy with despair, Tom began. "Sheriff, I first have to tell you about something that was in here earlier and that's gone now, because it appears to be the reason the senator was . . . attacked."

Tom related the story of his invention—what it was; where he was going with it; how it happened to be placed in the old carriage house during Polly Barnwell's funeral service; how he had shown the device to the senator, Cooper, and Nash Nottingham that afternoon; how he had come out with Tucker that night to put the cover back on the engine; and how they had found the invention missing, Barnwell murdered, and Cooper standing over the body. Tom led the sheriff outside to a horse in harness standing where he and Tucker had found it at one-fifteen that morning, when they had arrived at the carriage house.

"So you see, Sheriff," Tom said, walking back inside with Duran, "my invention was stolen, apparently hauled away by the horse, and a man who treated me like a son, a man who appears to have . . . defended . . . my device, was . . . killed."

"Now, why would anyone want to take your invention?"

"There's a fortune waiting for the man who develops a way to mechanize farming. An ambitious man could recognize the implications of my tractor, which I had described to Cooper, the senator, and Nash Nottingham earlier when I showed it to them. A clever mind would surely realize that the new device had the potential to transform the South. During our conversation, Cooper asked me if I had a patent on my invention. I told him I hadn't applied yet. So he knew there was as yet no legal protection for it."

Cooper listened, his arms folded in indignation, shaking his head.

"It seems Cooper saw an unusual opportunity. He knew my invention would be gone in the morning, so he had to act tonight while everyone was asleep."

"You were staying here overnight?" The sheriff asked his uncle.

"I was thinking of buying the Crossroads, and Wiley Barnwell was fixing to show me around the place in the morning. So after Polly Barnwell's funeral, I supped with Wiley and our overzealous inventor"—he pointed to Tom—"and then I settled in to stay the night."

"That gave you the opportunity to steal my device, hide it in the woods, then return to your room. In the morning, you could've acted as surprised as anyone that my tractor was missing—"

"That's *not* what happened. It's pure speculation, Robbie."

"I'll hear it out regardless," Duran told his uncle, then nodded to Tom to continue.

"I told Cooper that many modifications needed to be made to refine the design. So why not steal such a device in its infancy, then quietly enlist engineers to make the adjustments? After a series of improvements that would alter the device, and with my having no patent claim, how could I prove any ownership?"

"I had none of those thoughts! None at all!" shouted Cooper.

"After everyone had retired for the night, Cooper could have quietly left the house, harnessed his horse, and come here to haul my invention away. The senator could've heard him, because his room was on the first floor, facing the carriage house."

"Show me," said the sheriff.

Tom went to the door and pointed toward the big house.

"The senator had the room on the first floor with the open window there in the corner. It's near the parlor where we were conversing. I saw him go into it at the end of the evening."

Looking past Tucker, who was standing near the horses, the sheriff peered at the back of the big house. The open casement window in the corner of the house was visible in the moonlight, its drapery swaying in the night breeze.

"And where were you?" Duran asked Tom.

"I was on the opposite side of the house and up a flight, so I heard nothing," Tom continued. "But Senator Barnwell could well have heard noises through his open window when the thief put the cover on the motor and hitched the device to the horse. The senator might then have lit a lantern, put on his robe, and come out to investigate. He could have caught Cooper in the act of stealing the engine."

As his agitation grew, Tom's voice rose.

"If he caught Cooper, the senator would have been outraged. Because he was like a father to me and because he's an honest man, he would've tried to protect my invention. For Cooper, it would've been too late to retreat from his vile deed. The senator might have threatened to use his power and influence to smear Cooper's reputation and even harm him financially for his attempted thievery. The senator might have told Cooper as much when he caught him in the act of stealing."

"Utter poppycock!" Cooper injected.

"Being unable to retreat and faced with disgrace, Cooper could have panicked and attacked the senator," Tom continued. "Then he could've quickly hauled the engine away and hid it in the woods. The knife he used in the attack might have been traceable to him—perhaps it bore his initials or was in some other way distinctive—so he could have taken it with him and hidden it along with my tractor. Then, of course, he had to come back here, where he was spending the night. So he would have returned to put the horse in the stable and slip into bed. But on his way to the stable, he stopped where he had committed his crime. Maybe he was tempted to ensure that the senator—the tragic victim and sole eyewitness to identify him—was indeed dead. So he stepped in here, perhaps intending to stay only an instant. That was when Tucker and I walked in on him."

"That's all humbug! Preposterous!" Cooper shouted.

"Sheriff, there's a princely sum to be made in the development of that tractor. People have killed for far less. Why, the senator even joked earlier in the day that Cooper would sell his own mother for gold. His passion for wealth is well known."

"But my passion for crime is merely a fantasy of your perverted mind."

The sheriff's face was a stone slab. "How much time passed after the three of you retired for the night and you came out here?" Duran asked Tom.

"Let's see," Tom said, figuring. "I found Cooper here at one-fifteen, so two hours and fifteen minutes had passed since he, Senator Barnwell, and I had retired to our rooms at eleven o'clock. That could be time enough to execute the scheme I described. Furthermore, when I saw Cooper . . . leaning over the . . . senator . . ."—Tom's eyes closed painfully at the memory—". . . he tried to leave. He's here only because I forced him to stay."

"I was *leaving*, not *fleeing*. There was no point in staying here to subject myself to this boy's wild accusations. Robbie, you know where to find me, anytime, in the house where you grew up!"

The sheriff's eyes sank to a spot on the ground where he seemed to be staring at a torment of his own. Then he slowly raised his glance to meet the eyes of the man pleading with him.

"Mr. Cooper, how did you get the bruises on your face?"

"Robbie, it's me. You don't have to act so stuffy with your uncle."

"You will please answer the question," the sheriff said quietly.

"I scuffled with him, like he said."

"And the bruises on your face, Mr. Edmunton?"

"Cooper hit me."

The accused nodded in assent.

"Let's hear your side, sir." The sheriff turned to his uncle.

"Everything this crazy Yankee mechanic said is hogwash! I didn't covet that invention. I disapproved of it and all his wild, seditious talk of transforming the South. You should've heard him. It was treasonous, I tell you!"

Tom shook his head. "You had some misgivings, but you seemed quite interested. You asked questions—"

"Did you express your disapproval earlier, when Mr. Edmunton showed you his invention?" asked the sheriff.

"I did! But he was too raving mad to notice my displeasure. Besides, Robbie, I wanted a loan from his bank. I tried to temper my disgust when he rhapsodized on how his tractor would turn the earth topsy-turvy. I tell you, he's crazy!" Cooper sneered, waving his hands and pacing agitatedly.

"Then, sir, what were you doing in here?"

"Barnwell was my friend. I would *never* harm him. You know me, boy. I could never do this horrible deed."

The sheriff whispered to his deputy. The man left, then reentered with Tucker. The slave's wide black eyes glistened in the lamplight.

The sheriff turned to him. "Tucker, tell me what happened this evening."

Cooper was aghast. "Just what do you think you're doing, Robbie? You're going to have a *slave* speak against your own kin? You know a black man can't give testimony against a white in our courts."

"Regardless, I'm fixing to hear what he has to say."

The slave's gentle manner and soft voice lent an air of truth to his report. "I comes in here with Mr. Tom. I sees him." Tucker pointed without malice to Cooper. "He wuz a-standin' over the dead man—the senator—sir. And I sees blood on his hands."

"Did you see anyone else come in here earlier in the night?"

"No, sir."

"Did you see Senator Barnwell leave his bedroom?"

"No, sir. I wuz in the woodshed on the other side o' the house, gettin' wood fer the fireplaces."

"That's all, Tucker," said the sheriff.

Tucker looked around, quietly absorbing the situation, then left.

"Two men place you with the body. I think you'd better explain, Mr. Cooper." The sheriff's wooden voice revealed the awkwardness of the situation for him. "What were you doing out here at one-fifteen in the morning?"

Cooper stood before his listeners as the lantern cast his lanky shadow on the wall. He ran his hands through his hair, sighed in resignation, and began his tale. "I retired to my room at eleven, brooding over the impertinence of this Yankee recruit and his wild notions! I tried to dismiss my thoughts. I went to bed, but I couldn't sleep. It was then that I formulated a plan—a quite ill-conceived plan, as it turned out!—and I arose to execute it."

He flashed resentful glances at Tom as he spoke. "It galled me, the sheer arrogance of that boy and his traitorous utterances." He pointed to Tom, the shadow of his accusing finger elongated on the wall. "He was determined to shake up our world, by God, as if we didn't have enough worries right now with our meddlesome foes up North. The world of his wild imaginings has no use for slaves, so he was planning to clear the fields of men. *Poof*, I thought— our peace and serenity are gone, and our very society becomes a prey to his madness."

"But, sir, if you thought Mr. Edmunton a madman and nothing more, then why would his ramblings disturb you so?" asked the sheriff.

"Because I could see he was quite methodical. He had given the matter considerable thought. I believed he had something there with his device, and if *I*, a disapproving skeptic, found his invention plausible, there would surely be eager investors at the contest he was headed for who would believe his dreams quite willingly. Although I thought him mad, I also thought him dangerous because of his obsession. I decided to dash his wild scheme this very night, before it could become a plague on our lives."

The coroner had risen from his work. He stood with the deputies, the sheriff, and Tom. All listened intently, their eyes following Cooper as he paced nervously.

"It galled me that this madman would be cooking up the same kind of schemes that were once brewed right near this very spot—schemes that almost led to calamity. You know that old textile mill that's now in ruins just down the road by Cutter's Creek? You're too young"—he gestured to Tom and his nephew—"but Don, you remember how that confounded mill almost caused an insurrection."

"I remember the factory," replied the coroner noncommittally.

Cooper bristled. "That factory was going to transform the South too. Oh, it was going to open the area to manufacturing, just like up North. The owner wanted to employ our slaves. Now, everybody had extra hands that didn't do much, so it seemed like a good idea at first to hire them out, even to give them a share of the money we got for their work. That's when the factory got five hands from one planter, three from another, four from a third, and so on. Kept them a year at a time. Before anybody knew it, just as soon as those slaves got a taste of living away from their farms and mingling with the free workers, they formed a community, a 'factory town,' they called it." Cooper sneered. "Well, pretty soon the slaves were acting just like free men. Some wanted to open their own shops in their new village. Others wanted book learning, so's they could do the accounting or order the supplies or become supervisors and make more money. I tell you, factory life changed them." Cooper's voice hit low notes of fear. "They got . . . unmanageable."

He paused to observe his nephew and the others. No one offered a comment but simply waited for the rest of the story.

"I remember when the slaves started pressing us," he continued, "when they didn't want to come home, when they wanted a bigger cut of their wages, when they started asking for more license with their time, when their asking turned to demanding—with eight of them to every one of us!"

Tom knew about the abandoned cotton mill. He had seen its empty shell in the woods. He remembered how it had troubled him to find a factory in ruin, like a once-vital body that had succumbed to a fatal disease. He had wondered why the old factory failed.

"Come a time, we all knew the factory had to go. I was a lad of twenty-five then, running the family plantation with my father. Wiley Barnwell was a little older, serving on the town counsel. That proved *useful*." Cooper laughed shrewdly. "Wiley got a few laws passed—some taxes and fees on this and that, and regulations about manufacturing and shipping the goods, whatever. The new rules finally drove the factory out. You remember that, Don?"

"I do," said the coroner. "But Ted, what you're talking about happened twenty-five years ago."

"No matter!" continued Cooper. "When Tom here started with those wild notions about slaves working on machinery, about us farming with machines, about letting the field hands . . . go *free* . . . "—Cooper could barely pronounce the last word—"I knew he was *dangerous*." The planter darted an angry look at Tom. "His wild schemes had to be stopped. But this time, I couldn't count on Barnwell."

"Did you discuss your concerns with the senator?" asked the sheriff.

"'Twas no use. Wiley didn't seem to take the boy seriously. He acted as if Tom's treacherous plan was just a schoolboy phase he was going through and that he'd settle down to a planter's life. 'Twas obvious Wiley had his eye on Tom for his daughter. There aren't many eligible men of means around here to keep Rachel living well and keep her close to her daddy. There's Nash Nottingham, but Barnwell never thought much of him. I could tell that the senator was grooming Tom for his son-in-law. So with Barnwell turning a blind eye to the danger, I had to handle the matter myself. That's when I came up with my plan."

Cooper stopped pacing. He faced his audience and spoke solemnly, as if under oath.

"Yes, I came out here. Yes, I harnessed my horse. Yes, I entered this old building to take the invention."

"You see, Sheriff!" said Tom.

"But I came to haul it down to the bayou to sink it."

Surprised, the men stared at Cooper.

"Sir, let me get this right," said the sheriff. "You came here fixing to *destroy* the device?"

"Yes."

"Then what happened?"

"I got here. The door was open. I saw a lantern shining inside. I saw that the tractor had vanished. Then I looked down . . . and found . . . Wiley . . . lying there," Cooper said gravely, turning to the body. "I rushed to his side and searched for a pulse. But he was gone." Sadness gripped his voice. "I stood up, with his blood on my hands, trying to imagine what could've happened and what I should do. That was when the madman and the slave walked in."

The sheriff and his men were silent, thoughtful, digesting the story.

"The cover is missing," Tom noted. "The thief took precious time to put a heavy, bulky cover back on the engine. That risk would be taken only by someone who wanted to keep the engine intact, to protect it from mishaps in moving it and hiding it. There's no doubt the thief intended to keep the tractor undamaged so that he could exploit it himself."

"I walked into the same scene you did. I didn't see any cover or tractor. I didn't steal your wicked device. And I didn't kill Wiley!"

"You expect us to believe that?" Tom persisted. "You expect us to believe someone else was here tonight besides you? Where's the evidence? The only evidence is that *you* were here and *you* had blood on your hands. My invention was missing, and your horse was harnessed outside—"

"I never rode that horse. It wasn't even sweating. Did you notice that when you arrived?"

"It's a cool night," Tom observed. "And you couldn't have ridden very far with the tractor. Besides, the horse didn't have the machine to haul on the return trip, so it would've had a chance to cool down."

"But there wouldn't have been time for me to carry out your scheme."

The sheriff looked interested. "You may have a point. Mr. Edmunton, how do you figure Mr. Cooper would've had the time to do what you're suggesting?"

"Well, he had two hours and fifteen minutes, all told. So let's say he allowed thirty minutes to ensure that everyone was asleep," Tom reasoned. "And let's assume another twenty minutes to harness the horse, position the engine cover, and hitch the tractor. Then five minutes more for his . . . encounter . . . with the senator. That uses up fifty-five minutes and leaves an hour and twenty minutes to transport the invention to a hiding place and return here. It could be done in the time he had."

Cooper faced the cool stares of the men, then turned to his nephew.

"Robbie, you know I would never do anything like this. When your good-for-nothing father deserted your mother and you, who took you in? Who treated you like more than a sister's son? Who helped raise you, boy? And who had the connections to get you in as sheriff?"

The questions echoed in the hollow structure. The sheriff looked as stiff as the corpse.

"What are you going to do, Robbie?" Cooper said softly, affectionately, hopefully. "Why don't you let me go home now, while you think things over and investigate further to find the real culprit?"

The suspect's voice, tinged with fatherly affection, lingered in the air before the sheriff replied.

"Regardless of the reason," he said quietly, "whether you were fixing to keep the invention for your own purposes or destroy it or develop it up North, you did come here to *steal* it? You admit that?"

"Why, yes, but—"

"And the horse outside is yours, and you harnessed it to haul the invention?"

"Why, yes, but Robbie—"

"And you were standing over the body?"

Cooper did not reply.

"With blood on your hands?"

Cooper closed his eyes.

The sheriff shot an inquiring look at the coroner. Dr. Clark nodded, giving his answer to the unstated question. The evidence confronting them was sufficient for action.

Duran walked to the coroner's saddlebag, where a pair of handcuffs lay on the ground among the doctor's tools. The lawman picked up the manacles. He stood facing his uncle. Cooper stared at him helplessly.

The others watched the sheriff. A deputy stepped toward him and reached for the cuffs, as if to do the job himself, to spare the sheriff. But Duran pulled the cuffs away from his grasp.

Cooper's voice shook. "Now, Robbie . . . you can't believe . . . that I—"

The sheriff stared solemnly at the suspect before him. He walked behind Cooper, took his wrists, and drew them back. The iron shackles made a grating screech as he closed and locked them.

"Mr. Cooper, you're under arrest for the murder of Senator Wiley Barnwell." He turned to his deputies. "Take him in."

Cooper stared incredulously at his nephew. The sheriff held his uncle's gaze with a face that showed only a grim resolve.

The deputies flanked Cooper and escorted him to the door.

Tom stepped into the men's path for a moment.

"Where's my tractor?" he asked the suspect.

"In hell, I hope."

"Look, Cooper, your story doesn't wash. You say you didn't want to profit from the device, only to sabotage it, but why would you want to destroy an invention of great promise? An invention that could transform farming? That doesn't make sense. You're a planter and a businessman, aren't you?"

"I'm a Southerner first."

# CHAPTER 3

While the sheriff and coroner remained at the carriage house, Tom walked over the hill toward the fields to summon the overseer. From the vantage point of Polly's funeral earlier, he had seen the dwellings now coming into view in the moonlight—the rows of chimneyed brown blocks that were the slave cabins and, a short distance away, the overseer's cottage with the white picket fence. Behind him, the grounds of the plantation home were now punctuated with lanterns and busy with servants gathering for questioning. As he rounded the hill, the scene of the violence vanished from his view. But there was no way to block out the agony he felt—and the torment yet to come, when he would face Rachel and her mother.

When he reached the bottom of the hill, he saw a shadow in the moonlight. It was a human figure in the distance, stooping down at what appeared to be the slaves' garden, a small field of tilled earth near their cabins. He couldn't decipher any features, only the dark outline of a man who seemed to be digging something up from the soil and putting it into a small sack. Could he be retrieving something hidden there? Something stolen? Tom wondered. To his dismay, he thought that he might be witnessing yet another shady act in the night.

He took a few steps toward the stranger. The man looked up and seemed to spot Tom. Quickly, he ran away. As the figure darted off in the night, something on him flashed in the moonlight. It was a blue object that shined like a gemstone, perhaps the size of a large brooch. Tom rushed to the site, but the man had vanished, leaving only an empty hole dug in the ground. When he felt around in the dirt with his feet, Tom found nothing. He shrugged and continued on his way.

Was the stranger a runaway? he wondered. Or a slave living on the plantation? Slaves were known to bury stashes of money or other things to be used later when needed. Stealing seemed to permeate Greenbriar, Tom thought grimly. Masters stole the lives of their slaves, and the bondsmen in turn stole the possessions of their masters. Tonight someone had stolen the senator's life and the device that was key to his future. Theft and violence— were they the hidden blight under the lush lands and fortunes of the South? Tom's shock at the night's event had now turned to melancholy.

From outside the gate, the overseer's home had the charm of a cozy cottage. But as Tom climbed the front steps, he noticed overgrown shrubs, torn curtains, and tools cluttering the porch—the signs of a house in which a man lived alone. He knocked on the door and was startled when it opened instantly. Bret Markham, fully dressed and fully armed, seemed startled too.

"Mr. Markham, I believe we saw each other at the funeral, but we haven't met. I'm Thomas Edmunton, a friend of the Barnwell family."

The courteous bow of Markham's head seemed forced, whereas the suspicion in his voice seemed natural. "Whatcha want at this hour?"

"Something's happened, a . . . terrible . . . tragedy. . . ."

Tom relayed the news. Markham at first said nothing, merely staring at Tom like a dog ready to bite a trespasser.

"Lord!" he finally gasped. His astonishment quickly turned to worry. "The senator . . . he was fixin' to tell the new owner to keep me on. Now . . . what . . . ?"

"Were you just coming in, Mr. Markham?"

"Jus' goin' out. What's it to you?"

Tom smelled whiskey in the air around Markham. "The sheriff will be asking you some questions momentarily, Mr. Markham. As I explained, my property was stolen in the crime, so I'm involved with the matter too."

"I got nothin' to hide. You say you got the killer anyways."

"I said we have a suspect. Where were you going just now?"

"Check on the slaves, like I do every night."

"Where were you all evening?"

"Will you be runnin' the place now for the senator's missus?"

"That could very well be." Tom forced a tone of intimidation unnatural to him, trying to give the man what he seemed to respond to best. "Now, where were you all evening, Mr. Markham?"

The authority in Tom's voice seemed sufficient to loosen Markham's tongue. "Right where yer seein' me now."

"Was anyone with you?"

"Live by myself, and no one's been a-visitin'. Nobody ever's a-visitin' here," he complained. "My sister, she 'casionally comes from New Orleans and tidies up the place, but she ain't been here since Christmas."

"When I came over the hill, I saw a man in the field near the cabins. I couldn't make out his face or clothing, but he was bending down and seemed to be digging into the soil. Would you know who that was?"

"No, but it don't surprise me none. Slaves're always up to mischief at night, moseyin' 'round, stealin' an' hidin' things. They sell their pilfered stuff to the boatmen to git money for drink, or perfume and the like for their women, or just for runnin' away. Can't never trust a slave to be honest!" he said indignantly. "They got no respect for people's property. No, sir!"

Tom eyed Markham's whip and gun.

The overseer, in return, eyed his unarmed questioner. "Say, you talk like a Yankee."

Markham paused for a reply, but Tom offered none.

"Maybe you don't know this area, mister, but it's right foolish prancin' 'round unarmed these days." Markham glanced suspiciously at the slave quarters.

The first rays of daybreak lit the path that the two men took over the hill. Tom searched the sky. The distant clouds he had seen earlier were now larger and closer, shrouding the dawn in a dark gray that seemed to match the somber mood at the big house when he and Markham arrived. They found a group of the plantation's slaves—house servants, groundkeepers, stableboys, and others—waiting to be questioned, standing stiffly in the early morning chill.

With shoulders straight and eyes alert, Sheriff Duran showed little sign of exhaustion from the sleepless night. The focus on his work seemed so intense that it forced his body to comply. Tom brought Markham to him, and the questioning began.

"Did you know about an invention in the old carriage house?" asked the sheriff.

Markham shook his head. "No."

"Did you see anyone lingering around the big house?"

"Just folks payin' respects at the funeral."

"Did you talk to any of them?"

"No." The overseer frowned. "They don't mix with me," he added resentfully.

"Did you see anything or anyone unusual here during the day or night?"

"Nope."

"I saw something curious, Sheriff," Tom added. "As I was going to Mr. Markham's cottage, I spotted a man. I couldn't see his face, but he seemed to have a shiny object with him, like a piece of jewelry, a stone with a blue tinge that reflected in the moonlight. He seemed to be digging it up, or else maybe burying it, when he spotted me approaching and ran away."

"Oh?"

"I checked the area where he was, but I couldn't find anything except stirred-up dirt."

"Was he a slave?"

"I couldn't tell. I saw him just in shadow, with the moonlight catching the shiny object."

The sheriff turned to Markham. "What do you think?"

"Like I told the Yankee," he said, pointing to Tom, "I didn't see nobody. 'Twas prob'ly a slave with stuff he pilfered. It happens, 'specially here where the dis'pline ain't no good."

The sheriff continued his questioning, but Markham had nothing of substance to offer. Tom observed that the slaves who lived in cabins around the big house also had nothing unusual to report. When it seemed there wasn't anything more to learn, he summoned a servant to bring him a horse. He mounted the animal, his head low, his mood solemn. He would not be embarking on the exciting adventure he had planned but instead would be performing the most painful task of his life.

In the overcast dawn, he headed for Ruby Manor, the senator's plantation, to break the news to Rachel and her mother.

# CHAPTER 4

Tom began his ride to Ruby Manor vowing with renewed vigor to develop his tractor. Now he had to fulfill that goal not merely for himself but also for the man who had lost his life trying to protect the device. He owed it to the senator and his family to recover the invention and continue his work. He could not bring Wiley Barnwell back, but he could vindicate the senator's death by achieving his own life's dream.

Tom took the back roads to the plantation, hoping to find a clue to the invention's whereabouts. At the time of the crime, the ground had been hard and dry, making it difficult to detect the perpetrator's tracks. Now, a morning rainstorm intensified the problem, washing away any tracks that might have been discernible. Staring at the tangle of trees, shrubs, and rocks alongside his path, he wondered how many potential hiding places there were in the radius of the carriage house reachable by Cooper in the time he had to conceal the invention. Countless, Tom feared.

Soaked and chilled, he traveled along the lonely road. The saturated tree branches above his path seemed to arch lower and lower in the rain, closing in on him, shrinking his world to a raw contest with nature.

He plodded past the grounds of the Crossroads onto a ridge midway up a hillside. The old road there spanned from town to the plantations north of it like Ruby Manor. On one side of him was a sharp drop to Cutter's Creek, its stream racing in the storm to Bayou Redbird. On the other side was a steep climb to the hilltop, its runoff forming puddles under the horse's hooves and mud splatters on his pants. Could the invention be hidden around here? Tom wondered.

There were no roads going up the hill, with its thickets of foliage and wavy bands of clover, and it was too steep for a single horse to haul the engine up

36

the slope, so he dismissed that notion. He glanced downhill by the creek, but that was where the abandoned factory lay. Surely Cooper would not have hidden the engine around there, after he had explicitly mentioned the old cotton mill when questioned at the carriage house. Yet that plant was the closest building to Polly Barnwell's land and a good place to keep the tractor protected. As he rode along, Tom wondered if he should search it, but nature intervened to decide the matter for him.

The downpour was turning into one of Louisiana's late-winter storms, with lightning and thunder forcing him to seek cover. Through the stinging rain pellets, Tom spotted the turnoff to the switchback road down to Cutter's Creek. As he descended the deserted path, he imagined what it was like when draft animals hauled supplies and goods between the factory and the road on the ridge to town, bringing action and purpose to the sleepy hillside.

He reached the dormant plant by the creek that had given it power. The building stood desolate, not as an inanimate object that had never sparked with life but as a corpse that had lost it. The factory's prior human activities seemed to haunt the place, Tom thought, as he looked around. A giant waterwheel at the building's creek side was now raised above the stream's surface and immobilized, its power no longer needed. The factory's boat dock was vacant. Flatboats still used the creek to float crops and people downstream to the steamships at Bayou Redbird, but no one had reason to stop at this landing anymore.

Tom had explored the place once before, wondering if it could be reopened to manufacture his engine. It had disturbed him then to see an industrial building vacant, with rotting wood, shattered windows, and unhinged doors—a failed factory swallowed by the wilderness. Now, after hearing Cooper's story of how the company had been driven out, the old place disturbed him even more.

He tied his horse close to the building, underneath the roof's overhang and out of the rain. A twenty-five-year-old sign painted on a wood board was still nailed to the front door. He read the message despite the chipped letters: "Closed June 1834 by order of the town of Greenbriar for failure to pay taxes and fees."

When he entered through the creaky door, the field mice making their home on the floor scattered in the dust. He walked around the entry room, seeing nothing of note. There were fish scales, animal bones, and cooking implements in a fireplace, signs of hunters or runaway slaves taking shelter there.

On the factory floor, he saw remnants of the old machines, tools, and work bays, but no trace of his invention.

He could imagine the dozens of human voices and bustling activity that had once filled the place. He could visualize the workers cutting the cotton bales, straightening and aligning the fibers through carding machines, then spinning the lint into yarn. He could almost hear the gears humming and the hundreds of bobbins spinning—all to transform the balls of fluff on a small plant into thread for fabrics sought throughout the world.

He checked the warehouse but found nothing related to his device in the cold, hollow space.

He examined what had been the office, a room off the factory floor with a plain wood desk and other furniture apparently not worth salvaging when the place closed. A bookcase held musty volumes on mechanics and manufacturing, their titles faded by the years. On a table he found a stack of diagrams and manuals of the machines. He dusted them off and glanced through the stiff, yellowing papers, fascinated with how factories like this harnessed the principles of mechanics and energy to mass-produce yarn. He saw plans to add a weaving wing to the building and diagrams of powered looms that the owner had apparently planned to purchase, thereby expanding his operation to produce not only yarn but finished fabrics as well. Like a vibrant young man who dies suddenly, the factory seemed to have closed just when it was coming into its prime.

Waiting for the storm to pass, Tom sat at the desk and looked through the drawers. He found what was apparently the last item placed in the desk twenty-five years earlier, a local newspaper with a front-page article about the factory's closing. According to the report, much of the plant's land was purchased by Henry Barnwell. With the help of his bride, Polly, the new owner was going to tear down the cabins and shops that had comprised the workers' village, so that he could cultivate cotton.

The reporter had asked the factory's owner for a comment on why his company failed. The owner was described as looking despondent. "You can't change the soul of the South," he had said. "Anyone who tries is doomed."

The comment disturbed Tom. A budding industry, a workers' town, a burgeoning business, and a new age had been suffocated. That was twenty-five years ago. The soul of the South had remained unchanged. But the factory hadn't been killed completely, he thought, as he read the last paragraph of the story. The reporter mentioned that Henry Barnwell was naming his new plantation Barnwell Oaks. Reading this twenty-five years later, Tom realized that Barnwell Oaks was a name that somehow had never caught on with the townspeople. The owner of the factory, Tom thought, had seen the new age coming, because the name he had given his factory had attached itself to Henry Barnwell's plantation and endured through the years. The plantation, like the factory preceding it, was called the Crossroads.

When the rain stopped, Tom was as eager to leave the place as one might be to end a visit to a cemetery.

The storm had left its mark, he noticed, as he continued on the back roads to Ruby Manor. His path took him through a live oak forest, where the lightning and winds had wounded the great octopus-evergreens that seemed invulnerable. Among their sprawling trunks and tentacle branches, Tom saw trees split like barrels and branches broken like matchsticks.

He thought of another towering figure that had fallen, Wiley Barnwell, and how the women he left behind would need help managing their own plantation and selling the Crossroads. Tom would, of course, assist Charlotte and Rachel with their business and financial needs. But what about their grief at a loved one suddenly being ripped from their lives? He was helpless to fill that crater. For the first time, he felt responsible for the unhappiness of others. He could feel the women's sorrow and hear their anguish. Their cries were loud . . . vivid . . . frightful— He suddenly realized that the cries he heard were real. They were coming not from his imagination but from the woods ahead. He took off on his horse to investigate.

He soon discovered that the cries were the frantic whinnying of a horse in distress. A fallen tree lay across the midsection of the creature, a formidable black trunk slicing a roan body, the animal's limbs dangling helplessly in the air, its head bobbing up and down, its deep-throated wails reverberating through the quiet forest. A young mulatto woman was trying to free the beast. Her face looked as panicked as the animal's, but she was conspicuously silent and, Tom suspected, wouldn't dare cry for help because she appeared to be a slave caught in a runaway attempt.

She had devised a method for freeing the horse, using what seemed to be the only tool she had: a long rope. Tom visually traced the path of the rope from its one end tied to a tree trunk, then swung over a thick, low-hanging branch of a giant oak on one side of the animal, then curled around the trunk pinning the horse, then brought up around another low branch on the other side of the animal, and then brought down to its other end in her hand. The slim figure had tied a stick to the end she was holding in order to form a handle perpendicular to the rope for better leverage. She was pulling feverishly on it.

Tom looked in amazement at the makeshift pulley system that she had devised to reduce the weight she'd have to lift to free the hapless horse. He noted her intelligent effort as he watched her pulling on the rope. With the limited strength she had because of her small size, she could lift the trunk from the horse only slightly, insufficient to free the animal. She pulled again, adjusting her angle, trying to improve her leverage, but to no avail. She looked up from her rigors to see that the rope section around one of the branches was fraying and about to break. She gasped in horror.

Tom ran behind her, seized the rope, and gave one fierce tug. His superior strength proved decisive. He was able to raise the fallen tree high enough to extricate the animal.

"Grab the horse!" he directed.

The girl rushed to the frightened creature while Tom held up the tree trunk. She grabbed the reins and guided the animal to its feet, freeing it just before the frayed rope broke and the trunk came crashing down.

Tom was about to lend her a hand when he realized she was quite able to control the animal herself. She held the horse firmly by the reins, patting and soothing the barebacked creature until it settled down. Aside from copious bits of tree bark lodged in its coat, the horse appeared to be uninjured.

When she finished tending to the animal, the young woman turned to face her rescuer. She stood with her head high, staring at Tom distrustfully. He stared back, taking in the many contrasting qualities striking him at once. Her face displayed the glistening dark eyes and high cheekbones of one race in an arresting harmony with the tapered nose and delicate lips of another. Her skin was neither ebony nor fair but a golden-bronze mix of the two. Her hair was long and lustrous, a tangled mane tumbling down her back, tightly curled by the grace of one race and lightened to a reddish-brown by another. It was as if nature, in a moment of artistic inspiration, had blended on her great palette the fine features of two races to produce a stunning beauty.

He estimated her age at between eighteen and twenty, making her a cross between a girl and a woman. The wild hair and the penetrating eyes, the mud-splattered face and the proud posture, the hardness she showed him and the softness she showed the horse, the slave's frock and the runaway's spirit, the raw beauty and the keen intelligence—it all blended into a fireball presence.

He walked toward her, wanting to help. He was carrying a substantial amount of cash for his now-aborted voyage and was about to give her money. Had he paused to predict her reaction, he might have expected to be viewed cautiously or perhaps even feared. But he didn't expect to be punched in the face, then pushed in the chest and knocked down.

Before he could stand up and recover from his assault, she had jumped on her horse and was fleeing furiously, a vibrant creature riding bareback, strong-willed—and desperate.

He rubbed his chin, which smarted from her fist, and then he rose. As he dusted himself off, he watched her fading in the distance. Another bizarre event to perplex him, he thought. First his invention was stolen and an honorable man killed. Then he discovered that a factory bringing jobs, wealth, and the growth of a village had been driven out. Now a woman with a savage fear was running for her life. A common thread seemed to be tying these things together in his mind.

He remembered reading the factory owner's words: *You can't change the soul of the South. Anyone who tries is doomed.* Was the runaway doomed? He thought of the slave catchers who scoured the area, tracking the desperate, chaining them, returning them to their masters for untold punishment. *Will the patrols get her?* His eyes closed painfully in quiet protest at the thought.

# CHAPTER 5

The sun appeared that afternoon, drying the ground after the storm. But when Tom turned onto the path up the hill to Ruby Manor, a procession of oaks brought back the shade. He caught sight of the Barnwell home from spots where the branches thinned along the winding road, with each glimpse a reminder of the grim task ahead.

As he reached the top of the hill, the Greek Revival mansion came into full view. It was an imposing structure with massive columns supporting the first- and second-floor galleries in the front and back of the house. On more than one occasion Tom had heard the story of Greenbriar's most majestic plantation home. Early in their marriage, Wiley Barnwell had begun construction of a new house for his beautiful wife, and the couple and their one-year-old daughter, Rachel, had moved in twenty years ago.

Ruby Manor was named for the hundreds of rosebushes planted along the perimeter, surrounding its mistress with her favorite flower. Through the years, the hardy little plantings survived floods, droughts, frosts, and heat waves to mature into dense, fragrant bushes that created a spectacular sight— an alabaster-white Greek mansion inside a red picture frame of roses. Wiley Barnwell became known as Greenbriar's most romantic husband, and his gift of Ruby Manor to his wife was the envy of the townswomen. The celebrated story of Wiley and Charlotte weighed heavily on Tom as he approached the house that was a temple to a couple's love.

Tom knew that a carpenter who was a slave of the Barnwell family had been the principal builder of the home. Riding to the entrance, in a momentary reprieve from his problems, the inventor marveled at the splendor achieved by the talented craftsman.

On that February day, the rosebushes were bare. Would there be another spring, Tom wondered, after he said what he had come there to say? A servant took his horse and another escorted him into the foyer, and the dreaded moment had come. Waiting to be received, he hoped Rachel and her mother were made of as hardy a stock as the roses.

"Good Lord! Whatever is wrong, Tom?"

When Rachel entered the foyer, she gasped at the sight of Tom's unshaven face with its puffy, sleepless eyes, bruises from the fight with Cooper, and mud-stained clothing from the trip through the storm. She covered her mouth with her hands in horror.

"You'd better get your mother," he whispered.

She gazed at him, bewildered, then vanished to call Charlotte. In a moment, Tom stood before two women who had the same face and who stared at him with the same astonished eyes, their mouths agape.

Placing an arm around each woman's shoulders, Tom led them into the parlor, their skirts rustling against his weary legs.

"You'd better sit down."

The women sat on the sofa, anxiously leaning forward and looking up at him. He stood by the fireplace facing them. As the story of the past night spewed out, the women were appalled. He paused only for their gasps. When he finished, he was spent, with his arms on the mantel and his head buried in his hands.

When he looked up, his face was filled with pain. The women were speechless. They seemed to be stunned beyond tears, their horror producing a dry-eyed, numbing shock.

"My God!" whispered Charlotte. "Wiley's . . . gone?"

"Pa's gone? He's . . . gone?" a dazed Rachel asked Tom, who nodded grimly.

The women looked incredulous as Tom watched helplessly.

"How horrible!"

"I can't believe it!"

"This is terrible!"

Charlotte turned her white-marble face to her daughter. "What'll we do, child?"

In turn, Rachel looked at Tom, her face searching for an answer.

"Dear God! We could be ruined!" Charlotte continued. "Oh, what are we to do?!" She covered her face in despair. "We could lose our crop!" An even greater fear pulled her voice lower. "And we could lose control of . . . our people!"

Tom crouched down by Charlotte. He placed his hands on her shoulders to console her. "Mrs. Barnwell, I promise, I'll help in any way I can. I'll supervise the crop. You *won't* be ruined. I'll make sure of that!"

"And the Crossroads," said Rachel. "That's ours too now, isn't it? I suppose after what you told us, that utterly despicable Ted Cooper can't buy it now!"

"I'll help you find another buyer," said Tom.

"Father said the Crossroads had a bad year."

"The overseer blamed it on poor Polly. According to him, it was *her* fault he couldn't control the field hands! Imagine the impertinence!" said Charlotte. "I have my doubts about him. But what can I do? I never go to the Crossroads. The air there makes me ill." She threw up her hands in despair.

"I can handle Markham until you get a buyer. I'll visit there regularly. I'll go over the books and watch what he's doing," said Tom.

"Then we can put you in charge of the Crossroads?"

"Yes, Mrs. Barnwell."

He thought of how odd it was—how shocking, really—for them to mention such operational details at a time like that, but he was relieved to find something he could do to help.

"And your fee, Tom?"

"There's no fee. Absolutely not, of course not."

"Wiley said the Crossroads needs a loan—"

"I'll loan you the money you need, Mrs. Barnwell."

"Mama, do you feel better now?"

"Well, dear, I feel completely overwhelmed! This is horrible, just horrible!" Charlotte wiped her forehead with a handkerchief. She reached for her fan on a nearby table and cooled herself nervously.

"Whatever are we going to do about the funeral?" She lamented. "The town will expect something lavish for the *senator*. We'll have to have a headstone specially carved for him. And the reception! How ever will we handle that now, with planting coming on and no extra cash to spare? My God, we're in a fix!"

"There'll be planters and legislators from all over the state wanting to pay their respects," said Rachel. "The governor will want to come. We'll need music, flowers—"

"A special carriage and a custom-fit coffin!" added Charlotte.

Tom rose to his feet. "Under the circumstances, I must insist on paying for all the funeral expenses. I won't have any argument about it."

There was no argument.

"Why, that's right good of you," said Rachel.

"Yes, Tom. Thank you," added Charlotte.

Tom was astonished by the women's steely behavior. Theirs was said to be the weaker sex, but was it? The women before him certainly seemed to be the more pragmatic sex. While he was wracked with grief, they were able to plan soberly. He took it as a good sign that they could push aside their sorrow to deal with practical matters. Right now, he figured, they must be in too much shock to feel the full impact of their loss, and dealing with looming events gave them a sense of control over the sudden and violent change in their lives.

"With you helping us with the plantations," said Charlotte, "I shouldn't burden you with anything more, but . . . ." She paused for Tom's reaction.

"Mrs. Barnwell, I assure you, it's not a burden. The senator . . . stood . . . by me. He . . . defended my work, my dream . . . with . . . his life. It's my duty to help you now, my solemn duty."

"Well then, there's just one more thing we need, and I don't know how we'll pay for it. With Wiley just purchasing a new gin, and with the doctor bills we paid last month for delivering our weaver Callie's baby and for our cook Yancy's illness—"

"And there's the new horses Papa bought," added Rachel.

"I don't know where to turn!" said Charlotte.

"Turn to me, Mrs. Barnwell. Turn to me!"

"What I mean is, we'll be needing more mourning clothes." Charlotte glanced at her daughter. "Rachel, dear, look at you."

Rachel had already relaxed her mourning attire from her aunt's funeral the previous day. She still wore black, but her dress now had a bodice with transparent lace above her breasts, making her look more provocative than funereal.

"You'll need mourning clothes to wear for an extended time, child. What'll folks say if you're not in black up to your chin for months to come?"

"Mama, months in those horrible clothes? Really!"

This wasn't the first time Tom had heard Charlotte prodding Rachel about her attire. The mother dressed with a modesty and refinement that exceeded the already high expectations for a senator's wife. Though her red hair shouted of a still-youthful beauty, her braids and clips restrained the message to a whisper. Though her figure was still fetchingly trim, her wardrobe's muted colors and the high necklines she wore with a brooch at her throat choked off her feminine appeal.

Rachel, however, was a daring contrast. Despite her mother's pleas for modesty, the young Miss Barnwell loved bright colors and alluring dresses. Her necklines were provocatively low. Tom surveyed the beauty of her silky skin, the tumbling riot of red hair, and the small birthmark below her shoulder visible under the lace of her dress. His eyes paused on the reddish brown mark that was shaped like a heart and resting above her real heart like a beguiling little charm casting a spell on him.

Rachel sighed in resignation. "I suppose Papa would want me to be . . . proper."

"I'm glad you see things sensibly," said Charlotte.

"But I haven't any suitable clothes!"

Rachel's wardrobe was legendary. Her father had dedicated the plantation's best seamstress to making her dresses, and he had given her a room in the mansion to house her collection of gowns, day dresses, riding habits, carriage suits, tea attire, capes, cloaks, shawls, and robes, along with shoes, boots, hats, jewelry, and accompaniments of every kind. Tom had wondered if Rachel expected the man she married to match her father's indulgences.

But now, the young suitor's remorse wouldn't allow him to deny Rachel anything. If his invention had led to the loss of her father, then he felt responsible—unwittingly but undeniably—for the tragedy so cruelly thrust upon her.

"Rachel, I want you to get the clothes you need. You too, Mrs. Barnwell. I'll consider that to be part of the funeral expenses that I'm handling."

How small these gestures were, he thought, in view of their great loss. He'd use savings, which, after all, were replaceable. It was the beloved head of their family that was irreplaceable.

"We're mighty grateful for your help," said Charlotte.

Rachel nodded in agreement.

"Now, if you'll excuse me," Charlotte said, rising from her seat and walking toward the door, "I'll need to tell the slaves." She paused and look worried. "Whatever shall I say? They mustn't think that the strong hand directing them has weakened! They . . . three hundred of them . . . mustn't think . . . " Her eyes filled with the raw terror of someone facing physical danger. She looked up to the heavens. "Oh, Wiley, what'll I do without you?"

"Shall I accompany you, Mrs. Barnwell?"

"Mama, we'll both come with you."

Charlotte nodded. "That'll make it easier. I'll come for you after I gather everyone."

Tom observed her through the window as she approached the giant bell that summoned the slaves. When she pulled on the rope, the low tone of the iron gong sounded like a death knell.

He turned away from the window to find Rachel gazing at him like a wide-eyed child looking for support. He took hold of her arm, the whole of his sorrow visible on his face. He pulled her close to him. In what was the sole sweet moment in his bitter day, he embraced her, kissed her, stroked her hair, caressed her shoulders, moved a finger affectionately over the little birthmark. The fragrant scent and luscious feel of her carried him back to his first experience of these pleasures in Philadelphia, to their lusty days together at a time of abandon for both of them.

Tom had known Rachel when they were children. Their families, from the landed gentry of Greenbriar, had been neighbors and friends. He remembered Rachel as the child who sang to the town. Her natural talent, honed with voice lessons, made her the star of local gatherings, from church functions to plantation parties to the town's social events. Rachel eagerly performed at every occasion, and Tom had fond memories of watching the perky little girl, five years his junior, with the angel's voice.

Then at the age of fourteen, Tom left home to travel north for school. His father recognized a keen intelligence in the boy who took apart and reassembled every clock in the house just to see how it worked, who repaired their cotton gin and sawmill better than any mechanic, and who devoured every known book and periodical about machines. When Tom wanted to attend a science and engineering academy in Philadelphia, Colonel Edmunton could not deny his gifted son.

In the great northern city, an exciting world of science, formal education, urban life, and industry enthralled Tom. While in school, he worked part time for a machine-manufacturing company, and he remained there after graduation. He learned to design, assemble, and repair every kind of motor-powered device of the time.

One day he encountered an entirely new kind of motor that captivated him: an experimental engine powered by petroleum. The particular one he saw was inadequate. But it provided the hint that one day, with radical modifications and improvements, it could succeed. That day marked the beginning of Tom's project to develop such an engine, and with it a motorized vehicle for personal use in transportation and farming. Soon his project became a passion.

By the time he turned twenty-three, the inventor had all but forgotten his rural life and friends in Greenbriar. That was when his father wrote to tell him that their neighbor, Rachel Barnwell, now a young lady of eighteen, was coming to Philadelphia to attend a finishing school. Her parents had agreed to send their daughter for formal instruction on the social graces and cultural subjects in preparation for her future role as a plantation mistress. When Rachel arrived, Tom served as her escort, showing her the town and helping her get settled. To his surprise, the freckled child with the bouncy curls had blossomed into a beautiful young woman. What had begun as a childhood friendship became a romance.

The breathless year following Rachel's arrival was the happiest of his life. He began his days before dawn, laboring on his new engine and then working at his regular job. His evenings ended in the intoxicating world of Rachel and her newfound passion—the theater. Almost immediately, the red-haired beauty discovered the Philadelphia theater, and it discovered her.

Rachel auditioned and soon received her first roles. She endured tedious rehearsals, abrasive directors, and bit parts—all the indignities of the struggling artist. But she cheerfully prevailed, embellishing her talent with acting instruction, treasuring every role, proudly performing as if her character were the most important person in the world.

She told Tom that when she was acting, she felt more excitement than she ever had. "When I sang to the neighbors as a child, I never dreamed I could perform for an actual audience and feel such a thrill. I never dreamed I could be *onstage*!" She spoke as if she had discovered a cathedral and was blessed to stand on its sacred ground.

Rachel's vitality onstage was palpable to Tom. She was more exciting than any woman he had ever known. Her trials reminded him of his own passionate struggle—of the failed attempts at creating his new motor, the skepticism of critics, the scarcity of encouragement, the continuous push forward fueled only by his belief in himself and stubborn conviction that his idea would work. In Rachel he thought he saw a mirror of his own essence.

After her initial success at keeping her theater life hidden from school authorities, they discovered her secret and wrote to her parents of her shocking behavior. She tried to explain her newfound passion to them, but the innocence and joy with which she embraced the theater were not understood by her family. They considered theaters uncouth and actresses little more than prostitutes. By the code of conduct of Greenbriar, theaters were no place for the daughter of a senator and major planter.

Nevertheless, Rachel seemed undeterred, and Tom admired her pluck. Women were expected to be delicate, demure, and dependent first on a father, then on a husband, for their support. But in her pursuit of the theater, Rachel was the opposite—bold, daring, and strong-willed. She left school to throw herself into acting, and Tom saw her as a free spirit, breaking the mold that society had cast for her. He felt that she was buoyed by the same restlessness of the new age that lifted him, the sultry breeze that swept them off together toward love and adventure.

The Southern beauty cast off the conventional bonds of her upbringing not only for the lure of the theater but also for the passion of his arms. He'd watch her perform, and then they'd meet later for heady nights of laughter and love. To Tom, Rachel was a lily in full bloom whose fragrance permeated his existence.

But then something happened to blow the petals away. Charlotte Barnwell contracted a sudden illness when she learned that Rachel had decided to stay in Philadelphia to work in the theater. Rachel made what was supposed to be a brief trip home to be at her mother's side. But the recovery was long and the illness was vague, and Rachel never did return to Philadelphia. Tom was crushed.

His own busy life healed him. Yet he was left with a question that seemed unanswerable: Why? Why would Rachel abandon a life she loved, a city she loved . . . and him?

She wrote to him about how happy she had become at home and beseeched him to return too. Her parents had greeted her homecoming with extravagant gifts. They designated the services of one of the plantation's seamstresses as exclusively for her, and they set aside a room at Ruby Manor just to house her expanding wardrobe. They also provided trips to New Orleans for jewelry, perfumes, and imported fabrics, as well as an apparently limitless allowance to keep her happy. Rachel described in glowing terms the parties her parents had thrown for her, lavishing her with attention fit for a princess. She seemed to fall into the gaiety of being a Southern belle. She wrote of how terribly she missed him, but she wanted him to give up the opportunities that Philadelphia offered in order to live in Greenbriar with her. After a while, he stopped answering her letters.

Less than a year after Rachel had gone back to Greenbriar, Tom unexpectedly returned home also. The reason wasn't Rachel's entreaties but the death of his father and the need for him to take control of the family plantation and bank.

He found a subdued Rachel back in Greenbriar. In Philadelphia, she had sung exhilarating songs that stirred him. In Greenbriar, her taste had switched to quieter ballads that lacked the fire of her previous preferences. Her headlong lust for him had taken a cautionary step back also, so that she could discern his intentions before bestowing too many of her favors. He found her belated propriety to be a form of pressure on him to commit to something about which he now had growing misgivings.

She seemed to want more of his attention at a time when she was provoking more of his doubts. In Philadelphia, she never had reason to question his love for her, but now she had. In Philadelphia, she never viewed his invention as competing with her for his time, but now she did. In Philadelphia, he never doubted that she was the kind of woman who excited him, but now. . . . Something had happened to the prized flower that blossomed that year in Philadelphia. Was Rachel's spirit like the roses of Ruby Manor, with deep roots and perennial blooms, or was it more like the passing flowers that show their brilliance in one glorious summer, then perish in the autumn wind?

As he stood with Rachel in the parlor of Ruby Manor, he noted the one vestige of her former spunk: the alluring dresses that displayed her beautiful figure and tortured him with desire. He stroked such a dress now, feeling the pleasing curves of the body beneath it. He held her close, and for one thrilling moment, he felt as if they were back in Philadelphia. The tragic events of the past day seemed to intensify his desire to recapture their former joy.

Rachel lifted her head from their embrace and looked up at him. "You won't be going away now, will you? I mean, the invention . . . it's over, isn't it?"

He looked at her, dumbfounded. Was she in a state of shock and not thinking clearly?

"You won't be fixing to find that machine now, after all that's happened, will you?"

"I will."

She pushed away from him. "But hasn't it caused enough trouble already?"

His head dropped at the stinging remark.

"I'm sorry, Tom. I didn't mean—"

"It's okay." He told himself that she had a right to resent his invention—and him—after what had happened.

"I only meant that now, more than ever, I need you here with me and not roaming around the country." Her eyes flashed with a sudden idea. "Why, with Papa gone, there are new opportunities for you right here, Tom."

"Whatever do you mean?"

"You can go into *politics*."

Tom raised his eyebrows, repulsed by the prospect.

"Papa always said that to get what you want in life, you need to be well connected. I mean, it would be so wonderful, Tom, if you took Papa's senate seat!"

The thought left him speechless. He wanted to dispel her crazy notions immediately, because he had no intention of entering politics. But surely now was not the time to discuss *his* future—or his astonishment at how little she seemed to understand of it.

"Why don't you think about it?" she said to his unsmiling face.

Her voluminous hoop skirt brushed against the furniture as she walked around the parlor. The room had the static neatness of a painting, with every item in place, rather than a living space for active people who moved a chair, opened a book, tossed a hat on the sofa, or otherwise left their mark.

"It's lonely here." Rachel sounded pleading, as if Tom were to provide a solution. She paused to stare dreamily through the glass doors of a cabinet that held family mementos. "Aunt Polly's gone. And now Papa's gone." She pointed to pictures of them in the cabinet. Her eyes dropped to the bottom shelf, where a tattered old doll was perched in the corner. "My doll Sis was just a fantasy." She looked at him sadly. "And now, with you busy all the time with those projects you make for yourself—"

"In Philadelphia *you* were busy too. Remember how I used to wait for you to finish your classes and rehearsals and performances before you found time to look at me?"

She smiled at the memory.

His eyes brightened with a sudden thought. "Say, let's start a theater here! You and me. I'll invest in it, and you can run it—and star in it. I'll bet you won't be lonely then!"

"Oh, no, I couldn't."

"When you were performing, you weren't lonely. The theater made you glow, Rachel."

She gazed out the window, reminiscing. "I don't know where I got the energy I had then. Why, I was downright delirious. You can't stay feverish like that for long. You have to come back down to earth."

"Why is earth a place where you're bored?"

"*Philadelphia.*" She pronounced the word affectionately. "My life there seems so distant now, like a dream."

"You were happy then. *We* were happy."

She nodded wistfully.

"Then you went home and somehow things changed. Why didn't you come back?"

"At first, I intended to. I was angry with Mother when she said she would have Papa cut off my money if I continued in the theater—"

"What? You never told me you were threatened."

"I was *not* threatened," she said indignantly. "They were trying to help me."

"You could've come back to me. I would've helped you get by."

"I didn't want to just get by. Life in the theater was so . . . grueling. No sooner did I get back home then my friend Margie Gainsworth read me an article about how actors got nervous conditions and ruined their digestion after years of those horrid auditions with all the rude directors. Then if you get the part, there are the nasty critics. The struggle and grind of it all, well, my goodness, it changed the actors. They weren't themselves anymore. They were ill and . . . unhappy. And Lord knows, the odds they'd ever get the leading roles they wanted were unbelievably slim." She sighed. "As I listened to Margie reading, I thought that being an actor was like climbing a mountain . . . barefoot." She gazed out the window introspectively. "I was afraid I'd slip and fall. After all, what was so special about *me*? Golly, Tom, there were so many other actors to compete with."

"But you were good, *really good*. It's no disgrace to slip and fall, but you stood out from the crowd. I think you would've reached the top."

"But I *have* reached the top. I'm a star *right here!*" He wondered if the forced cheerfulness in her voice was to convince him—or herself. "I still sing. I just performed at the Harringtons' barbecue."

He listened, confused. His mind wandered to the day that the talented figure before him had performed patriotic songs in a public square at an Independence Day gathering of thousands, with her soaring voice and magnetic presence moving many to tears.

"And I also sang at Mrs. Kipling's pumpkin-pie contest."

He had no reply.

"You don't understand, Tom. When I came back, the people in Greenbriar gossiped about me, with their nasty tongues wagging all the time. I couldn't stand it!"

"Maybe they were jealous of you."

"That shriveled old witch Mrs. Garner whispered about the *senator's daughter* living wild and loose in Philadelphia. And Mrs. Jeffreys asked me to please assure her that what she'd heard about me wasn't true. I had such a fright!" Rachel lowered her voice to a whisper. "I thought she had found out about *us*!"

"Just how would that be her business?"

"Turns out, that wasn't it. She said she'd heard that I joined a *theater*. That was worse than an affair. She made it sound as if I'd joined a brothel. You see, the folks here have a different view of things than we did."

"A very close-minded view."

"Now, Tom!"

"We don't have to walk down the same dusty old roads people walked in the past. The world is changing, Rachel."

"Not here it isn't."

He stared at her silently, at a loss to find the magic words that would make her the person she used to be.

"So I left the theater." She glared at him. "Tell me, Tom, what's so wrong with that?"

"By all means, leave it. But not out of *fear*."

"You make it sound as if I committed treason."

"Only to yourself. I mean, you shouldn't betray yourself."

"I was causing Mother to fall ill, and I was an outright embarrassment to Papa in the senate. And what was I doing to *myself*? My friend Abby, bless her heart for trying to help me . . . well . . . she told me terrible stories about what happened to a woman she knew in the theater in New Orleans. Her parents downright cut her off for her wayward life. Then crooked managers robbed her and fickle audiences deserted her for a newer star. She was pushed out to walk the streets, penniless." Her eyes looked dark and troubled. "It was a steep climb and a hard fall. So you see, when my parents offered me anything I wanted to stay in Greenbriar, I realized it was for the best."

"But you have to live *their* way."

"It's not *their* way. It's our traditions. And they serve us well."

"I just want you to be happy, Rachel."

"I'm happy."

She might have said that she was bored or sleepy with the same indifference. This was the girl who had run into his arms, danced with joy, screamed with glee at the smallest of pleasures in Philadelphia—at a dessert she liked, a new play opening, a morning walk through the park. The fire in Rachel had somehow dampened.

"When I decided to stay here, the thing I missed most was you. I missed you terribly, you know." She looked up at him in her alluring way. "But now you're home too."

His eyes searched hers as he tried to understand. Was she really happy? he wondered.

"You said you wanted to help Mother and me. You said you felt *responsible*. . . ."

His eyes closed in anguish.

"I don't want you to suffer, Tom. I just want you to stay here with us and help us preserve what Papa worked so hard to provide for us. Now that he's been taken from us . . . so suddenly . . . so horribly."

His head fell as if a knife in his chest had just been plunged deeper. He took her hands. "Of course," he whispered painfully, "I'll stay here with you. For as long as it takes to get you and your mother through this."

He was relieved when Charlotte appeared at the door.

"We can go out now and talk to the slaves," said Mrs. Barnwell. "I want to be soothing. That's how Wiley always spoke to them. He told them he'd look after them and protect them. We must assure them they'll be fed, clothed, and cared for just as they've always been. That's what's always kept them . . . manageable."

A sudden thought struck Tom. Is that what Charlotte and her husband had been doing to Rachel? Keeping her fed, clothed, and cared for so that *she* would be . . . manageable?

As he walked out of the parlor with Rachel and Charlotte, he paused to notice an oil painting of the senator by the front door. Tom had seen the portrait on many occasions, but this time it held a special significance to him. He looked admiringly at the kind face, the intelligent eyes, and the dignified bearing of the man who lost his life defending the invention. He recognized the signature of a local artist in a corner of the painting.

"Mrs. Barnwell, may I ask the painter if he can make me a reproduction of this portrait? I would love to have a remembrance of the senator."

"Why, yes, of course, Tom."

"It would mean so much to me. The senator meant so much."

"By all means, have a copy made, Tom," said Charlotte.

"The senator believed in me."

"We believe in you too, Tom. You're a good young man. You'll provide a comfortable life for a wife"—Charlotte's eyes darted to Rachel—"and a family of your own." She patted his arm fondly. "You have a solid future here in Greenbriar. We believe you'll do very well running your father's bank and plantation."

"But Senator Barnwell believed in my other work—my *invention*—and he . . . bravely . . . defended—"

"The vicissitudes of an inventor's life weren't what I was speaking of," said Charlotte.

"Whenever I'll look at this painting, Mrs. Barnwell, it'll serve as all the more reason why I *must* develop my invention, not only for me but now also for the brave man who gave . . . everything . . . for it. My success will be my tribute to your husband's memory."

Charlotte stared at him. "Good Lord, Tom, what if that thing of yours is *cursed?*"

"How can *progress* be cursed?" Tom asked incredulously.

"What if Wiley's death is an *omen?*"

"An omen . . . of what?"

Charlotte seemed to stare through Tom at a disturbing image of her own. "People who tried to defy fate are no longer here."

"What do you mean?"

Charlotte didn't seem to hear him, captured by a haunting memory that tugged at her.

"Mrs. Barnwell, are you all right?"

"No one can tamper with our way of life. Those who tried are no longer around to talk about it."

"Tom," interjected Rachel, "you've been away so long, you don't remember that our traditions are our soul. You can't change that. No one can change that."

# CHAPTER 6

The Greenbriar sheriff's office was barely larger than a slave's cabin, but the man occupying it didn't seem to care. His tavern-like furnishings—a desk, a table, and a few chairs made of rustic planks—appeared to provide all the comfort he needed. A copy of the state and local statutes on top of a trunk filled with legal papers composed his library. Sheriff Robert Duran sat at his desk in shirtsleeves, writing notes about the case that consumed him. Out the front window, he could see the main street of the town he protected. Out the back window, away from public view, he could see the means by which he protected it—the brick jail and the courtyard with the scaffold in the corner, ready for use when needed.

His eyes drifted to the jail, where his uncle Ted Cooper stood at the barred window of his second-floor cell. The prisoner seemed to be staring across the courtyard between them, directly into his office—and into his eyes. Could his uncle really see him at that distance, he wondered, or was it his imagination? He lowered his head to his notes, avoiding the window.

It was the second morning since he had been called to the murder scene at the Crossroads. He glanced at his pocket watch. The men he had asked to come to his office to discuss the Barnwell case should be arriving soon. The overseer, Bret Markham, and the plantation's slaves had said they knew nothing about the invention in the old carriage house or the crime committed there. They had seen guests attending the funeral, but nothing that looked suspicious. The sheriff was unaware of anyone having contact with the invention, aside from the three men to whom Tom had shown it: the senator, Cooper, and Nash Nottingham.

Duran had questioned Tom, who said he was alone in his room, writing, after the senator and Cooper had retired for the night. One servant said he'd brought logs, and another had taken tea to Tom's room late that night, corroborating his whereabouts. Although a slave's testimony had no legal standing in a case against a white man, the sheriff had no reason to doubt what he'd heard.

Yesterday he had visited the Nottingham plantation, where he spoke to Nash and his mother. They both seemed genuinely shocked to learn of the senator's death. Nash explained that after Polly Barnwell's funeral, he'd left the Crossroads to have supper and spend the night at his own plantation. Mrs. Nottingham confirmed that her son had been at home with her the entire evening; she'd retired early and seen her son before going to bed and again in the morning at breakfast.

Also yesterday, the sheriff had visited Ruby Manor, where he found Tom, who had already broken the news to Barnwell's wife and daughter. The sheriff had learned that Charlotte and Rachel Barnwell knew about Tom's invention and its whereabouts at the Crossroads, but they couldn't conceive of anyone who'd have a motive to commit the horrible crime. After Polly's funeral, they had returned home, where they had spent the evening in the company of neighbors until past midnight. When he left Ruby Manor, the sheriff dropped in on those neighbors, who verified the story.

Duran uncovered no loose ends and no conceivable suspect for the crime other than his uncle, who had been found standing over the body. Nevertheless, he had called Tom Edmunton, Bret Markham, and Nash Nottingham to his office that day. The inventor and the overseer were at the Crossroads at the time of the murder, and Nottingham was the only other man besides the inventor, the deceased, and the suspect who knew the nature of the device in the old carriage house. Duran had spoken to each of the men separately. Now he wanted to question them together to see if he could learn anything more.

He saw the first of his visitors coming up the front steps to his office and rose to put on his vest. Pinned to it was the silver badge he kept polished and wore proudly. His eyes paused on the emblem on the badge, a replica of a blindfolded goddess holding the scales of justice. He had always thought of her cause as his also. He glanced up at the man in the cell window whose eyes haunted him, the man he loved and couldn't believe guilty. He silently vowed to uncover any information that might lead to a different interpretation of the crime. But because of his loyalty to the lady on his badge, the facts would have to fall where they might on her scales.

After the three men arrived and everyone took seats around the table, Duran searched the men's faces. From Nash to Markham to Tom, he saw expressions from coolness to distrust to curiosity.

"I called you here to go over some things and ask a few questions," he said simply. "First, Mr. Edmunton, tell me a little more about how your invention happened to get to the Crossroads on the day of Polly Barnwell's funeral."

Tom began his story. "I wanted to start a company that would develop my tractor and later sell it. This was a big venture, and I needed more money than I had, so I entered a contest in Philadelphia that was a showcase for new inventions where I hoped to find backers. I continued to make improvements on my invention until the last moment before I had to depart, which left me with little time to spare. It was at this time that Polly Barnwell died, and her funeral was set for the day I was going to leave on my trip, so I planned to miss the service."

As he spoke, Tom looked at the sheriff, glancing occasionally at the others.

"The day before the funeral, I went to Ruby Manor to pay my respects to the Barnwells and apologize for having to miss the service. Rachel was upset with me. I had been courting her, but I was also neglecting her to work on my tractor. I hadn't expected her to respond so . . . unfavorably. I was puzzled for a moment about what to do. The senator, who was present during the discussion, inquired about my plans. He consulted the steamboat schedule in a newspaper that he had handy and came up with a solution."

"And what was that?" asked the sheriff.

"I could catch another steamer the morning after the funeral, which would get me to Philadelphia in time for the contest. Because the Crossroads is so much closer to Bayou Redbird, he suggested I take the invention there, attend the funeral, stay the night, then immediately head for the docks the next morning. The delay would be inconsequential, he suggested, and I could make Rachel happy while still carrying out my plan. I agreed to his alternative plan, and he sent his most trusted servant on his fastest horse to the docks with a note to reserve a place for me and my cargo on the steamboat leaving the day after Miss Polly's service. The servant later returned with my new reservation."

The sheriff nodded.

Tom continued. "The senator came up with a further suggestion. He needed to go to the Crossroads early on the day of the funeral. So if he hauled the tractor there for me, then I could do him the favor of riding with Mrs. Barnwell and Rachel in their carriage later, to console them, he said. He didn't want to leave them grieving without the benefit of his comfort, yet he wanted to arrive at Miss Polly's plantation well before the ladies would be ready to leave. It also seemed as if he wanted to help me smooth things out with his daughter before I left town."

"Why was Senator Barnwell arriving early at the Crossroads?" asked the sheriff.

"He said he wanted to look over the plantation journals and see that everything was in order because Ted Cooper was coming to inspect the place with an eye to purchasing it. The senator explained that the Crossroads had come into his hands upon Polly Barnwell's death. At his age, he said, he couldn't take on another plantation and would rather sell it."

The sheriff nodded.

"Nash was there," Tom continued. "He heard all of this."

"Is that so?" The sheriff turned to Nash.

"I was at Ruby Manor to pay my respects," said Nash. "I heard the senator offer to haul something to the Crossroads for Tom, so he could ride with the ladies. Now, had the senator asked *me* instead, I would've been quite happy to accompany the women, and I daresay I would've been more interested in them than in a chunk of machinery." Nash, whose manner toward Tom oscillated between politeness because Tom was his banker and jabs because Tom was his romantic rival, smiled pleasantly, but Tom wasn't amused.

"So, Mr. Edmunton, you agreed to let the senator take your invention to the Crossroads?"

"I was hesitant, Sheriff. Truthfully, I didn't want to let the tractor out of my sight for a second. That's why I wouldn't bring it to the docks beforehand for storage or let a servant take it there. I was reluctant indeed. The senator seemed to read my thoughts, because he assured me he would take the utmost care of the thing. I trusted him above anyone, and if I hadn't agreed, I feared it would seem I lacked that confidence. So I felt obliged to say yes. Early the next morning, the day of the funeral, I brought the tractor to Ruby Manor, which is the next turn off the main road to town from my place, and I entrusted it to the senator. Indeed, he was most careful, and the invention arrived quite safely at the Crossroads."

The sheriff said nothing. He stared soberly at Tom, digesting the story. Then he turned to Nash.

"Mr. Nottingham, when did you arrive at the Crossroads?"

"I rode there early on the day of Miss Polly's funeral."

"When?"

"In the morning."

"Why did you arrive so early, when the service wasn't till the afternoon?"

"After I heard the senator say he was going there early, I figured it'd be a good time to have a conversation with him . . ."—he glanced at Tom— ". . . in private."

"A conversation about what?" asked the sheriff.

"Well, it's really no one's business."

"Sir, you'll please answer the question."

"But I do have personal affairs, Sheriff."

"Either in private or at this meeting, you'll please answer."

"Why should I?"

"Because you're one of only three men who were shown an unusual object. And one of those men is dead."

Nash sighed in resignation. "Okay, Sheriff, if you must know, I'll tell you. After all, my affections are no secret. I was going to ask for Miss Rachel's hand."

"Were you?" said Tom.

"And I was going to ask for the Crossroads as a wedding present."

Tom looked incredulous.

Nash smiled pleasantly, as if unaware of any impropriety. "Is that any more crazy than giving Rachel's hand to an inventor who goes tinkering with dirty machines and blazing around the country with his wild schemes?"

"You mean you were going to address your courtship suit to the senator on the day of a family funeral?" asked the sheriff.

"The Crossroads was part of the deal. I heard the senator say he was fixing to sell the Crossroads to Cooper, so I had to act fast."

"So you wanted to get Rachel as part of a land deal?" snapped Tom.

Nash laughed, unperturbed. "Look, old boy, I should think we could discuss this matter civilly. Before you moved back here, Rachel and I grew rather fond of each other. If I could obtain her father's blessing, I had reason to hope she'd . . . well, see the folly of her ways with you and open her heart to a more suitable arrangement."

"Suitable for whom?"

For a moment Nash dropped the glossy smile and replied earnestly, as if he understood something his rival had yet to learn. "Suitable for everyone concerned. Even for you, Tom."

"How's it suitable for the senator to give his land and daughter away to someone who's already depleted his own fields and whose financial mismanagement is no more a secret than his affections?" asked the man who was Nash's banker.

"I beg your pardon," said Nash, his coolness returning. "By giving the Crossroads to me, the senator could secure his daughter's future by his side. Our children would grow up sitting on their grandpapa's knee."

"Did you ask the prospective mother what she thought of your scheme to produce babies for the senator's knee?" asked Tom.

"What was the alternative? To give Rachel's hand to someone who was less . . . shall we say . . . *stable?*"

Tom stared at his rival contemptuously.

"With you as his son-in-law, a time could come when the senator would never see his daughter again. Why, she might have been hauled to the North, just like the tractor!"

Nash then turned to the sheriff to press his case. "With Tom courting investors more ardently than he courted Rachel, what future did she have with him? I could offer Wiley Barnwell assurance that I'd *never* leave

Greenbriar, and I'd *never* subject his daughter to the vagaries of an inventor's life." Nash turned back to Tom. "Look, old boy, even if you *are* my banker, for Rachel's sake these things had to be said."

"And when you arrived at the Crossroads on the morning of the funeral, did you talk to the senator about your proposal?" asked the sheriff.

"I had a few words with him. I told him I wanted to . . . acquire . . . the Crossroads. He said he thought my funds were strained. I told him I had a unique plan that might be amenable to him. He told me about Cooper's interest in purchasing the place. But then he paused and added that he supposed it was good to have more than one potential buyer. It might raise the price."

"Did you tell him your plan wasn't to *buy* the place, but to get it as a present, along with his daughter?" the sheriff blurted out.

"No!" Nash seemed perturbed as he recalled the encounter. "I didn't get a chance to explain the full nature of my innovative plan and its benefits to him. The senator said he had to go to town on a matter, so he instructed this man here"—he pointed condescendingly at Markham—"to show me around the place. The senator said that after I'd gotten a tour of the fields, we'd talk sometime soon."

"And did the senator go into town that morning?"

"Why, I assume so," said Nash. "I was feeling a touch of *mal de mer* from the coach ride, so I went into the house for a glass of claret before my tour commenced."

The sheriff turned to Markham for an answer.

"Yeah, the senator, he gone to town that mornin'," Markham offered.

"Why?"

"To sell a slave girl," said the overseer.

"You mean the senator went to town to sell a slave on the day of the funeral?" asked the sheriff.

"'Twas Miss Polly's servant. She was a whole lot o' trouble anyways, and she warn't needed no more. The senator said he was goin' to Stoner's. To find her a suitable place, was what he said."

Since Greenbriar was a distance from the slave markets in the large cities, the local planters were known to meet informally to trade slaves at Stoner's Saloon in Bayou Redbird.

"So the senator went to the docks?"

"He was gone for a bit, then he came back without the slave. Said he found her a nice family."

"Did this matter have anything at all to do with the invention?"

"None far as I know," said Markham.

The sheriff turned to Nash. "Mr. Nottingham, could there have been any other reason the senator declined to talk to you? I mean, what was your relationship with him like?"

"Oh, excellent. I had a fine relationship with the senator—even though he pushed me off to waste my time with someone who had no bearing on my affairs," he said, offended, "and who couldn't possibly be of any value to me." As a king might scorn a pesky subject, Nash glared at the overseer.

Markham bristled. The resentment he constantly held in his eyes now made its way out of his mouth. "If the senator liked you so much, why'd he throw you outta the kitchen?" The overseer leaned over the table to Nash, sneering like a dog baring its teeth. "Why don't you tell the sheriff 'bout that?"

Duran turned sharply to Nash. "You had a *dispute* with Barnwell?"

"Oh, that?" Nash laughed. "That was nothing, just a trifle!" He turned to Markham. "How *dare* you insinuate—"

"You had some words with Wiley Barnwell? In the kitchen?" The sheriff pressed.

"It was later that day, after the funeral service and the little engineering lecture from our Yankee-schooled friend. It seemed the senator was bent on courting Cooper as a buyer that evening, so I figured I'd best be on my way home. I was ready to leave and looking for my coachman. He was nowhere to be found. He wasn't in the stable, and since I know he has a fondness for food, I surmised where he might be. I wanted to catch him at his dalliance myself, you know, put some fear into the lazy scoundrel, so I went into the kitchen to look for him. The senator observed me, and I'm afraid he got the wrong idea." Nash laughed. "It seems he had the preposterous notion that I was chasing after a slave girl! He told me to leave."

"Throwed you out, I'd say," Markham volunteered.

"How very rude of you! Why, Sheriff, it appears this crude man wants to misinterpret my activities out of sheer malice."

"I seen what I seen," Markham insisted. He turned to the sheriff to explain. "The Barnwells offered me food after Miss Polly's service. But they didn't say to join the reception and mingle with their kind, no sir! They pointed to the kitchen, so I told one o' them slaves there to run a platter to my cottage. Then I left the place to go back 'cross the hill, when I seen fancy boy here headin' into the kitchen. Caught my attention 'cause his kind don't never go near slaves. Couldn't hear nothin', but I seen Barnwell watchin' him, and the senator, he don't like what he sees one bit. I remember the senator frownin' when he seen fancy boy that mornin' too. He was none too happy with the likes o' him from the first. Next thing I know, the senator follows him in the kitchen. Then he shoves him out the door so hard he skids to the ground and gets a good dustin' on his purty suit."

"Perhaps the senator got a bit ruffled," said Nash unperturbed. "But then I explained the matter. I told him why I was there. I apologized for the misunderstanding, and the incident was over. I found my coachman and left on amiable terms with the senator, *quite* amiable."

"Didn't look none too friendly to me," Markham grumbled.

"Did you see the incident, Mr. Edmunton?"

"No, Sheriff, I didn't."

"Mr. Nottingham," said the sheriff, "did your chasin' a slave girl around the kitchen have anything at all to do with the invention?"

"The incident had nothing to do with Tom's machine. And I most certainly was *not* chasing a slave girl!"

"Were you angry with the senator for treating you like he did?"

"No, Sheriff. The senator might have sometimes failed to accord me the esteem I deserve, but I was always confident that he would recognize my value to him in the end." He looked pointedly at Tom.

"Was there anything else you did to anger Wiley Barnwell?"

"Good heavens, no." Nash looked at Markham crossly. "Sheriff, you might want to direct your suspicions elsewhere, because I saw Mr. Markham come out of the old carriage house that morning when I arrived." He turned to the overseer. "Did you tell the sheriff you were in there with the machine?"

Nash seemed pleased that he had gotten the stone-faced Duran to arch his eyebrows.

"What about it, Mr. Markham?" The sheriff's voice hardened. "I thought you knew nothing about the invention."

"I don't."

"Then what were you doing in the old carriage house?"

"I seen the thing. Looked like a heap o' iron junk with wheels. Was nothin' to me. I paid it no mind."

"Then what were you doing in there?"

"The senator said a slave needed a little educatin', so I done it."

"You mean you whipped a slave?"

"A few stripes, Sheriff." He waved his hand dismissively. "I did it in the ol' carriage house, but it had nothin' to do with the machine there. The wench was disobeyin' orders, not doin' her chores, nothin' out o' the ordinary for that place. I tell you, some o' them slaves need educatin' bad. 'Course, Miss Polly never allowed it! That didn't stop her none from gripin' to me how the hands didn't work hard 'nuff. Why, I was glad to see the senator had more sense and some discipline was bein' enforced." Markham's eyes suddenly came alive. "I was happy to help on that score!"

"And where were you all evening?"

"Like I told you before."

"Tell me again."

"In my cottage, like always, where the gentleman here found me later and told me 'bout the killin'." He gestured to Tom.

"I understand you were dressed and about to go out when Mr. Edmunton came for you. Where were you going at that hour?"

"Checkin' on the field hands. Seein' they was in their cabins and not makin' mischief, like I check on 'em every night. Just like I told the gentleman." Markham forced an anemic smile at the man who apparently was to be his new boss, at least until the Crossroads was sold.

Tom listened quietly, having nothing to add. He was convinced that Cooper was the murderer and hadn't heard anything at the meeting to the contrary.

When the sheriff had exhausted his list of questions, he rose to end the meeting. "Thank you for your time, gentlemen."

Tom lingered after the other men had left. He wondered if he could get a clue to the tractor's whereabouts from Cooper. He went to the jail, but predictably, the prisoner refused to speak to him. It would be tantamount to admitting guilt if Cooper let slip any information leading to the recovery of the device. He would have to find it himself, Tom figured, sighing at the daunting task.

Walking toward his horse, he observed the people of Greenbriar. A man in a wagon carrying sacks of cornmeal passed him on the road; another man entered the general store; a woman with a small parcel left the post office; a few neighbors chatted pleasantly by an open carriage. As Tom stood high on the bluff, away from the rowdy saloons, gambling dens, and noisy steamships of Bayou Redbird, he thought that Greenbriar, with its sleepy streets and sprawling plantations, seemed to be a place of calmer waters. Or was it? he wondered. Though he saw a tranquil surface, his thoughts were pulled by the undertow of violence at the Crossroads.

After his sleepless night at the murder scene, Tom had spent the past night at Ruby Manor. With Mrs. Barnwell overwhelmed by the prospect of handling the plantation's business affairs and Rachel showing no interest in doing so, he had stayed the evening to discuss the most urgent matters weighing on Charlotte. Then, too exhausted to ride home, he accepted the women's offer to stay the night. He had come directly from there to the sheriff's meeting. Now, as he was about to return home for the first time since departing for Polly's funeral, he felt a sudden uneasiness, wondering what new mischief he would find from those who were tied to him against their will.

As he reached his horse, a quiet figure down the street caught his attention. It was a young woman sitting in the open wagon of the town's slave patrol. He recognized the runaway whom he'd helped in the woods. Gone was her proud stance and fiery spirit. She stared numbly, with her mouth gagged, her hands tied in front of her, and her feet bound. Her horse was tied to the side of the vehicle, its muzzle stretching into the cart to nudge her face. The animal seemed to sense its mistress's distress and to want a comforting pat from her to dispel its uneasiness. Tom saw one of the slave catchers go into a tavern. His partner stood near the wagon with their bloodhound, while the captive grimly awaited her fate.

Soon the first slave catcher walked back to the wagon, accompanied by an unkempt man, about forty years old, carrying a saddle. The man paid the slave catchers, who then deposited the girl on the road, untied the animal from the cart, and rode off with their hound.

The large, dirty man saddled the horse. Then he towered over the girl's slim frame. He walked around her slowly, ominously. A sneer on his unshaven face made the girl tremble. With a pocket knife, he cut the rope around her ankles. He yelled at her, smacked her across the face, then pulled her toward him lecherously. Tom grimaced, guessing the reason why she had run away. Her tormentor untied the cloth gagging her mouth and cocked her head for a kiss. The girl snapped her face away in revulsion. The gruesome man forced it back. She bit his hand. That enraged him. He scowled, swore, and smacked her again. Blood dripped from the side of her mouth.

The man reached for a rope hanging on his saddle. He made a noose and swung it around her neck. As he tightened the noose to fit snugly, her eyes flashed in horror. Then he mounted his horse, grabbed the reins, and glanced at her slender form standing helplessly alongside him. She stood still, with her hands tied and a distant stare of the doomed in her eyes. She straightened her shoulders and breathed deeply in what seemed like an effort to control her terror and brace herself for the coming ordeal. Wretched with dirt and mud, she looked like an animal captured after a fierce fight and now left with no escape possible. Tom was held by the intensity of her face, for she seemed to be making an extraordinary attempt to focus coolly on the road ahead and to survive—if she could.

The man held two ropes: one attached to the horse and the other to the woman. Two passersby said nothing, unmoved by the sight of a woman on a leash. The owner tugged on the rope, jolting the girl.

"So, ya wanna run off, do ya? Now you're gonna do some real runnin'!" he roared maliciously.

As he was about to ride away, with her on foot and tethered to him, he seemed to have another thought.

"Wait," he said, dismounting. "There's somethin' we need to do first."

Her giant eyes followed his every move.

"What if you git more crazy ideas 'bout runnin' off while I'm sleepin' agin? There's somethin' we need to do first, before we git goin'."

He reached into his saddlebag and took out a small pair of pliers. "I'll make it so's you ain't never gonna pull that stunt again!" He snapped the tool's python-like jaws at her. "I'll pull that purty front tooth o' yours, so you won't git far if you try that agin! You be a marked woman from now on."

The girl screamed in terror. He grabbed her head in a vise grip with one hand, forcing her mouth open. She kicked him, hit him with her bound hands, and tried to pull her head away, but she was no match for a man of his size. With great effort, he fixed her front tooth in the pliers. Then, his elbow high, he readied himself to pull with all his might.

Tom was already running down the street toward them, an explosion rising within him.

"Stop! Stop! Stop this unspeakable act! Stop this instant!"

He was protesting not only the violence before his eyes but also the violence that had swallowed Barnwell and his tractor, the current of violence that he felt flowing through the town. He felt an urgent need to act against the insidious undertow before it pulled down yet another victim.

He lunged at the fiend who was his same height but twice his girth, and he wrestled the pliers from him, throwing them on the ground.

"Just what d'you think yer doin'?" The stench of alcohol wafted across Tom's face.

The man tried to grab him by the throat, but with quicker reflexes and a sober mind, Tom knocked him to the ground. As the man's face twisted in fury and his hand moved toward his gun, Tom pulled out a roll of bills and flashed it in the man's face.

"I'll relieve you of this woman right now."

The man's hand stopped midway to the weapon. He rose, staring at Tom in bewilderment, his anger cooling at the sight of the cash. He took it and counted in disbelief.

"Eight hundred? For *that wench*?"

In handing over the large sum of cash he was carrying for his journey, Tom had just done something he had never done and thought he would never do. Instead of buying a ticket to the new age, he was buying a parcel from the old one.

"Why, fella, that's a price ya might pay for a decent plowman, but for *that* piece o' trouble . . ."—he pointed to the girl—"that spiteful . . ." The man stopped. He seemed to think better of telling Tom he was paying too much. "Say, you don't come from 'round here, do ya? You sound like one o' them Yankees."

Tom hadn't seen the man before. Bayou Redbird brought strangers in and out of its docks, some of whom made their way up the bluff to Greenbriar.

"Just take the money and go."

The man smiled, flashing his decaying teeth. He removed the rope from around the girl's neck.

"All right, Yankee, she's all yours." He stuffed the bills in his pocket, picked up the pliers, and rode off.

The parcel and the purchaser looked at each other. Both seemed astonished. Tom untied the rope around her hands. Her wrists were red from the burning cord, but she paid them no attention.

He walked toward his horse with her following him. He offered her a canteen of water. The eagerness with which she drank told him it was from need, not pleasure. When she'd had enough and returned the vessel to him, he took a cloth from his saddlebag, spilled some water over it, and held it out to her. She rubbed her face with it, removing mud, grime, and blood to reveal the bronze glow of her skin beneath. She put the cloth in her pocket and stared at her new owner.

He realized he had exchanged no information about his purchase and had no . . . receipt.

"What's your name?" he asked.

She gave no reply. With her immediate ordeal ended, the abject terror drained from her face, and the defiance he had seen on their first meeting returned. She offered no words of gratitude.

"Who are you?" he persisted.

The only response he received was a contemptuous stare, as if all white men were the same rot to her. He took this as a sign that her condition had improved to its normal state.

He took hold of the horse's reins and gestured for her to mount. He waited, but she remained on her spot.

"It's a long way to walk," he said.

She remained motionless, so he mounted. He made room in front of him for her to ride sidesaddle, as women did, and extended his hand to help her up. When she didn't respond, he started off at a slow pace. She finally ran up and leaped on behind the saddle, straddling the horse like a man.

Cheerlessly, they rode together in that fashion. With her feathery light weight and keen sense of balance, she endeavored to stay on the animal while avoiding the revulsion of touching him. She succeeded, except for the wind that kept blowing disorderly strands of her long, wild hair across his face.

# CHAPTER 7

The clip-clop of Tom's horse was amplified in the silence of his ride with his companion. Greenbriar's countryside, lush even in February, draped the two travelers in its primeval beauty. After the previous day's storm, the resurrection fern that attached to the oak branches had turned from brown to green. The plant possessed the amazing capacity to endure dry periods in which it appeared to be dead, only to regain its color with a new rainfall. Tom felt no such resurrection of his parched mood as he rode along the main road through the town's plantation country. He had lost the man who was like a father to him and the machine that was to launch his future. And now, a precious sum of money was also lost, replaced by the hostile body behind him.

The young woman proved to be a good rider. Despite the brisk pace that Tom set, she ably kept her balance without reaching to hold on to him.

As they neared the turnoff to Indigo Springs, he wondered what he might find there. Even though he had been gone only two nights, he felt uneasy. Although the field hands were managed well by his trusted overseer, Nikolaus Bergen, what worried him were the servants in the big house and its dependencies, who were under *his* direction—or lack of it.

He felt in constant tension with the slaves he managed. The spark of choice, the great igniter of human energy, had been stolen from their lives, and they, in turn, took what they could from him. He was their enemy, and they were his nemesis. He could harness fuel to produce mechanical power, but he couldn't harness the human spirit. Perhaps no one could—or should. His overseer had promised to monitor the servants and craftsmen who lived and worked around the big house, but Tom knew that Nick would be kept busy ginning and baling the remainder of last year's crop and plowing for this year's planting. What liberties would his servants take? What tasks would they leave undone? What would they steal? He would soon find out.

He observed a wagon ahead, coming from the opposite direction and turning onto his plantation trail. One of his slaves was hauling a pile of bricks that Tom had purchased to build a new smokehouse. He bristled thinking of the time his servants spent idle while he bought bricks from the outside instead of making them with his own labor. He thought that the bricks would long be mass-produced by machine and hauled with a motor wagon before he would learn the secret of getting first-rate work from people who toiled without will, without gain, without hope, people whom it was against the state laws in 1859 to free, and against his nature to compel, making him feel as chained to them as they were to him.

Alongside the road, some of his fields came into view. He saw plow teams turning the soil, with the men looking as indifferent as the earth they tried to stir. His workmen would soon be planting a few hundred acres of corn and other crops consumed on the plantation, then a few thousand acres of the white gold, cotton. In a budding industrial age, these crops would be grown using manual methods of the ancient past, he thought, envisioning the day when a single man driving a motorized tractor could plant an entire field by himself.

He saw Nick on horseback, presiding over the field hands. Nick and his three brothers had come here from Germany for greater opportunities and were working as overseers on different plantations to earn enough money to buy their own land. The thirty-five year-old immigrant was too busy watching the hands to notice his employer. Growing cotton with gangs of unwilling men required constant scrutiny, Tom thought grimly, but it was better than the whip, which he forbade. He owned their bodies, but how much more would be possible if he could tap their will?

He took the turnoff to Indigo Springs, traveling along a path lined with towering trees whose seedlings were planted sixty years ago by his grandfather. In spacing the little plants many feet apart, his grandfather must have envisioned the spectacular growth that Tom now saw. He wondered if one day someone would travel this road in a motorized vehicle, realizing the future that he imagined.

He rode along a path that sliced through some of the richest soil deposits in the world, where his grandparents had started a modest family farm that had grown into one of the largest cotton plantations in the state. Now he planned to create a different and greater future through his invention. Would he ever recover it?

Through the trees, he glimpsed the roof of a solitary cabin high on a plateau away from the big house and its dependencies. It was the place where he had spent all the time he could spare. To anyone's casual glance, the simple wood structure looked like an old shack, but to Tom the place was a sanctuary for escaping the old world and a factory for building a new one. It was his workshop.

Tom had chosen a secluded spot to assemble his invention, with a shed to house the device and an arable field outside to test it. The hands lived a distance away, by the cotton fields, and had no contact with the shed. The household servants paid little attention to the small building removed from their living and working quarters. The pains he took to ensure his seclusion might have been unnecessary because none of the slaves had shown any curiosity about his endeavors. They seemed as content to be left alone by him as he was to be free of them, so his work had proceeded in privacy. When he had left with the invention for his trip, he shuttered the windows and locked the doors. Now, with the product of that shop lost, he felt no urge to ride up the hill and reopen the place. It was the first time he'd passed his workshop feeling no desire to be there.

The shop vanished from view as he headed toward the big house. He saw four servants walking out of the well house, plodding along lifelessly, hauling two buckets of water among them; it was a job for one person. He saw the laundress carrying a basket of clothes, with two helpers who carried nothing. The faces he saw looked blank, distant, bored. At that moment, when his grief had smothered his desire to do anything, he felt as listless as the servants. Is this what they felt like every day, he wondered, as they faced life without the spark of a goal, a purpose, or a dream?

Like the fern that covered the oaks, their spirit seemed never to die actually but rather to go dormant. It was resurrected in their leisure time, with the wild revelry of their music and dancing that seemed as much a need as a pleasure. He liked knowing they had an escape. The new numbness he felt seemed inescapable.

As he rode on the path around the front garden toward the big house, the servants walking about didn't yet notice him. His arrival was obscured by overgrown shrubs spilling onto the road, shrubs he had directed his servants to prune—how many times? The garden also needed tending, yet the grounds team was nowhere to be found.

The home up ahead looked fit for a painting: a two-story plantation house, with arching trees brushing the upstairs windows, a gallery wrapping the main level, and a pond partly visible behind the home with ducks wading across the water. Like so much of Greenbriar, he thought, the sight was one of untroubled beauty. A landscape artist would capture nothing more. But what picture lay beyond the painter's brush?

He thought of the young woman riding behind him. The scene of her torment was something that never made it onto artists' canvasses. He wondered how she viewed the site of her new captivity and what he was going to do with her.

Just then he saw a sight that vexed him. His stable hand and the chief factotum of the plantation, Jerome, was dressed in a satin vest and dress shirt, a carryover from his days as head of Colonel Edmunton's household servants before Tom had taken charge and demoted him. The lanky slave in his late twenties was neither dressed for the stable nor anywhere near it. In fact, Jerome was coming out the front door of the big house and holding a glass of sherry, looking like the owner. He also held a small object in his hand, which he inspected closely, then placed in his pocket. He availed himself of the rocker that was the colonel's favorite seat, and began swaying leisurely, enjoying the view—until he spotted Tom approaching.

In one frozen moment, the rocking stopped and Jerome stared at Tom in utter surprise. Then the resourceful slave sprang to his feet, casually hid the drink behind a pot of ferns, and began shaking the rocker, sitting, standing, shaking it again, as if testing its stability.

He leaned over the rail and called to another slave who was sawing wood nearby. "Lawd sakes, Sammy, the colonel's rocker, it's a-dancin' 'stead o' standin' still. You needs to fix it 'fore Mr. Tom come home—" He was shouting loud enough for Tom to hear. As the inventor rode up, Jerome feigned surprise.

"Well, well! What we got here? Mr. Tom! Ain't you went to Philerdelfi?"

"I had a change in plans." Tom stopped the horse in front of the house. "I hope I'm not interrupting your afternoon sherry."

Jerome laughed smoothly from the gallery. "I wuz inspectin' the big house, sir. Makin' sure them good-fer-nothin' maids keepin' it clean. Yes, sir, Jerome watch everythin' when yer gone," he said with great self-importance as he walked toward Tom. With his fine clothes and shiny boots, he looked ready for a Sunday social, but the day wasn't Sunday, and he was supposed to be in the stable.

"What about the drink that's behind the plant?"

"Oh!" His lips pursed as he pondered what to say next. "You see, Mr. Tom, I wuz testin' it, and it gone a tad sour, so I be gittin' Jimmy to replace it."

Jimmy was the butler. Either from their memory of Jerome as their boss under the colonel or from Tom's failure to supervise them himself, Jimmy and the other servants tended to take orders from Jerome.

"What's in your pocket?"

"Nothin' to concern you none, Mr. Tom. Jus' somethin' I's meanin' to do 'fore you return." He smiled charmingly.

"Come on, Jerome, let me see what you've taken this time."

Reluctantly, Jerome removed a small silver object from his pocket.

"The colonel's bookmark! How could you, Jerome? You took it from the library. You stole a keepsake from my father!"

"Why no, sir, I jus' inspectin' the house and sees this gotten tarnished, so I takes it to put a shine to it. The colonel, he don't let his stuff git tarnished, no sir! That disrespectin' to his memory. You needs to put a strap to them house servants so they be keepin' things better fer you."

"I'm not amused," Tom said curtly. "Not about this or with the watch or the ivory comb or the scarf pin that're also missing."

From his saddle, Tom stretched his hand down to Jerome, demanding the object back. Jerome gave it to him.

"And what about the ham that went missing from the smokehouse before I left?"

The slave sheepishly confessed. "Jerome jus' move Mr. Tom's ham from inside Mr. Tom's smokehouse to inside Mr. Tom's slave."

Tom wanted to punish him roundly. But how? He realized that Jerome's assessment of the situation was right. If he had stolen Jerome's entire life, how could he punish the slave for stealing a ham or a bookmark or anything else?

Tom wished that the attempt he'd made to get rid of Jerome had worked. Some time ago, through contacts at the docks, Tom had learned of a safe house in Cincinnati and of a steamship captain who could be persuaded, with sufficient inducement, to carry a slave there from Bayou Redbird on his route to and from the northern ports. When Tom suggested the possibility to Jerome, the slave was eager to leave, so Tom made the arrangements. He hired Jerome out to work on the captain's ship and gave him one hundred dollars to deliver secretly to the captain in exchange for leaving him behind in Cincinnati. Then he had Jerome memorize the address of the safe house. Both of them needed to be extremely careful. If Tom were caught aiding a slave to escape, he could go to prison for years, and if Jerome were caught, the consequences could be . . . worse.

Jerome eagerly embarked on the trip, and Tom thought he had finally seen the last of the incorrigible slave. But then Jerome unexpectedly returned home—without freedom and without Tom's money given to purchase it.

Jerome had never boarded the ship to Cincinnati. Instead, he'd spent a few days frequenting the shops at Bayou Redbird and lodging with a free man of color whom he knew. Then he returned to Indigo Springs with a new wardrobe for himself and gifts for his lady friends. To Tom's exasperation, Jerome resumed all of his old tricks. Although he was assigned to the stable, the unruly slave was often in the big house, bossing the servants, availing himself of Tom's food and liquor, and stealing little items along his way. The bondsman who managed to fleece Tom of his money and have the run of the house was a chronic reminder of his failure as a slave owner.

Jerome seemed to sense that his master struggled with the unhappy choice of either being a patsy or a brute. Since Tom rejected the latter, Jerome seemed bent on making him the former.

"Why didn't you go when you had the chance?" Tom had scolded Jerome at the time.

"Jus' afore I wuz s'posed to go, I sees a snake in my dreams, sir. A snake wid two heads. One head pointin' north, the other south." Jerome became agitated, as if he were reliving the dream. "The head pointin' north wuz hissin' and flashin' its tongue. It wuz fixin' to bite me somethin' fierce."

The ready grin on Jerome's face had vanished. He looked sincere and troubled. "You see, sir, I wuz more afeared o' the head pointin' north than the head pointin' south."

"Did the snake also point you to the shops to spend my money?" Tom sighed, exasperated. But his anger at the theft was tempered by pity at what appeared to be a genuine, paralyzing fear.

Tom had demanded the money back. He told Jerome to use the area around his cabin to plant crops and raise livestock of his own to sell. That way Jerome could recoup the money he squandered. "Give it back to me, and I'll hold it for the time when you're ready to make a second try for freedom," Tom had said. "I'll give it to you and write you a pass when you're ready. I spoke to the captain, and the deal's still open."

But Jerome never did generate the money—or the will—to make a second try for freedom. As Tom now stared at the slave whose sole ambition, apparently, was to irritate him, he thought of that old incident.

"I'm prepared to write that pass anytime, Jerome."

The slave smiled, knowing what Tom meant.

"If you'd just save the money you get from stealing my stuff and selling it at the docks, you'd have quite enough by now, you know."

"I reckon I likes stayin' put, sir."

Of course Jerome liked staying put, Tom thought, because his work output was sparse, while his benefits were plentiful. As long as Tom remained lax with him, why would the bondsman want to trade his happy indolence here for the demands of freedom elsewhere? Oddly, this slave at the bottom of Greenbriar's social structure reminded Tom of a man at its top. In idleness and pretension, Jerome bore an uncanny resemblance to ... Nash Nottingham. In Greenbriar's peculiar interplay of masters and slaves, Tom saw that the distinctions between the two groups were sometimes blurred.

"Say, whut's that muddy thing?" Jerome, in his impeccable attire, looked aghast at the vagabond peering at him from behind Tom on the horse.

"I thought we needed a woman's touch," said Tom.

"C'mon down, girl." As Jerome approached the damsel and reached for her waist, trying to help her dismount, she placed a dainty foot on his chest and kicked him down. Then she slid off the back of the horse, with Tom dismounting after her.

"Hey, whut ya think yer doin'?" Jerome got up, brushed himself off, and moved toward the girl, ready to grab her arms and shake some sense into her.

Tom stepped protectively in front of her, and Jerome backed off.

"Whut name this wench got?"

"Don't call her that."

"Say, Missy, whut name you got?"

The young woman's only answer was a disapproving stare at Jerome.

"What *is* your name?" Tom asked more politely, but was equally ignored.

"Well?" He glared at her, waiting. She glared back, offering nothing.

"Okay," he sighed, "we'll call her . . . hmm . . . " He pondered the matter. The two slaves stared at him curiously as he stroked his face, considered possibilities, then made up his mind.

"*Solo*. We'll call her *Solo*."

"Whut?" said Jerome. "That ain't no name."

"It's a good name for someone who wants to be left alone." Tom looked sympathetically at the silent woman with the big eyes and the slender figure. "Until you're ready to tell us your real name, you'll go by that."

Not given to lengthy ponderings, Jerome moved on to other matters.

"Well, Missy, there be things you gotta know 'bout yer place here. Ol' Jerome'll learn ya good. First, ya calls the genelman"—he pointed to Tom—"*mistah*. Not *marse* or *massa*. He don't like bein' called that, no ma'am. And next, you needs to earn yer keep. Ya gotta *work*, and work *hard*!" He pointed his finger at her sanctimoniously. "Mr. Tom, he be a fine genelman, he don't use no whip, so you can't take 'vantage o' that, no Missy. Jerome don't let you take 'vantage o' Mr. Tom!"

Solo stared at Jerome, then at Tom, her forehead wrinkled as she tried to assess the two new characters in her life.

"Now, Mr. Tom, I thinks Missy here kin help Aunt Bess in the kitchen." Bess was Tom's elderly cook. "Bess gettin' too old fer cookin'. She forgettin' the sugar in the cake and the eggs in the bread—"

"And do you eat my food too, Jerome?" Tom inquired. "Never mind. I know the answer."

"If not fer Jerome tastin' and directin' Aunt Bess, yer food be mighty hard to swallow, sir."

"And is that why you drink my sherry? Do you worry that there's an Aunt Bess in Spain botching the sherry too?"

Jerome laughed briefly, then continued with his theme. "Us go to the kitchen now, Missy, and see yer new job." He turned to Tom, as if remembering who had the final word. "Mr. Tom, if you 'low me, I takes care o' this, sir."

Tom hesitated, as he often did when it came to managing the slaves, which led Jerome to take charge by default. The inventor, who was decisive about where to place every nut and bolt on his tractor, had no preference at all for what the new girl, or any of them, did.

Jerome tried to lead Solo by the arm, but she pulled away from him.

"Ya can't jus' stay here and do nothin', Missy! Now, c'mon!"

Solo stood firm.

"Let her be," said Tom.

"But this little squirrel, she gotta do somethin', and we needs a cook, sir. Why, Aunt Bess, she shaky. She forgettin'. She can't make yer mama's dishes no mo'. Us needs young hands there, so's us kin eat good." He turned to the girl. "C'mon, now, Missy."

Jerome grabbed her arm and prodded her forward. She kicked him in the shin.

"Ow!" he wailed, clutching his leg. "You hellcat!" Taking great offense, he raised his hand to slap her.

Tom caught his arm and bent it behind him with a force that made the slave double over in pain.

"I said let her be."

Tom twisted the arm a little tighter, making Jerome wince, then he finally released it. Jerome was stunned by a side of Tom he had never seen.

"If you *ever* touch her, I'll send you to the fields to work there forever."

The ruthlessness in Tom's voice and the fear in Jerome's eyes were equally unprecedented. Tom's threat caught the slave by surprise. In the fields Jerome would actually have to work hard, a far cry from his current situation. For once speechless, he backed away from the girl, as if seeing for the first time a line drawn by Tom that he could never cross.

"We can decide what to do with her later. Right now, I'd like to see what *you've* been up to."

Tom walked toward the stable. Jerome took the reins of his horse and walked with him.

Solo cocked her head in curiosity at the two men, then trailed behind them.

On the way, Tom saw the wagon full of bricks that had just been hauled up the road. Someone had unhitched it from the horse by the site of the new smokehouse. Tom's three slaves who were supposed to build the new structure stood around the pile of bricks, talking and joking, while no one made any effort to unload them, lay them out, or begin work.

As the young master reached the stable and walked around, he gasped in exasperation. There was no water in the horses' buckets and barely any hay left in their stalls. The animals looked parched and weak. The horse that had just hauled the bricks up the road was standing in the middle of the stable. The poor beast had been left sweating, unattended, with saliva dribbling from its mouth.

"Damn it, Jerome, this animal looks terrible! They *all* look neglected!"

"I wuz jus' gettin' to them, Mr. Tom!"

As Jerome approached the sweating horse, Solo pushed him aside. She rushed to the animal, removed its harness, threw a blanket over its back, patted it reassuringly.

She pushed an empty bucket at Jerome. "Get water," she said.

"Why, you little tick! For Gawd, Mr. Tom, you tells her to hold her tongue wid Jerome!"

Solo turned to Tom, staring at him pointedly, as if his next move would set the limits—or liberties—on hers.

"But she's *right*, Jerome. You need to get water. You needed to do that a while ago."

The girl turned back to the slave, triumphantly. "Go! And be quick about it!"

She preceded to rub the animal down.

"Darn that Willie! Comin' back wid that big load," Jerome whined. "It too much for one po' beast! Why don't he take two? How's it be Jerome's fault that horse sweatin' so?" He turned to Solo. "Now, I handles this, Missy. I works here. *You* git to the kitchen!"

"*You* get to the kitchen! I'm staying here," said Solo.

She turned to the horse, rubbing it down and patting its nose. The animal seemed to like the petting, because when she stopped, it nudged her with its muzzle for more.

"Whut you doin', woman?" Jerome persisted. "This here Jerome's bizness. You stays out!"

"Get the water. Now!" she replied.

Tom noticed that the new addition to his household spoke correct English.

"Mr. Tom, this she-beast need whippin' bad!"

"Get the water, Jerome."

"Everybody 'round here mind Jerome, 'cept *her*." He punctuated his remark with a finger jabbing at her face.

When no one paid any attention, he left with the bucket, deflated and grumbling. "Maybe Jerome get lucky and this she-beast run away."

"Maybe *I'll* get lucky, and you'll both run away." Tom sighed.

# CHAPTER 8

The planters' church in Greenbriar was the tallest structure in town. Its steeple rose higher than the town's other buildings, and its pointed arches pierced the sky like spears above the softer curves of the trees around it. With its towering presence, the church seemed a fitting place for Wiley Barnwell's memorial service.

The thick stone cross embedded like a tombstone at the entrance cast a shadow over the winter camellias at its base just as the day's event cast its shadow on the arriving guests. Ornate carriages deposited plantation families and prominent public figures at the front steps. Tom stood at the door in top hat and tails, alongside Charlotte and Rachel in black bonnets and mourning dresses. As the wealthy and politically powerful guests entered the church, they offered condolences to the widow and daughter.

"Charlotte, dear," said plantation mistress Emma Turndale, a stout woman with a kindly face. "I can't believe he's gone!" The women embraced. "Why, just recently I was telling my niece from New Orleans about Ruby Manor, and how our senator built a home for his wife that surrounded her with roses! How can we ever forget him?"

"Thank you, Emma." Charlotte smiled gently beneath her veil.

Then Claire Winfield, a descendant of one of the town's oldest families, approached. "Oh, Charlotte, I'm heartbroken for you!"

"Hello, Claire." Charlotte embraced her friend.

"My dear, you've volunteered so much of your time through the years for our social activities and charity drives. Now it's our turn to relieve you of these tasks in your time of sorrow."

"Oh my, Claire, I forgot all about the events coming up in March!"

"Of course you did, and well you should. I spoke to Millie Browning, and we're ready to pitch in. We'll arrange the church fair and the spring dance."

"Thank you, dear. That's a big help," said Charlotte.

"Don't worry about a thing, honey. Of course, we can never fill your shoes, just as no one can ever fill Wiley's shoes in the senate. But we'll manage. You needn't give it a thought." Mrs. Winfield clasped Charlotte's hands in sympathy.

"Claire, you're a dear friend."

The next guest to pay his respects was a person whom everyone recognized and many knew personally.

"My dear Mrs. Barnwell," said the man, taking Charlotte's hand.

"Governor, it's so good of you to honor us."

"It was Wiley who honored us, Mrs. Barnwell, by his distinguished service to the people of Louisiana. And he couldn't have found a wife of greater poise, grace, and gentility to adorn his life than you."

Charlotte inclined her head at the compliment.

"I'm deeply saddened for *your* loss and *ours*." He bowed solemnly and kissed her hand.

"I appreciate your kindness, Governor."

He smiled, taking leave of Charlotte, then turned to Rachel. "Miss Barnwell," he said, bowing to kiss her hand, "let me offer my deepest condolences."

"Thank you, Governor."

"We will profoundly miss your father in the state senate. That chamber will not be the same without his leadership."

"He would be honored by your presence here today."

"My God, child, it infuriates me to think that your father met an untimely end over some foolish, harebrained invention!"

Rachel's eyes darted to Tom, and she fidgeted nervously. The governor looked from her to Tom, as if expecting an introduction. The newspapers had reported the story but without photographs of the people involved, and Tom and the governor had never met.

"Governor," she said, her voice suddenly tentative, "this is . . . uh . . . our neighbor."

The governor paused, expecting Rachel to provide a name. When it was not forthcoming, he shook hands with Tom.

"Governor," said Tom, "I should mention that *I'm* the in—"

"He's a planter! A planter, like Papa!"

"I see. How very nice." The governor looked confused.

Rachel changed the subject. "And how's your family, Governor? I remember the lovely dinners we had together."

"They're very well, thank you."

The governor tipped his hat to take leave of them, and then walked into the church.

Tom looked at Rachel, his face hurt and disappointed, but she avoided his eyes. Then he reproached himself for feeling slighted. After all, *he* wasn't the one who should expect consideration at this tragic time. It was his obligation to provide comfort to the real victims: Rachel and her mother.

"I'm going inside," said Rachel.

He curled her hand around his arm, wanting to escort her. But Rachel removed her hand and walked in without his assistance.

As she entered the church, a man approached to pat her arm reassuringly. Walking behind her, Tom overheard them speaking.

"You poor dear, having to go through this terrible ordeal! How are you holding up?"

"I'm doing well. It's nice of you to ask," said Rachel softly.

The pale face above the collar ruffles belonged to Nash. He and Tom looked at each other without greeting.

"I want to be here for you, Rachel, to help you recover from this most unfortunate ordeal," Nash continued. "When you feel up to it, I'd like to take you to our place for a stroll through our peach orchard and a taste of Mother's fine peach brandy. It'll relax you, dear, and get your mind off this terrible business, this truly . . . *senseless* tragedy." His eyes slid to Tom.

"That's very kind of you," said Rachel.

"I want to be sure you maintain all the comforts your dear father gave you."

Rachel smiled politely.

"You need to be in the company of a man like your father was, a man who can properly provide for your needs."

As his banker, Tom knew that the one man who did not fit that bill was Nash.

The women's skirts rustled against the pews, their giant hoops swaying to and fro, as the guests filled the church. Rachel and her mother sat in the front, with Tom and Nash in the row behind them.

Only one planter in the area was missing, Ted Cooper, who sat in a cell, awaiting trial. The evidence against him was deemed to be strong, providing grounds for holding him without bail.

Ushers gave songbooks to the guests, the church organist took his seat, and the ceremony opened with the group singing hymns. The solemn music moved Tom. His sorrow, grief, and admiration for the man being honored seemed to converge on his throat so that he couldn't find his voice to join in.

When the singing stopped, Greenbriar's mayor, a short, stocky man with shrewd eyes that were the same cool gray as his tailcoat, took the podium to deliver his eulogy.

"Where do I begin to honor my close friend, the man who was like a brother to me since childhood? Perhaps I should commence by honoring those who gave us Wiley Barnwell. His parents came here from Virginia and cleared a spot in the vast alluvial forest, where they built a home, raised a family, and started a successful plantation out of the wilderness. Then they passed their land on to Wiley and his generation."

The audience listened attentively.

"But the man who was to become a leader of our town and state wasn't content merely to take what was given him by his kinfolk. Where his papa planted a good crop, Wiley planted a great one. Where his papa built a simple cottage, Wiley built a mansion. Wiley Barnwell was a planter and businessman second to none!"

Tom's face showed admiration for the master planter who had generously reached out to him after his own father's death, teaching him the fine points of cotton farming that were instrumental to his own success.

"But Wiley Barnwell was far more than our leader in farming, my dear friends. He was also a moral compass to guide us through turbulent seas. He had an unshakable belief in the goodness of our society. He spoke out proudly about the South. Why, he was the most persuasive and prolific among us to uphold our customs—in our town meetings, in the halls of our legislature, and in newspapers throughout the South *and* the North. His was the proud voice we depended on to silence those incorrigible Yankee tongues, wagging at us with their wild notions about changing our way of life. Wiley was like a powerful tonic that braced us to withstand their fanatical attacks."

The crowd listened somberly. They showed no surprise at the turn taken in the eulogy, as if they had come to expect public gatherings of all kinds to lead to the one mounting concern on everyone's mind in 1859.

"Our beloved senator taught us why we cannot merely remind our Northern foes of how the greatest good of mankind is served by the world cotton economy that we make possible with our domestic institutions. Our enemies dismiss that as mere economic calculation, which they claim cannot right a human wrong. But Wiley Barnwell knew how to answer them. He insisted on holding up the moral character of our cause, because what we do here stems not only from economic necessity but also from our *humanity*.

"The senator never tired of explaining to our touchy challengers how we do far more for our bondsmen than the North does for its wage earners. While we work our laborers not unduly hard, we also feed, clothe, and shelter them; we minister to their medical needs; we care for their children; and we support them in their aging years, after their productive days are over. Wiley never failed to remind us of what decent and noble folks we planters are. We look after the little people! We relieve the needy and unfortunate class from the pressures of want! While the North offers nothing more than wages to their workers, we offer benevolence, caring, and a lifetime of security to our bondsmen. Why should such a humane society as ours rile the delicate sensibilities of the Northern busybodies?"

The mayor's voice was rising, his face reddening, and his hands tightening into fists. "Why must they persist in their brazen intrusions into our sanctity that can only lead to *peril*?" He banged his fist on the podium like a hammer. "The senator often said: 'I think of my slaves as my children, and they think of me as their father.' Yes, my friends, there was no kinder, gentler, more beloved master than Wiley Barnwell."

Tom remembered the faces of the slaves when Charlotte had told them of the senator's death; not one had shed a tear for their humane master. Why? he wondered. At Polly's funeral, her slaves had cried openly. He glanced at Rachel and Charlotte. He hadn't seen them cry, either, for the senator. But then he pushed away his guilty suspicions. After all, he reasoned, the senator's death was immediate and horrific. Rachel, Charlotte, and their slaves must still be numbed by the shock of it all, he concluded.

"Besides giving us the moral shield to hold high against our foes, Wiley also gave us the spears to repel them," the mayor continued. "In our town and later in the state legislature, he was a driving force in banning the subversive books and pamphlets bombarding us from the North and fomenting discontent. And he fought ceaselessly to end all manumissions, to increase the penalties for educating the slaves, and to stiffen the sentences for those traitors who give aid and comfort to runaways. Thanks to leaders like Wiley, we now have the laws we need to protect ourselves from any uprisings. We can punish the rogues who commit seditious acts. We can even call for their death!"

A collective gasp was heard from the pews. The women in the audience fluttered their fans, and the men wiped their sweating brows as the tension in the hall became palpable. As if finally sensing he had gone too far, the mayor stepped back, took several calming sips of water, then continued with a softer tone and a smile.

"In conclusion, my dear friends, let us pick up the banner that our fallen leader waved so proudly."

Tom's head dropped and he stared down at his hands as disturbing images flooded his mind. He had admired Wiley Barnwell as a cotton planter, but he was unfamiliar with the side of him described by the mayor. He thought of his first encounter with the desperate runaway he later named Solo and how he had wanted to give her money to aid her escape. He thought of how he had done everything possible to help Jerome get to the North. He thought of a dank cell with a hard floor, iron bars, and a dim light floating in from a small rusted window. That cell now housed Cooper, a man charged with murder. Tom wondered about his own fate with the laws enacted. If he had been caught helping Jerome or Solo, would *that cell* be the place where he would waste away precious years of his life? He thought of the scaffold in the courtyard outside the jail. Could he have met an even worse fate? He wasn't a slave—he was a free man—yet the tentacles that gripped the slaves seemed to be stretching out to grab him too.

He thought of the coming era and its great promise: to clear the fields of slaves and raise the level of work to heights never before imagined, heights demanding a worker's free choice and free effort. Was the senator a prime force in thwarting this future?

"To bolster us for whatever trials may lie ahead, we must always remember our beloved statesman. We must always remember the grandeur and glory of the South that he extolled and that we will forever honor and defend!"

After the mayor finished his eulogy, others gave their tributes, but Tom wasn't listening. His own thoughts preoccupied him. How could the man who fought to defend his invention—and the modernization it promised—be the same man who had enacted measures to punish those who challenged the old ways? Could he cast doubt on the man who had given his life for the tractor? Or did the fault lie with the messenger?

The mayor clearly had his own banner to wave. Invoking the senator's prestige at such a poignant moment surely helped him further his *own* cause. Painting the senator in the colors of his own banner helped the mayor spread a message of his own. That must be it, Tom concluded, rubbing his eyes as if clearing away a foreign object that had impaired his sight.

At the end of the service, Tom walked along the street before heading home, feeling an urge to dissipate the tension that had built inside him during the ceremony. As he passed the printer's shop, he saw stacks of the latest newspaper being loaded onto a wagon. Nothing could bring the senator back, he thought sadly, but there was still one thing that could—and must—be done. The emblem on the sheriff's badge, the goddess with her scales, flashed across his mind. The newspaper's headline gave him hope that justice would soon be done to close the matter and give them all peace.

The headline read: *Barnwell Murder Trial Set for Late March.*

# CHAPTER 9

In the weeks following the murder, Tom felt a growing isolation from the townspeople. There were those who blamed their beloved senator's death on Tom's invention, a contraption they called foolhardy. Some snubbed him, others criticized him in newspaper columns, and a few withdrew their money from his bank. As a result, he had little interest in dealing with them. He stopped buying the newspapers and limited his reading to farm periodicals. He avoided social functions and went to town only when necessary to manage his bank, retrieve his mail, and buy necessities.

Tom also felt uneasy around Rachel. His visits to her home focused on business matters, such as arranging a loan for Charlotte and helping her manage Ruby Manor and the Crossroads. After his meetings with Charlotte, he made excuses to leave, rather than linger there with Rachel. He was wounded by her curious behavior toward him at the memorial service. Where did she stand, he wondered, with him or with his detractors? But her tragic loss—and his involvement in it—stopped him from raising the issue with her.

He spent all the time he could spare searching for his missing device. He explored potential hiding spots off trails, in clearings, on dry mounds near the swamps, and in other places he thought were accessible by horse in the range Cooper could have covered on the night of the murder. But he found no trace of his tractor. The sheriff conducted his own search, also without success.

Would Cooper's voice be choked by the hangman, with the secret of the invention's whereabouts still inside him? Tom wondered, as he rode his horse up to Indigo Springs on a morning in early March. Returning home from one of his overnight searches, he saw the roof of his workshop on the hilltop, and his mind traveled through the locked doors and shuttered windows to the tools lining the walls, his worktable, and the shelves containing his notebooks, experiments, and drawings. It had taken him years to design and fabricate every part of his tractor. He sighed at the prospect of having to repeat the arduous process if he couldn't retrieve his lost treasure.

With the device missing, there was no reason to enter the workshop now. His journey to the new age had hit a roadblock. The empty space in the center of the shed was matched by a gaping hole in his life. For as long as he could remember, his life had always contained activities that excited him and that he energetically pursued, but now he lumbered through the tasks he *had* to perform and was left with nothing he truly *wanted* to do.

In the distance he saw his overseer with a slave team harrowing the fields for the massive cotton-planting operation to begin in a couple of weeks. He thought of the arduous process involved in putting a cotton seed into the ground. It took three laborers: one to make a hole, a second to drop the seed, and a third to cover it with soil. This laborious work was performed for each and every plant sown over thousands of acres.

To streamline the process, Tom had begun using a device developed by prior inventors: a seed drill, which was a small, horse-drawn wood hopper on a wheel chassis. The hopper was filled with seeds that could be dropped into the ground at intervals. He needed to make adjustments to its design to plant cotton more effectively. He also hoped eventually to hitch the seed drill to his tractor, instead of to a draft animal, and advance his dream of mechanizing the planting process.

The seed drill. *That* was what he could work on. Even with his invention missing, he still could make progress by speeding up the planting operation. He picked up his pace and soon arrived at the big house. After leaving his horse with Jerome, he went directly to the carpenter's cabin. There he found the seed drill he'd been adjusting and brought it outside to examine it.

Before leaving for his trip, Tom had begun modifying its parts to improve its performance. He stared at the three components of the device designed to plant seed in rows: the blade in front to cut a furrow in the soil for the seed, the hopper that held the seed and released it at fixed intervals to space the plants properly, and the harrow in back that covered the seed with soil. With the blade, the hopper, and the harrow, the seed drill replaced the manual work of three field hands on foot, requiring the work of only one man on horseback to haul the implement. *That amounted to reducing labor by two thirds.*

He thought of how such a device could enable crops to be grown cheaper and faster. He thought of how customers could buy less-expensive crops and have money left to spend on other things. He thought of how humans freed from the back-breaking toil of manual planting could engage in more intellectual work. He thought of the even greater progress that could be achieved with the development of an advanced type of seed drill, one that consisted of several hoppers over multiple planting rows. Then he thought of the superior new source of power, his tractor, which could drive, perhaps, a *dozen* seed drills, with one person in the tractor *replacing the work of . . . thirty-six . . . human planters—*

"'Skuse me, Mr. Tom . . ."

His mind was fathoms away, trying to grasp the profound implications of his reasoning.

"Mr. Tom, sir . . ."

He turned from the device to see one of his house servants, Fannie, who had approached him while he had been deliberating.

"'Tis 'bout my garden, sir."

The household slaves planted their own vegetable gardens behind their cabins.

"I wuz thinkin' to start 'nother plot on the side o' the cabin an' grow mo' stuff, sir."

Tom looked puzzled at the question. "That's fine, Fannie. But why ask me?"

"The colonel, yer daddy, he wuz fussy 'bout how much we grows. He allow jus' small plots in back, sir."

"Oh?" He looked out toward the row of cabins near the big house. "So that's why all your gardens are in the back." After eighteen months, Tom was still uncovering rules from his father, which he learned from the slaves as he went along.

"Yer daddy, he wuz a-frettin' 'bout us takin' too much time wid our plots an' sellin' our stuff at the dock, 'cause then us be neglectin' our work fer him."

Tom nodded as if it didn't surprise him to learn that the slaves would work harder on their own plots than on tasks for his father.

"Maybe I kin grow a little mo' 'taters an' carrots an' corn, sir? Lawd, my boys eat 'nuff fer a small army."

He frowned at the irony of the predicament he and his slaves were in. They seemed to blatantly disobey his orders on important matters and to ask his permission for trivialities.

"Why don't *you* decide? Okay?"

"You mean, you wants *me* . . ." Fannie looked surprised.

"Yes, yes!" He tried to curb his impatience. "Plant whatever you want around your cabin. Use the front, the back, the sides. It's up to *you*."

Fannie looked confused as if grappling with a new thought.

"Go on, now, Fannie."

When she walked away, Tom returned to the seed drill, inspecting the parts, considering the possibilities of improving the little device before him. He had an idea—

"Mr. Tom?"

He turned to see another slave approaching him. "What, Hadley?"

"Sir, when you gives out blankets, we don't need all you given the wife and me. 'Stead, we needs mo' shoes. Kin us give back a blanket for one mo' pair shoes?"

Tom stared, expressionless.

"I needs 'nother pair cuz what happen the day o' the big storm—"

"You don't have to go into all that, or trade any blankets—"

"Don't you needs to know? You mean, I kin jus' ask for somethin' and I gits it?"

Tom frowned. How could he verify the legitimacy of such requests? Why would he want to spend his time doing that? Was it fair to the slaves if he refused requests for things they really needed? Was it fair to him if the slaves feigned a need and drained his supplies, then sold what he gave them at the docks? He rubbed his hands over his face, as if he wished to wipe away the matter from his mind. How could he end this quickly, so he could get back to his work?

"Tell Corey to make you another pair."

Corey was the slave who made their shoes.

Hadley seemed surprised at Tom's reply. "But him needs a *order* from *you*, sir."

Tom nodded wearily. "Right. I'll tell Corey to make you another pair."

"Why, thank you, sir!" Hadley smiled and walked away.

Tom returned to the seed drill. He thought of how cotton planting was complicated by the need to drop several seeds in every spot. This, in turn, required an additional laborious task: thinning the seedlings. After the first leaves appeared, workers had to comb the fields again to remove the less hardy plants at each spot and leave the most vigorous one to take a stand and grow to maturity. Tom wondered if the planting could be improved to the point at which only *one* seed would need to be dropped, a seed with a near-certain chance of hardy development, instead of just one chance in three. That would eliminate the thinning process, saving an *enormous* amount of labor. What if he modified the harrow on the seed drill—

"Say, Mr. Tom . . . Mr. Tom?"

He looked up to find two more slaves, Lucinda and Patty, awaiting his attention.

"Yes?"

Lucinda spoke first. "I's sorry, but I can't be washin' the laundry no mo'."

Tom waited to hear more.

"Lucinda, she havin' a baby," said Patty.

"I's a-needin' rest, sir. Pleez don' gimme them heavy baskets t'haul down the stream in my condition," said Lucinda.

"'Tis too much fo' her, sir," added her friend.

"Then why don't *you* carry the basket for her?"

"Oh, no, sir!" wailed Patty. "I ain't strong 'nuff."

"Then put the basket in a wheelbarrow and move it that way," offered Tom.

"But I feels sickly, sir," said Lucinda, who looked quite healthy.

Involuntarily, Tom's eyes dropped to her midsection. Was she or wasn't she? He couldn't tell. He frowned, unable to decide what to do. Frustration and guilt were wrestling in his mind, as they often had since his return home.

Lucinda could easily be faking her illness, he thought, because she knew he wouldn't beat her and couldn't abandon her. He felt he should order her to work. But could he blame her for dodging a job she had never chosen to do? Wouldn't he, in her place, do the same?

Then there was the possibility that she really *was* telling the truth. Had he gotten so cynical that he assumed every plea of his slaves was a lie? He sighed at the tugging factions that left him indecisive. Though he dreamed of changing the future, he felt mired in the present.

He disliked having to depend on someone who was eminently unreliable, but at times like this, he saw no alternative. Whenever he tried to demote the person who was his major vexation, he found new reasons to use his services. "Jerome!" He looked at the stable and called to the lanky slave, who was directing a stableboy unloading a wagon of hay.

When he heard his name, Jerome looked pleased at the prospect of being needed. He walked eagerly toward Tom and the two women.

"Jerome, Lucinda has a . . . situation." He turned to the women. "Talk to Jerome." Then he said to his grinning stableman, "And let me know the outcome."

Jerome seemed to increase in height, enjoying the moment. His neck stretched like a proud rooster, and his eyes suddenly came alive as if he were calculating how he might use Tom's need of him to best advantage.

"You gals, you comes wid me. Mr. Tom, don't you worry none. Jerome take charge o' these good-fer-nothin' servants, so they don't cause you no mo' trouble!"

Jerome's authoritative words and general swagger seemed to impress the women sufficiently. They followed him without a fuss.

After being rescued by Jerome, Tom returned to the seed drill. He studied the harrow that covered the seed after it was dropped. He wondered if a wood block to compact the soil would be superior to the harrow in covering the seed, or if using *both* implements could result in a better-planted seed, which could reduce the quantity of seeds that had to be planted and in turn reduce and ultimately eliminate the arduous thinning-out later. He had been thinking about this before and had already made a wood block to attach to the seed drill. He looked around in the carpenter's cabin and found it. He crouched down at the drill to install it. He wanted to test his ideas—

"Mr. Tom?"

One of his gardeners, Rubin, now appeared.

"I wants to ask iffen me an' yer housekeeper Ally kin git married." Although slave marriages had no legal standing, Tom's slaves bonded to each other the same as all other people did.

The inventor looked stunned.

"Kin we, Mr. Tom? Kin we? Oh, pleez, sir!"

Rubin stood there timidly, pleading as if his life rested on the answer. He held a trowel, which he gripped fiercely, the whole of his anxiety coursing through his hand.

"Mr. Tom, sir?"

Tom was speechless at being asked to decide such a personal matter between two people. He had been home for eighteen months, but matters like this never ceased to unsettle him.

Rubin's shoulders slouched; his head jutted forward; sweat formed on his brow.

Tom realized that his silence was intensifying the gardener's anxiety, so he stood up, smiled, and patted the man on the shoulder. "If it's okay with Ally, then it's okay with me."

The man grinned, tremendously relieved. "Oh, she haves me, all right!"

Tucking the trowel under his arm, he took Tom's hand in both of his and squeezed it vigorously, just as a subject would grasp the hand of a ruler who had granted a wish.

Tom turned the gesture into a handshake. "Congratulations." Grit from the garden transferred from Rubin's palm to Tom's.

"Thank you, sir. Thank you! I tells Ally us got yer say-so!"

Tom watched his gardener bow to him, then scurry away. Why, he wondered, would he ever want to have this kind of say-so? When he could design a better seed drill to produce a crop cheaper and easier, why would he instead want to manage someone's carrot patch? When he could design a new motor to transform farming, why would he instead want to manage someone's footwear? When the mysteries of harnessing science lay waiting for men to discover them, how could anyone instead want to control the gardens, the blankets, the spouses—the lives—of others? He felt as if his slaves were shrinking his world just as surely as he was shrinking theirs.

He didn't understand men who wanted to harness other men, but he did understand the seed drill. He attached the wood block to the back of it and gathered the materials he would need to test his modification in the field.

After changing into work clothes in the big house, Tom stepped out the front door to feel the sun hitting his face, promising a rain-free afternoon for his work. At the entrance, the sunrays hit Jerome too as he lay stretched out, fast asleep, in the horse-drawn wagon that Tom had ordered.

"Okay, Jerome, nap's over."

Jerome opened his eyes, looking dazed for a moment. Then he jumped out of the wagon, smiling confidently, as if nothing were amiss.

The inventor checked the objects in the wagon: the seed drill, a bag of cottonseed, and some additional tools. "Looks like everything's here that I asked for."

Jerome looked aghast at Tom's clothes. He seemed shocked to find his master dressed in the coarse trousers, bulky shirt, and floppy hat that the slaves wore. Tom returned the disapproving look at Jerome's attire; his ruffled dress shirt and satin vest were hardly suitable for the stable. Or perhaps Jerome planned on skipping his work there that afternoon.

"Mr. Tom, you ain't fixin' to work in the fields?"

"I am."

"Then you be needin' hands?"

"No."

"You goes youself?"

"Yes."

"But you can't do that."

"Why not?"

"'Tain't right, sir."

"Why not?"

"You needs to stay here an' sit in that chair," he pointed to the colonel's rocker on the gallery.

"And do what?"

"Wait fer visitors."

"Why would I waste time waiting for imaginary visitors when I have work to do?"

"'Tain't proper, sir. Massas don't work no fields." He pointed with urgency to the colonel's rocker. "Somebody gotta sit there! Entertain folks that come a-callin', like yer daddy done, and his daddy 'fore that."

"I'll tell you what, Jerome, since you seem to have nothing to do and you're decked out for it, why don't *you* sit there and wait for visitors? *You* can entertain them when they arrive. I have better things to do."

Jerome, in dress clothes, stood speechless as he watched Tom, in work clothes, head to the fields.

The place Tom chose for his experiments was recently plowed and prepared for planting. It lay next to Greenbriar's main plantation road, where he could see the progress of his plants when he traveled to and from town. He removed the seed drill from the wagon and surveyed the rich alluvial soil before him. With his field hands sowing corn in another area of the plantation and the main road quiet, he was happily left alone. He recaptured his concentration on the absorbing problem of how to improve cotton planting.

He filled the hopper with seed, and then, using a harness, he pulled the device on foot across the field, stopping at various times to make adjustments. Soon he had the first few rows planted. He was so intent on his task that he was unaware of the sweat slowly soaking his shirt, the dirt marks smearing his face, and the soil splattering his pants. If anyone had traveled past him on the main road, he was unaware of it—until an open carriage stopped alongside him and a voice called out from a few feet away.

"Look here! We have a new bondsman." A white-gloved hand pointed to him as a male voice said mockingly, "Why, it's Mr. Edmunton!"

Tom looked up to see Nash Nottingham, his formal suit and frilled shirt fit for a courtier.

"Is this what you've been up to, Tom? Is this why we've hardly seen you?" A hint of anger heated the sweet voice that used to sing to him in Philadelphia. Rachel was sitting in the carriage beside Nash, with her servant and his driver on the bench in front.

Tom stared at the woman whose sparkle had once dazzled him. Three weeks after her father's death, she still wore a black dress and bonnet in accordance with the rules of Victorian mourning, but with a low neckline reminiscent of the feisty spirit that had set its own rules at a time that seemed long ago.

"My dear, it seems your good friend here would rather be in the company of little gadgets, nasty flies, and grimy soil than be in your exquisite presence," said Nash.

Rachel frowned at the remark. Nash grinned smugly, looking pleased that his words hit a nerve.

"A cotton planter," he added gaily, "knows how to live, old boy. He enjoys the company of beautiful women." He bowed to Rachel, who smiled at the compliment. "And a cotton planter enjoys a life of amusement, indulgence, and finery far removed from grimy fields."

"How can you be a cotton planter and be removed from grimy fields?" Tom asked.

"But really, Tom, you don't have to labor in the dirt yourself, you know!" said Rachel.

"I'm trying to figure out how to *save* labor, lots of it. Doesn't that seem like a good way to spend an afternoon?"

"Good heavens!" said Nash. "We don't need to *save* labor. We have too much of it already. Whatever would we do with all of it that you saved?"

"I suppose this is part of that new age you dream about," Rachel added.

"It is."

"And whenever will you find time to join us in the *current* age? You remember, don't you, the world we actually live in?" Her voice was teasing, but her mouth pouted reproachfully. "In case you haven't noticed, some of our fruit trees are in bloom. Nash was taking me to see his orchard and to taste peach brandy. Why don't you come along?"

The crescent curve of Nash's grin abruptly turned downward into a frown. "Why, Rachel, dear, I don't believe Tom is interested in such niceties. I mean, look at him in those outrageous clothes with dirt on his face. He seems to revel in being an outcast."

"Do you, Tom?" asked Rachel. "Do you revel in being an outcast?"

Tom stared at the young beauty with the red hair and satin-white skin. As his eyes dropped to the heart-shaped birthmark he knew so well, the memory of their past surfaced on his face.

"You know," she added, "outcasts make other people feel . . . uncomfortable."

"If people . . . two people . . . are happy being what they are, then why would they care if others felt uncomfortable with them?"

"We all need people," she replied. "Even *you* can't escape that, Tom Edmunton. We need our family, and friends, and the pleasure of . . ."—she scoured the sky for a word to name her feelings—". . . *belonging.*"

"And our dreams? Where do they belong?"

The two of them stared at each other as if there were an ocean between them.

"Where do *you* belong?" Rachel asked pointedly. "Can we claim you in *our* world, Tom, at least for the afternoon?"

"But Rachel, dear," said Nash, "how could you want this fellow coming along? Why, he must reek of fertilizer!"

"That doesn't stop you from banking with me," said Tom.

The remark jolted Nash, who suddenly remembered his delinquent loan. "Oh, no offense, old boy. Between us, I think you're a fine fellow."

"Between us, I didn't know *my* standing was in question."

"Now, Tom, don't get sore. Of course, you're welcome to join us . . . if you must," said Nash. His voice gave the invitation, but his face showed his distaste for it. "We can wait at your house while you . . . er . . . perhaps clean up a bit."

"Oh, do come, Tom!" added Rachel. "What could be so important about that field of dirt that you can't take a few hours off to relax . . . with us?" Her face said: *with me.*

"I'll wait for another time of *our* choosing—you and me."

"You mean, another time when you have a minute to spare from the Holy Grail that's your work—and you can deign to consider matters of much lesser importance!" Rachel snapped.

"Look, old boy, you've lived too long in a strange place. Allow me to give you some advice." Nash glanced at Rachel, as if more concerned with conveying his message to her than to Tom. "Down here, we planters know how to live like gentlemen. Labor is for the lower classes."

Nash smiled haughtily at Tom, then tapped his cane on the driver's shoulder, and the carriage drove off.

Where had he seen anyone as indolent as the man riding away with Rachel? Tom wondered. He instantly thought of his stableman. But Jerome was robbed of his self-direction and forced to labor against his will, so he had an excuse for his indolence. What was Nash's excuse for a laziness that he practiced as diligently as others honed a profession? Tom wondered about the two men whose lives seemed as cool as ashes from which a fire had never raged. Why did the man at the top of society's ladder seem as devoid of passion and purpose as the man at the bottom?

And what happened to the fragrant vision that had stirred his own passion? Where was the exciting woman he knew in Philadelphia, with the bold dreams and joyful laughter, with an inner fire as vibrant as her tumbling red hair? Why was the bright splash of color that was Rachel so muted now that she had returned home?

When he finished his work, the matter still lingered in his mind. He thought of the words of the factory owner who had been forced to close his business: *You can't change the soul of the South.* Does the South stake a claim on its souls and recapture those that stray from its grasp? Does it hunt down not only its slaves but also its wayward sons and daughters . . . like Rachel?

As Tom drove the wagon back to the big house, he saw another puzzling spirit, one that seemed engaged in its own clash with the soul of the South. He saw Solo riding one of his stallions around a large pasture.

Her riding had begun shortly after her arrival at Indigo Springs. Despite being assigned to the kitchen, she had ventured into the stable one day in the late afternoon. She had declared that her tasks were finished and now the horses needed exercising. Then she proceeded to mount one and ride it around the pasture. Jerome protested such liberties taken on his turf, but she ignored him. The slave complained bitterly to Tom, but the master posed a question to his indignant stableman that he couldn't answer: "What harm is she doing, Jerome?"

After that, whether it was the horses or instead the rider who needed a spirited jaunt through the field, Solo exercised one of them each day as her self-assigned task.

Tom wondered where she had come from, but she never offered any information. Often slaves of mixed race didn't know their origins themselves. A planter or overseer would deny committing any indiscretions, so a child born of one could grow up ignorant of who its father was. And pressure to remove such an offspring from the reach of a suspecting wife could be so great that a mulatto child might be sold from its original plantation and separated from its slave mother as well. If Solo had been as unruly in childhood as she was now, she could have been sold repeatedly, shuffled from plantation to plantation.

Approaching the big house, Tom watched the young woman ride. She was absorbed in her task and unaware of his wagon on the road. He thought he detected a quiet exhilaration coloring her otherwise mysterious face. The fear and contempt that hardened her features when she was among humans seemed to soften in the company of horses, a species she obviously preferred. It seemed as if she could drop her guard with the large, benign creatures that sought nothing from her except a little kindness.

Despite repeated scolding from Aunt Bess and the other elder servants, along with shocked stares from the younger ones, Solo liked to wear men's clothing, which allowed her the comfort to move around and ride in the manner she preferred. As she jaunted along bareback, straddling the horse like a man, she looked strangely alluring in her oversized shirt and baggy trousers, with her white sleeves rolled to reveal the metallic sheen of her arms and the sash holding up her pants tightened around her waist, stressing its trimness. Tom saw lustrous rosewood hair tumbling down the coarse shirt and slender legs outlined under the pants. He sensed the whole of this beguiling image in an instant emotional reaction, which he hastily suppressed before it could lodge inside him.

But he couldn't stop himself from contrasting the sight of Solo in trousers to Rachel in crinolines. Solo was tied by slavery and had nothing, yet her spirit somehow seemed free. Rachel was free and had everything, but her spirit somehow seemed . . . constrained.

He wondered what to do with the odd new addition to his plantation. In the four weeks since her arrival, he had tried giving her different tasks, but she failed at all of them. In the kitchen, she displayed an uncanny bent for overcooking and underseasoning the food. This enraged Tom's declining octogenarian cook, who still had sufficient faculties to demand the girl's removal. Solo did a stint at housekeeping, which came to an end when she broke a prized vase passed down from Tom's grandmother. She was assigned to ironing but burned an heirloom tablecloth. She proved equally inept at weaving and sewing.

Unable—or unwilling—to find a place in the household, she was returned to the kitchen, where she remained recalcitrant. To Jerome's vexation, she liked being near the horses and gravitated to the stable. No doubt feeling protected—and emboldened—by Tom's edict against any physical attack on her, Solo found fault with Jerome's care of the animals and argued with him constantly.

"What Jerome gonna do wid that she-beast hangin' 'round the stable, sir?" Jerome had complained repeatedly. "Her don't like this nor that, tellin' Jerome how t'do his job. 'Tain't right, Mr. Tom. She needin' to git to the fields!"

The problem weighed on Tom as he reached the big house and brought the seed drill back to the carpenter's cabin. He set it on the worktable to make another adjustment. As he worked, his thoughts wandered to the problem with the girl. It would be unfair to the others if he allowed Solo to continue shirking work. With cotton planting about to begin in earnest in a few weeks, now was the time to send her to the fields. But he couldn't do it. He had discovered something about the girl that prevented him from sentencing her to a life of field labor. To his astonishment he had learned that unlike any other slave at Indigo Springs, this odd misfit of a girl was *literate*. Although he operated a major agricultural business engaged in international trade, in the whole of his labor force he had no job for the literate.

It was by accident that he had discovered she could read. After her arrival, he noticed late at night from his second-floor bedroom that a light was burning in the kitchen cabin behind the big house. That light burned long after the slaves had finished their tasks and gone to sleep. Then late one night, he went downstairs to use the library, the great study on the main level that held his parents' sizeable collection of books. To his surprise he saw a light filtering out of the room. From the hallway, he saw the slim figure of Solo at the bookshelves. A lamp flickered near her on a table. It highlighted her face as she gazed with the wonderment of a child at the musty volumes.

He thought of classical paintings of woodland scenes with a huntress whose physical appearance matched the setting. In the same way, Solo seemed to match the setting of his library. Her bronze skin blended with the earth tones of the room's drapery, and her red-brown hair matched the massive rosewood bookcases in color and luster. The huntress who forayed into his library seemed to belong there.

She skimmed through several volumes, decided on one, then extinguished the light and left through an open window. She carried the book delicately in her arm as if it were a newborn. By the next morning, he noticed, the empty space left by the book was filled again. Solo had apparently read it overnight in the kitchen, then returned it before it could be missed.

The next night he observed the same scene in the library. This time Solo was holding a little book he recognized; it was one of his favorite plays, a comedy. As she read a passage, for the first time he saw her laugh. He walked toward the room from the hallway. Startled, she looked up at him standing at the door. The soft radiance on her face vanished, and her eyes filled with terror.

He approached her, wondering what passage had made her laugh. As he touched the small volume and leaned toward her to see the page she was reading, she dropped the book into his hand and reached down for an object strapped to her lower leg, hidden under her clothing. In the next moment, a knife was pointed mere inches from his throat.

He recognized the weapon, a hunting knife from his saddlebag. He stood motionless while his eyes studied her, the astonishment on his face turning to understanding. He guessed the reason why she feared his coming so close to her; he could only imagine the past horrors she had endured to provoke that fear.

For a long moment, he observed the knife pointing at him. Then, ignoring it, he turned to the book and read the page she had been reading. He laughed too. "That's one of my favorite scenes," he said.

She remained frozen. The knife stayed poised at his windpipe. He remained on his spot.

"Where did you learn to read?"

A hostile stare was his only answer. Sometimes plantation mistresses taught slave children to read, despite the laws forbidding it. He wondered if she had encountered a kind mistress in her past.

"Here, take it." He held the book out to her. When she didn't take it, he dropped it on the table nearby.

"I came to tell you that you don't have to sneak in here through the window at night. You have my permission to borrow the books you want. And you can come in during the day and use the door."

He could read no other reaction on her face, except a terror that apparently would not disappear until he did. He turned his back on the knife and walked out.

On another evening, as he came out of his room and was about to descend the staircase, he saw her downstairs in the parlor. She was looking in fascination at picture cards, gazing through the binocular lenses of a stereoscope, a small, handheld device kept there for viewing photographs. The stereographs presented two slightly different images of the same picture, side by side, one in front of each eye of the binocular viewer. The two images when viewed that way were perceived as a single picture with three-dimensional depth. In the parlor there were a stack of stereographs showing artwork, famous landmarks, and street scenes from cities around the world.

He watched her viewing the cards, holding the device up to the window, straining to catch the last blue light of the day. He saw her read the descriptions of the scenes given on the cards. He remembered that he had stereographs of Philadelphia in his bedroom, and he returned there to retrieve them. He put the cards in his jacket pocket and went downstairs.

As he reached the parlor, he could see the stack of picture cards spread out on the table near her. He knew well the photographs she was viewing— an outdoor market in London, a railway station in Paris, lively scenes with horse-drawn vehicles bustling down tree-lined boulevards, shops with windblown awnings and windows filled with merchandise, sidewalks jammed with busy pedestrians. The human activity captured in the pictures seemed to represent everything in the world that was closed to her.

She was unaware of him. Her back was to the door as she gazed intently at a stereograph that held particular interest to her. In an effort not to startle her, he spoke softly as he entered the room.

"Say, I thought you might be interested in something."

She whirled toward him. In her nervousness she dropped the stereoscope. It landed on the table, and the picture in the viewing slot fell to the floor. He bent down to retrieve it. When he straightened up, he found the hunting knife pointed at his chest.

His eyes traveled from the knife to her face. Her enchantment with the pictures had turned to terror. He glanced at the picture he had retrieved. It was a photograph of a painting hand-tinted to show the vivid colors of the actual artwork. The scene was of a grand ballroom where beautiful women in bright-colored gowns danced with handsome men in tails. The artist had captured the lively sweep of their movements and the laughter on their faces. Tom observed the gaiety of the scene, then the desperate eyes of the woman before him.

He dropped the card on the table and was about to reach into his pocket for the pictures he had brought. But his arm paused in midmotion when she raised her free arm up to grip the knife with both hands. For a long moment, the two stared at each other—a tall man with strands of gold hair spilling into his eyes and a petite woman with yards of wild russet curls—with the silver knife blade flashing in the twilight between them. He slowly continued with his action and took out the stereographs.

"I thought you might like these pictures of Philadelphia."

He offered the cards to her, but she declined to take them, her fiery eyes locked on his, her fists white-knuckled as she grasped the knife.

He dropped the cards on the table. She didn't look at them but remained motionless. Then he turned around so that the knife was pointed at his back, and he walked out.

At other times, he spotted her reading a weekly agricultural newsletter that he picked up in town. When she brought trays of food to and from the dining room, she made detours into the library. She checked the shelf where he stacked the newsletters after he'd finished reading them, and when a new issue appeared, she grabbed it. But the articles on planting times, plowing methods, soil preparation, hoeing, and the like didn't seem to interest her. Instead, she turned to the back page, which carried advertisements for farm implements, along with notices of field hands for sale or hire . . . and rewards for capturing runaways. He wondered if she was looking for someone.

Once late at night, he had returned home after another futile search for the invention. As he went upstairs to his room without having eaten, his despair mixed with his hunger to form anger. He swore silently at Ted Cooper: the thief, the killer, the man who was a trespasser in his life.

He approached his bedroom and was startled to find . . . a trespasser. He had never before seen Solo in his room, and he sensed this was the one place she would definitely avoid. But there she stood, leaning over a lamp on his dresser, reading something he had left in his room. It was the latest issue of the agricultural newsletter. Apparently, she was so eager to see it that she couldn't wait for him to finish his reading and bring it to the library. From the open door, he saw her face through the dresser's mirror, her eyes moving intently across the back page. Hearing him approach, she looked up to catch his face in the mirror, staring at her.

The image of her in the looking glass held him. He saw the dark eyes, the wild mane, and the auburn skin of a grassland filly unbridled. And yet he saw an intelligence that caused her to devour books, a curiosity that made her yearn to see pictures of the world, and a pressing need to find something . . . or someone.

Slowly, he walked toward her. In a flash, she pulled out the knife she carried with her and whirled around to face him. He walked closer, until the blade was mere inches from his chest. Then he walked closer still, till the blade touched his shirt. His nerves frazzled from his long, fruitless day, in a split-second move he grabbed her arm with one hand and seized the knife with the other. Roughly, he pulled her against him and dug his fingers into her arm. She winced.

"If I were what you think, do you really believe this knife would protect you?"

She stood before him, trembling helplessly. Her eyes—dark, moist, and filling with stark terror—seemed to look through him, to an inner horror, a nightmare of her own that was scorched onto her memory.

He too felt a horror as he towered over her with the knife. How could anyone stand this? he wondered. How could anyone want to make someone else feel helpless and afraid? How could anyone feed off that? He thought of the murder, the theft, the mayor's words, the factory owner's warning—the fear and violence around him that he couldn't escape. Her terror seemed to weigh on him in the same way.

She lowered her face, unable to bear her inner torment, to shake it off, or to hide it from him.

The sight of her plight drained the anger from him. He sighed. He loosened his grip on her arm and took her hands in his. He put the knife back into them. He aimed it at his throat. She looked at him, astonished. He squeezed her hands reassuringly, then released them.

"There, do you feel better now?" he asked softly.

She kept the knife pointed at him, but her face became calmer and her grip on the blade softer.

He gestured to the newsletter, with its ad page flickering in the light on the dresser.

"Are you looking for someone?"

There was no reply.

"Someone who might've run away?"

The nightmare was receding; her composure was returning. Her face was once again becoming mysterious, her feelings unreachable.

"Can I help you find who you're looking for?"

His voice was lost in the tangle of curls that brushed against him as she turned and rushed out of the room.

He could still feel the cool breeze that her whirling hair left in the air. It was still palpable . . .

He realized it was the cool wind of the early March day blowing across his face as he left the carpenter's cabin. But his mind still lingered on that incident in his room. Was it just something from a violent past that had resurfaced to frighten her that night, or was it also something in him . . . in the way he looked at her? That evening in his room, he had glimpsed his own reflection in the mirror, and he was surprised to see on his face a feeling he hadn't acknowledged to himself—and emphatically didn't welcome. As he stood outside the carpenter's cabin, he resolved to avoid the volatile new presence in his household.

Just then he heard her arguing with Jerome.

"You need to brush the knots out of their manes," she said, agitated, coming out of the stable with her adversary, "and wash the mud off their legs, and clean their hooves better. You keep the horses scraggly, and you groom yourself like a prince, when it should be the opposite. At least the horses are worth something."

"An' you needs to put mo' molasses in th' gingerbread, so it be sweet like you ain't. An' stew the meat longer, so it be tender like you ain't!" Jerome jumped around, pointing an angry finger at her. "Jus' 'cause you sour and tough don' mean yer food gotta be too."

"If the gingerbread was sweeter and the meat more tender, how would that help the horses?" she asked.

Jerome spotted the inventor watching them. "Mr. Tom! This hellcat, she need to hold her tongue!"

Tom sighed as they walked in his direction. He felt as if he were watching a play unfold from a seat in the audience. There was no director of the action, he thought, feeling no urge to assume that role.

"Stablin' ain't woman work. Git back to the kitchen!"

"Why don't *you* go to the kitchen? You're always talking about it. You're always eating Mr. Tom's food. You're always telling me how to make it better." She paused, as if suddenly realizing something. "It seems *you* want to be there."

Jerome stopped walking, struck by the words. Tom stared at him, struck by the words too. The three of them were speechless. Solo had observed something that was obvious, yet it had never occurred to any of them.

She continued, her voice showing her own surprise at the notion. "Yesterday you chopped almonds and added them to the cake batter. The day before you added more onions to the stew. Today you put herbs in the soup. You do something like that every day."

"Cookin' ain't man work, Missy!"

"The hog doesn't care who cooks it," she replied.

"'Tain't done. I ain't never seen no man in th' kitchen." He turned to Tom. "Ain't that right, sir?"

"Why, no, Jerome. Men *do* cook." Tom seemed surprised at the slave's remark, but reminded himself that Jerome had seen little of life outside of Indigo Springs. "There are male cooks in taverns, on ships, in hotels, and even on plantations."

"The best ones work in fancy places," added Solo.

"You little squirrel, how's you knowin' 'bout them fancy places?"

"Men who cook in fancy places are called *chefs,*" she said. The last word sounded as if she'd said *kings*.

Jerome listened curiously.

Tom watched a change occurring in the two of them. Jerome's ready grin and sweet-talk were vanishing; he seemed earnest. Solo's crusty aloofness had softened; she seemed friendly.

"Didn't you ever see the picture cards in the house?"

Jerome stared at her blankly.

She turned to Tom. "May I . . . ?" She pointed to the big house.

Tom nodded.

Like a butterfly, she vanished soundlessly and just as swiftly returned, holding the stereoscope and a few picture cards.

She placed the first card in the viewing slot. "Here's a famous restaurant in Philadelphia, where people go for fancy eating."

The slave looked through the viewer at an opulent room with a glass chandelier and small linen-covered tables set with sparkling silverware and flowery china.

She placed another card in the slot. "These are the cooks who prepare the food for this restaurant."

Jerome carefully examined a row of men in white uniforms with white hats standing proudly behind a table filled with platters of food. There was a black face in the group.

"Say, that be a slave there in Philerdelfi?"

"I think he's free," she whispered somberly.

They looked questioningly at Tom. "That's true," he said, a touch of pity in his voice.

Jerome peered through the lenses, studying the image with a childlike fascination. It seemed as if Solo had stirred something buried under the cool façade that was Jerome.

She lifted the card and pointed to a caption on the photograph. "It says, 'Executive Chef William Roberts and his culinary staff.' "

"You kin *read?*" Jerome seemed as astonished as Tom had been to learn that. The stableman's eyes panned to Tom; his eyebrows arched in an unstated question.

"That's what it says, Jerome." Tom confirmed.

"Which one be Mr. Chef William?"

"He's the one with the tall, straight hat. He's the head of all the cooks. The others have short, floppy hats, but Chef William's hat is different."

Jerome took another look through the lenses at the man with the hat that looked like a tall, white crown.

"I can make you a hat like that," she said enticingly.

"I thought you couldn't sew," said Tom.

She flashed one of her rare, brief smiles.

"Here's another picture of the chef," she said to Jerome.

She changed the card in the viewer. The new one showed a closer image of the leader of the kitchen. Chef William was alone in the shot, holding a beautifully decorated layer cake. The man's proud face and the imposing toque on his head created a regal presence.

Jerome scrutinized the pictures. When he finally put the stereoscope down, the rings around his eyes showed how tightly he had held the viewer to his face.

"I can make you a hat like Chef William's, so you can be the chef of *that* kitchen." She pointed to the little cabin behind the big house. "Then I can get out of that hot, greasy place and be with the horses instead. I can trade places with you." She turned to Tom, as if suddenly remembering that his opinion might be important. "If that's okay."

Jerome turned to him too. Their dark probing eyes stared into his blue ones.

"If the hog doesn't care who cooks it, neither do I. Whoever *wants* the job should be the one to do it," said Tom.

He and Solo looked at Jerome. There was a long pause, a furrowed brow, and an intensity in the eyes of the slave who seemed to be engaged in a new mental activity: making a choice about his life.

"I reckon that be me."

Tom looked at Solo. "I suppose the horse doesn't care who feeds it either."

She nodded, and the matter she had engineered was settled.

The next day, Solo made Jerome a handsome toque. She had removed the rim from an old top hat of his and used it as a frame. She lengthened it and covered the top and sides with a starched white fabric. Sensing there was something important about the hat, she and Jerome waited for Tom to appear outside the big house to make a little ceremony of its launch.

Tom wondered about the change that the affair had brought about in them. Her open hostility and Jerome's stealthy defiance seemed tempered. He wondered about the thing inside them that all the laws and whips of the South couldn't touch, the thing that gave them dignity and made them masters of themselves.

"This hat has twenty pleats," she said, counting aloud the vertical folds she had placed in the hat.

"Whut them fer?"

"I once read that they can stand for the number of recipes the chef creates. Some chefs have a *hundred* pleats on their hats."

Jerome's eyebrows arched in wonderment. "Don't the chef make recipes already there?"

"*Cooks* make recipes that are already there. But *somebody* has to create them. That's how the chef earns his pleats," she said.

"Tha' so, Mr. Tom?"

"It sounds reasonable to me, Jerome. It seems there are pleats to earn in every line of work." He smiled at a new, speechless Jerome, who beamed like a peacock about to fan its feathers.

"If you create more than twenty recipes, I'll make you another hat—with forty pleats." Solo stood on her toes, raised her arms, and placed the toque on his head. "You are now *Chef Jerome*."

"Why, thank you, Miss Solo." Jerome bowed to her as if he had been knighted.

From the moment she placed the toque on his head, Jerome's nicknames for the girl vanished. She was no longer a squirrel, a tick, a she-beast, or the like. She was now *Miss Solo*.

"There's just one small matter left, Jerome." Tom looked at his slave, who had grown a foot taller with his new hat. "The chef usually gets his hat and title *after* he's cooked something worth eating. So when you get around to it, maybe you could make your way to the kitchen."

Jerome looked eagerly at the little cabin behind the house. It was the first sign of genuine interest that Tom had ever seen him display in anything.

# CHAPTER 10

The Greenbriar courthouse stood across the street from the jail. Greek columns in front gave the white building stature, and azaleas blooming along the side gave it color. While the wall of pink flowers announced a new spring, a prisoner inside faced the darkest days of his life.

A somber Tom Edmunton walked toward the entrance. Ahead, Rachel and Charlotte Barnwell lifted acres of crinoline to climb the front steps. Witnesses, reporters, and onlookers filled the courtroom that late March day for the beginning of the murder trial that had jolted the town, snaring two of its sons: their esteemed senator killed and one of their wealthiest planters accused.

The courtroom was quiet and the mood solemn as an attendant assisted the town's respected plantation mistress, and now its most recent widow, to a seat in the front row. Rachel slid onto the bench next to her mother. Tom sat behind them, looking on sympathetically. The unadorned walls of the room were as pale as the women's faces.

Two days of testimony followed.

Prosecutor Will Drew was a tall, thin man in his forties with unusual, probing eyes on an otherwise average face, giving him both a forthrightness and simplicity that combined to inspire trust. He methodically presented the state's case.

The jury listened as the prosecutor developed his interpretation of how the crime occurred. He painted Cooper as a man driven by money and power, who saw a unique opportunity to amass a fortune through an unpatented new invention and so tried to steal the device; then when caught in the act, he committed murder to carry out his avaricious deed. The jury remained attentive as they heard the testimony of Tom, the sheriff, the coroner, and other witnesses.

Defense attorney Sam Potter was a short, stocky man in his fifties with graying temples and a deep voice that suggested wisdom and authority. He endeavored to raise doubts about the prosecution's case and to present Cooper's account of the night's events.

Potter highlighted the fact that the murder weapon had not been found and made the point that for all anyone knew, it could be discovered at a location impossible for Cooper to have reached in the time available. The invention too had not been located, after it had been searched for in the radius of the murder site reachable by the defendant. If it was eventually located farther away, Potter noted, that would exonerate the accused, who not only was limited in the distance he could travel on the night of the crime but was also held in custody without bail thereafter.

Potter questioned Nash, establishing that he knew the nature and location of the invention. Here was a man who had quarreled with the senator on the day of the crime and who wanted to court the senator's daughter but wasn't favored by Barnwell.

Potter also questioned overseer Bret Markham, establishing that he was yet another man who had seen the invention at the Crossroads, a man who lived there and was on the property the night of the crime. This was a man who was found fully dressed in the middle of the night after the murder was committed.

Prosecutor Drew countered by showing that both men saw the invention hours earlier and that there was no evidence that either of them was anywhere near it at the time of the crime.

Potter pointed out that the inventor himself was on the premises on the night in question and at the murder site soon after the victim's death. Tom arched his eyebrows at the prospect of becoming a suspect in the theft of his own property.

Potter introduced witnesses to attest to the defendant's character, then called Ted Cooper himself to testify. The defendant gave his own account of his actions and motives on that tragic night. He maintained that he had arrived on the scene only *after* Barnwell had already been killed. Cooper admitted that he had intended to steal the invention. "That device had to be destroyed, and I was going to do it," he said unapologetically.

His attorney stressed that the perpetrator had taken valuable time at the murder site to reattach the cover to the motor, something that never would have been done by someone intent on destroying the device but only by someone wanting to protect and profit from it. And that person, the defense claimed, could not be Cooper.

"I'm a Southerner *first*." Cooper leaned toward the jury as he fought for his life. "Whoever took that device is *not* of Southern mind or spirit, but is a traitor in our midst. By the inventor's own words, his new machine *will clear the fields of men.* Think of it. What will happen if tractors work the fields in place of men? What will happen to our bondsmen? Why, of course, they'll be *emboldened.*"

Cooper seemed frightened by his own dire predictions.

"They'll want to acquire other skills and jobs. They'll want to live away from our farms. They'll want to be educated. Before you know it, they'll want to do everything *we* do." His voice rose, his fist hit the arm of his chair, and his body stiffened. "They'll *demand* we set them free! And if we don't, they'll storm our towns and homes, riotous and uncontrollable, and outnumbering us *eight to one.* I tell you, there'll be an *insurrection!*"

A buzz shot through the crowd. The polarizing times and the gathering storm were on everyone's mind, and remarks like Cooper's discharged some of the sparks. The judge struck his gavel for order.

"If the South knows its own son, it knows I would *never* want that invention to succeed. I would *never* covet that device, as the killer clearly did. As sure as I'm a Southerner, I'm *innocent!*"

He stared at the jurors. The faces of those who held his life in their hands were solemn, alert, and unemotional.

Will Drew cross-examined Cooper, forcing him to admit that he intended to take the invention, he left his room in the night to do so, he hitched a horse to haul the device away, he entered the place where the invention was kept, and he was discovered standing over the senator's body with blood on his hands.

The jury listened intently. After each side rested its case, the trial ended with closing arguments. The prosecutor presented his in simple terms.

"This case is about a man who encountered a new invention, who learned it was not yet under patent protection, who recognized the potential worth of it, and who seized an opportunity to steal it in pursuit of riches. Driven by his own obsession for wealth, Mr. Cooper was tempted that night, and he crossed a line. When Senator Barnwell caught him in the midst of his vile act, he crossed another line. Once he slipped into the quicksand of evil, he could not extricate himself. He descended still deeper. This is why he plunged a knife into the chest of Wiley Barnwell!"

He paused to allow the jurors to digest the words.

"Whether any of us approves or disapproves of the invention or wonders what it can or cannot do or what it will or will not lead to," he continued, "we're *not* here to judge the device. We're here to judge one thing only: Who killed Senator Wiley Barnwell?"

He pointed to Cooper each time he mentioned him. "It is the *defendant* who was staying overnight at the Crossroads and had the opportunity to steal the invention. It is the *defendant* who schemed to steal it. It is the *defendant* who hitched a horse to haul it away. It is the *defendant* who returned to the

Crossroads to reoccupy his room. It is the *defendant* who felt it safe, with everyone asleep in the dark of night, to check that his victim was indeed dead and wouldn't recover to name his attacker. And, members of the jury, it is the *defendant* who was caught standing over the senator's body, his hands stained with blood."

Drew paused to move his eyes across the jurors, then returned to his seat.

Cooper's attorney rose to give the closing argument for the defense.

"The prosecution would have you believe this is an open-and-shut case," he told the jury. "But look at all the reasonable doubt we've exposed for you. First, the circumstances: Why would a man *return* to the place where he had earlier stabbed someone? And where's the murder weapon? And the missing invention? Finding them might shed an entirely different light on the crime. We also know that there were other men besides Mr. Cooper who knew about the invention, knew of its whereabouts at the Crossroads, and could have had access to it as well."

He studied the faces of the jurors, one by one, as if wanting to imprint his perspective on their minds.

"Beyond the circumstances, I call your attention to the man himself. We've established that the murderer went to considerable lengths to protect the invention, to put a heavy cover on the engine at the scene of the murder, an act that would delay his escape and increase his risk of being caught. The perpetrator had to have a compelling reason to want that cover on the engine. The reason can only be that he *valued* that device. He wanted to protect it, to develop it, and to profit from it."

Potter searched the jurors' faces for an indication, a clue, a nuance. There were none.

"This is a case in which the *character* of the man accused precludes him from having the *motive* to commit the crime. Mr. Cooper is a son of the South. We've presented solid testimony to establish his loyalty to our cause in words and deeds. Mr. Cooper, by his very character, could *not* be the thief who wanted to profit from the invention. That means he could *not* be the man who murdered Senator Barnwell."

At the end of the closing arguments, the jurors departed the courtroom as expressionless as they had arrived and had remained throughout the trial.

After two days of deliberation, the jury announced that it had reached a verdict. It returned to the courtroom that was once again packed with witnesses, reporters, and townspeople eager to learn the outcome.

"Foreman of the jury, have you reached a verdict?" asked the judge.

The foreman stood up. "Yes, we have, your honor."

Cooper rose to face him.

The eyes of Tom, Charlotte, Rachel, and the dozens of others present were pulled to the two men standing.

"How do you find the defendant?" the judge asked.

"We find the defendant *guilty*."

The crowd gasped. Charlotte's head fell in a sudden release of two months of tension. Rachel stared numbly ahead. From his seat behind them, Tom's arms curled around the women in comfort. The inventor closed his eyes, feeling relieved that justice had been done. But would he ever see his tractor again?

As two guards flanked Cooper to escort him back to jail, the prisoner whirled to Tom, his eyes hateful, his voice a subhuman snarl. "One day, when you find that wicked device, you'll *know* I was innocent!"

The guards cuffed his hands. "You'll *all* know!" He bellowed to the room at large.

As the guards pushed him toward the door, he delivered a parting shot to Tom: "Fate won't allow a patriot to die while a traitor lives. Fate will avenge me!"

That fate was to be tested presently. Two days later the judge pronounced the sentence: Theodore Cooper would hang by the neck until dead.

# CHAPTER 11

Ted Cooper appealed his case to the state's highest court. It agreed to take up the matter, with a decision expected in early May. For the man in the cell, as well as the man with the padlocked workshop, it was a time of waiting, first for the trial to occur and then for the appeal to run its course.

During that period, the household affairs at Indigo Springs were changing in unexpected ways. The month of March brought a happy improvement to Tom's dining. The chef's hat placed on Jerome's head gave the slave a stature he had never before known. He found an area in which *he* could be the master, and it was a field that suited him. The newly designated chef restored order to the kitchen and taste to the food, rescuing Tom from the culinary mishaps of the plantation's declining Aunt Bess.

Under the new management, the smokehouse was better stocked than it had been in recent years. And the storehouse next to the kitchen was more orderly and well supplied. Jerome kept cornmeal, flour, and other dry goods in ample amounts and protected them from moisture and insects. He ensured that enough milk, butter, and eggs were always on hand. He caught fowl and fish from the plantation's pond, and made fine meals of his catch. He mastered Aunt Bess's roasted chicken, turtle soup, and other dishes. With a fondness for sweets, he learned to make her almond pudding, lemon cake, and gingerbread cookies.

He bought imported items such as tea and coffee in town. Because Bayou Redbird was a major port town between New Orleans and Natchez, this brought to the riverfront, as well as to Greenbriar up the bluff, a brisk commerce and variety of shops that made it convenient for Jerome to find the ingredients he needed. He rewarded Tom's outlay on spices and extracts by reviving a dish recently dropped from Aunt Bess's collection: cinnamon buns with vanilla cream.

For the first time, Tom was pleased with Jerome's work. In retrospect, the inventor realized that his slave always had a keen interest in the kitchen and a rudimentary knowledge of its operation, which accelerated his learning. With the openness of a child eager to be complimented, Jerome solicited Tom's opinion of his dishes and relished the praise he received. Tom gave him latitude, and Jerome's talent rose as handily as his kneaded breads. The new chef's primary job was to cook for his master, but he also made dishes for the servants at the big house and its dependencies, supplementing the food they prepared for themselves from their rations and vegetable gardens. Amazingly, Jerome seemed too absorbed with his newfound interest in cooking to indulge in his former pastimes of indolence and theft.

Jerome delegated tasks to a few kitchen assistants, freeing time for him to expand his sphere. With Tom lacking interest in culinary affairs, Jerome took to managing the field hands' cook and the other servants involved with food production, just as he had previously assumed the management of the household servants. He oversaw those who tended the hogpen, cow pasture, smokehouse, henhouse, pigeon cote, corncrib, big-house vegetable garden, and other food-related areas. He pressed them to do their jobs properly so that he could have a well-stocked kitchen.

Soon Jerome was eager to try new recipes. He remembered a few dishes he liked that Aunt Bess no longer made. They were from the housekeeping journal of Tom's mother, which the mistress would read to her cook. Jerome asked Aunt Bess about these dishes, but she no longer remembered the book or its recipes, and Pearl Edmunton had died several years ago.

As soon as Jerome displayed a good grasp of the cooking and squeezed all he could from the shriveling fruit that was Aunt Bess's memory, she was sent to join the other elderly slaves, who watched the children while their parents worked. When she took off her kitchen apron for the last time, it seemed to be to everyone's benefit.

One afternoon in late March, when Tom was returning to Indigo Springs after a few days away, he was hungry—and surprised to realized that he missed Jerome's cooking. Tom had been attending to bank business, supervising Ruby Manor and the Crossroads as he'd promised Charlotte, and searching in vain for his invention.

Headed home on horseback, he glimpsed his workshop on the hilltop. He had not yet entered it. While his own project was on hold, he was pleased that a padlock of another sort had somehow swung open to release the initiative of his most incorrigible slave.

Within a system that didn't allow him a choice, Jerome had found something he wanted to do. Within a system that didn't allow him to learn, Jerome had found a subject he wanted to understand. The unexpected change in Jerome was another step on the path to a future era, Tom thought, when all people would be as self-starting and self-fueled as the new engine he wanted to bring to that age. Could he somehow tap the will of the *other* slaves—for their benefit and his? He thought of one slave in particular who had gazed longingly at a picture card of couples dancing around a ballroom, a literate young woman who seemed to him terribly miscast in her new role as Jerome's replacement in the stable. What would he do with Solo?

Riding toward the big house, he pictured her. Dressed in a man's shirt and trousers, her sleeves and pants cuffs rolled up to fit her small frame, she spent her days raking the hay and tending the horses, looking like the young slave boys who assisted her. At night, in her cabin near the stable, she read voraciously. She made frequent trips to Tom's library for books. She returned her selections promptly and always in the same condition she'd found them, as if the dusty old volumes were sacred texts not to be crimped, bent, or soiled. By the location of the latest gap on the library shelves, Tom could tell the category of book she was reading—an ancient history, a biography of a distinguished person, a collection of poems, a novel, a travel journal, a geography of the world. She displayed a keen interest in every kind of book—and no interest in any person. She kept to herself, declining to socialize with the other slaves or to accompany them to town on errands. Within a group that was limited in its human interactions by outside forces, she was even more so by choice.

Tom was drawn to the mysterious girl who seemed to be such a misfit. Wasn't he too an outsider? Was that why she aroused his . . . curiosity?

When he arrived at the big house that afternoon, his horse was tired and he needed food. However, no one was there to help him. He walked the animal to the stable, but Solo was not in sight. He looked for Jerome in the kitchen, but the cavernous brick hearth was dormant and the room was empty.

He heard voices coming from the storehouse and walked there to investigate. Through the window he saw two figures standing by a table, one wearing a chef's hat. Intent on their business, they failed to notice him.

"This next entry is something entirely new!" said Solo.

Her dirt-splattered pants and shirt gave her the look of a farm boy at work, but her long tangled hair was emphatically feminine.

"Whut the missus mean?" asked Jerome.

Solo was holding a bound volume of more than one hundred handwritten pages. Tom recognized his mother's housekeeping book. Jerome had recently asked him about the book, but he hadn't been able to find it in his mother's room. It must have been placed in the library, where the room's newest visitor apparently had located it.

Pearl Edmunton, like many other plantation mistresses, kept a journal of helpful tips for managing the domestic affairs of the estate. The book contained items as diverse as remedies for soothing sore throats and for treating cholera, techniques for dying fabrics and for polishing furniture, and recipes for making soups, meats, stews, breads, cakes, preserves, brandies, and other foods. Watching Solo read from the book, Tom was carried back in time, held for a moment by an image of the mother he loved, who had died six years earlier.

"Mrs. Edmunton said she discovered something new to eat while she was traveling around the North," said Solo. "She said it was delicious."

"And whut that be?"

Glancing in the window, Tom was astonished by what he saw. To his surprise, the items in the room were *labeled*. Common cooking measures and ingredients were spread out on the table as if a lesson were in progress, with the name of each item written on a scrap of paper near it: *teacup, teaspoon, tablespoon, pint, quart, mixing bowl, eggs, butter, milk, sugar, flour, yeast*. On the shelves, he saw labels adhered with a spot of glue to containers of foodstuffs: *raisins, molasses, peach preserves, pepper, vinegar*. Tom also saw labels on cooking equipment: *cake pan, soup kettle, sieve*.

"Mrs. Edmunton came back from her trip with a recipe for a new kind of cake," said Solo.

Jerome looked at the page she was reading. His face crinkled with the mental labor of deciphering the words.

"Hmm," said the chef in deep concentration, pointing to words in the recipe, then searching the items on the table to find the objects they named. His eyes moved back and forth, from the page to the labels, looking for matches. Finally, he found one. "Eggs!" he said in triumph.

"That's right," said his teacher.

He picked up a small basket of eggs and moved it in front of him. He repeated the process for a second item, then a third, and so on. In that manner, he gathered in front of him butter, sugar, and flour.

"Good." Solo nodded her approval.

His finger paused on an ingredient in the recipe that had no matching object in the room. He scrutinized the table and shelves, trying to match the word that appeared in the recipe, and indeed also in the title of the dish, but without success.

"This ain't here. Whut this say?" Jerome pointed to the puzzling word on the page.

"*Chocolate*," said Solo.

"Oh, that be cocoa. But that fer drinkin', ain't it?"

"Actually, Mrs. Edmunton's recipe is for a chocolate *cake*."

Jerome and his teacher looked surprised. Although cocoa was widely used as a beverage, they had not heard of anyone eating food made with it.

"She has a note about it." Solo read to Jerome from the book:

*There is a growing interest here and in Europe in using chocolate for eating. Through better roasting and grinding methods, companies are manufacturing a smoother, richer chocolate that brings out more of the flavor. Shops sell this chocolate in one-pound bars, which can be cut into smaller pieces and melted, then used to make quite delicious bonbons, candy sticks, and other confections.*

Solo looked up and smiled about this pleasant new discovery.

Jerome's eyes flashed with interest. "I's gonna make this cake!"

The man at the window felt sure that the chocolate cake from his mother's book would soon appear on his table. He sensed what Jerome was feeling; he had felt the same eagerness in moments of surprise and discovery that had sparked his own life. In fact, he was having such a moment right then because, finally, he knew what to do with Solo.

He stepped up to the open door to face the culinary explorers.

They turned to him in awkward silence, with their book open, looking like two burglars caught with goods that didn't belong to them.

It was Solo who broke the silence. "I'll tend to your horse."

"No, don't go back to the stable." Tom walked toward them.

"I fix yer dinner, Mr. Tom."

"No."

Jerome seemed taken aback by Tom's remarks. There was no trace of the slave's ready smile and cheerful manner. He dropped his head as if expecting a reprimand. Solo didn't follow suit; she kept her eyes on Tom, more curious than fearful—and perhaps more attuned to his nature than was her friend.

"But Mr. Tom, you jus' gittin' home; you needs yer dinner—"

"I don't want you to go back to the kitchen, Jerome."

"But—"

"And she's not going back to the stable."

"Whut?!" Jerome looked terrified.

Tom, intent on a new idea, didn't notice his cook's panic. "Somebody else can get me dinner and take care of the horse."

"But, Mr. Tom, you can't send us to the fields! Fo' Gawd, pleez, sir!"

"What?" Tom was astonished. "The fields? Why would I do that?"

"I knows Miss Solo can't be learnin' me. Pleez don't send us to th' fields! We gives back yer mama's book and won't do this agin."

Jerome took the housekeeping journal from Solo, closed it, and handed it to Tom. The slave then started to take the labels away from the items on the table.

"No, stop, Jerome." Tom spread his arm over the table to block the action. "What I meant was, you can stay here and finish your lesson."

Jerome stared at him.

Tom held the book out to his confused slave. "I'd like to taste that new chocolate cake."

Slowly, Jerome's smile returned. He reached for the book and grasped it gingerly with both hands as if it were a prized manuscript.

Then Tom turned to Solo. "And I just realized what you could do here."

She looked at him, her eyes of melted chocolate waiting to hear his recipe.

"You can give classes to the servants. Teach them to read and write. Teach them to want to learn about something. Teach them to *care* about something, *anything*. I want you to make me more Jeromes."

Her stunned silence suggested that she realized the proposal was unheard of, outrageous . . . unlawful.

"And teach the children too. Of course, teach them." Tom continued matter-of-factly, as if he were in another time and place, arranging a normal activity.

Solo remained speechless with the dazed look of someone hit in the head and knocked off balance.

"Would you want to do that? The job's yours if you want it."

She cocked her head, assessing the matter. The proposal itself and being asked for her assent seemed to take her completely by surprise.

"Well?" Tom waited.

With his eyes searching hers, he wondered if he could reach something vital within her, as she had reached in Jerome, and as they both had reached in him. Out of the stagnant waters that trapped the three of them, their will and choice in how to deal with one another seemed to be surfacing like a current to carry them into a fresh new stream.

When she said nothing, he finally turned to go. As he reached the door, he heard her reply.

"I'll make a list of what I need."

\* \* \* \* \*

The stores were open and business was brisk when Tom drove a wagon through the main street of a town ten miles from Greenbriar. He hoped the distance from home and his wide-brimmed hat would protect his anonymity. He hitched his wagon to a post, then walked past the display windows of various shops until he came to the general store. He paused at the entrance to lower his hat over his face, feeling like a criminal. He was buying items that would be used to commit a crime: slate pencils and boards, primers, and other supplies for Solo's school.

The new teacher had moved into his childhood tutor's room in a secluded area of the big house. There she found items useful to her new role—a desk, a blackboard and chalk, and a bookcase containing Tom's early lessons and schoolbooks. Slaves working at the big house and its dependencies were to comprise her first class. She would add the children and other adults later . . . after Tom traveled to other towns for more supplies.

When she had asked to use an outer building for her classroom, he offered an alternative. "If you're going to teach them to read, why not meet where the books are—in the library?" The offer of his house to the slaves for their meetings left her too shocked to reply.

"Those books are just sitting on the shelves collecting dust, kind of like people who waste away with their potential untapped. Don't you think we could tap that?"

"Tap the people—or the books?" she asked.

"Both."

She laughed, a quick puff of air with a sweet sound that was too rare an occurrence for his taste.

Her expression quickly changed to worry. She sensed danger, and she surprised the two of them with her concern—for *him*. "If we meet outside, maybe you can pretend you don't know about the class . . . if . . . anyone—"

"And leave *you* to take the blame? In case you don't know it, I would never do that."

She quietly absorbed his words of protection.

"If anyone comes around, I have a plan to conceal the class. If it doesn't work, then *I'm* the teacher and you're just one of the students. And you can't read or write."

"But—" she protested.

"No buts."

She looked uneasy but accepted his resolve. She would give her class in the place she liked best, the palace of her life: the library.

He felt he had a personal stake in the school. It was linked in his mind to the missing invention, the boarded workshop, the halted project—to the new age he couldn't yet reach. The class was a step he *could* take along that road.

The school created to liberate the servants almost began as an act of utter tyranny. The school's self-appointed sergeant at arms and first student, Jerome, wanted to fill Solo's class by *ordering* the slaves to attend. This required that they complete their tasks earlier than usual and give up some of their precious free time in the evening. When Tom heard of the plan, he shook his head. "You need to try for *volunteers*," he advised. "You can force their legs to walk and their hands to work, but you can't force this."

Heeding Tom's words, Jerome tried persuasion, and Solo helped with the effort. To their surprise, they soon found enough servants willing to attend. Whether it was out of curiosity, constant prodding from the two advocates, or the added inducement of a piece of Jerome's new cake—for by then he had gotten the chocolate and produced a fine product—nine servants arrived at the back door of the big house on the evening of Solo's first class.

111

Before the class began, Tom appeared at the library door. He inspected the empty room, checking to be sure the drapes were drawn, as he had instructed. With the bookcases stretching to the ceiling with musty tomes and the lamplight casting a golden tinge over the room, it looked like a scholar's hideaway.

While Tom observed the new classroom, its teacher appeared. He turned to her, amazed at the new image before him. She had broken with habit by wearing a dress. The feminine clothing looked surprisingly well suited to her. The dress was a simple slave's frock, clean and ironed, but she wore it with a quiet dignity that made her look like a handsome farm woman. The frock's high collar gathered in a simple tie at her neck looked demure, while the figure the dress hugged looked womanly. A ribbon fastened her voluminous hair, lifting it off her face. With her hair swept back, the lines of her face were even more striking.

Tom broke with his conscious policy by letting his attention linger on her. Against his will, his glance traveled from the glistening almond eyes that dominated her face, then to the gaunt cheekbones, the pleasing slope of her nose, the etched lips, the tapered chin. Her face was still too arresting to evoke calm emotions, but the fury that was part of her usual countenance had vanished. She looked almost genteel.

In answer to the surprise on his face at her newfound civility, she looked as if she were about to smile. Then thinking better of it, she simply stared back at him.

"If you need me, I'll be around," he said, turning to leave.

She looked astonished at the prospect of his being at her service.

As he walked toward the front entrance, he heard Jerome on the back porch welcoming the new class. "Yer clothes gotta be clean. Lemme see them shoes! Hold out them hands! Git that dirt off yer knuckles! Y'all's gotta be clean, clean, *clean*. And don't be touchin' nuthin' in there!"

After passing Jerome's inspection, the slaves quietly passed Solo one by one at the library door. She gave them each a slate pencil and board, with a cloth for an eraser. She directed them to seats on the couch, on chairs, and on the floor. They formed a crescent around the tutor's blackboard, which had been moved into the room. Their dark eyes glistened in the lamplight as they glanced up at the walls of books, absorbing a world completely new to them. They sat in unbreached silence as Solo closed the door and began her class.

Outside on the gallery, a lonely figure sat in a rocking chair, a rifle resting across his lap. From his perch in the moonlight, Tom could see the road approaching the big house.

The slave patrols that scoured the town appeared on his grounds infrequently, but always at unexpected times, to search for runaways. He had never heard of a planter chasing them away, and he didn't intend to arouse their suspicions by being the first.

Tom could also see the light filtering out through the drapery in the library. Close enough to see through the curtains, he noticed Jerome's figure by the window. Tom had arranged in advance for his cook to sit there. Should anyone ride up the road toward the house, Tom would alert Jerome. The slave would then erase the blackboard, quietly get the students out the back door, and gather them by the pond. He'd direct them to begin singing hymns, and Tom, if necessary, would explain that they habitually gathered around the pond in the evening for songs. That was the plan if someone appeared whom he couldn't turn away. The plan for dealing with strangers who needed persuasion to leave was simpler. He glanced at his rifle.

He could see Solo's lithe form through the curtain, standing before the group. From the dark veranda, unseen by the others, he heard her begin the class.

"Before we get to your lesson for tonight, I want to say something." She pointed to the bookcases that formed a literary cave around them. "You see these books? What do you suppose is inside them?"

The class stared at her hypnotically, as if she were the priestess of this new temple.

"The answer is: *everything*. The whole world is inside these books. Would you like to take a trip across the ocean? This book is an adventure story written by a sea captain." She pulled out a volume and held it up to them. "Would you like to see what people and places there are up the river, where the steamers go? That's in this book." She selected another title, this one displaying a steamboat on the cover, and held it up to the group. She placed her selections on a table and continued searching the shelves. "Would you like to know what it's like to be a princess in love with a duke who's plotting to kill your father, the king?" She made another selection and held it out to the women in the class. "This book is called a novel, and it tells a story about that. You see, all of these books sweep you away from here and bring you to an exciting new place."

Like the proprietress of a shop who knows the merchandise well, she brushed through the shelves with ease. As she spoke, she looked into the eyes of the servants in the room—the butler and maid, wearing the white gloves they used for formal dinners; the gardener sitting on a chair next to his girlfriend, the housekeeper; the weaver and spinner sitting together on the couch; the blacksmith and carpenter sitting on the rug; and Jerome at the window. They turned their heads to follow her as she moved among the books.

"Would you like to know how people in history lived? How great empires of the world grew and crumbled? That's in this book." She took out one of the thickest tomes.

"And did you ever think about how pretty a rose is? There's a poem in here that describes that. This is a book of poetry." She held up one of the thinnest books.

"Did you ever wonder what goes on in the theater? This book takes you there. It's a book of plays, which are performed onstage." She held up the selection. "See how you can know the answer to *everything* in these books?"

She picked another volume. She thumbed through it and displayed one of its illustrations to the group. It was of a beautifully dressed man and woman at a table dining; the couple displayed correct posture and a refinement in handling their silverware. "Would you like to have manners? This book is called *Etiquette*. It teaches you the manners that make you gentlemen and ladies. Manners mean that no one can be better than you. Now, you might not always want to show people your manners . . ."

Outside, Tom wondered if perhaps she was thinking of her own outrageous behavior.

". . . but you'll have your manners when you want them. And no one can ever take them away from you. These manners travel from the pages of the book straight to you. And they're yours to keep."

The class members looked thoughtful as they heard about things that were theirs to keep and the magic of the books that awaited them.

"Speaking good English means nobody is better than you. It means you're a full person who can stand tall with anyone. This book teaches you how to speak." She held up another book.

"This book is about bookkeeping and arithmetic. It teaches you how to handle your money, how to buy a farm, how to manage a shop, how to order your supplies, how to pay your bills, and how to count your profits." She held a volume up in front of the carpenter and the blacksmith. "After you read this book, you'll be ready to run your own farm or shop . . . maybe . . . one day . . ."

The two tradesmen stared at the mysterious volume in her hands that was about a subject they had never imagined or thought possible.

She took another book and leafed through it purposefully, looking for a certain page. "Here's a book about Paris and the shops there that sell so many pretty things."

She opened the book to the page she wanted and moved it across the group, starting with Jerome. The page showed an artist's illustration of the outside of a Parisian pastry shop. The drawing captured a store window filled with cakes, cookies, cream puffs, and other treats. A boy stood in the corner, holding his mother's hand, looking eagerly at the display, pointing to an item of special interest to him.

"Hmm." Jerome seemed unaware that he had uttered anything or jumped up from his seat to study the drawing.

"In the meantime, you can have a shop here . . . almost. You can make things in your free time and sell them in town," Solo continued.

Slaves of Indigo Springs and other plantations sold items they raised or produced, such as broomsticks, baskets, hens, eggs, hogs, or vegetables. They sold these goods to their masters or to the locals and steamboat travelers in Bayou Redbird.

"I'll cover arithmetic in class, so you'll be able to buy and sell things for money and make change."

She looked at some of the slaves whom she knew had children.

"And you'll want to teach your children what you learn, so they can know what's out there beyond these fields. They can learn what any other person can learn, so they'll be able to do useful things . . . and take care of themselves."

Her students glanced at each other, their faces attentive, as if they were considering the matter put before them.

"Books make you a master of yourself."

Her words seemed to lift her listeners in their seats.

She moved her hands fondly across the books she had accumulated on the table, as if she were caressing them.

"If you can't go out to the world, the world can come here to you— through these books."

She reached into a cabinet in the corner and pulled out the primers that Tom had bought. Jerome helped her distribute one to each student. "This book is *yours*. It's your first book."

The slaves took their books and looked curiously through the pages.

"This book will teach you letters. Then it'll show you how to form words with the letters, and sentences with the words. You'll write the letters and words and sentences on your slate board, as I'll write them on the blackboard. And you'll read from your book."

The slaves' eyes traveled back and forth from their teacher to the pages of their first book.

"If you know how to speak, and read, and write, then you have something no one can ever take away. Inside yourself, you're . . . *free*."

The last word seemed to linger in the air.

"Miss Solo?"

The rich timbre of the carpenter's voice reached her. Like Jerome, he instinctively addressed Solo with the title reserved for free women. Being someone who enlightened them, she seemed to merit the respectful *Miss*, regardless of her social status.

"Yes?"

"Does it say in any o' dem books dat us gonna . . . one day . . . be free *outside* ousselfs?"

115

Her voice was solemn. "I've read that the world is changing, new ways are taking root . . . like new seeds in the garden . . . and *that day* is coming."

Dark, glistening eyes widened as minds seemed to open to a topic of significance like no other.

"When the time comes, you'll be ready." She held up a copy of their primer. "*This book* is your ticket to the new day."

Tom's figure formed a dark outline on the veranda, topped by a sparkle of gold hair catching the moonlight. He looked relaxed on the rocker, his long legs stretching up to the porch rail, his arms falling limply in his lap. From a distance he might have seemed to be napping. But a closer look revealed alert blue eyes intrigued by the lesson drifting out to him. To his amazement, the mysterious creature he had named Solo was describing the new age.

# CHAPTER 12

By early April, Jerome's confidence and skill at his new job had grown. He could be heard directing the objects under his command as a captain might lead a charge:

"Boil now, dang ya!" he told the soup kettle.

"No burnin', ya hear?" he warned the pancakes.

"C'mon, c'mon! I ain't got all day!" he ordered the egg whites as he beat them furiously.

He deployed an arsenal of kettles and a regiment of pans to the fireplace where he simmered stew, boiled ham, roasted duck, heated vegetables, fried crullers, and griddled waffles.

With his love for desserts and sweets, he soon gravitated to baking. He gave an assistant the job of fireplace cooking so that he could concentrate on the large open mouth in the wall with the charred brick mustache that was the oven. Early in the morning on baking days he built a fire in the oven, then stoked the wood until it burned fiercely. When the bricks had absorbed an intense amount of heat, Jerome was ready.

He shoveled his prepared batters in and out of the oven with military precision. His ever-present wood peel slid the pans around. He made room for all his soldiers, covered the field evenly, and removed them when they were done to make room for replacements. First he sent in the pies and loaf cakes, which needed the most intense heat. Then came the breads. Finally, with the remaining heat, he put in the smaller items like tarts, biscuits, and cookies. On baking days, Jerome's battlefield smelled of smoking-hot lemon tarts, pumpkin pies, and raisin breads. His production was becoming too much for his plantation family of one diner, Tom, and for the specialties allowed the bondsmen. It seemed that either Tom would need to marry and have twelve children or Jerome would need to find another outlet for his energies.

With Solo's help, he was learning to read Mrs. Edmunton's housekeeping book, which provided a trove of recipes, as well as guidelines on cooking methods and food handling. He learned that every ingredient needed special care and attention for the best result. He tackled the flour, ridding it of impurities, drying it, and sifting it to a fine consistency for baking. He checked the eggs for freshness. He washed the butter to remove its preservative salt. He chopped the pecans diligently and added them to his cakes and breads. He was rewarded for his care with fine baked goods, and he learned a lesson important to any chef. "Recipes is like people," he told Tom. "Whut ya git out o' them depend on whut they got inside."

In his foray into baking, Jerome developed a fascination for one ingredient about all others: chocolate. He obtained chocolate baking bars from Bayou Redbird's general store, which stocked them from a northern manufacturer. Using Mrs. Edmunton's recipe, Jerome created a tasty chocolate cake. With his latent creative bent now released, Jerome was an innovator from the start. He added a touch of vanilla to the chocolate cake and improved it; then he added chopped walnuts and improved it again.

"How's you likin' yer mama's cake?" he asked his master.

Tom smiled. "I think it's *your* cake now."

When Jerome melted the chocolate bars, something magical happened that served as an announcement of his new presence at Indigo Springs. An incredible aroma of chocolate permeated the air. The irresistible scent lured the house servants, the craftsmen, and even Tom to the kitchen door to investigate. The hogs and cows were also curious, as they wandered toward the little cabin that was emitting the enticing scent. The smell of chocolate cake fresh from the oven aroused Solo's students, who were allowed a piece once a week after their lesson. Jerome basked in their oohs and aahs over his cake as if they were admiring his newborn baby.

The eager chef tried adding chocolate to other recipes, sometimes with questionable results. The guinea pig for his experiments was his unfortunate master. One morning Jerome added his favorite ingredient to scrambled eggs and biscuits, turning them a dark brown. He served them to Tom and waited hopefully for his response. But the chef was disappointed. "You don't have to put chocolate in everything," said Tom, after tasting a breakfast that was the same color as his walnut dining table.

The maddening scent of his favorite ingredient drove Jerome to further explorations. On a day when he was to bake his cake for Solo's class, an idea occurred to him. The chocolate had its most intense taste and aroma when it was warmed in melted butter and sugar, before adding the other ingredients. What would happen, he wondered, if he added more of the sweetened chocolate and as few additional ingredients as possible, so the taste would be richer? He began the recipe by doubling the amount of chocolate and increasing the sugar as he melted them in butter, then he brought the warm batter to his worktable. To bind the ingredients, he added eggs, and for richer taste, vanilla. Then to keep the batter thick and the chocolate intense, he left out the milk and added only half the amount of flour he normally used in the cake. Before baking, he mixed chopped walnuts into the batter, which had worked well for him in the cake recipe.

The result was a thick, compact batter, almost a paste, that barely covered the bottom of a rectangular cake sheet. After it baked, the lack of any rising worried Jerome, but the chocolate aroma that the new recipe exuded while it baked was incredibly richer than that of the cake. He shrugged his shoulders, dubious about his new concoction, as he left it to cool while he attended Solo's class.

Afterward, the class piled into the kitchen, awaiting their taste of Jerome's cake. But there was no cake, high and fluffy, inviting them to take a slice. There was only a pan of something mysterious. Although the sides of the pan were four inches high, the oddity inside barely rose above an inch. The slaves hesitated.

"Dis fer eatin'?" said one.

Jerome nodded hesitantly. The unappetizing item in the pan had a dry brown crust, with cracks in the surface.

"Look like dirt," said another slave.

Jerome's eyes widened apprehensively. He took a knife, but his hand paused over the pan before he had the courage to cut a piece. Solo took the knife from him and completed the action. The little square she cut held firm on the knife, without the need of a plate. She grasped it with her fingers. The group watched their teacher silently, a concerned expression on their faces, as she studied the chocolate square, smelled it, and finally, cautiously tasted it. The slaves' eyes followed the piece into her mouth. Then she smiled.

She cut a piece for Jerome. He tasted it. Then he smiled.

He cut pieces for the others, who stepped up, tasted the new treat, and gave their assessments.

"Hey, dis mighty good!" said one.

"Dis *real* good!" said another.

"'Taint no cookie. It too thick."

"'Taint no cake. It too small."

"It's Jerome's *chocolate squares*." Solo named the item that looked like the dry Louisiana ground cracking during a drought but tasted more intensely chocolate than a cake and more chewy than a cookie. She nodded approvingly at the creator.

One slave slapped Jerome on the back. "Say, man, dis whut chocolate appose ta be!"

The others nodded in agreement.

Before the pieces were gone, Solo grabbed one and dashed into the big house. She found Tom reading in the parlor. She bent down by his chair and held the piece out to him.

"Taste this!"

It was hardly the way a slave would act toward a master, but neither one seemed to notice. His eyes moved from her to the two-inch square morsel, amused; then he took it and tasted.

The next instant, he sprang up and walked out the back door to the kitchen, with Solo following. In the darkness he saw the shadows of the class members as they were returning to their cabins. In the kitchen he found Jerome alone, standing tall in his hat, an empty pan with a few chocolate crumbs before him.

"What did you do, Jerome?"

"I change couple things. You likes it, sir?"

Tom took another bite. He cocked his head as he chewed slowly, savoring the taste. The man with the chef's hat stared at him eagerly. Solo also waited.

"This is *outstanding*, Jerome."

The chef face brightened. So did his teacher's.

"I've traveled a lot, but I've *never* tasted anything like this." Tom took a third bite, drew out his enjoyment of it, and then held the remaining morsel up to the lamplight.

"It's almost a cake, but not quite. And it's almost a cookie, but not quite. It's something different that has its own unique character." He looked at the proud man in the tall hat. "Jerome, you created something entirely new."

As he consumed the last bite, Tom surveyed the shelves and found one of the chocolate baking bars in its package. He picked up the item that was the size of a small brick.

"Is this what you used?"

Jerome nodded.

"Hmm . . ." Tom read the label aloud: *New and improved flavor. Smooth, velvety texture.*

His companions watched him with interest.

"I've read there are new machines coming out for grinding and smoothing the chocolate inside the cocoa bean, so more of the flavor is captured." He held the package up. "This chocolate must be made with the new methods."

Tom looked in earnest at the man society had deemed beneath its notice. "You saw a potential in this chocolate that no one else has seen. You created something new. That makes you an *inventor*."

Jerome looked as if he had received an award.

The two inventors smiled at each other. They didn't know that years later Jerome's recipe, as well as countless variations of it, would be created in kitchens around the world and eagerly consumed by millions. They didn't know that Jerome had created one of the earliest—perhaps the first—example of the food that would one day be called a brownie.

"A new age is coming," Tom announced to the intelligent faces watching him. "I didn't realize till now that it includes chocolate." He grinned. "And it apparently includes Jerome."

Tom held the chocolate baking bar out to the man who had used it to make something new and remarkable. Jerome accepted the bar with pride, as a sculptor might accept a block of stone waiting to be shaped.

Tom's eyes wandered to a vision of his own. "Important new things in any field need to be introduced to the world." Then his face brightened with an idea. "Say, why don't you come to the bank with me tomorrow and bring a pan of these?"

"Huh?"

Whether it was due to his being asked, rather than ordered, to do something, or the outlandishness of the suggestion, Tom couldn't tell, but his slave looked astonished.

"You can set the pan on a table outside and sell pieces to my customers. And it'll attract new people to the bank too."

There was a long-standing practice of slaves bartering and selling things in town. Tom didn't know how much of this commerce was legal and how much was custom. He knew only that a worthy discovery needed marketing.

Jerome seemed unable to find his voice.

"Just be sure someone's in the kitchen to make me a little food and handle things—and not burn the building down."

"And be sure you come to class," said Solo.

Jerome stared at Tom agape.

"Well?" asked Tom.

"Jerome, do it." His teacher nudged.

He gave his answer as a broad smile.

\* \* \* \* \*

The next day, decked in his chef's hat and the fine clothes from his days as Colonel Edmunton's head of the servants, Jerome established his stand outside Tom's bank. A long rectangular pan containing his new creation sat on a table. Solo had provided the sign: *Jerome's Chocolate Squares, five cents.*

The squares were easier to transport than cake, stayed fresh longer, held together firmly, and could be eaten with one's hands. They provided an ideal snack for the people bustling through the streets of Bayou Redbird.

Soon Jerome's first customers came: a hungry shopper, a sea captain, three slaves with a few coins in their pockets hauling a wagon of cotton to the docks, a couple traveling with two children, a customer entering the bank. Before long, ten of the sixty two-inch squares were sold, and Jerome had made fifty cents. The seductive quality of the chocolate took effect, and several of the customers returned for seconds. The sea captain bought ten squares to take back to his ship and sell for twenty cents apiece onboard. A plantation mistress wanted ten more squares to bring home to her family.

With the squares being compact and easy to carry away, customers made purchases for future consumption, which opened up an additional sales opportunity that sent Jerome to the general store for brown paper and string to wrap orders.

From the window of his office in the bank, Tom saw the chef's hat bobbing around as the animated figure underneath it talked to people, smiled, laughed, drew them to his stand, and sold his product. Tom imagined a time in the future when *he* would stand beside a new invention, one that also generated excitement, made life more pleasant, and was addictive once it was tried. What other creations could be spawned, he wondered, if the few in charge didn't have a monopoly on ideas and if everyone were free to think, dream, create, and act?

He felt a bond with Jerome—and with the slender teacher back at his home. Somehow the force within each of them—the twin engine of intelligence and will—was the power needed to drive the new age.

That evening, when he walked out to the veranda to guard Solo's class, he realized that what had started as an obligation to protect the school was now a pleasure. He liked hearing the voices that filtered out to him, voices rich with a teacher's excitement for her topics and her students' satisfaction at mastering their lessons. As he walked toward the rocker that was his lookout post, he saw Jerome standing there waiting for him.

"How did it go today, chef?"

"I sells all sixty squares."

"Really? At five cents apiece, you made three dollars."

"I sells two pans mo'."

"You what?"

"Miller Tavern order a pan fer sellin' in the saloon at ten cent apiece, and Mrs. Weatherby order pan fer a party she havin'. So I got two pans to make fer them folks tonight."

Tom stared incredulously at Jerome.

"You mean, you made *nine dollars*—in one day?"

"I buys some supplies with it and got this left." Jerome took seven dollars out of his pocket.

"Why, that's more than the overseers make!" An overseer might average twenty dollars a week.

Jerome fidgeted for a moment as if something were on his mind, then blurted out: "Since you own Jerome, then you mus' own Jerome's squares." He held the money out to his master. "This mus' be yers."

Tom's eyes dropped sadly. He hated to feel the way he did at that moment and wondered how anyone could stand it. Then he looked up and spoke quietly.

"But I didn't make the squares. And I didn't make you either."

Jerome stood with his hand out, the money in it untouched by Tom. "Beside, Jerome owe you from a ways back."

Tom knew what he meant. It was the first time the slave had ever mentioned the money Tom had given him to reach the Cincinnati safe house. Back then Jerome had changed his mind and returned home sheepishly, squandering the money and his chance at freedom. Now Tom felt as if he were looking at a different person.

He pushed the money back to the slave. "How about if you buy your own ingredients and supplies? Then you can keep whatever profit you make from your business."

"My . . . *bizness?*" Jerome's voice was barely a whisper.

"That's what it's called when you make a product and sell it." Tom smiled. "Just keep the kitchen running for me, and you can go to town and tend to your own business whenever you want."

"Yes sir." The words were a gasp.

"*Nine dollars* in one day! Come here. I have to show you something."

The slaves were beginning to file into the library for class when Tom brought Jerome to the blackboard.

"How many days will you make the ride into town? Say, two days a week?"

"Least three. I kin do three," said Jerome.

"Okay, three days a week times nine dollars a day means you could make *twenty-seven dollars* a week. And that's just for starters. That's taking your sales on the first day, which surely will grow." Tom scribbled the numbers on the board. "Times, let's say, fifty weeks a year. . . . Good God, Jerome, you could make $1,350 a year." He wrote the total and circled it on the board.

Jerome's eyes darted incredulously from the board to Tom. The amount was like an ocean to a man who had only seen puddles.

"You'll have to subtract your costs, but there's still a big profit to be made here."

Jerome studied the numbers, speechless.

"You're on to something big, Jerome!" said Tom.

Solo entered carrying her primer. She and Tom acknowledged each other in what had become their standard greeting: a quiet exchange of stares. Her simple dress and ribboned hair reflected in Tom's eyes for one lingering moment. She paused to gaze back, then continued to the desk as he left the room.

Jerome stood where Tom had left him, entranced by the number circled on the blackboard.

\* \* \* \* \*

By the beginning of May, Jerome had a steady stream of customers. Several steamships, a tavern at Bayou Redbird, and the general store in Greenbriar bought pans of chocolate squares to resell at a profit in their locations. A dress shop bought the squares to serve as complimentary treats to customers to gain an edge on its competition. Then there were the bank customers who bought a square on the way in and another on the way out. Children especially loved the squares. And plantation mistresses bought pans of them to serve at parties.

Every shop in Bayou Redbird and up the road in Greenbriar knew about Jerome's chocolate squares. He gave away some as free samples, he traded some for the supplies he needed, and he sold the vast majority. He put his talent for talking to people to good use and became an effective salesman for his product. He kept his recipe to himself and enjoyed a brisk business.

True to his word, Jerome also kept the Indigo Springs kitchen running. He had an assistant and other kitchen workers who helped him keep Tom fed well and helped perform his other duties. And he prepared a pan of chocolate squares once a week for Solo's class.

Tom had given the class permission to look at the library books, and Jerome availed himself of that. One day Tom found him at the shelves, staring at a page in one of the books. It was the drawing Solo had passed around during her first class, showing the bake shop in Paris.

Jerome smiled awkwardly, as if caught in a moment that was personal. Tom put a sympathetic arm on the slave's shoulder.

"I reckon it be nice a-bakin' an' a-sellin' all them things in that winder . . ."—he pointed to the shop window full of cakes and other sweets—". . . sellin' them in a . . . shop . . . like that."

Tom thought of the obstacles thrown in the way of Jerome's dream. There were the laws prohibiting manumission. There were the laws requiring the return of fugitive slaves. There were the kidnappers in the North who seized blacks, whether they were free or slave, and brought them South to sell into slavery. There was the treacherous journey to reach Canada to escape the threat of being returned. As Tom's affection for the slave grew, so did his concern for his safety, should he ever decide to take that second chance offered him. But Tom tried to hide his trepidations so that Jerome's dream could live. What would his own life be like, he wondered, without *his* dream?

"Yes, Jerome, it would be nice to make all those pastries and sell them in a shop . . . one day."

Before, Jerome had no yearning. Now he did. That put him above certain free people Tom knew. He thought of the lifeless face of Nash Nottingham, the man he'd once compared to his slave. But Jerome, with his energy, his business, and his dream, could never be compared to Nash again.

Later that night, there were two lights burning at Indigo Springs. One was in the kitchen, where Jerome was baking chocolate squares to fulfill customer orders. The other was in the library, where Solo was preparing the next day's lesson. No longer feeling like an interloper, she now openly used the place that was her classroom and her treasure trove. On the hill, Tom's workshop was dark. Where was the light that had burned there through so many heady nights of experiments—of making parts, of seeing them fail, of disassembling them and trying again, and of finally solving problems, with each one that was solved spurring new ones to challenge him? Would he recover the device that had been born in that place? Would the only man who knew its whereabouts ever reveal his secret?

# CHAPTER 13

"We searched clear down to the other side of Myrtle Road, then up past Morton's Landing, then through Clearwater woods . . ." Grant Sayers, a tan, athletic-looking man, pointed to places on a topographic map.

Standing with the speaker and two other men, Tom looked down at the map on his desk at the bank. His three visitors all had a few days' stubble and wore clothes suited for camping out in the woods.

"We waded on foot through Robin's Creek, thinking maybe the thing had slipped into the water, but nothing was there," said the second man, pointing to another area of the map.

Tom nodded. "I see."

"We asked permission and looked through the brush on the Johnson, Straithmore, and Billing plantations," said the third man. "Of course, we also checked the wooded areas at the Crossroads."

"Me and my men covered all the areas you laid out," said Sayers. "I'm sorry, Mr. Edmunton." The leader of the team that Tom had hired to find his invention looked earnest and regretful. "There was no hint of a mechanical device or a motor of any sort."

Tom looked at him and the others. "Thank you for trying."

He opened the door of his office and escorted his visitors to a clerk at a desk. "Please pay Mr. Sayers and his men from my personal account," he instructed the clerk.

Tom shook hands with the men, then exited the bank. His face grim, he mounted his horse and headed up the bluff to Greenbriar. He was too distraught to notice the spectacular puffs of pink and blue hydrangea blooming along the road that first week in May. His only awareness of time was that it was running out.

The high court had upheld the guilty verdict against Ted Cooper. The sole person who knew the whereabouts of his invention was to be executed the next day.

\* \* \* \* \*

Tom climbed the steps two at a time on the stairway to Cooper's cell. There he found, sitting on a straw bed, a thin, drawn, bitter, and hateful Ted Cooper.

"Now's the time, Cooper. Now's the time to honor Wiley Barnwell and the friendship you once had. As a last act of contrition toward him, as an act of justice, as an act of honor toward his memory, now's the time to tell me where you hid the invention that he died for."

"Go to hell."

"Wiley Barnwell wanted that device to get its hearing. He gave his life for it. In the name of anything he once meant to you, now's the time to atone for his death by enabling my tractor to live."

Cooper rose and walked to the bars of his cell, his eyes darting like daggers at his visitor, his mouth curling in contempt.

"You know as much as I do about how and why Barnwell died that night. If that humbug you spew about Wiley defending your contraption is true, that brings *dishonor* to his memory."

"In the name of a new discovery that you'll never be able to claim, in the name of letting its rightful owner bring it into the world, in the name of its immense importance, which you recognized by taking it, you *must* tell me its whereabouts."

"I had no intention of bringing that confounded device into the world. If I had my way, it'd be buried on the bottom of the bayou. That's *my* honor." He smirked. "You dare speak to *me* of honor? *I'm* the one who'll die with it tomorrow!"

With all the strength remaining in his emaciated body, the once-vibrant planter thrust his clenched fist between the bars. Tom backed away, missing the punch. The convict clutched the bars, casting a long shadow that crept over Tom. With a shaky voice, Cooper gave his farewell:

"May you burn in hell for the mistake you're making!"

\* \* \* \* \*

The grandfather clock in the dining room chimed six. Tom sat alone, his untouched plate of food pushed away, his elbows on the table, his hands over his face. His despair contrasted sharply with the cheerful vase of spring roses on the table. Cooper's execution the next day would dash his hopes of finding his own budding centerpiece, the invention that was to bring a fresh season to mankind.

When he raised his head, he realized that Solo had been standing at the open door, observing his silent agony from the hallway. The layout of the house—the main hall slicing through the center of the first floor—with the parlor, dining room, library, and other rooms opening onto it—made for frequent encounters between them.

She seemed concerned about him, with questions on her face that didn't reach her voice. She knew nothing of his invention, the murder, the trial, or the impending execution. He brought home no newspapers and said nothing of his personal affairs. Since the night of the crime, he had received no visitors. His life apart from their interactions, he realized, was as mysterious to her as her past life was to him.

"If you're not feeling well, I could cancel the class tonight—"

"Why, no. I'd like to see the class go on." A softness seeped into his voice, breaking through his despair.

She nodded and went on her way.

His manner toward her bore no resemblance to that of a master addressing a slave or even of an employer speaking to an employee. The fact that he never ordered her to do anything but rather let her do whatever she pleased as an equal living in his home tempered her hostility. Without a target, she had to put down her arrows.

In the six weeks since her class had begun, it had more than doubled in size. Tom had made more trips to nearby towns to buy additional primers and other supplies. Some servants were permitted to bring their well-behaved children to class with them. In all, twenty-five people now crowded into the library for Solo's lessons. Finishing their daily tasks properly was their ticket of admission, so the quality of their work had improved as well. By the eager way the teacher prepared and delivered her lessons, Tom knew she would welcome a chance to add more classes. He was determine to find a way to expand what was a growing school, as well as to keep it hidden from the outside world.

He enjoyed seeing the students engaged in their lessons, writing words on their slate boards—*cat, dog, chair, table*—and reading simple sentences that appeared with matching illustrations in their primers—*See Mary skating. See Anne sewing. John and William are hard at work. John has a hammer. William has an ax.* The teacher would intersperse a poem about a beautiful scene, an essay about a major city, a few pages of history, a scientific experiment—whatever suited her. The group listened, their faces aglow, like eager travelers being taken to new attractions. The teacher described sights and events she had never seen, sounding as knowledgeable as a seasoned traveler and with the spirit of an adventurer. This was how Tom discovered that beneath the charred lives of his bondsmen, their souls still flickered. And this was how he got to know the unusual new presence that in some way had stoked him and them alike: Solo.

Early on, he had observed her giving a lesson on a topic that he hadn't requested but was grateful she addressed. "This lesson is on the meaning of something important, called honor," she had explained to the class. "When you give a person your word on something, and you keep your word, that means you have honor. And if you have honor, it means that no one is higher than you. Someone who has a million dollars or twelve thousand acres of land isn't any higher a person than you are, because you have honor. You know, honor isn't something you have to show to a slave catcher, or to anyone who's trying to hurt you. Honor is something you show to someone who's trying to help you, and whom you don't want to harm.

"Now, I want you to show honor toward me and toward the person who makes these classes possible. I want to ask for your word of honor about our school, that you'll keep it a secret among us here, a secret that doesn't leave Indigo Springs. Will you keep that secret, on your honor?" She looked all of them, one by one, and they each nodded to her, pledging their honor. By the solemnity on their faces, they understood what she was trying to convey.

As he sat in the dining room, unable to eat, he thought painfully of someone else's honor. Senator Barnwell had promised to protect his invention when he transported it to the Crossroads. He had been honorable and kept his word . . . protecting the invention far more than merely on his trip. He had protected it with his—

"Excuse me, Mr. Tom . . . Mr. Tom?" The butler appeared at the door.

"Yes?"

"You have a visitor. Mr. Kenneth Gale is here for you." Tom noticed the improved quality of speech of Solo's student.

"Oh, yes. Show him to the parlor."

As Tom rose from his seat, Solo reappeared at the door, concerned. "I saw a man come in. The library's set up for the class," she whispered.

"Don't worry; I know him." He straightened his tie and coat. "He's just coming to bring me something. He won't be going anywhere near the library."

Down the hallway, the butler was placing a hat on the table in the foyer and escorting a man who carried a large painting into the parlor.

\* \* \* \* \*

Tom was so eager to see the painting that he neglected to close the parlor door behind him or to greet his guest properly.

"Why, it's beautiful!" he exclaimed, taking the painting from the artist and holding it up before him.

"I'm delighted you're pleased, Mr. Edmunton."

Tom moved an antique clock from the fireplace mantel and put in its place the picture. Then he stepped back to observe the effect. "That's the perfect spot for it!" he said, observing the portrait of Wiley Barnwell that he'd commissioned.

"It was good of Mrs. Barnwell to make her painting available to me, so I could produce this copy for you. She told me how much it means to you."

"Yes." Tom's eyes lingered on the work. "You did a fine job, Mr. Gale." The host reached for a decanter of brandy that sat on a tray with glasses. He poured two drinks and handed one to the artist.

Tom extended his glass toward the figure of Barnwell, whose vivid eyes were eerily staring out at them, making his presence palpable in the room. The artist also raised his glass to the painting.

"To a most admirable man, a man who was my father's friend and who became like a father to me," Tom said solemnly. "Long may his image grace this home!"

Tom began to lower his glass, as if he were finished. The artist lowered his and was about to drink when Tom raised his glass again as if a sudden impulse drove him to say more. The visitor followed suit, looking curiously at Tom, whose calm was vanishing, with anger lines now crossing his brow and fury filling his eyes.

"To the man whose life was suddenly . . . tragically . . . ripped from us!" Tom moved closer to the portrait and looked deeper into the painted eyes. "Tomorrow, your death with be avenged when your murderer hangs by the neck for his merciless crime!"

The men downed their drinks.

In that moment, three months of inner torment found an outlet. In one violent stroke, Tom flung his glass into the fireplace, shattering it.

He regretted the act when he noticed Solo staring at him from the hallway, looking alarmed. Was she startled by the anger inside him . . . an anger that surprised him too? She vanished before he could read anything more on her face.

Recovering, he took out his billfold and paid the artist. The men shook hands as Tom escorted his visitor to the foyer and out the door.

The inventor summoned Jerome and arranged for the slave to replace him on the gallery that night as the guard for Solo's class. Then, weary and despondent, Tom climbed the staircase and retired to his room. He remained there for the rest of the night.

# CHAPTER 14

The candles were generating too much heat for what was already becoming a hot, humid day. In shirtsleeves and vest, Tom could feel the sweat forming on his forehead as he sat in the dining room for breakfast the next morning. The crystal candelabra, the fine china, the impeccably polished silverware—all from his mother's best collection—were part of the setting Jerome had arranged for the service of his chocolate squares. Like many of Greenbriar's residents, Tom had become addicted to the new food, and a few squares downed with a pot of coffee was now his standard breakfast fare.

Soon the chef entered to serve these items himself. Though he kept late hours tending to his many tasks and newfound business and he delegated work to his assistants, he made a point of serving breakfast himself to Tom, who rose at dawn.

Although Tom allowed him to wear his kitchen clothes in the big house, Jerome arrived in his finer threads, adding to the formality of a meal that Tom viewed as a mere cramming of something into his mouth so that he could get on with his day. Tom observed the chef's hat on the slave's head, stressing the stature of the person who made his breakfast and of the dish that was perfuming the air with chocolate.

"Mornin', Mr. Tom."

The inventor nodded, watching Jerome pour his coffee with a flourish, then serve the squares with a bow, as if they were a delicacy and Tom a king. The inventor sighed. He decided not to spoil Jerome's moment by having the candles extinguished; he would endure the heat.

He watched the tapers send curls of smoke into the air for a few lively seconds before they vanished. He thought of Cooper's life now flickering in its final moments, about to fade into the stillness within hours. The treachery of Cooper, the demise of the senator, and the loss of his invention had drained all joy from Tom's face and mood.

He pushed the squares away and gulped down his coffee.

"Mr. Tom, are you feelin' ill?" Jerome's speech, though not perfect, had improved with six weeks of Solo's classes.

"I'm fine."

Jerome looked concerned. "You want somethin' else? Muffins, biscuits, or waffles?"

"No."

"I have leftovers. Cold ham or chicken fricassee?"

"I'm not hungry."

As Jerome refilled Tom's coffee cup, a house servant, Charles, entered holding a letter.

"Excuse me, Mr. Tom. This came for you."

Tom noticed the improved speech of another of Solo's students. Charles also seemed to stand taller than usual, as if straightening out his grammar did the same for his posture.

Tom took the envelope. It was from a standard line of stationery sold in the general store and in widespread use. His name was written on it in block print letters: *Mr. Edmunton.* Tom glanced at both sides of the envelope, looking for an indication of the writer's identity. There was none.

"Who sent this, Charles?"

"I don't know, sir. 'Twas on the table by the front door this mornin'. 'Twasn't there last night when I put out the lights and gone to my cabin."

Tom shot a questioning glance at Jerome, who shook his head, indicating he too knew nothing about the matter.

The front door was often left unlocked and the window at the entrance open. Could someone have dropped the envelope off in the night? Curious, Tom thought, as he opened it. He removed a letter that was unsigned, written on the same stock stationery, and with the same block letters, making it impossible to recognize the handwriting.

Holding the letter in one hand and his coffee cup in the other, he read:

*THE MAN WHO IS TO BE HANGED IS INNOCENT. THE KNIFE THAT STABBED BARNWELL IS A MILE UP THE TURNOFF TO WATKINS LANDING. LOOK BY THE DEAD OAK IN THE CLEARING AT MANNING CREEK.*

Tom leaped from his chair. His coffee cup slipped through his fingers and shattered on the floor as he rushed out of the room.

* * * * *

A slave who was hauling a wagon of wood to the big house veered sharply off the road to avoid colliding with a wild figure galloping at blinding speed toward him. The slave was stunned to see that the crazed man was his master. Tom's horse whinnied its distress as it struggled to make the sharp turn onto the main road at full speed. The dirt stirred by the hooves sprayed Tom's face and clouded his vision. Trees and fields along his path whizzed by him in one liquid smear. The horse tried to oblige Tom's urgent need for speed, flying along, its tail straight out, its eyes bulging in high alert.

Tom leaned forward and drove the animal hard on the main plantation road headed north. After riding eight miles, he came to the turnoff for Watkins Landing. He headed northwest on the old Indian trail that led to an abandoned trading post. He jumped over a downed tree on the unkempt path, then another, and then he splashed through mud. Soon he heard the rippling waters of Manning Creek. He meandered off the road through a tangle of vegetation to reach the stream, with branches tearing his shirt and insects biting his hands.

Just as the letter in his pocket described, he came to a clearing and spotted the trunk of a dead oak. The once-living giant had apparently been struck by lightning in a past storm, leaving only a hollow, decaying trunk. Tom dismounted and combed the area by foot. He looked through the fallen dead branches of the tree, the ground cover around it, and the roots exposed and rotting along the bank of the creek. Then he saw a silver object shining in the dull brush.

Tom picked it up carefully. It was a carving knife. Embedded on the handle were two flowery initials, the same ones he had seen on the cutlery and china served at a funeral reception: *PB*. Caught in the blade were traces of what looked like dried blood and a torn piece of fabric the color of Wiley Barnwell's robe on the night he was killed.

Indigo Springs was four miles north of the murder scene at the Crossroads. The spot where Tom stood was nine miles northwest of Indigo Springs. That placed him thirteen miles from the Crossroads, or twenty-six miles roundtrip. It was *impossible* for Cooper to have covered that distance, hauling and hiding the invention for part of it, in the approximately eighty minutes he had on the night of the murder. And it was *impossible* for Cooper to have come here afterward, because he had remained in custody since that night.

Tom didn't need to analyze the distances; they were clear to him in the one shocking instant when he had read the letter. Now, holding the knife, he had to face the inescapable conclusion: Cooper could not have put it there.

# CHAPTER 15

Sheriff Robert Duran stared at the document on his desk. It was a warrant signed by the governor, and it was his sworn duty to carry it out. His eyes locked on the words *to be hanged by the neck until dead.*

Out the back window, he saw the setting for the duty he had to perform: the courtyard between his office and the jail. He saw the simple wood platform that had been pulled out of the corner for the day's event. At the top of its steps were two posts and a crossbar with a noose hanging motionless in the stagnant air.

Out the front window, the sheriff caught sight of a youngster from the town, a boy about ten years old, walking along the street with his father. The man went into the shop next door, and the boy sat on a bench outside to wait for him. The youngster settled himself comfortably and began to read a book he was carrying.

The sheriff noticed how quickly the child became immersed in the book. With his face lowered to the pages and his hair spilling into his eyes, he seemed oblivious to passersby and street noises. The sheriff marveled at the boy's apparent preference for reading rather than shopping with his father. The youth reminded the lawman of himself at that age because as a boy, Robert Duran was an oddity; he loved book learning.

He was about the same age as the boy outside on the day he found his mother crying inconsolably. She was in their small farmhouse, standing before the empty dresser that belonged to his father, who had just left them. His mother had married the man in defiance of her parents' admonitions, and they, in turn, had disowned her. She and her husband became yeoman farmers who grew cotton on their small acreage, tilling the fields themselves. Thanks to his mother's scrupulous savings and determination to give her son an education, Robbie was able to buy books and attend school. The boy tried to console his mother in that desperate moment when she wondered aloud how they would manage their farm. As he hugged her and wished desperately that he could make her stop crying, he pledged to leave school to help with the crop. She could count on him. He was strong and could do the work of a man, he told her.

Robbie was spared from his own death sentence—a life of back-breaking drudgery on the family farm—by the man named in the warrant before him. His mother's brother, Ted Cooper, stepped in to help them begin a new life of comfort on his plantation. Under the protection of his uncle, Robbie completed his basic education and found a calling in the law.

Outside the sheriff's office, the boy's father left the shop and returned to the young book enthusiast. The boy stood up and grinned at him. The man patted his son's head affectionately, and they walked away. Watching their happy exchange, the sheriff recalled his own fond moments with the man he came to regard as his father.

When the man and boy vanished from his sight, the sheriff turned his glance to another object of interest: the whisky bottle on his desk next to the death warrant. He closed his eyes in flat refusal of his need. That would be for later, he told himself. Right now, there would be no relief.

He got up, straightened his tie, and pinned to his vest the badge with the blindfolded lady and her scales.

A small, somber group of witnesses gathered before the scaffold. Some arrived on horseback and hitched their animals to posts in the back of the yard. Others arrived in carriages that they left on the street, then walked the narrow path to the courtyard hidden from public view.

The witnesses included newspaper reporters, planters, shopkeepers, other townspeople, and relatives of the victim and the convict. Greenbriar's coroner and town doctor, Don Clark, was there to make the final pronouncement on the doomed man after the task was done. Bret Markham was there from the Crossroads Plantation.

Charlotte Barnwell, dressed in black, fanned herself limply, looking drained by the heat and tension of the day. Rachel, standing next to her, wore a dress of muted gray with a white bodice that formed two scallops over her breasts, her neck and shoulders bare. A black lace shawl falling around her arms was a remnant of the mourning attire that she had relaxed in recent weeks.

Nash Nottingham stood next to Rachel. His admiring glance at her soft breasts suggested that she looked alluring to him, even at a hanging.

"Where's Tom?" he whispered to her.

"Darned if I know. He never came for us this morning, like he said he would." Rachel's voice was heated with anger. "He never showed up, on this horrible day!"

Nash took her hand reassuringly. "*I'm* here for you, dear. And for your mama too."

* * * * *

A dust cloud swirled around Tom as his horse galloped along the dirt road. The airborne particles stuck to the sweat on both of their bodies, making a single bronze figure out of the man and his horse. They had traveled miles in the blistering heat. Could they go a bit more?

There were multiple tears in Tom's shirt, making visible bloody streaks on his skin from his duel with the bushes at Manning Creek. His face was flushed from the toxic mix of scorching heat and lack of water. But *his* condition was not the chief problem.

Just as he took the turnoff to Greenbriar's main street, his horse stopped its constant whinnied pleas and slowed its pace. The overworked animal was breathing rapidly and sweating uncontrollably, sure signs of heat exhaustion. The animal needed rest and water, but Tom could only give it the whip. The poor creature could no longer oblige; it would rather endure the sting than move another step. The animal suddenly began to tremble, its legs wobbled, and then its belly hit the ground with a thump. The horse seemed in the throes of fatal heatstroke.

Tom slid off the animal and began running. He was at the outer edge of town and not yet near the shops and people. Ahead he could see the town landmark, a clock tower near the jail, with a great bronze bell that rang to signal every hour. Tom ran furiously toward it. From his distance and angle, he couldn't see the time, but he knew the next hour would be ten o'clock. He raced ahead, wishing desperately that he would not hear the tower bell, because if he did hear it, the event he was trying to stop would begin. Then in mere seconds it would be over.

* * * * *

There was silence in the courtyard when the door to the jail opened. A small group came out and walked toward the scaffold. Sheriff Robert Duran led the procession. Next came Ted Cooper, his head down, his hands tied behind him, a guard on each side. A chaplain in a robe walked behind the doomed man, reading from a Bible and blessing him.

The sheriff looked as grim as the prisoner, realizing that somewhere among the witnesses, his mother would be standing, once again suffering an immense loss—and once again crying. This time he could do nothing about it, except add to her grief. As he walked, he resolved not to look at anyone. At the scaffold, he glanced at the clock tower visible above the yard. Within moments, it would strike ten, the time set for the . . . event.

He mounted the steps to the platform. Cooper and one of the guards followed. The other guard moved to the side of the platform, where he took hold of a lever. The sheriff positioned Cooper's feet on the trapdoor.

The noose cast a looming shadow on the ground. The prisoner stared at his nephew in indignation and hopelessness. The nephew did not avoid his uncle's eyes but stared back in sadness, resolve, and quiet agony.

The guard on the platform observed the pair. Knowing their relationship, he stepped forward to reach for the rope and handle the matter for the sheriff. But Duran put a hand on the guard's arm to stop him and took the rope himself.

With his uncle's unblinking eyes locked on him, eyes that were hardened in scorn at everything and everyone, the sheriff positioned the noose around the prisoner's neck and tightened it.

There was another set of eyes that never left the sheriff. The prison guard at the base of the platform waited for Duran's signal. The guard's hand gripped the lever that would release the trapdoor. He held the handle in white-knuckled tightness. The sheriff thought he could hear the guard's teeth grinding.

Duran turned to the prisoner. "Do you have any final words, Mr. Cooper?"

"May Tom Edmunton rot in hell."

The sheriff picked up a white hood on the platform and raised his arms to place it over Cooper's head. The prisoner shook his head, emphatically refusing it. Duran stared at Cooper, the hood in his hands, as if wishing the prisoner would change his mind. Cooper shook his head again, and the sheriff tossed the hood aside.

The tower bell began sounding its ten gongs to announce the hour. The sheriff turned to the guard at the lever and was about to nod.

Suddenly, an urgent cry filled the courtyard, drowning out the town's bell, and a body shot through the crowd like a bullet.

"Stop! Stop! Stop at once!"

A collective gasp came from the group as the shouting man raced toward the scaffold. Panting and about to faint, he faltered. Two men propped him up, and he yelled, pointing at the accused, "He's innocent! *Innocent!*"

Disheveled and weak, with no jacket, his vest torn, his shirt streaked with blood, his pants splattered with mud, and his face soaked with sweat, he was almost unrecognizable.

The first official to reach him was Dr. Clark. "It's Tom!" The coroner exclaimed.

The sheriff stared at Tom from the scaffold in utter astonishment.

"My God!" Rachel screamed. Charlotte looked ready to swoon. Nash, their pillar of strength, curled a comforting hand around each woman, and he too looked shocked.

Trying to catch his breath and steady his legs, Tom reached down for the knife tucked in his boot and the letter in his pocket. He gave the items to the coroner, who examined the weapon and read the note.

To the stunned gathering, Tom told his story. He described the anonymous letter found that morning in his home, how it had directed him to a location thirteen miles away from the scene of the crime, how he had followed the instructions and found what in all likelihood was the murder weapon, and how impossible it was for Cooper to have made the round trip from the Crossroads to the knife's location on the night of the crime, or thereafter while he was in constant custody.

"Sheriff," Tom concluded, his voice rising as if delivering a proclamation, "since the prisoner could not have delivered that note to my house, nor could he have disposed of the murder weapon at Manning Creek, someone else has to be involved."

A man in the group handed Tom a canteen of water, and he drank greedily.

"Was any person seen on your property who could have left that note?" the sheriff asked Tom.

"The servants didn't see anyone, nor did I. The block printing of the words makes it impossible to identify the handwriting."

A tall man who ran the general store peered over the coroner's shoulder to inspect the letter. "I sell that paper and ink in my shop. Everybody buys it. Could've come from anyone."

"Sheriff," said Dr. Clark, "this is a carving knife that bears Polly Barnwell's initials and evidently came from her plantation. It appears to have the right dimensions to be the murder weapon, and I can do measurements to confirm that. And, Sheriff, I also see fabric particles on the knife that I believe can be matched to the decedent's clothing."

With great consternation Dr. Clark reached up to the platform to hand the items to the sheriff. All eyes turned to Duran as he examined the knife and read the letter. He paused, silently weighing the matter as he studied the new evidence, the prisoner, and the gathering. Then he gave the items back to the coroner. The group studied their lawman for his response, searching for a break in his marble composure.

"In view of the new evidence, this matter needs to be investigated further. The warrant will *not* be carried out."

The sheriff tried to maintain his even keel, but his relief at the change of events was evident in the sudden spark of life in his eyes and in the more spirited motions he used now than he had in his earlier preparations. He promptly removed the noose from Cooper's neck and untied his hands.

Cooper's eyes lost their doomed stare. His face dropped into his hands in utter relief from his ordeal.

"The guards will take the prisoner back to his cell," said the sheriff. "I'll take the letter and knife into evidence and get the sworn testimony of Mr. Edmunton and Dr. Clark. And I'll notify the court and the governor."

The coroner gave the evidence to one of the guards. Another directed Cooper off the scaffold. As the prisoner was escorted back to the jail, he passed Tom, and the two men glared at each other.

"You really *were* telling the truth, weren't you?" Tom asked incredulously. "You really did arrive at the carriage house *after* the crime, didn't you?"

"Why is that so hard for you to understand?" replied Cooper. The deathlike stiffness of his body had relaxed, but his voice remained hardened with resentment for Tom.

"You really were aiming to *destroy* my invention, weren't you?"

Cooper smiled contemptuously. "You fool! You don't understand us at all, do you?"

# CHAPTER 16

The stunned group in the courtyard watched Cooper being led back to jail.

Tom smoothed his hair and wiped the dirt from his face and clothes, trying to temper his shocking appearance. He and Rachel looked at each other in silent greeting. His eyes held sorrow at her distress; hers seemed resentful, as if he were to blame.

Stepping off the scaffold, the sheriff directed the crowd to leave but asked the coroner and several others to stay. Those he wanted to remain—Tom, Nash, Markham, and the Barnwell women—were the ones, aside from Cooper, who had knowledge of the invention and its whereabouts and who were at the Crossroads on the day of the murder.

The sheriff's probing eyes seemed to be searching for a person or clue among the people remaining that would indicate what new direction he must take on the crime.

"Somebody killed Senator Barnwell. If it wasn't Mr. Cooper, then who?" He began the discussion by stating the obvious. "Who left the knife at Manning Creek? And who wrote the letter?"

The people in the group glanced suspiciously at one another.

"It seems we have a murderer with a sudden pang of conscience who wrote a note at the last minute to prevent an innocent man from hanging for his crime," the coroner added.

"So what do we know?" The sheriff asked, throwing his questions out to the group, his eyes sweeping from one person to another to enlist a response and study their reactions. "Let's take the knife. Where did it come from, and who took it?"

Tom was cooling off, and his energy was returning. Now that the emergency had passed, he began pacing as he began analyzing. "The knife I found at the creek definitely came from the Crossroads."

"How can you be sure?" asked Duran.

"The monogram on that knife was on all the silverware at Polly Barnwell's funeral reception. I saw carving knives on food platters that were going in and out of the kitchen that day that were identical to the knife I found this morning," Tom replied.

The sheriff turned to Markham. "You live there. What do you say?"

"Miss Polly had a collection of carvin' knives just like the one he brung here," Markham affirmed.

"The murderer could be someone who was intent on stealing the invention and who had Polly's knife with him as a precaution," Tom added. "If he met resistance in his thievery, he couldn't shoot a gun, which would wake up the household, but he could use a knife to thwart anyone interfering with his scheme. If the weapon were found later, a knife from the plantation would throw suspicion on a person who was there and had access to it. That would be convenient for a culprit who no one thought was at the Crossroads when the crime was committed."

"But them knives are locked up at night," said Markham.

"Maybe someone had access to the knife earlier." Tom stopped pacing, as if coming to a conclusion. "Someone who was seen in the . . . *kitchen*."

The sheriff raised his eyebrows and nodded subtly, as if he was coming to the same conclusion.

"After the reception, someone was seen in the kitchen and indeed was thrown out of it by the senator. That person could have stolen the knife, left the plantation with the other guests, then returned with the weapon later to steal my invention."

Tom and Sheriff Duran both turned their heads to the same person: Nash. The others followed their glance.

"Nonsense!" Nash scowled. "These wild fantasies are insulting! If this little affair is over, I have other things to do!"

Nash bowed his head to the Barnwell women, taking leave of them, then walked indignantly toward his horse at the back of the yard.

As he untied the horse from its post and was about to mount, an object on his saddlebag caught Tom's attention. Shining in the late morning sun was a large ornament above the buckle on the flap of the leather pouch. Typical of the extravagance of its owner, the ornament was composed of gemstones and glittered like a large, showy brooch. The gemstones were *aquamarine* and gave off a flashy blue sparkle.

"Wait! Just wait a minute!" cried Tom.

He rushed toward Nash and examined the decorative bag that hung from the saddle. "Sheriff, this is the same blue stone that I reported seeing on the night of the murder! I told you about the stranger with a sack that I saw on my way to Markham's cottage, and the shiny blue object that looked like jewelry flashing in the moonlight. The sack I saw was this saddlebag. And the shiny blue object I saw were these gemstones. They caught the moonlight and sparkled with the same blue color."

Rachel and her mother looked at each other, mortified.

In a flash, the sheriff was toe-to-toe with Nash. "What about it, Mr. Nottingham?"

"I don't know what you're talking about. Gemstones aren't uncommon on bags and other accessories used by people with fine taste." He turned to Tom, his voice low and hateful. "I don't know what you saw that night, but I was home sleeping, as my mother told the sheriff."

"Your mother said she saw you when she went to bed and again at breakfast. That doesn't include the middle of the night," said Duran.

"You lied to the sheriff, and you lied at the trial, under oath," Tom charged. "You were at the Crossroads that night. It was *you* I saw. The shiny blue ornament was that one on your bag."

"Poppycock! That's sheer poppycock!" Nash laughed dismissively.

"You were just steps away from the murder scene that night, with this bag," Tom continued. "You were seen in the kitchen arguing with Wiley Barnwell earlier. And you were one of only three men who knew what my invention was, where it was, that it wasn't yet patented, and that it had the potential to make a fortune. The only other two men who knew these facts were the senator, who's dead, and Cooper, who's innocent."

"How dare you!"

"Mr. Nottingham," said the coroner, moving close to the accused, joining the sheriff and Tom in cornering him, "I think you'd better explain."

"This humbug's gone far enough. I've nothing more to say."

Nash reached for the reins of his horse, but Tom grabbed them first.

"Mr. Nottingham, were you at the Crossroads Plantation on the night of the crime?" Duran pressed.

"I never saw the senator. I never saw the invention. I never harmed anyone or anything."

"Were you *there*? Was it the blue ornament on your saddlebag that Mr. Edmunton saw that night?" Duran continued.

Nash removed the bag from his horse. "There's nothing suspicious in there. Look for yourself." He offered the bag to the sheriff. "There's no blood, no fabric, nothing that would tie me to the weapon or the crime."

The sheriff and coroner inspected the saddlebag, found nothing of interest, and gave it back to Nash.

"Were you at the Crossroads that night?" Duran repeated.

"There's nothing in my bag, Sheriff."

"There's nothing in it now," interjected the coroner.

"You have no evidence to accuse me of anything. I'm leaving." Nash tried to grab the reins of his horse from Tom.

"Not so fast." The sheriff dropped an arm like a dead bolt in front of Nash's chest to stop him. "Were you prowling around near the murder scene with that bag?"

"I didn't harm anyone."

"Were you *there*?"

"Sheriff, I can explain—"

"Answer the question."

Nash was trembling. He looked at Rachel and her mother with embarrassment. But then his eyes moved to other objects of more pressing concern. He looked with dread at the jail, and he looked with terror at the noose hanging from the scaffold.

"Answer right now or face arrest!" Duran demanded.

Nash closed his eyes.

"Were you at the Crossroads on the night of the crime?"

"Yes," he whispered.

# CHAPTER 17

Duran led Nash and the others across the street to the courthouse to continue the meeting out of the sun. The group gathered around a table in the trial room where Ted Cooper's guilty verdict had been issued, death sentence pronounced, and case closed. Now that case would be reopened. The group looked like unhappy members of a disgruntled family forced to interact at the dinner table.

"I did *not* commit any crime!" insisted Nash.

"At the very least, you committed perjury when you told us you spent the night at your house, and I can charge you with that," said the sheriff, his eyes scouring the suspect. "What are you hiding?"

The hot day added physical discomfort to the emotional stress of the occasion for the Barnwell women. Rachel sat fanning herself, her red curls swaying with the motion. The high collar of Charlotte's mourning dress rubbed against her skin, forming red marks under her chin. The little burns seemed as abrasive to Charlotte's skin as the events of the past three months had been to her nerves.

Dr. Clark sat next to the women. Bret Markham sat opposite them, staring suspiciously at everyone. The guards standing off to the side added body heat to the room.

Sheriff Duran, Nash, and Tom circled the table, too nervous to sit.

"Sheriff, I assure you, I had nothing to do with the senator's death," said Nash.

"Mr. Nottingham," Duran replied, "you were in the kitchen at the Crossroads on the afternoon before the murder; that gives you access to the weapon. You knew about the invention, *and* you were seen arguing with Senator Barnwell; that gives you motive. And contrary to your sworn testimony, you went back to the property during the night; that gives you opportunity. If you have any explanation, now's the time to share it."

Sweat formed a dark ring around Nash's white collar. His grand airs now gone, he nervously wiped his face, sighed in resignation, and sank into a chair to begin his story.

"That night, after my mother went to sleep, I quietly left my house and rode back to the Crossroads."

"Now, why would you do that?" asked the sheriff.

"I was miffed at the audacity of a man who had left our town as a youngster, never kept in touch with any of us, lived among our adversaries, and then came back to upset us." Nash brooded. "To understand why I went back to the Crossroads, you have to understand what weighed on my mind. And to understand that, you have to know something about the peculiarities of Tom Edmunton."

Tom quietly took Nash's complaint.

"Tom's thinking has been twisted from living so long in the North. He doesn't understand us and our ways. To my vexation, he doesn't care to know how his father managed our local bank and showed more patience with his customers. Yes, Tom's coldhearted way of banking peeved me. But that wasn't all."

Nash pointed an accusing finger at his banker.

"Anyone who's ever been to his plantation can see how unseemly he is. I tell you, his slaves take outrageous liberties. One of them drinks Tom's liquor and has the run of the house as if *he* were the owner." The thought made Nash's voice shrill. "And you should hear the way Tom talks to his servants, so polite-like. Well, *of course* he can't control them. When I was there a while ago, the house was in disarray, the stable was in shambles, and there was no servant around to show me in. But there's something even worse." He leaned across the table and whispered to the others, as if revealing a shocking secret. "His slaves aren't allowed to call him *master*."

Nash paused to allow his audience to absorb his words.

"It's a scandal, I tell you!" He turned to Duran. "How do you suppose I felt when this outsider reappeared in our town to steal my woman and meddle in our business with his wild schemes?"

Rachel, flustered, admonished Nash. "I trust you'll mind your manners and not be discussing my personal affairs."

"He chose his machines over you," replied Nash. "He chose his Yankee life in Philadelphia over you. He came back only through the sheer accident of his father's death, not for you." Then he turned to the sheriff. "And the senator encouraged *his* courtship of her over mine!" The thought evoked a visceral anger in Nash.

"Really, now! How very rude of you to say all this!" said an embarrassed Charlotte.

"I regret that I'm forced to explain myself here. But please know that I was thinking only of Rachel's good, Mrs. Barnwell. I was thinking that you could keep Rachel near you if she would accept my fervid wish to be her humble servant. I so wanted the senator to see that." He bowed his head to Charlotte. "Why, I feared that with Tom more interested in scientific oddities than in being a proper match for your daughter, he could get homesick for the North and up and take Rachel away with him. Would you want your grandchildren brought up as Yankees?" He pleaded.

"Sheriff, I think this discussion has gone far enough!" said Charlotte.

Duran looked sympathetic but firm. "I'm sorry, Mrs. Barnwell. I would like you and your daughter to be close by, in case I need to question you. But if you'd rather wait outside . . ."

The women looked at each other, coming to a silent conclusion. Charlotte spoke for them, her voice sharp with irritation. "We'll stay, Sheriff. That way we'll know what's being said about our family, so we can defend our good name, if it comes to that!"

The sheriff looked puzzled by Charlotte's need to defend her name. "You and your family are not on trial, ma'am," he assured her, then turned back to Nash. "You were telling us your state of mind, Mr. Nottingham?"

"What could my state of mind be, Sheriff, after Tom told us he had a new invention that would turn our lives topsy-turvy? It looks like Cooper's story about wanting to put a stop to that contraption was true. I'm not surprised," he said, his voice heavy with resentment. "I had those very same thoughts too."

"What do you mean?" asked Duran.

"After Tom told us his grand plan to transform our lives, I went home that night with his words festering in my mind. While I was with him that afternoon, I pretended to be amused. After all, he's my banker, and I needed a little time on my loan. But I was disturbed by a ruthlessness in him that, well, reminded me of the Yankees in their sheer arrogance. Nowadays, no one can deny they're hell-bent on destroying us. Like those scoundrels, Tom spoke about a future that dismantled everything we hold dear for a world of machines, factories, and slaves running amuck. I tell you, Sheriff, he riled me good!"

Tom listened, his face questioning but his voice remaining silent.

"Tom spoke *their* language, not ours. I wanted to push him back, to wipe him out, to get what was *mine*."

"So what did you do?" asked the sheriff.

"I rode to the Crossroads that night and left my horse in the bushes. I walked out to a patch of soil in the slaves' garden that had been turned for planting. I brought my saddlebag with me and bent down to gather some of the loose soil in it."

"Whatever for?" asked the sheriff.

The others sat quietly. The coroner was absorbed in the tale, the Barnwell women looked wary, and Markham's eyes darted around the room suspiciously.

"That afternoon, Tom had shown us where the fuel was kept on his confounded machine. There were two tanks: for gasoline and kerosene. I was fixing to pour the soil into those tanks so the engine wouldn't work." Nash smiled sardonically. "I figured that when Tom tried to demonstrate the device at his big meeting in Philadelphia and the darn thing wouldn't move, he'd be the laughingstock of the place. I reckoned his hopes would be shattered, and he'd come back a defeated man." Nash's face livened at the prospect. "Then Rachel and the senator would see him in a different light . . ."—he grinned— "as a fanatic . . . a dreamer . . . thwarted in his wild quest. Then the senator would look elsewhere to secure his daughter's future."

He exchanged hostile looks with Tom.

"You see, Sheriff, I didn't *covet* that contraption. I didn't want to steal it and make money off it. I wanted to *destroy* it."

The sheriff studied his subject without expression.

"But I never got that far. As I began to gather the soil, I saw a man looking at me in the distance. I didn't know then that it was Tom, but I ran away. I went to the other side of the hill where the big house was, fixing to reach the invention from that route and perform my deed, but I saw lanterns on and people outside. I knew something strange had happened, so I cleared out and went home. I didn't learn what had occurred till you came to my home the next day, Sheriff."

"That can't be!" said Tom.

"It can be, and it was," said Nash. "That was all there was to it. I went to the Crossroads that night fixing to damage your invention, but I ended up leaving without doing anything."

"But it wouldn't make sense for you to sabotage the invention. It makes more sense for you to have stolen it to profit from it yourself. That would've brought you financial stability and made you look good to Rachel and the senator."

Rachel looked flustered when the conversation turned to her personal affairs. "Hush up, Tom!"

But Tom was undeterred. "Look, somebody stole the device. If it wasn't Cooper, then who? You were there. You could've taken the prototype to investors and made an arrangement with them to develop it further. You could've done it secretly, and profited, then made up a story about coming into some money. You would've been able to pay off your debts and appeal to Rachel and her family as a serious suitor. It makes more sense that you went to the Crossroads that night to steal a new device that could make you wealthy."

"What ravings! It's clear modesty isn't one of your virtues," quipped Nash.

"You would've put the cover back on the motor to protect the invention. It was vital for you to keep everything intact as you hauled it off, so you could sell it to investors for a good profit."

"Well, Tom, since you're so smart, tell me: Why would I still be there at the Crossroads *after* the crime was committed? The senator was already murdered when you saw me by the slaves' garden. Isn't that so?"

Tom stroked his chin in concentration, then offered a theory.

"Maybe you first hid the tractor somewhere in the brush, then you came back to bury the knife, which you put in your saddlebag. Maybe you were trying to plant the weapon near the slaves' quarters, so the murder would be pinned on one of them, on someone you deemed your inferior, so you'd feel no compunction when a poor bondsman was executed for your crime. A slave would provide a decoy that would be very easy to prosecute and convict, and thereby end the investigation, so no one would ever suspect you. Everyone would believe that a slave who was fearful of new master, someone much stricter than his old mistress, could be driven to a desperate act. And everyone would believe that a slave could also steal property out of sheer rebelliousness, or steal it to redirect suspicion to a white man."

As Tom spoke, Nash shook his head.

The sheriff seemed content to let Tom continue with his theory and to study the exchange between him and Nash.

"But when I spotted you, I would've thwarted your plan to hide the weapon by the slaves' quarters and pin the crime on one of them. So later, you disposed of the weapon in the woods where I found it."

Nash bristled. "Pure poppycock!"

"Then when Cooper was accused instead of a slave, you would've had a sudden pang of conscience at the last minute and written the note to reveal the weapon's location and exonerate an innocent man of your crime."

"You're mad!"

"The night of the crime, when you tried to slip the cover back on, you made noise, which the senator heard from his open window. He came out and caught you, and you were disgraced in his eyes. You would have had no chance ever for the wealth and marriage you envisioned. So you killed the senator and went on with your scheme. Isn't that what happened?" offered Tom.

"I hated that invention. I went there to destroy it, but I never got near it," Nash bellowed. "Besides, why would I carry a murder weapon clear to Manning Creek? Why not just toss it in the bayou?"

"Well," said Tom, thinking aloud, "when you couldn't bury the weapon at the Crossroads and pin the crime on a slave, maybe you decided on another plan. If you planted the knife a great distance away, then you could reveal its location later, if necessary, to make me believe that the invention also could be hidden over so large an area that a search was futile. I might've given up searching. Then you could've waited a while, and when interest in the case died down, you could have secretly gotten the device out of the South."

"Sheriff, there's no evidence *whatsoever* for Tom's wild accusations."

"That's quite true, Mr. Nottingham," the sheriff agreed. "But we do have you spotted at the Crossroads that night, and we have your animosity toward Mr. Edmunton, and the senator's animosity toward you."

"Maybe you would've welcomed Senator Barnwell coming in to spoil your burglary as an excuse to do away with him," said Tom.

The sheriff raised his eyebrows.

"Now, this has gone too far—" Nash snarled.

"You knew the senator was staying at the Crossroads that night. You knew he might be closing a deal with Cooper the next day to sell the place, foiling another one of your schemes"—Tom laughed contemptuously—"to have him give you Rachel's hand and Polly's plantation as a wedding present."

"What? Merciful Lord! How could you, Nash Nottingham?" Rachel scolded. "I take great offense, I'll have you know!"

"Maybe you intentionally made noise by the senator's room to draw him out," Tom continued. "Not only did you have a motive to steal the invention and use it to get out of your financial difficulties and into Rachel's good graces but you also had a motive to do away with Senator Barnwell. You were angry with him. You were continually frustrated in your attempts to court Rachel. The senator didn't like you. He saw through your pretensions. He saw nothing in you for his daughter. Indeed, he and I were both in your way."

"You're crazy!" cried Nash. "You're obsessed with that invention. It's deranged your mind."

"Maybe you saw a once-in-a-lifetime opportunity to enrich yourself, to defeat me, and to do away with the senator all at once. That one night you had your chance to accomplish all that." Tom's voice was hard.

"That's rubbish! Besides, I was on fine terms with the senator. We had a little misunderstanding that day, that's all."

"A misunderstanding you neglected to mention until Mr. Markham told us that he saw the senator throw you out of the kitchen after the funeral," interjected the sheriff. He turned to the overseer. "Isn't that so, Mr. Markham?"

"Like I said, Sheriff, I seen the senator throw him out o' Miss Polly's kitchen that afternoon."

Nash swept a handkerchief across his damp forehead.

"And the kitchen is where you would've found the carving knife," the sheriff added.

"I didn't touch any knife!" Nash waved his hands in protest.

"Why were you in that kitchen?" asked the sheriff. "And why did you argue with the senator on the day of his death?"

"My words with the senator had nothing to do with the invention, *nothing at all.*"

"You lied when you testified that you weren't at the Crossroads that night. You held animosity for Mr. Edmunton and his invention. You argued with the deceased. And you wanted Miss Barnwell's hand, but the senator wouldn't permit it," pressed the sheriff. "All of that we know. Now tell us the rest."

"I didn't take any knife or harm anybody."

"Why did the senator throw you out of the kitchen?" repeated the sheriff.

"I told you. He misunderstood me. I was in the kitchen looking for my coachman, but he thought I was chasing a female servant."

"You wouldn't be giving even a hint of pursuing a slave girl while Miss Barnwell's father was around," said the sheriff, his voice harder.

"And you'd never get your clothes dirty in a greasy kitchen to look for your coachman," added Tom.

"Why were you in the kitchen?" the sheriff repeated, his voice harder.

A silent agony played out on Nash's colorless face. The sheriff waited, but the suspect remained silent.

"All right," said the sheriff, "maybe you'll talk after spending the night in jail."

He gestured to the guards. "Arrest him."

The two guards moved toward Nash.

"Wait!" Like a child afraid of the dark, Nash seemed gripped by terror. "Don't put me in that disgusting rat-hole! I couldn't stand that!"

"Then talk," said the sheriff.

Nash sighed in resignation.

"Okay, I *was* chasing a slave girl."

"Good gracious!" exclaimed Charlotte.

"How could you!" cried Rachel.

"Now, now, it's not was you think, ladies! Not at all." Nash said.

"And Senator Barnwell, no doubt, didn't like you chasing the girl," said the sheriff.

"He didn't like it at all, but it had *nothing* to do with the invention."

"What did it have to do with?"

"She was a young mulatto woman. I had seen her earlier that day when I arrived. I had approached her that morning. I suppose I frightened her, because she ran into the kitchen. The senator first noticed my interest in her that morning. That's why he frowned at me when I had just arrived, as Markham told you at our meeting after the crime, Sheriff."

The sheriff nodded, remembering the matter. Markham also nodded, frowning at everyone.

"After the reception, I looked around for the girl, and I entered the kitchen to inquire about her whereabouts. The senator, I realized, was observing me and followed me in. He knew that I had stumbled on something. He got angry and threw me out."

"What did you stumble on?" prodded the sheriff. His ruthless eyes locked on Nash's pleading ones.

"A secret."

"What secret?"

"Something I wasn't supposed to know."

"What?"

"It has nothing to do with the invention."

"Come on, Mr. Nottingham," the sheriff said tiredly. "What did it have to do with?"

"I had discovered something about the girl, and I wanted to see her close up to be sure."

"What did you discover?"

Nash hesitated.

"Mr. Nottingham. You're trying our patience. It's time to come clean." The coroner interjected his older, respected voice to help the sheriff. "What did you discover about the slave that caused you to look for her in the kitchen and that caused the senator to throw you out?"

Nash glanced anxiously at Charlotte and Rachel.

"Answer, Mr. Nottingham, or face arrest." Duran threatened. "What did you learn about the mulatto girl?"

Nash dropped his eyes to the floor, avoiding the women's glances. When he spoke, his voice was barely a whisper. "I learned that she . . . was a . . . Barnwell."

The women gasped. Rachel's hands covered her face in disbelief. Charlotte's head dropped in a swoon. The coroner reached into his pocket for smelling salts.

# CHAPTER 18

Charlotte's eyes opened after she inhaled a whiff of spirits from the coroner's small flask. She and her daughter were given cups of water. Sweat glistened on Rachel's bare shoulders, and her shawl lay in limp folds in the crooks of her arms. Charlotte's face was pale from her light-headedness.

"Ladies, I'm deeply sorry . . ." Nash began, his head down.

"If you're sorry, then shut up!" said Rachel, channeling her anger into vigorous waving of her fan.

". . . but necessity compels me to speak as an honest man must to defend his honor."

"To defend your honor, you'll take away ours!" cried Charlotte.

Nash sighed helplessly.

Charlotte glared at him, then turned to Duran. "Isn't it clear that this pathetic man will stoop to anything to get himself out of a fix?"

"I'm sorry, Mrs. Barnwell," replied the sheriff, "but I intend to hear him out."

"It's lies you'll hear. All lies!" The widow's cries filled the courtroom.

"Now, now, Mrs. Barnwell. You must try to calm down," Dr. Clark instructed.

"I'm very sorry, ma'am," said the sheriff. His eyes paused on Charlotte briefly, then moved on. "Now, Mr. Nottingham, let's hear your story."

Avoiding the women's stares, Nash spoke. "As you know, I arrived earlier than the other guests. My coachman let me off at the house, but there was no one there to greet me. The slaves seemed at a loss with the death of their mistress. I felt a touch of *mal de mer* from the ride, so I was impatient standing there, looking for someone to escort me in and get me a claret to settle my nerves, Sheriff."

Duran nodded. "Then what?"

"I noticed a young mulatto. She was dressed like a house servant. She looked weak and disheveled, as though she had just been beaten. A ribbon that tied the front of her dress at the neckline was undone, as if she had loosened her garment for a few lashes to her back. She was leaning against a marble statue near the entrance, in pain, unable to stand. I called to her to show me in and fetch me a claret."

"You mean you asked a beaten woman who could barely stand to fetch you a drink?" blurted out the sheriff.

"She was a *slave*, after all," Nash replied. "The girl seemed unable to comply. That was when I noticed something. With her garment slipped off her shoulder, I saw . . ."

Nash hesitated.

"Come on, you saw what?" the sheriff prodded.

Nash glanced out the window, where he could see the top of the jail behind the sheriff's office, and a shot of panic flashed on his face. When he spoke, he seemed oblivious to the people in the room, speaking only to the barred windows across the street.

"I saw on the girl, just below her shoulder and above her heart, a little birthmark, just like that one right there." He pointed to the tiny heart-shaped mark on Rachel's body.

"What in tarnation!" shrieked Charlotte. "Liar!"

She quickly lifted her daughter's shawl to cover her bare shoulders, but it was too late. Everyone's eyes had already darted to Rachel and seen the birthmark.

"It was the very same mark in the very same place as Rachel's. It was so distinctive, a fetching little heart! What could explain that? I immediately concluded it must run in the family," Nash said.

"Lies!" Charlotte shook her head in vigorous denial. "All lies!"

She shot up and hurled her cup so its contents splashed in Nash's face. He took the attack quietly, wiping his face.

"Mrs. Barnwell, now calm down!" directed the coroner, pushing her by the shoulders back to her seat.

"I declare to goodness!" Rachel said, scowling and pulling the shawl up to her neck. "How could you suggest this girl has anything to do with us, Nash Nottingham? It could have been a piece of dirt you saw, and for that, you disgrace us. Why, I'll never speak to you again!"

"Ladies, please, quiet down," said the coroner.

"I saw what I saw." Nash shrugged his shoulders helplessly. "I walked toward the girl to examine the birthmark more closely. I asked her what that little thing was below her shoulder. But she was frightened of me. She quickly tied her frock to cover the little reddish mark. Then she mustered her strength and ran. She disappeared into the kitchen."

Charlotte and Rachel fumed.

"During this interlude, the senator appeared. He was walking with Markham. The senator seemed to notice my interest in the girl and my attempt to see the birthmark. He looked displeased. Just what did I think I was doing, he asked. I told him that I had come early in the hope of speaking to him. About what, he asked me brusquely. I told him it was about acquiring the Crossroads Plantation. This part of the story I told you previously, Sheriff."

Duran nodded.

"The senator said he thought my funds were strained, and I replied that I had a plan. He said that Cooper might purchase the place, but he supposed it was good to have more than one buyer interested."

"That's when you didn't tell the senator that you wanted him to give you Rachel, along with the Crossroads as a wedding present?" Tom asked sharply, knowing the answer.

"Nash, you scoundrel!" cried Rachel.

Nash squirmed guiltily in his seat, then continued. "That's when Senator Barnwell said he had to go to town, and he asked Markham to show me around the place."

The sheriff looked at Markham, who nodded his head in agreement with Nash's story.

"Then after the reception that afternoon, I looked for the girl again. I wanted to examine the birthmark. I went into the kitchen and asked about her. The senator, I soon realized, was suspicious of me. He followed me in, and then, well, encouraged me to leave."

"He threw you out. I seen that part," said Markham.

"So that's what I was doing in the kitchen, Sheriff. I was looking for the girl with the curious birthmark, the identical marking to Rachel's. It had nothing *at all* to do with Tom's confounded invention or plotting to murder anybody or stealing any knife."

The sheriff pulled out a chair and sat across from the coroner. "Dr. Clark, what do you think about this business of the birthmarks?"

The coroner stroked his face thoughtfully. He leaned back in his chair, reflecting on the matter. The others watched him and waited.

"It's rare, but it does happen," said the man who was also the town doctor. "Here in Louisiana, we have a strange mix of people. We find things here that you don't often see elsewhere. With the English settlements in these parts, and the isolation of the plantations and the intermarriages of cousins and the like, I've seen cases of rare traits running through families."

"Like what?" asked the sheriff.

"I know of a family with an extra bone that juts out of the side of one foot, between the ankle and toe joint. Several family members have it.

Another family has a parent and several children with extra teeth impacted in their lower jaws behind their molars."

"What about birthmarks?" asked the sheriff.

"I've seen birthmarks run in certain families. I know brothers who have the same birthmark in the same place on their legs. And cousins with the same birthmark on the back of their necks. If a birthmark is passed on by a parent to one offspring, it could be passed on to another."

"Did Polly Barnwell have that birthmark?" asked the sheriff.

"My heavens!" said Charlotte.

"I treated Polly for consumption. No, she didn't have any such marking," said Dr. Clark. "Besides, Polly wasn't a blood relative of Rachel."

"We take offense at this questioning!" Rachel glared at the sheriff, who was undeterred.

"Did Polly's husband, the senator's brother, have the marking?" asked the sheriff.

"He wasn't my patient. I wouldn't know," Dr. Clark replied.

"Didn't Polly's husband die twenty-four years ago?" asked Nash. "I remember the senator mentioning that at the funeral."

"That sounds right," said Dr. Clark.

"This girl looked younger to me, maybe nineteen," said Nash.

The sheriff nodded. "Well then, did *Wiley Barnwell* have this birthmark?"

"Sheriff, really!" cried Rachel.

"You must stop these insinuations at once!" scolded Charlotte.

The sheriff acknowledged the women with a brief, sympathetic glance, then turned his attention back to the coroner for a reply.

"Wiley Barnwell was never sick a day in his life. I can't recall ever examining him while he was alive. After the crime, I didn't see any birthmark on his body—"

"You see, Sheriff! You see!" Rachel said triumphantly.

"*However*," Dr. Clark continued, "the knife wound tore the tissue over his heart. So because of the damage caused by the murder weapon, it's impossible to know if there was a marking on the skin in that area."

The sheriff nodded, then turned to the women. "Mrs. Barnwell, did your husband have that marking?"

"Certainly not!"

"Miss Barnwell, did you ever see that birthmark on your father or any other relative?"

"No, Sheriff, I most emphatically did *not!*"

"Do either of you women know anything about the girl that Mr. Nottingham described?"

"No!" they said in unison.

"It's a lie!" Charlotte added. "It's only the word of a coward and a scoundrel who'll say anything to keep himself out of jail. If it's just him who says it, Sheriff, then it can't be proven."

The sheriff slowly turned to Brett Markham. "Mr. Markham, do you know the mulatto female that Mr. Nottingham described?"

"Yup," he replied.

"Is she the slave that the senator directed you to whip and that you gave lashes to in the old cottage house on the morning of the crime?"

"Yup."

"Did she have a birthmark above her heart, as Mr. Nottingham says?"

Markham surveyed the group suspiciously.

"Did the slave have the birthmark, Mr. Markham?"

"I never whipped her before. Miss Polly never allowed that, no sir. But that day, the senator was in charge. I ordered her to loosen her dress. She done it. I lashed her back, just a few stripes to teach her good."

"Did you see the marking?" repeated the sheriff.

"I seen her outside later when this feller did." He pointed to Nash. "I seen her staggerin'. I seen her dress fall off from her shoulder, like he says."

"Did she have the birthmark?"

Everyone in the room stared at Markham.

"Yup. I seen it."

"Liar!" Charlotte's arm shot across the table, her finger pointed at Markham's face. The coroner, in the gesture of a doctor giving comfort, gently put her hand down and held it for a moment.

"Where is this girl, Mr. Markham?" asked the sheriff. "Can we see her and verify the birthmark?"

"Nope."

"Why not?"

"She's the girl the senator sold that day."

"What!" Tom gasped.

A look of astonishment cracked the sheriff's marble face, sending furrows across his brow.

"The senator up and gone to town with her," Markham added. "Seemed sudden, but then the wench was Miss Polly's personal servant and of no use no more."

The sheriff spoke slowly, as if digesting the full implication of his words. "You mean Senator Barnwell suddenly had to go to town that day to sell the very slave who had the birthmark, after Mr. Nottingham noticed her?"

"Seems so," said Markham.

"Why didn't you mention *before* that the slave he sold was the one you whipped?"

"Nobody asked me, Sheriff," said Markham dully.

"Did you notice that Mr. Nottingham had paid special attention to her?"

"I didn't pick up none on that, Sheriff. Only that the senator didn't like purty boy here." Markham pointed to Nash.

"Did this matter of the girl, as far as you know, have anything to do with the invention, Mr. Markham, anything at all?"

"I don't reckon so."

"Do you know anything about this girl's parents, or how she got to the Crossroads?" the sheriff continued.

Markham shook his head. "I been there jus' five years. The girl was there when I came. Nobody ever said nothin' 'bout her parents to me. I managed the field hands. Didn't know much 'bout the house servants."

"In the afternoon, when Senator Barnwell went into the kitchen and argued with Mr. Nottingham, did that have anything to do with the invention?"

"Nothin' I can tell," said Markham.

"Did you hear the invention mentioned by either man?" asked Duran.

"Nope."

The sheriff weighed the matter, then spoke to the coroner. "From what I can tell, the quarrel that occurred seems to be a . . . personal . . . matter between the senator and Mr. Nottingham."

"I agree." Dr. Clark nodded.

"For now, you can go, Mr. Nottingham," said Duran.

Nash gave a great sigh of relief. He sprang from his chair and bowed to the women, who were looking daggers at him.

"I assure you, I am most deeply and humbly sorry," he whispered. Then he turned to leave.

Tom was incredulous. He approached Nash, standing eye-to-eye with him.

"You mean you really did want to *sabotage* my invention?"

Nash rolled his eyes irritably, but Tom pressed on.

"An invention that would've given you a chance to make the profits you have trouble making as a planter, to have the idle time you crave, to pay your debts, to buy your clothes at the finest shops, and to support your lavish tastes? That night, you took a big risk in coming to the Crossroads to sabotage my invention. Since you were willing to go that far—to break the law—I don't understand why you didn't try to go for the big prize. How could you choose to *destroy* the invention instead of to exploit it for your benefit?"

With a tremendous weight lifted from his mind, a more relaxed Nash could afford to laugh dismissively. "You don't understand us, Tom. Actually, it would be good for everybody if you just went away, old boy, and left us alone."

# CHAPTER 19

A portrait of Polly and her husband painted twenty-four years earlier hung in her library. Tom looked up at the canvas from Polly's writing table. Three months after her death, a pair of reading glasses still lay on the table as if she had just left for a moment and planned to return. Next to the glasses, a letter was tucked inside an envelope that had not yet been addressed or sealed. Tom felt as if he were observing one of Polly's last acts, cut short by her illness.

Charlotte Barnwell had not yet visited the Crossroads to handle Polly's affairs since her funeral. The mistress of Ruby Manor had long declared that the air at the Crossroads made her ill. In fear for her daughter's health, she had even discouraged Rachel from visiting her aunt. Thus, it had become customary, Tom gathered, for Polly to visit her relatives at Ruby Manor rather than the other way around. Now Charlotte seemed to be continuing the same habit after Polly's death.

Because Charlotte had appointed him to manage the Crossroads until a new owner was found, Tom took the liberty of looking through the plantation's old journals in search of clues. Sitting in Polly's library, a few days after Cooper was saved from the hangman, he wondered if he could uncover any information to help him find the person who stole his tractor and killed Wiley Barnwell.

In a cabinet underneath a bookcase, he found stacks of the yearly bound journals of the plantation's operations. They contained records of the supplies purchased, fields planted, crop yields, prices of cotton, weather conditions, and many other details. Each book also chronicled the activities of the slaves: their names, jobs, marriages, births, illnesses, doctor's visits, special events, and deaths. He spread out the books of prime interest to him.

Two large globes hung in walnut stands on either side of the writing table. One mapped the earth's continents; the other, the celestial bodies. Tom felt as if he were spread between two worlds as dissimilar as those painted on the globes: the familiar world inhabited by everyone around him and the new world that he saw on the horizon.

There was someone else who saw the great potential of the new realm. It disgusted him to know that the person was a thief and murderer. By stealing the motorized tractor—while taking special care to place the cover on the beating heart that was its motor—the culprit showed that he recognized the coming age and the machine's great value. Tom wondered what perversion within a man could make him appreciate a device born of science yet stoop to primitive aggression.

His thoughts turned to the only other man—besides himself, the senator, Cooper, and Nash—who had seen the invention at the Crossroads and was on the property that night: Bret Markham. Tom recalled how Markham had opened the door of his cottage in the middle of the night, after the murder, fully dressed and armed. What was he doing that night? Was he coming in or going out? Was he really about to patrol the slaves' cabins as he stated?

Tom absently looked out the window, thinking. It was Sunday, and the field hands were walking about the property on their day off. He had brought Jerome with him to question the slaves. Jerome had brought his charm and his chocolate squares—both appealing—to accomplish the task. Outside, Tom saw the slaves gathering around the new chef to taste his special recipe.

Tom had told Jerome that a murder had occurred at the plantation, and he wanted to find out what the slaves knew about it. In particular, he asked if Jerome could find out whether the overseer, Bret Markham, really patrolled the slaves' cabins at night.

"I want to know the truth, Jerome," Tom had said, "and that might be different from what they told the sheriff."

Jerome had replied with his usual self-confidence. "If they know somethin', Jerome'll git it outta them."

Inside, Tom heard a kind, able voice directing the servants in the parlor. It belonged to Bret Markham's sister, Kate, who was staying in the big house. After Polly's death, Markham had urged Tom to employ his unmarried sister, a tutor in New Orleans, to come to the Crossroads temporarily to manage the house servants. Tom spoke to Charlotte about the matter, and the arrangements were made. The capable, energetic teacher soon brought order and efficiency to a household that had fallen into disarray since its mistress's death. With Charlotte's approval, Tom asked Kate to stay on until a new owner was found, and she arranged to do so.

Kate was half the size of her younger brother, but when they were together she seemed to tower over him in authority. At first Tom was startled at the resemblance between Kate and Bret and even more startled at their striking differences. Although the prominent brows, wide eyes, and firm jaw of Bret formed a perpetual scowl, those same features on Kate caused her to look forthright and intelligent.

As Kate directed the servants to arrange the parlor for a meeting called by Sheriff Duran, Tom examined the journals. He read the entries pertaining to the slaves, going back eighteen to twenty years: five males and four females born in that period, various cases of influenza and other illnesses, three deaths, four marriages, outings to neighboring plantations and church gatherings in town, a funeral that some of them attended for Daniel, a slave at Ruby Manor who had drowned. He could find no record of the birth of the mulatto female who had caught Nash's attention; the slave births for the period recorded the names of both parents, and they both were slaves. He examined a couple of books before and after that period, found nothing of interest, then closed the journals and put them away.

Despite his curiosity about the girl's lineage, there seemed to be no connection between her and the crime. The heated exchange between Nash and the senator regarding her seemed to have been centered around Nash's discovering a family secret, but that secret had nothing to do with the invention. Tom sighed, wondering where to look next. If chasing Nash led to a dead end, then what trail should he follow instead? He walked outside, pondering the matter.

"Mr. Tom," Jerome called to him. "Farley here has somethin' to tell you."

At the brick post that held the plantation bell, Jerome and a tall, young slave were talking. As Tom approached them, the teenager dashed behind the post. His glistening eyes peered out at Tom.

"Come on," Jerome coaxed. "Tell him what you tell me."

There was no answer. The youth only looked out from behind the post, his head tilted sideways, his eyes expressive.

"Farley, I won't hurt you," said Tom.

The slave cautiously stepped out.

"What do you do here, Farley?"

"I's a field hand, sir."

"Do you remember the night when a man was killed here, last winter?"

Farley nodded.

"Where were you that night?"

"In my cabin, 'cross the hill."

"Does anyone patrol those cabins at night?" Tom continued.

Farley hesitated.

"Does Mr. Markham, the overseer, come out at night to check on things?"

"He say he do, sir."

"What do *you* say, Farley?" Tom asked sympathetically.

"Why, sir, I say whut he tell me to say."

"If you could say what your eyes tell you, instead of what Mr. Markham tells you, what would your eyes tell you to say?" Tom's voice was kind yet persistent.

The slave stared at Tom in what looked like a silent plea. Then the boy turned away in fear.

Tom touched his shoulder reassuringly. "I promise, I won't let anyone hurt you."

Farley looked at Jerome, who nodded to him, vouching for Tom.

"Does Mr. Markham patrol your cabins at night?"

"No, sir."

"Does he come out at night?"

"Him drinks at night." Farley's voice was stronger now, as if he were easing out of a choke hold.

"Does Markham ever come out of his cottage after dark to check the cabins?"

"No."

"Not on the night the man was killed?"

"Not then. Not never."

"Are you sure, Farley?"

"I . . . I—" The slave's voice suddenly lost its confidence.

Farley was looking at something behind Tom that gave him a start. The slave whirled around and ran away.

"Farley, wait!" said Tom.

It was too late. The slave was gone.

Tom looked behind him to see someone watching them from a distance. It was Markham.

\* \* \* \* \*

The harp and the piano stood dormant in a corner of the parlor, with Sheriff Duran having no need for music or levity at his meeting. Those summoned sat around the room facing the sheriff and the coroner, with two deputies standing nearby.

Nash Nottingham and the now-exonerated Ted Cooper looked imposed upon, Bret Markham looked guarded, and Tom looked somber. Charlotte Barnwell sat on the sofa. Rachel, sitting next to her, wore a dress with an uncharacteristically high neck, masking the little birthmark that had caused a great stir.

The sheriff gestured to the widow. "I want to thank Mrs. Barnwell for allowing me to hold this meeting here and for coming at my request."

"The air here makes Mama ill," said Rachel resentfully.

"Goodness knows I have to be here, to protect my family from lies and rumors you allow to be spread, Sheriff," added Charlotte.

Duran took the reprimand quietly, then turned to the others. "I wanted to be by the murder scene in case we needed to verify anything that might come up. Thank you all for coming."

He studied the uneasy group. Except for a quiet nod from Tom, no one offered a courteous reply.

"I want to continue where we left off the other day in the courthouse, when our meeting brought out new information that was previously withheld." He looked pointedly at Nash. "I have a feeling there's more that some people know but haven't yet told."

The people in the room glanced at one another suspiciously.

"Dr. Clark, do you have anything to add?"

"After a careful examination of the knife from Manning Creek, I found it to be the right size to have been used in the stabbing," the coroner said to the group. "It definitely came from Miss Polly's silverware set. And the bits of fabric stuck on the blade precisely match the robe that the victim was wearing. It's the murder weapon, all right."

"This means we're looking for the person who planted that knife at Manning Creek." The sheriff concluded. He paused for a reaction.

"That leaves just one man," said Tom, rising to his feet. "There's only one man besides the senator, Cooper, Nash, and me who knew about the invention at the Crossroads. And that man also had access to the knife, was here at the Crossroads that night, and could have later brought the knife to Manning Creek."

His head turned sharply to Markham.

"And this man, I have just learned, also lied about his activities that night."

"Sez who? A slave?" Markham shot back.

"You touch him, and I'll smash you," Tom threatened.

Markham leaped toward Tom, a fist cocked at his accuser's face. The deputies quickly wedged themselves between the two men.

"Tom! What impertinence! Whoever said you could threaten *my* overseer?" said Charlotte.

She raised her eyebrows at Tom, expecting an apology. But he didn't offer one, only a look of surprise at the side she took.

"Sit down, gentlemen!" ordered the sheriff.

The men complied. The deputies stepped back.

"Go on, Mr. Edmun—"

"He spoke to a slave, Sheriff. A *slave*," Markham griped. "That don't count as no evidence, an' you can't hear it out!"

"I *will* hear it, Mr. Markham." He turned to Tom. "Go on."

"When I went to your cottage after the crime to tell you the news, I found you fully dressed and armed in the middle of the night. You said you were going out to patrol the slaves' cabins and that you do that every night. That wasn't true. You were up to something else that night."

"You believe a slave over me? You rotten Yankee!"

"Why did you lie?" Tom asked sharply. "What were you doing that night?"

"'Cause a worthless slave says somethin' don't make it true. They all got a' ax to grind."

"If you won't give an answer, I can supply my own theory," said Tom. He looked at the sheriff.

"Go on," said Duran. "Maybe your theory will prod Mr. Markham here to tell us the truth."

Tom leaned forward in his chair, looking grimly at Markham.

"On the day of the crime, you went into the old carriage house to whip a slave. There you saw an invention, something you had never seen before. You were curious. You poked around, examining it. You could've found the drawings and calculations I had in a box near the driver's seat. They showed how to operate the device, what it could do in the field, and the tremendous work output it had over manual farming. From the device, the drawings, and the numbers, it would be easy to figure out what the invention was and its potential to revolutionize farming."

"Them's lies, all lies!" bellowed Markham.

"You could've figured that the invention was just what you needed to solve your own problems. You blamed the slaves for your low yields. With the machine, you could get high yields. You blamed Miss Polly for not letting you beat the slaves so the crop would be better. With the machine, you wouldn't have to beat any slaves to get a good crop. You could be far more efficient and have hardly any field hands to supervise. You could be more valuable to any employer if you had a tractor instead of slaves."

Markham's lips curled as if he wanted to bite Tom.

"And you could make even more money, a great deal more, if you could *sell* the tractor. In fact, if you could steal the invention and sell it to someone with a lot of cash to develop it, then you could quit working altogether and live off the proceeds. That thought could have occurred to you as you stood there in the old carriage house, marveling at an invention you'd never seen before. With your poor yields from recent years and a new owner coming to the Crossroads, well, your future employment is less than certain—"

"Hogwash!" said Markham.

"You could've come back that night to steal the device. In the process, you could've awakened Senator Barnwell, who tried . . . valiantly . . . to rescue . . . it." The horror of the event surfaced in Tom's voice. "You could've had a knife with you from the plantation, which you obtained beforehand. You could've performed the vile deed, taken the device, hid it nearby, and left the senator on the floor where Ted Cooper found him. Later, after you returned to your cabin, I knocked on your door before you'd had a chance to undress. So you lied about why you were dressed and what you were doing at that hour, and you feigned surprise at the terrible news I brought."

"I *was* surprised fer real!" roared Markham.

"You would've had plenty of time after that night to hide the device and weapon farther away, to make them nearly impossible to find."

Tom sat back, looking at Markham. The women fanned themselves nervously. Everyone waited for the overseer's reply.

"Okay, Mr. Markham. Tell us your side," said the sheriff.

"That's all humbug, beginnin' to end, Sheriff."

"Then what's the truth?"

"The Yankee's a fool. That's the truth."

The sheriff persisted. "Then tell us what really happened."

"Nothin' to tell."

"You did see the invention in the old carriage house, as you told us previously?" asked the sheriff.

"I seen it."

"You were dressed to go out in the middle of the night, and you told Mr. Edmunton and later you told me that you were going to patrol the slave cabins as you do every night. Correct?"

"What of it?"

"Do you really patrol those cabins, Mr. Markham?"

"Who sez I don't?"

"Come clean, Mr. Markham," the sheriff continued. "You weren't patrolling any slave cabins. You were dressed to do something else, weren't you?"

"It's not what yer thinkin'."

"Why were you going out that night? Did it have something to do with the invention?"

"I didn't kill nobody, Sheriff. And I ain't never got near the contraption."

"What happened that night?" asked the sheriff, growing impatient.

"I was about to do somethin', but I never got the chance. The Yankee here come to my door jus' as I was leavin'."

"What were you about to do?" the sheriff prodded.

"It warn't my idea. I was workin' fer somebody else."

"What wasn't your idea?"

"To take the machine."

"To take it and do what?"

"Somebody wanted it smashed. Paid me half a year's wages to do it."

Tom's head shot up.

"Continue, Mr. Markham," said the sheriff.

"Somebody paid me two hundred dollars up front and was givin' me 'nother two when I done it. You can see the money yerself. It's in a bag given to me."

"Exactly what were you being paid to do?" The sheriff persisted.

"To take the invention away. Smash it to smithereens. Bury the parts. I was about to git the ax and my horse, then go over the hill to haul the thing away. That was when he come to my door." Markham pointed hatefully to Tom.

"That can't be true, Markham," said Tom. "It makes no sense."

"No? Somebody tol' me what that thing was, that it'll do farmin', that it'll replace the slaves and maybe even replace *me*."

"Who told you that?" Tom continued.

"The person that wanted it smashed. I tell ya, I was happy to do it. I was double happy to get paid fer it. Why would I want a bunch o' no-good slaves runnin' wild, takin' my job?"

The sheriff stood up and walked close to Markham, towering over him. "Who paid you?" he said.

"Somebody who wanted the engine chopped up."

"Who?" This time it was Tom who was on his feet grilling Markham.

"I don' want it held against me. I was just gonna do what I was told."

"Who told you to take the invention and smash it, Mr. Markham?" Duran pressed.

The sheriff's voice was stern. His deputy put his hand on a pair of handcuffs tied to his belt, as if getting ready to use them. Markham's eyes darted from the deputy's cuffs to the sheriff's face. He stood up and pleaded with the lawman.

"Lord's sake, Sheriff, don' ask. I got my job to think of."

"You've got your *life* to think of, Mr. Markham. Who gave you money and put you up to stealing the invention?"

Markham looked at Charlotte. "Please don't hold it against me, ma'am. Please!"

"Who wanted the invention smashed and was willing to pay you a half year's wages to do it?" Duran demanded.

Sweat from Markham's forehead sprinkled on the rug as he lowered his head and shook it in refusal. Then he slowly raised it in acquiescence.

"'Twas Wiley Barnwell."

# CHAPTER 20

Tom looked shaken by Markham's words. He walked up to the overseer and pointed a finger at his chest. "You're lying!"

"Oh, yeah?" Markham slapped Tom's hand down and grabbed for his throat.

"Sit down, gentlemen!" ordered the sheriff, wedging himself between them.

The coroner stood too, ready to assist the sheriff.

Exchanging angry stares, the men complied. Duran and Dr. Clark returned to their seats also, in an effort to ease the building tension.

Tom's head dropped. With his face hidden, he looked like a boy encountering his first disillusionment. "The senator wouldn't do that to me," he whispered, as if talking to himself.

"Oh, no?" Cooper smiled at Tom's discomfort. Life had returned to the man saved from the hangman's noose. "Sounds just like old Wiley to me."

"It's certainly more in tune with the man I had the great honor of knowing!" Nash looked pleased by the turn of events. "The senator was always the first one to defend our traditions against outsiders." He glanced at the women, as if hoping to impress.

"You think it's okay to destroy a new invention?" Tom raised his head in astonishment. "I have a higher opinion of the senator. I know he'd never do that."

Duran looked at Cooper and Nash, "Did either of you actually *hear* the senator express any opinion of the invention?"

The men shook their heads.

"Mrs. Barnwell," said the sheriff, "did you ever hear your husband say anything about Mr. Edmunton's invention?"

"I don't know if Wiley was fixing to do any mischief to that machine or not," said Charlotte. "If he was, he didn't share his thoughts with me."

The sheriff's face was drawn tight and his eyes were bulging, on heightened alert to everything said.

"I don't know if Wiley realized what was troubling me," his widow added. "Even before the . . . crime . . . I feared that Tom's device might be . . . *cursed*."

Tom looked as if he'd been slapped.

The sheriff turned to Rachel. "What about you, Miss Barnwell?"

"Papa didn't say anything to me, Sheriff. Of course, I urged him to talk to Tom about his obsession with that machine. Seemed downright unhealthy, it did."

Tom looked as if he'd been slapped again.

"To tell the truth," Charlotte said, reflecting, "I worried that Rachel would be taken away from us and moved to the North because of Tom's wild ideas. The senator assured me he'd see to it that Tom wouldn't pursue that path. He said Tom was young and a bit brash, and without a father, he needed guidance."

She looked at Tom, her eyebrows raised, as if she were hoping to impress her words upon him. "Of course, Tom's quite a nice young man. I don't mean to say we didn't like him very much, but he just needed a little *grooming*."

It was Tom's turn to raise his eyebrows, not liking to hear himself described the way someone would describe a horse.

"Ladies, are you saying that Mr. Markham's story about the senator fixing to harm the invention makes sense to you?" asked the sheriff.

"It does," said Rachel, nodding.

"It wouldn't surprise me," added Charlotte.

Only two people in the room—Tom and the sheriff—looked surprised that the women nonchalantly considered their patriarch capable of betrayal and theft.

"But do you have any *evidence*?" Duran asked.

The women shook their heads.

"Sheriff, they're wrong about the senator." Tom stood up before the group. "We can't forget the meaning of his tragic death," he said painfully. "He fought to *save* my tractor, not to destroy it. Doesn't the evidence show that the senator tried to ward off the robber?"

The sheriff listened without comment.

"Markham lied about his activities on the night of the crime," Tom continued. "Now that we've caught him in his deception, he belatedly admits he intended to steal the device. He's certainly not going to admit to the actual theft and murder, so he's made up a story."

"'Tis the gospel truth," the overseer insisted.

"Markham went to the old carriage house to steal the invention for his personal gain. He put on the cover. The senator heard rumblings, came out to investigate, and defended the invention with his life. Markham then stabbed him, took the device, hid it somewhere, and returned home, where I later found him. Doesn't that seem like the logical theory that fits the evidence?"

"'Taint so, Yankee!" roared Markham, rising from his chair. Any pretense at cordiality toward the man who was his acting manager was no longer possible. "When the senator got to the Crossroads that mornin', he called for me. He shown me the contraption. He told me what he wanted me to do. Gave me money. We made a deal."

Tom shook his head. "The senator said he was going to the Crossroads early that day to inspect the place before Cooper's visit—"

"He didn't inspect nothin'. He come to see me and make a deal. That mornin' when he shown it to me was the last I seen o' the contraption. The crime was done 'fore I could git to do my business that night."

The sheriff stood up and walked to Markham. He faced the overseer squarely.

"You saw the invention," Duran said sternly. "You knew its location, and you were told what it was. Isn't that so, Mr. Markham?"

"Like I said."

"You made a deal to steal it?"

"But I didn't hurt nobody."

"You were up and dressed to do the deed that night?"

"But I never got to do it 'fore the Yankee here knocked on my door."

"You lied to me about your plans for that night?" Duran continued.

"I didn't see no reason to mention—"

"You took the invention?"

"Somebody stole it 'fore I left the house."

"Who?" asked the sheriff.

"How am I to know?"

"How is it that the man who supposedly hired you to steal the invention is dead, Mr. Markham?" Duran's voice was hard.

The overseer had no reply.

"Look, Markham, you had access to the weapon," interjected Tom. "You had knowledge of the invention. And you had the opportunity to commit the crime. Later, when Cooper was about to be hanged, some vestige of guilt seeped into your conscience, so it was *you* who wrote the anonymous letter to free a man from paying for your crime. You were the one who left that letter at my house in the night, so I would stop the execution. This was what you did to relieve your conscience from a second death. Wasn't it?"

"Them's lies! All lies!" thundered the accused. His fists tightened, eager to contact Tom's face.

"What do you think, Dr. Clark?" The sheriff turned to the coroner.

"Let's take him in," replied the coroner grimly.

Duran nodded in agreement, then turned to his deputies. "Cuff him."

One deputy placed Markham's hands behind him; the other curled manacles around his wrists. The clicking of the iron locks filled the room.

"Wait!" The urgent voice of a woman came from outside the room.

Kate Markham stepped into view in the narrow opening between the two panels of the pocket door. She slid the panels open further and walked into the room. She faced the group solemnly, without any attempt to hide or excuse the fact that she had been eavesdropping.

"Did you say the murderer wrote a *letter*?" she asked.

"Yes, Miss Markham," said the sheriff, who had been introduced to her earlier. "Haven't you been following the case?"

"No, Sheriff. I'm afraid I haven't been reading the newspapers, but I do know that my brother could not have committed that crime."

"Stay outta this! They got nothin' on me. I kin clear myself," barked Markham.

Ignoring her brother, Kate continued. "You said the murderer wrote a letter—"

"Hush up!" yelled Markham.

"My brother couldn't possibly have written that letter or any other document."

"What do you mean?" asked Tom.

"He told me he kept the plantation journals," added Cooper.

"He couldn't have kept the journals, either." Kate frowned at her brother.

The sheriff cocked his head as he appraised the woman. "Why not, Miss Markham?"

"Shut up, Katy!"

"Because he's illiterate."

Like a creature who gets a sudden glimpse of what it means to be fully human and of how far short he falls, Markham's face flushed and his eyes dropped in an embarrassment that was awkward for the others to watch.

"Damn you!" he mumbled to his sister through gritted teeth.

"Sheriff, my brother never had any inclination for book learning. When our mother sent us to our little town school, Bret paid no attention to his lessons, and the other students surpassed him in every subject. But where he excelled was in beating them up after class."

The sharp glance she shot at her brother suggested that time had not tempered her reaction to the events she described.

"And Brett especially enjoyed beating up those who couldn't fight back, like the slave children he encountered when my father took a job as an overseer. So you see, Bret never learned, never wanted to learn."

Markham was silenced by his sister's rebuke. He listened docilely, as if he were still a boy and her voice had the power of their mother.

"After Miss Polly died, my brother downright *begged* me to come here and stay for a while—not to manage the house servants, as Miss Charlotte and Mr. Edmunton were concerned about, but to keep the books." As she spoke, her brother fidgeted like a boy caught stealing cookies. "I didn't realize he was lying to folks about that, but it seems to me Miss Polly kept those journals."

"We can find out easily enough," said Tom. Impelled by a sudden idea, he rushed out of the room and returned moments later with a book and an envelope in his hands.

"This is the plantation journal from last year. And in this envelope we'll find a letter Polly apparently wrote just before she died but never mailed. I discovered it earlier on her writing table."

The sheriff took the documents. He removed the letter from the envelope. "It's signed by Polly Barnwell and dated just a week before she died." Then he flipped through the journal, comparing the handwriting in it to that of the letter. "Looks identical to me."

He turned to the coroner, who had come to his side and was also examining the documents. Dr. Clark nodded in agreement.

"You don't read at all?" the coroner asked Markham.

"I can read the cotton scale an' write slave names by their pickin' weights good as anybody."

"That's about all he can do," Kate added.

Cooper turned sharply to Markham. "Why did you tell me *you* kept those books?"

Markham's head sunk into his shoulders.

Kate shook her head reproachfully at her brother. "Bret may be a liar and a fool, but he's no writer."

Tom faced Markham incredulously. "What would you have done if Ted Cooper had bought the plantation, then discovered that you can't keep records after all, and that you lied to him?"

Markham shrugged his shoulders. "Then's then. Now's now."

Tom knew that the man before him, who couldn't project the consequences of his actions over mere weeks, was not someone who could have projected the consequences of an invention into the far future.

The others were silent. Somehow, they also knew this was true.

Kate stated what they all were thinking: "Sheriff, if you're looking for a murderer who had a conscience and wrote a letter so somebody else wouldn't be punished, well, I don't know about the conscience, but as far as writing the letter, Bret's not your man."

The sheriff nodded. He turned to his deputy and gestured to Markham. The deputy removed the handcuffs.

"Now I understand where that purse came from," Kate told the sheriff. "Bret didn't have any money when I visited him at Christmas. Fact is, he was trying to squeeze some out of me. But when I came back in February after

Miss Polly's death, he had two hundred dollars in a purse. He claimed it was his bonus for a good crop."

Kate darted an angry look at her brother, who lowered his head in silent admission of yet another lie. The powerful overseer who made slaves tremble in fear was himself cowered by his older sister's scolding.

"Sheriff, I know my brother likes to gamble and drink. That's why I wouldn't let him touch the money until his position with the new owner of the Crossroads was secured. I have the purse with the two hundred dollars, if you'd like to see it."

"Before we leave, you can show us, ma'am," said the sheriff without urgency, evidently moving on in his hunt.

Tom stood nearby, in unblinking shock from the revelations. He walked slowly toward Markham.

"I can believe *you* didn't appreciate my device. But the *senator*?" His eyes dropped painfully to the floor. He added, as if talking to himself: "The man who treated me like a *son*?"

Sporting a rare smile, Markham replied: "He was only playin' with you, boy."

# CHAPTER 21

As Kate excused herself and left the meeting, Bret Markham sank into his chair, relieved by the sheriff's loss of interest in him. Duran and the coroner also took their seats; with the tension of the moment past, they observed the others, wondering where the trail would now lead.

"I'm rather proud of the senator." Nash looked at Tom with an air of insolent satisfaction at beating a rival.

"It seems old Wiley didn't let us down after all," gloated Cooper. "I should've known he'd have a plan to deal with an outsider who comes here hell-bent on revamping everything." He smirked at Tom. "The senator might have wanted you in his family, but it was definitely going to be on *his* terms."

Markham seemed to be enjoying a rare moment of camaraderie with the class that paid his salary but otherwise ignored him. Proving that self-control was not among his talents, he joined the chorus against the man who was his acting manager. "Right proud I was when the senator trusted *me* with smashin' that thing. I reckon we woulda got along jus' fine, me and the senator."

"Tom," said Rachel, "Papa was only doing what he thought was right."

"It was for your own good, Tom," Charlotte announced.

The inventor, the only one who had remained standing, now faced the group as if *he* were the culprit and they were the firing squad.

"No offense, old boy," said Nash, proceeding to offend, "but it would be best for everybody if you never found that machine of yours. You can see all the trouble it's brought us." He looked at Rachel, who rewarded him with a nod.

"Nash is right," she said.

Tom looked at her blankly, as if she were a stranger.

"I hope it's at the bottom of the swamp," added Cooper, "that confounded device of Yankee gall."

"It's *cursed*," said Charlotte.

Tom looked curiously at the woman whose eyes held a hint of derangement.

"It's brought innuendoes and suspicions—lies, all lies!—on our family," Charlotte continued. "I declare, that machine could do the farmin' for Satan!"

Markham smiled maliciously at the dressing-down of his superior. Encouraged, he added to the chorus: "Slaves make crops. Always have, always will."

The verbal bullets kept flying for a few minutes. But they seemed to miss their mark. Rather than fatally wounding the young inventor, they emboldened him. He stood tall, his head high with pride in himself and his eyes heavy with contempt for them.

When they were finished, he spoke. "So none of you are surprised by the senator's behavior?"

Waiting for an answer, he pensively looked out the window like a scientist forming a conclusion, then turned back to the group. "None of you are dismayed to learn that your town's distinguished statesman, a man of great standing among you, was engaged in deception, bribery, thievery, and destruction?"

No one denied the charges.

"Face it, Tom, your invention was just a delusion, anyway," said Cooper. "There was no proof it would work the way you claimed. Why, our dear Wiley was doing you a *favor* before you made more of a fool of yourself. He was helping you come down to earth by getting rid of the senseless thing."

"People don't commit crimes for things they think are senseless." Tom shook his head. "New devices that don't work die by themselves. Nobody would have a motive to steal and destroy something he believes is useless."

Tom paced before the others like a bobcat they couldn't shoot down.

"Tell me, Cooper, were you also doing me a favor by attempting to steal my tractor that night? Was Nash doing me a favor when he tried too? Were you both going to risk getting caught and going to jail for the theft of something you thought was useless—in order to do me a favor?"

There was no reply.

"I'd say you all took the device very seriously." His eyes traveled from Cooper to Nash to Markham, while his mind also saw a fourth face on a portrait hanging in his parlor. "Yes, indeed, you took it seriously! But not for the reason I thought." His voice dropped grimly. "I didn't understand you at first. I thought you wanted to *develop* the invention and realize the dream of the new age. But now I see what really drives all of you." His eyes reached Rachel, including her in his statement.

The sheriff listened patiently, allowing Tom to continue. The lawman watched everyone. He looked interested in letting the interplay proceed among those closest to the invention and the deceased, as if hoping it might lead to a new clue and direction.

"I had mentioned my invention to the senator on previous occasions, but he didn't know how far along I was until the day before Miss Polly's burial when I told him I was going to Philadelphia to unveil it and couldn't make the funeral. Now I realize why he insisted on delaying my trip. He wanted to get at the invention before I could take it away. That's why he offered to bring it to the Crossroads. He wanted it in the place where he was going to be that night. And that's why he pressed me to show the device to Cooper and Nash that afternoon. The more men who knew about it, the harder it would be to pin the theft on him. Sheriff, I think the senator concocted an excuse to bring my device to the Crossroads early that day. He told me he wanted to review the plantation records, but it seems he really wanted to see the overseer and make his deal, as Markham claims."

The youthful disillusionment had vanished from Tom's face. The scientist in him was now in charge, dispassionately firing off conclusions. The puzzle pieces were now fitting together to form a clear picture.

"None of you are surprised at the senator's behavior—because you're just like him. *All* of you wanted my tractor smashed."

No one denied it.

"It appears none of you actually stole the invention or killed the senator, but you're guilty of crimes just the same." His targets now fidgeted in their seats. The men looked vexed, and the women looked puzzled. But the sheriff and coroner looked merely curious. "You're guilty of crimes against *yourselves.*"

"Robbie, stop this drivel now!" Cooper looked about to jump out of his chair.

"You all had your chance to speak. Now I'd like my chance," said Tom.

The sheriff motioned to his uncle to sit back. Cooper seemed surprised to see how little sway he now had over the young lawman who once treated him like an oracle. "Mr. Edmunton and his invention are critical to the case. I'll hear him out."

Sparks flew from Tom's eyes. "You, Cooper, you pride yourself on being a businessman, but you committed a crime against business. You want to make as much money as possible, yet you tried to sabotage an invention that promised to make you more money in less time and at a lower cost than ever before."

"You traitor! You know how we farm here," argued Cooper. "Why do you taunt us? Our system was fixed on us; we didn't make it."

"But you like it the way it is, and you would destroy anything that upset it."

Tom recalled the day he tried to improve the seed drill, when his attention was pulled away to deal with the most mundane details of other people's lives. He recalled too many of his days spent like that.

"Instead of engaging yourself with the latest discoveries and innovations to reduce your costs and labor and improve your business—instead of that— you throw away your mental energy on arranging how many blankets others have, the frocks they wear, the kind of shoes they get, the food they eat, the beds they sleep in. When you control every detail of others' lives, you not only shrink *their* horizons but you also shrink *your own*. You gloat over the destruction of a farm invention that could enlarge your profits, while you glory in a world where you dispense molasses rations and keep others helpless. You betrayed business for the sake of power. That's your crime against yourself."

The faces around the parlor reddened. In the Louisiana of 1859, no one ever said the kind of things the group was now hearing.

"Watch it, Yankee," warned Cooper. "We have laws here—"

"Yes, yes, you have laws," Tom said contemptuously. "Like the ones you and Barnwell used to shut down the factory? Like the ones you use to block your fellow citizens from freeing their bondsmen or even schooling them— because the self-reliance of others threatens your power? That's the other crime you committed, the crime against the law. You took off the blindfold of justice to make the law give you benefits at others' expense, and those others aren't just the slaves. They're also your fellow citizens, like me. When I can't speak my mind or educate my servants or free them without getting thrown in jail, then aren't you using *me* against my will to serve *you*? Isn't that also slavery?"

The man whose badge displayed a blindfolded lady looked disturbed by the notion.

"Shut your insolent mouth, or I'll have you prosecuted!" Cooper looked to the sheriff for support, but his nephew offered none.

The inventor turned to another man, one whose face was drawn tight and who stared at him resentfully.

"You, Nash, you spread your feathers like a peacock who's all fluff and no mass. Where's your *passion* to do anything? Where's your *skill* at doing anything? The only thing you excel at is idleness."

Nash shot up in his chair. "What gall!"

Tom continued pacing as he gestured to Nash. "You live off not only the backs of the slaves but also off anybody else you can cajole. You lived off your father's efforts. And after his passing, you lived off loans, like the ones you got from me. Then you wanted the senator to gift you with the Crossroads, so you could live off the product of Miss Polly's work."

Nash turned to Duran. "Sheriff, really now!"

The sheriff didn't reply. He looked engrossed in Tom's words.

"You want someone else to do the work. Yet when you learned of a new invention that had the potential to make you lots of money in farming with much less effort, you wanted to sabotage it. What you really want, Nash, is to be an aristocrat in a dying age. That's your crime against yourself. In your quest for a life free of effort, you made for yourself a life free of purpose, a life of laziness, incompetence, and debt."

"You're not fit for Rachel!" roared Nash. "Go back to the North where you belong!"

"And . . . the senator—"

"Stop, before you disrespect the dead! Have you no shame?" cried Charlotte.

"Senator Barnwell was your salesman for the dying age." Tom stood still, his restless pacing subdued, his voice heavy with sadness and bitterness. "Barnwell put the mask of goodness on something bad. He told himself and all of you that the dying age is kindness; it's caring; it's looking after those who can't help themselves." Tom thought of the intelligent face of a young teacher and the eagerness of a chef with a tall white hat. He thought of how proud and capable they stood. "That's Barnwell's crime. He tried to bend and twist morality to justify power."

Tom's eyes grew more intense as a further thought occurred to him.

"And he tried to control *me* the same way he controlled the slaves. He tried to push me to lend Cooper money to take the Crossroads off his hands, against my own lending practices. He wanted me to marry his daughter and give up inventing, against my own wishes. An appetite for power doesn't stop at one prey but hungers for more. Barnwell was closed to the great challenge of nature that the new age presents. He was too busy trying to expand his control of people in the dying age."

"Well, I declare! In all of God's kingdom, *you* are the most arrogant beast of all!" said Rachel, aghast.

She seemed to have lost her self-consciousness at having her personal affairs discussed in the group. A perverted intimacy seemed to have developed among those involved in the sheriff's meetings, like a bickering family unable to break away from conflict.

"When Senator Barnwell, your great moral leader, learned of an invention that could have created the most moral society ever—one in which nature's awesome power was tamed and men were set free—what did he do? He tried to destroy it."

"Good gracious God!" cried Charlotte.

"And others here," Tom looked directly at Rachel, "gave up their dreams for the comforts and conveniences of the dying world. They didn't mind going along with the corruption, didn't give it a thought, as long as they got their own inducements. They committed crimes against their own spirit.

When someone has to rein in her will and inclinations to conform to what the town wants her to be . . . who's the real slave?"

Rachel crossed her arms and whispered venomously, "You monster!"

"And you, Markham, you want your own niche of power. It's not brainpower you want but the power of the whip. You never cared for schooling because you think intelligence doesn't matter. You say you were happy to smash an invention that could free up the field hands to compete with you for work. Why? Because you've held yourself back; you've made yourself unfit to compete. The new age requires brains, not muscle. Your crime is that you never tried to beat your mind into shape—only your field hands."

"I's right itchin' to beat *you* into shape, Yankee!" Markham's lips curled into a snarl.

Tom pressed on. "In fact, you're *all* Markhams. That's what you've become. You're *all* bullies. Only Markham makes no pretense at being anything more, while you fancy yourselves as upper class."

The three men Tom had insulted shot out of their seats and leaped at him.

"Swine!"

"Madman!"

"Traitor!"

Nash reached for his throat. Markham raised his fists. Cooper lodged the first blow. Tom threw off their hands and ducked their punches. The women screamed. The sheriff sprang up, and the deputies and coroner rushed into the fray. The lawmen wedged themselves between Tom and his attackers.

The sheriff was silently grateful for his earlier insistence that guns be left with a deputy outside the meeting so that only the law enforcers were armed. As he and his men pushed and shoved both sides back, Tom was still defiant.

"Why did you commit crimes against business, against justice, against morality, against your own characters? Because you're clinging to something whose time is up."

"It's *your* time that's up!" yelled Nash.

"By keeping your slaves down, you're keeping yourselves down too. Being masters over men doesn't destroy just your subjects. *It destroys you too.*"

"Seditionist!" yelled Nash.

"That's treason! Arrest him!" added Cooper.

"Get back! Get back! Get back!" ordered the sheriff.

The riled men pushed forward to break the lawmen's defense. The sheriff and his men peeled the attackers off Tom.

The inventor backed away as he had the last word: "You're at a crossroads. The new age is at your door. It needs men to be masters over nature, not over other men. And it requires all men first to be masters over themselves."

"Your confounded device—and your poisonous ideas—aren't welcome here," said Cooper. "Either you leave on your own steam, or we'll run you out of town."

"I'll get my tractor back, or I'll make another! The world's going to change, and you can't stop it!"

"Maybe the Yankee needs schoolin', Southern style." Markham smirked, eager to do the job.

"This is sedition, Robbie! I demand you arrest this man!" Cooper looked suspiciously at his nephew, who had done nothing to silence Tom. "Or do you *agree* with him?"

Duran paid no attention to the imposing man who had reared him, as if his respect for his uncle was a fading memory.

"Arrest him, Robbie! He's committed sedition ten times over! If you don't, then you're complicit in his treachery."

The sheriff backed away from the pack and pulled out his gun. "Sit down! Sit down! Sit down, or I'll run you all in!"

The attackers slowly backed away.

The sheriff turned to the inventor. "That's enough, Tom."

Tom was astonished that the sheriff addressed him by first name and in a sympathetic tone. At that moment, the inventor realized he had an ally. He wondered how many others thought as he did about the great injustice surrounding them, people who didn't speak out for fear of reprisal.

"Everyone, sit down—*now*," the sheriff repeated.

With shoves from the deputies and urging from the coroner, everyone finally did sit down. But they kept their fiery stares fixed on Tom in the quieted room.

"Let's get back to the matter at hand. We're looking for a suspect," said the sheriff, putting away his gun. "Someone who stole the invention, who took pains to cover and protect it, and who murdered for it."

The sheriff's searchlight eyes swept across the group.

"We're looking for someone who was literate and could write the letter *and* had access to the murder weapon *and* knew the whereabouts of the invention. Who would that be?"

"No one we know of from our investigation." The coroner shook his head.

The sheriff gestured to the others, one at a time, for their answer to his question.

"There was no one else with us," said Cooper, "when Wiley, Nash, and I saw the invention and Tom explained it."

"Nobody I know of," said Nash.

"I didn't show the invention to anyone else," said Tom.

When the sheriff got to the women, they shook their heads.

The sheriff turned to the last man in the group.

"There *is* somebody," said Markham.

All heads turned to the overseer.

"Who?" asked the sheriff.

"There was a slave at the Crossroads who could read and write and saw the invention in the ol' carriage house."

"Oh?" The sheriff tensed, taken by surprise.

"What?!" Tom looked astonished.

"And that slave coulda stole a knife and hid it a-forehand. Miss Polly warn't too careful. Fact is, she was lax. They all stole, and they all hid things."

"Who is this slave who was literate and who saw the invention? I want to talk to him now!"

"'Tain't a *he*," Markham explained. "'Tis a *she*. Miss Polly musta learned her 'fore I arrived here, 'cause she read to the missus and even wrote passes fer the slaves. She was hidin' in the shed, curled up inside the old coach that was in thar when me and the senator was talkin' about the contraption."

"Are you serious?" The sheriff looked incredulous.

"Yup."

"How could you not have told me this before?"

Markham shrugged his shoulders. "Didn't pay it no mind."

"Bring her to me right now!"

"She ain't here no more, Sheriff."

"What do you mean?"

"She's the slave with the birthmark, the one the senator sold that day."

# CHAPTER 22

The women gasped. Everyone looked astonished.

The sheriff's alert eyes met Markham's unfocused ones. "Am I to understand that the female slave that has a . . . connection . . . to the Barnwells—"

"I'll not have you insinuate what you're insinuating!" Charlotte demanded.

Rachel subtly glanced down at the neckline of her dress, as if to check that the little birthmark over her heart was fully covered, then she echoed her mother's displeasure with the lawman. "Sheriff, you'll please not insult us, sir!"

The sheriff looked at the women, sighed, then turned back to the overseer. "Let me begin again. Mr. Markham, you told us previously that the young mulatto woman who had the birthmark that Mr. Nottingham noticed was taken to the docks on the morning of Miss Polly's funeral and sold by Senator Barnwell, right?"

"Yup."

"*She's* the one who was hiding in a coach in the old carriage house, with the invention there?"

"Yup."

"So she had knowledge of the invention. *And* she can read and write?"

"Yup."

"This is the girl you whipped?"

"One an' the same."

"Mr. Markham, when you told us previously that you whipped a slave in the old carriage house, it appeared you took her in there for the lashing. You didn't mention that she was *already* in there, hiding." The sheriff looked exasperated at the sheer density of the man. "Didn't you think this might be important to mention?"

"Didn't occur to me none, Sheriff."

Duran rubbed his eyes wearily. "Never mind. What's her name?"

"Ladybug."

"Is that a nickname? What's her real name?"

"That's what everybody called her. Only name I knowed."

"Are you saying this slave named Ladybug, after she was sold, could have later returned to the Crossroads to kill the senator?"

"Could be."

"Why was she hiding in the old carriage house where the invention was? You told us previously that the slave Mr. Nottingham pursued had nothing to do with the invention."

"Nothin' I can see. The senator and me found the wench in the shed while we was discussin' the invention. She was in there prob'ly to slough off her tasks, take a nap, daydream, somethin' like that. Then when we come in, she musta tried to hide, 'cause we found her curled up in the old coach that was near the invention."

"Did she overhear you and the senator talking about the invention?" the sheriff continued.

"Reckon she did, 'cause we was talkin' and she was hidin' thar."

"What were you and the senator saying?"

"Not much. He told me the contraption was a new invention, a dangerous one, and he wanted me to haul it away, take it apart, and make the pieces disappear, so they'll never be found. He give me two hundred dollars. Said I'd get two hundred more when I finished. He said it had to be done that night, 'cause in the mornin' the invention would be gone. That's all I know. Then he noticed the girl hidin'. He got mad, pulled her outta the coach, told me to whip her, and he left. I gave her a few stripes and left the shed too."

"Was that just before Mr. Nottingham arrived and ran into her?"

"Yup."

"Then after the senator noticed Mr. Nottingham's interest in the girl, he decided to take her to town to sell her, right?" the sheriff continued.

"Seems so."

The sheriff glanced at the coroner, who looked puzzled. "Mr. Markham," said Dr. Clark, "since the senator sold the girl, wouldn't it be impossible for her to come back and kill him? And why would she?"

Markham straightened his spine and seemed to rise in his chair like a person of importance about to give a valued opinion.

"Well, let me see. The senator warn't no Miss Polly, allowin' servants to run wild. That day the girl got her first taste o' the lash, then she got sold. That musta miffed her darn good!" He seemed amused at someone's life suddenly thrown into chaos. "Now, Ladybug, she's a smart one. She's a house servant, so she coulda knowed the senator was fixin' to spend the night here. She coulda made her way back that night to get her revenge on him. She coulda wrote herself a pass and sneaked away for a bit while her new massa was sleepin'. She coulda maybe took a horse from his stable. Or she coulda got one from the livery, if the new massa was stayin' at the docks that night. Why, she could talk some young buck, a slave or a free person o' color, at the livery inta givin' her a horse fer a spell. She's a sweet one when she wanna be. Her favors could go far fer her."

"Let's say she wrote herself a pass, got a horse, and snuck away that night. Then what happened, according to your hypothesis?" pressed the sheriff.

"Hmm." Markham thoughtfully stroked his chin, looking like a man of distinction, except for the two-day stubble of whiskers covering his face. His sudden stature as a man with an important hypothesis seemed to awaken whatever mental faculties he possessed.

"Well, I reckon she coulda come back here. Maybe she grabbed a knife she already had hidin' here, a knife she stole and stashed to do evil with at some time, in some way. She knew that this was the time. She made noise outside the senator's window to wake him up. Then she drawn him into the shed where nobody could see her vile deed, and she stabbed him. Then she took the invention to make it look like a white man's crime fer a white man's machine, instead of a wench's revenge against her massa. When she was through with her mischief, I reckon, she gone back to her new massa, iffen it was a nice family she was sold to, like the senator said. Good chance runaways git caught after the massa puts out notice on 'em, so I reckon she gone back."

"What would she do with the device?" asked the sheriff.

Markham crossed his legs and leaned back as if he were the owner of the Crossroads, entertaining guests with his stories.

"She coulda hid it in the woods so nobody can never find it—never!" He looked at Tom and seemed pleased that his remark gave the inventor a start. "Slaves got hidin' places in them woods that we won't never know 'bout. They disappear fer a while and go to them when they get the urge, slippin' away or claimin' they're off a-huntin'. They hide fugitives and bring 'em food too, them slaves. 'Specially the ones here, with nary a sting o' the whip. Yup, Miss Polly's slaves, they took liberties, they did."

"And you think Ladybug would have stopped to put the cover back on the tractor?" interjected Tom.

"She's a strong thing. She coulda did it. Cover was on the contraption when the senator and me was talkin'."

The sheriff pondered the matter. "What do you think, Dr. Clark?"

"If the girl is the culprit, maybe she thought it was worth a couple of minutes and would've made a good case for the *invention* being the reason behind the crime, and not *her* being the reason," said the coroner. "After she was sold that day, she might have worried that she could be a prime suspect and so wanted to deflect attention away from that."

The sheriff looked flabbergasted. "You mean we could've gotten the case *all wrong?*"

"This could have nothing at all to do with the invention and everything to do with a slave's vengeance toward a new master. Tom's device could have been just a decoy," the coroner said grimly.

Markham chuckled. "Maybe Ladybug got all you smart folks to go down the wrong trail, Sheriff." He seemed to relish the thought of the gentry before him being flummoxed by a slave.

"Who was she sold to, Mr. Markham?" asked the sheriff.

"The senator, he didn't say."

"I'll get the plantation journal." Tom rose from his chair. "Maybe the senator made a note about it."

He disappeared into the library and returned with a large ledger. "This is the current year's book."

The sheriff and coroner rose, took the volume, and thumbed through the pages.

"Here's the entry," said the coroner, jabbing his finger on a page. "It was made on the day of Polly's funeral."

Cooper and Nash gathered around the sheriff, the coroner, and Tom to examine the page. The women remained in their seats, looking indignant about the entire discussion. Markham, having no reason to examine a record he couldn't read, was the only man left sitting.

The coroner read aloud the terse entry: *Ladybug, age 19, sold to Fred Fowler of Baton Rouge, $500.*

"That's Wiley's handwriting, all right," remarked Cooper.

The sheriff looked around. "Anyone know Fred Fowler?"

The others shook their heads; none knew the new master who lived thirty miles south of Greenbriar.

"This Fred Fowler was in Bayou Redbird that morning," Cooper remarked. "Maybe he stayed in the area overnight, which gave the slave a chance to write her pass, slip away, and travel just a few miles back here to do her devil's deed." Cooper paused as further thoughts took shape. "If Ladybug then went back to Fowler, and he continued his travels north, maybe that's how she got to dropping the knife at Manning Creek."

The sheriff looked pensive. "There's a whole lot of speculation going on here. None of it resting on anything. We need to question her."

Cooper didn't look at all pensive. "Why fuss about the fine points?" His face looked alarmed as the impact of the new information hit him. "*A slave killed a master!* That's what this comes down to, doesn't it?"

"We can't let her get away!" said Nash.

"She could knock off her new massa too." Markham's voice sounded as though he was disturbed by the prospect, but his face carried a subtle smirk. "That bad apple could give other slaves ideas."

"If she's a troublemaker, she could be emboldened by thinking she got away with her crime. Why, she could start an *insurrection!*" said Nash.

He and Cooper looked as if the fear they kept bottled in the cellar of their minds had suddenly popped out.

"She'll pay for this!" added Cooper.

"Quiet!" ordered the sheriff. "Hold your tongues!" His command had the brief calming effect of cold water splashed on feverish faces. "There's no proof yet at all. Just lots of questions to be asked. Now, let's continue."

He turned to Markham.

"What about the note delivered to Mr. Edmunton the night before the . . . sentence . . . was to be carried out?" The memory of the worst day of his life seemed to shake the sheriff. His voice broke for a moment, then steadied again. "How do you explain that, Mr. Markham, if the slave was in Baton Rouge?"

"Well, Ladybug, she coulda read about the trial in them newspapers they get in Baton Rouge. She coulda got the Yankee's name"—he gestured to Tom—"and wrote him the note. Maybe she got friendly with a free man o' color, or even a white, workin' on the ships that dock at our port and down thar in Baton Rouge. Maybe Ladybug got one o' them to deliver her note."

"That's more speculation," the coroner commented. "Even if she's a vixen who can manipulate a man to do her bidding, why would she take a risk in writing that note? Why would she want to save Mr. Cooper, a planter, from the hangman?"

As he heard that last word, Cooper studied the sheriff as if searching for a hint of weakness that he might use to his advantage later. But the sheriff's face held firm. Any remorse he might have felt seemed to have passed.

"Could we have here a slave with a *conscience?*" the coroner added.

"Maybe a slave with a conscience is no more surprising than the many free folks I've known without one," the sheriff replied. "I'll find out soon enough. I'm going to Baton Rouge."

He walked up to the women sitting on the couch and spoke softly. "Mrs. Barnwell, do you know something about this girl, Ladybug, that you haven't told us?"

"Certainly not!"

"I also know nothing, Sheriff, because there's nothing to know," said Rachel, flashing an angry look at the sheriff.

"I'll have you know I most emphatically resent your insinuations about my husband!" added Charlotte.

The sheriff was unmoved. "When I get back, I'll be paying you a visit, ma'am, so we can talk, just you and me, in private."

"You know what I think, sir? I think you're harassing me," Charlotte said indignantly. "I believe you're *unfit* to be sheriff."

Duran looked startled at the veiled threat from a member of the all-powerful class that ran the town.

"Sheriff, you're upsetting my mother!" Rachel looked around the room for help and turned to an obliging figure. "Isn't there something you can do . . . *Nash*?"

Two faces in the room reacted to the name Rachel uttered. Tom looked resigned to a prospect he had lately come to consider possible. Nash looked delighted at a prospect he had feared was impossible.

"We'll just see, Rachel, dear," Nash said, rushing to the women like a crusading knight. He looked scornfully at the sheriff. "We'll see what can be done about the abuse of power that seems to be occurring."

"A slave killin' a massa! I hear 'bout cases where they kill overseers too," mumbled Markham. "You take guns and whips to bed with you, and it still ain't 'nuff against that trash." He looked around nervously as if expecting an attacker to appear from behind the drapes or beneath a table.

"A slave killing a planter who might be her—" Cooper looked shocked. He glanced at Charlotte and caught himself before uttering the unmentionable.

The coroner too looked apprehensive. "There could be another dimension . . . a personal angle . . . to this case that we hadn't considered."

Duran thought of the others he had investigated: The Barnwell women had an alibi; they were in the company of friends that night, and he had confirmed their story. The inventor had an alibi; servants confirmed he was in his room, where they had delivered pots of tea and fire logs that night. The trails on the other three men—his uncle, Nottingham, and Markham—had led to dead ends. He had run out of other suspects.

"We'd better get this girl," Duran said, looking grim at the thought of picking up a new trail on a case three months old. The clock in the parlor chimed three times. With the mood of the group playing on his nerves, the sounds were magnified in his mind like a warning that time was running out.

"This meeting's adjourned," he said. "I'll ride down to Baton Rouge to find Fred Fowler and bring the girl back to face questioning."

"If she lives long enough to face anything!" Cooper snapped. His words stirred the already turbulent air.

The women rose to leave, their faces grave. Rachel walked up to the sheriff. "Maybe it's best if you *don't* bring her back here at all. This whole matter is unseemly, and I think Mother and I would like to put it behind us."

"It'll be put behind us, Miss Barnwell, as soon as we get to the bottom of it."

"Any public attention about this would be dreadful—*just dreadful!*—for our family. Don't you think we've suffered enough, Sheriff?" Charlotte asked reproachfully.

The sheriff didn't reply. He seemed sympathetic to their desire to avoid a scandal yet unable to assure them that it could be prevented.

"Everyone knows there's only one outcome for a slave who killed my father," Rachel continued coldly. "So what's the difference if we . . . settle . . . the matter there or bring her back here?"

Tom was stunned. "You're asking what's the difference? Between murder and justice?"

"Now whoever said that?" Rachel replied innocently. "Why, I declare, Tom Edmunton, you don't understand us at all!"

"No, I don't!"

"The girl must be *hanged!*" Cooper seized the idea hovering in the air like a ball in play. "We have to send a *clear message* to the rest of the slaves. And the sooner the better."

"Sheriff, you can spare us any further unpleasantness by taking care of the matter *there!*" Rachel repeated. "Maybe Nash can help . . . handle . . . things." Rachel tilted her head down, looking up coquettishly at Nash, the way she used to look at Tom.

Nash hesitated. He smiled to give her hope but stopped short of saying whether he would commit murder on her behalf.

"Now see here, all of you! There will be no talk like this as long as I'm sheriff. I'll bring the girl back. If she proves to be a suspect, she'll be charged and get due process."

"Robbie, you know a slave won't get a jury trial here. A few local slave owners and judges will hear the case and decide it for themselves." Cooper smiled cynically. "They'll all be our friends and people Wiley and I got appointed to the bench."

Among the Southern states, Louisiana was especially harsh toward slaves accused of crimes, providing for special tribunals of judges and slave holders to decide their guilt or innocence rather than giving them a trial by an impartial jury. And the ominous possibility loomed for Judge Lynch to open and adjourn the court, especially when the crime was egregious and stoked the planters' fears of insurrection.

"The outcome has to be what it has to be," Cooper added softly, like a father instructing a son on a difficult matter, "or else the others will get *dangerous* ideas."

The sheriff responded sharply. "We haven't even *questioned* her yet, and you're out for blood. *I'll* handle the matter. And *you* keep out of it."

"Robbie, how you talk to me!" Cooper's face bore the disappointment of a father unaccustomed to being contradicted by a son.

"*All* of you keep out of it."

"Sheriff," said Tom, "this woman may be able to lead me to my invention, which I'm most eager to recover."

"You can be sure we'll question her about that."

"And what if you find his confounded invention, Robbie?" asked Cooper.

"If we locate the device, it'll be returned to its owner."

"No, Sheriff, you mustn't return it!" cried Nash.

"That thing's evidence of sedition. It has to be confiscated, so we can throw the Yankee in jail," said Cooper.

"We'll give him a trial first, just to make it look good," added Nash.

The sheriff stared incredulously at his uncle and Nash.

"Go home!" he ordered. "This meeting's over. Everybody *go home.*"

Tom remained while the others left the parlor. His eyes were distant and his face introspective as he assessed the situation. He felt an isolation beyond the empty room in which he stood. He realized there was no one around him—not even the woman he had loved—who recognized any glory in his invention. The crime now appeared to be related to a slave's revenge against a man she had reason to hate, nothing more complicated. His device, the harbinger of a new age, seemed to be the accidental victim of a dying one.

Would he ever retrieve his machine, and would the new age get *its* fair trial?

# CHAPTER 23

As Tom left the big house, a fragrant whiff of wisteria provided a welcome relief from the stale air of the meeting. In front of him, standing by their carriage, Rachel and Charlotte conversed with Kate Markham. The well-groomed women, the shiny black carriage, and the purple wisteria arching on a bower by the road created a scene of gentility.

Behind the house, a scene of violence was playing out. From the gallery Tom heard the snap of a whip and a victim crying out in pain. He rushed to the back of the porch, where he saw a man who had rearmed himself after the meeting and who lacked the self-control to wait until the guests had left to launch his attack.

"Shut up! Shut up! You good-fer-nothin' snitch!" Furious, Markham towered over Farley.

Tom leaped off the veranda and jumped on Markham. The overseer broke away and in a fit of rage lashed the whip at Tom, leaving a burning slit across his cheek, from which blood trickled down his face. Markham gloated at what he appeared to see as one of the more pleasing moments of his tenure at the Crossroads.

Tom wrestled the whip away from him and gave the overseer two swipes across his knees. Markham fell to the ground, groaning.

The three women rushed to the back of the house to see what the commotion was.

"My God!" gasped Charlotte.

Tom stood with his face swelling where he'd been lashed. He brandished the whip in his hand, hovering over Markham. He could have struck the man repeatedly with it. Instead, he called out Jerome's name, and the slave, who was investigating the operation in the nearby kitchen, heard and walked toward Tom.

"Take Farley away. He's coming home with us."

Farley's shirt had several tears from the lash, but Tom had intervened before the damage was extensive. Jerome put a reassuring arm around Farley's shoulder.

Markham rose to his feet. "Who do you think you are, Yankee? You can't take my field hand!"

"Who do you think *you* are, beating up a man for speaking the truth?" said Tom.

"He ain't no man. He's a slave."

"He spoke the truth, and you lied. If anyone should be whipped, it's *you*."

Now in Tom's protection, Farley apparently felt it safe to look at Markham with dark, shining eyes filled with contempt, too probing for Markham's comfort. "Get back to yer cabin!" he roared.

Farley looked at Jerome. Jerome looked at Tom.

"Get the wagon, Jerome. You and Farley get in. I'll be right there." He took out a handkerchief and wiped the blood from his face.

"That's slave stealin', Yankee. I can shoot you fer that," said Markham.

"Go on, Jerome," said Tom.

Suddenly, Markham reached for his gun. Before the women had time to gasp, Tom snapped the whip over Markham's hand, and the gun dropped.

"Pick up the gun, Jerome," said Tom.

"Yer givin' a slave a gun!" yelped Markham, his wrist beaded with red where the whip sliced it.

Jerome calmly picked up the gun and gave it to Tom. Then he escorted Farley away.

"Tom! Whatever are you doing?" cried Charlotte.

"I'll bring Farley back after Markham is gone."

What do you mean, *gone*?" Charlotte bristled.

Tom turned to Markham. "You're fired! Take the money Barnwell gave you to destroy my invention, and clear out. Now."

"Yer not my boss! Mrs. Barnwell, you see him stealin' yer field hand. I was jus' defendin' yer property. You can't let him get away with this, ma'am." Markham pled his case to the new owner of the Crossroads.

"What on earth do you think you're doing, upsetting us all like this, Tom Edmunton?" Rachel crossed her arms in indignation.

Markham shot a hopeful glance at the young woman.

"I gave the field hand my word that he wouldn't be harmed for speaking the truth." Tom replied.

"You don't have to keep your word to a *slave*," said Rachel.

"But if *he* told *me* the truth, why would my word to him be anything less?"

"The overseer handles the slaves. We don't interfere, and we didn't give you permission to interfere either," Rachel continued, her mother nodding in agreement.

"Don't you care to protect a man who spoke the truth in the case of your father's murder, instead of the man who lied?"

Rachel's eyes flashed angrily. "Let me tell you something, Tom. My father was a kind master. He treated the slaves like his own children. But he knew when punishment was necessary, and he didn't flinch from it. Will you ever be the man that he was?"

"No, I won't."

"You have to stand up to the slaves."

"Do you really think it's a good idea to be at war with your workers—or to treat them like children?"

"That's not how we look at things. Mr. Markham knows how to keep the . . . workers, as you call them . . . in line."

"Your Aunt Polly wouldn't approve of what he did. He has to go, Rachel."

"No."

Tom looked at her in disbelief. "You want him to stay? After he pulled a gun on me?"

"But we can't do without him! Have you forgotten in your arrogance that you and your invention got us into this mess? It ripped my poor father away from his family. And it foiled our plan for Mr. Cooper to buy the Crossroads. You know, Mother has spoken to him since he was released from jail, but he's no longer interested."

"That's correct." Charlotte scolded Tom: "Mr. Cooper isn't buying the Crossroads because *you're* managing it, and he refuses to deal with you."

"You mean he's not buying because I won't give him a loan with no collateral," Tom retorted.

"After you chased away our buyer, you now want to leave us without an overseer too?" Rachel snapped. "After your foolhardiness led to Papa's death, don't you owe us some respect?"

"Rachel, I don't know what killed your father. All I know is he made a deal to kill my invention, and he treated a slave pretty badly, a slave he sold, who might be related—"

"Oh, sweet mercy! What a horrible thing to say!" Rachel's reproaches fell on a man who no longer was weighed down by them, a man whose face now was free of guilt for the death of her father.

Tom turned to Charlotte. "Mrs. Barnwell, I have a capable overseer, Nick Bergen, whose brothers are also overseers. I think one of them is available for hire. He could come here temporarily, and if you like the job he does, he could be your man. If he's half as good as Nick, he'll give you a fine crop. And he'll treat the slaves well too."

"I'm not interested in the least! Mr. Markham will stay. You have no right to fire him against my wishes, no right at all!" replied Charlotte.

"That's true, Mrs. Barnwell, I can't fire Markham, but I can withdraw my loan offer to get you through the growing season."

"What!" yelled Rachel.

"I don't give loans to pay for the likes of Markham."

"Lord in heaven! How could you? That's blackmail, pure and simple!" Charlotte put her hand on her heart, and her eyes rolled to the sky in despair. "Besides, if Mr. Markham leaves, then we'll lose his sister too, and God knows, I haven't a clue how I'd manage without her."

"Miss Markham is certainly welcome to stay. I have no quarrel with her whatsoever." Tom bowed his head graciously to Kate.

"My sister'll stick with her kin. That's how we do things here, Yankee."

"Certainly she'll leave with her brother," Charlotte said to Tom, "after you humiliated and degraded him. If he's fired, she'll go too."

"No, I won't!" uttered Kate.

"What in tarnation, Katy—"

"Hush!" Kate ordered, and the man twice her size was silenced.

Charlotte and Rachel looked astonished.

Kate reassuringly placed her hands on Charlotte's. "Mrs. Barnwell, trust me, you'll be much better off without my brother. The servants were fond of Miss Polly. She treated them kindly." She cocked her head in displeasure toward her brother. "Bret's . . . sort . . . doesn't belong here."

Kate's comforting tone calmed the widow. Charlotte's anger was cooling; she looked thoughtful.

"I'll help Mr. Edmunton and the new overseer get your crop planted, Mrs. Barnwell. Believe me, I can get in the field myself and manage the gangs if I have to," Kate added, her cheerful self-confidence sweeping away Charlotte's desperation.

"As for you, Bret," Kate said sternly, "before Polly Barnwell's even cold in her grave, you're trying to make trouble here! I'll give you the two hundred dollars, and you can clear out before sunset. If you're smart, you'll take it and find another line of work."

She turned to Tom. "The furniture in Bret's cottage belongs to Miss Polly. He came with nothing and will leave with nothing. Only the clothes—and the weapons—are his."

The women were speechless.

Tom smiled. "I guess that settles it."

Charlotte sighed wearily. "Okay, Tom. I'm in too much need of your help and your loan to argue." She turned to the overseer, whose mouth was agape and eyes were bulging in utter dismay. "Mr. Markham, I'm afraid you'll have to leave."

"But . . . but Mrs. Barnwell—"

"The decision is final, sir."

"That ain't right, ma'am!" Markham growled at Charlotte.

The new mistress of the Crossroads silently stood her ground.

Finally, Markham shrugged resignedly, then turned to his sister. "Get yer stuff together. Yer comin' with me."

"No, I'm not! I'm going to stay on here and help Mr. Edmunton and the Barnwells." She turned to Tom. "I'll be sure he clears out before sundown."

"Katy! How could you desert yer own kin?"

"And you can leave Farley with me, Mr. Edmunton. I assure you he *won't* be harmed."

"I'll do that."

Tom trusted the woman who seemed more like his own kin—in sentiment, if not in blood—than like Markham's. He called to Jerome, who was waiting in their wagon at the front entrance. "Bring Farley to Miss Markham."

Farley walked toward Kate, who flashed him a kindly smile. "You stay here with me tonight and help the house servants." That seemed to allay his fears.

Kate turned to her brother and pointed in the direction of his cottage. "Go now. Pack your things. Find a laborer's job that keeps you away from the slaves. You have enough trouble managing yourself, without having to handle them."

Markham walked up to Tom and held out his hand for his gun and whip. Tom appraised him thoughtfully, then decided to give him the weapons.

Markham grabbed them, his eyes filled with hate.

He turned to gape petulantly at Charlotte, giving her a start. "This soil here's been planted with my sweat. You wronged me, ma'am. You done me wrong!"

"Is that a . . . threat . . . Mr. Markham?" Charlotte's voice was reduced to a whisper.

Markham didn't reply. He turned to Tom.

"You don't belong here, Yankee. You're the one should be clearin' out. You're gonna pay fer this."

# CHAPTER 24

Tom returned home with the throbbing cut on his face a constant reminder of his abrasive encounter with Markham. His head throbbed too with the stinging revelations of the day. The man he most admired had betrayed him. The four men who knew about his invention had tried to destroy it. A man who had spoken the truth was lashed for it. A woman who might have information about his tractor was in danger of being lynched. And the woman he thought he loved had sided against him.

There wasn't any noble ally who had given his life to save the invention. Apparently, there wasn't even an astute, albeit perverted, thief who had grasped the promise of the tractor and committed murder to attain it. It seemed there was only a badly treated slave who sought revenge. Tom now knew that everyone in his circle was against him. The realization was like a blanket of gloom smothering him in loneliness.

What could he do to shake off this intrusion choking his spirit? he wondered. With his invention missing and his work halted, how could he breathe fresh life into his dream?

He sat down to a late-afternoon tea prepared by Jerome's budding apprentice, Brook. Still reeling from the day's events, however, he found he had little appetite. After half a cup of tea and a few morsels of cake, he headed outside to see what the slaves had been doing in his absence. Passing the open door of the library, he saw Solo at the desk. He recognized the latest agricultural journal in her hands. As was her habit, she had turned it to the back page of advertisements, where rewards were posted for runaways. He paused to observe the woman who had shared nothing about herself with him.

She no longer scurried away when he spotted her in the library, as if she had no right to be there. Now she looked at him calmly from what had become her classroom. Her expression instantly turned to shock when she saw the lash across his cheek, but he volunteered no comment on it.

Seeing her with the journal, he thought of his own fruitless hunt for his invention and wondered if she too were engaged in a painful search. "It's sad to be looking for something without any luck, isn't it?"

She nodded solemnly as if she understood how that felt.

He pointed to the journal. "Can I help you find . . . someone . . . you're looking for?"

She suddenly seemed uneasy. "No," she whispered, offering nothing more.

The curls of her hair formed an ornate rosewood frame around the oval cameo of her face. Her strange mix of mystery and beauty held him for a moment, then he continued on his way out the door.

He walked past the areas where the slaves under his direct supervision worked, his steps quickening with a growing anger as he observed their work product. In what had been his mother's prized English garden he saw weeds two feet high. In the tack shed he saw costly saddles haphazardly strewn on the floor instead of hung on the racks, with the corner of one chewed away by a mouse. In the stable he saw unkempt stalls and thirsty horses. At the equipment shed he saw a harrow and plow needing repair, the same as they did a week ago, with no progress made.

He sighed, weary of the shoddy work that seemed as much a feature of the dying age as a withered body was of a dying person. The lack of choice, interest, payment, and reward for their work, he thought, shut down the engine within his slaves. Neither Markham's use of the whip nor his own restraint from it could make that motor run. It required its own will as its fuel, he thought.

Yet there were ways in which some of his people were getting better results than he was. Solo's school had helped improve her students' work because their tasks had to be completed properly as the condition of entry to class. And attending of their own choosing spurred them to do well with their lessons. The slaves working under Jerome's watch had also become more industrious. The vegetable garden, ice house, storage room, hen house, barn, and other areas that the new chef supervised were remarkably well tended. What was Jerome's secret? Tom wondered.

It was the Sunday in May when the slaves were given materials to make their summer clothing. He saw his weaver, Kitty, and her assistants setting up fabrics on a table outside the big house where he would distribute the rations. The women carried rolls of fabric in their voluminous aprons, with the folds of their dresses swaying as they trudged along, their spirits as subdued as the pale-colored cottons they held.

At the fabric table, Tom surveyed the rolls of homespun, calico print, and a somewhat finer cotton called plains. There were also small bundles of needles, buttons, and threads ready for the slaves to take.

Paying little attention to customs like this, which had long been established by his father, he depended on the people who received the rations to guide him in giving them. "Kitty, how did we do this last time?"

"Mr. Tom, you given four white roll, two blue, an' two brown fer Ida and Adam, and they take two small roll fer little Timmy. You given four small roll to Lavinia fer Lily and Carl, four brown and four white large to Lottie and Helen. Same four white, two blue, two brown fer Murphy and Terina, wid four small roll fer Becky and Jeb. That the homespun, sir. Fer the calico—"

"Hold on, Kitty," he said, exasperated. "Can't they just work this out for themselves?"

"Why no, sir!" Kitty looked shocked at the thought. "Yer daddy, the colonel, he have his rules." Sternly, she pointed to the fabrics as she educated Tom. "Two white homespun and two blue fer shirts and trousers fer the men. Two white homespun and two brown fer women work dresses. One calico print fer Sunday frock and cotton plains fer men Sunday meetin' shirts and pants. Chillun gets half."

The slaves were milling around, waiting for Tom to figure things out. The man who had assembled the systems of the internal combustion tractor seemed bewildered by homespun and calico.

"All right, let's get this over with," he said.

As he doled out the rations, he observed the slaves walking to the table. The prospect of making low-grade clothing that looked the same as everyone else's gave their procession all the joy of a funeral march.

The first to approach him, Sherman, routinely neglected his work, while Ben, behind him in line, did a fine job. Yet they were both getting the same rolls for their shirts and trousers. Toya, who found constant excuses to take sick days and fall behind in her tasks, and Caroline, who never missed work and always finished on time, were both getting the same material for their frocks. Was it fair to deny his workers their due as individuals? he wondered.

After his cheerless task was done, Tom heard chatter behind the house and walked around to investigate. He saw the lanky figure of Jerome, imposingly tall in his chef's hat, distributing clothing rations to the slaves under his supervision. But Jerome's fabrics were causing quite a stir. He had a variety of fabrics spread out over two tables, with a long line of slaves eager to get at them. Curious, Tom approached.

The slaves were counting brown-colored, oval objects they had in their hands. Looking closer, Tom observed that these objects, the size of grapes, were dried cocoa beans, and a sack of them sat at Jerome's feet.

Tom remembered when Jerome, who was as curious as a scientist about anything related to chocolate, had purchased the sack of beans, which the town's general store had gotten for him. He tried roasting and grinding them himself to see if that would enhance the flavor of the chocolate. The manual process, however, proved too arduous and yielded a gritty product inferior to the velvety texture and rich taste of the manufactured chocolate. So Jerome was left with a sack of the beans. Now he'd evidently found a use in circulating them among the slaves.

Intrigued, Tom watched the proceedings. Jerome stood in front of the tables, directing his assistants in spreading out the fabrics and sewing accessories. Solo too was there, placing paper signs by the various fabrics that read *one bean, two beans, three beans,* or *four beans.*

"Okay, you good-fer-nothin's. C'mon up!" Jerome shouted.

The slaves in the front of the line approached the tables, inspected the merchandise, chose the fabrics they wanted, then paid Jerome the required beans for them. When they left, another wave followed.

Jerome displayed the usual white, pale blue, and brown homespun, as well as calico and plains on one table. But the real attraction was in the rich colors and textures of the items on the other table: velvet ribbons for dress trimmings and hair ornaments; lace for shawls and ruffles; soft muslin for finer clothing; silk for neckties; satin for vests; and sewing patterns for elegant dresses, men's clothing, and accessories. Although these materials were limited in quantity to what would serve as luxury items for the slaves, the fabrics themselves were of the same fine quality as those worn by a planter's family. The slaves eagerly searched through bold greens, vibrant reds, rich pinks, and lively prints. They rubbed smooth velvet against their cheeks and stroked shiny satin with their hands. Women held fabrics against themselves for their men to see, and the men expressed their approval. One man placed a blue silk up to his neck, and his wife shaped it into a cravat. An older woman marveled over a piece of black lace, wrapped it around her shoulders like a shawl, and lifted her head like a duchess.

A teenage girl draped a strip of velvet across her shoulders, shaping the neckline for a dress. "Look, Mama, look!" she called excitedly. Another woman wrapped white satin around her head and tied it in a bow under her chin, like the trimming for a bonnet. A man held a piece of blue muslin across his chest, measuring out a shirt to be made. Observing the slaves going through the line, Tom was struck by their enchantment with the fabrics.

Everyone seemed to understand the system except him. The slaves used various numbers of beans to pay for the fabrics, depending on how much they took and how costly their chosen materials were.

One man, Tom noticed, hardly bought anything. He chose a couple of homespun rolls along with cotton plains to make a few shirts and trousers. He had beans remaining in his hand, which he fondled like doubloons. He presented them to Solo, and she gave him a card that said simply: *day off.* The man presented the card to Jerome, who took out a pencil and ceremoniously signed the card as if it were a king's proclamation.

No one assigned fabrics to the slaves. They simply took what they wanted and paid for it with their beans. Families returned to their cabins with their materials, pleased with their choices and eager to make their clothing.

Had Jerome gone mad? Tom wondered, surveying the fine merchandise. How much was this costing? Jerome hadn't asked for or received any money to do this. What was he doing?

As the last of the slaves made their selections, Tom approached the table. "Jerome, explain to me what's going on here."

"Why, Mr. Tom, Jerome can't have lazy good-fer-nothins' like who work fer you. Jerome got his kitchen an' chocolate bizness to run. Jerome had to do somethin' else than yer doin'."

"What did you do?"

"I start out with food rations. 'Do one day work,' I tell the wastrels, 'and get yerself one cocoa bean.' That bean give 'em food rations fer one day. They can leave their work anytime after they done their task for the day. When I say that, sir, well, some of 'em up and finish their task at noon. Lordy, I think to myself, *noon*. So then I tell 'em, 'Do two days' tasks in one and get yer food rations fer two days and next day off.' So, some of 'em do that."

"Really?" Tom pondered the matter. "And what about the clothing rations?"

"Few weeks ago, with the clothing ration comin' up, I say, 'Do one day task and get one bean for one day food ration *and* another bean for yer fabric. Do more work, make extry stuff I can sell, an' get more beans for finer threads for some real nice clothes. You can have it, brother,' I tell 'em."

"And where did you get money to shop at Greenbriar's finest fabric shop?"

"From the surplus they're makin', sir. They get time off if they finish their task early. Some o' them been pickin' berries, huntin', fishin', diggin' up vegetables, makin' baskets and the like in their extry time from finishin' their task early. I give 'em cocoa beans for their stuff, then I sell it in town, and buy the fabric."

"You mean this isn't costing me anything more than before?"

"Why, no sir. The extry stuff comes from theirselves and their own work."

"But you must be working them to death, Jerome. If they're gardening, hunting, and basket weaving, in addition to their assigned tasks, why then—"

"Oh, no, sir. They ain't workin' no ways near to their death, Mr. Tom. They're jus' doin' less chatterin', less day dreamin', less sleepin', less mopin' on the job."

"And you're somehow making money on this venture, I assume?"

Jerome smiled. "Somebody gotta sell their stuff in town, sir. Jerome, why, he be their agent."

Tom eyed one of the slaves lingering at the table. She held a piece of muslin across her figure. Unlike the dull colors of their normal clothing, the fabric was dyed. Its brilliant pink color seemed to shout out to the woman, daring her to wear it.

The slave showed the fabric to her teacher, standing nearby. "I remember the story you read, Miss Solo. The one 'bout the princess. She had a dress made of muslin!"

"I think it was pink too, just as yours will be," Solo said, embellishing.

The woman spontaneously hugged her teacher, then she paid Jerome for her fabric and walked away, the pink cloth spread across her arms.

Watching her saunter, almost dancing with the fabric, Tom was fascinated.

He turned to look at Solo. The coarse cotton of her homespun frock was a jarring contrast to the smooth sheen of her bronze skin. His imagination strayed from his guard to envision the comely figure before him in a daring silk dress, with wild hair tumbling over bare shoulders.

"Where are *your* beans?" he asked.

"I don't have any."

"Why not? Why can't *you* have a nice dress too?"

"Because I work for you."

He recalled her standing in his line earlier, taking her homespun from Kitty with all the eagerness of getting a bottle of tonic to cure ringworm. Suddenly, he laughed. It was the hearty laugh of someone who had just found the answer to a problem perplexing him.

She seemed drawn to the first sustained laughter she had ever heard from him. She studied his face, and the smile that formed on hers seemed involuntary.

"That's it! That's what I can do!"

"What?" She looked confused.

"I can give you cocoa beans! I can give you *all* cocoa beans!"

He felt the heavy gloom lifting from his spirit. He sprinted to the stone tower that held the plantation bell. He pulled the cord, and the gong rang through the fields. The bell was like his cry of rebellion against the people from the dying world who wanted to pull him down. *No! No!* the resonating tone of the great bell seemed to announce. He wasn't going down.

As the slaves gathered in the grassy field in front of the big house and garden, wondering why they were being summoned, they saw their young master laughing as he rang the bell, as happy as if calling them to a wedding.

Standing before the growing group of slaves sitting in the field, he felt like a conductor ready to lead his players in a new score; their theme would be *man's* engine. Jerome had shown the way to spark the imaginations and productive energies of those who were plodding along, forgotten in the dying age.

Tom saw a simple truth in Jerome's experiences with the chocolate squares and the slaves' rations, which had awakened the cook's own energies and those of others. A man's work can't be separated from his choice to perform it or from the fruits of his labor. The dying age separates him from both and shuts him down. Once his will, his actions, and their rewards are reunited under his control, then he's a master of himself, and the results are amazing.

The slaves coming to hear Tom sat on the grass, leaned against the tree trunks, and sprawled across the dirt paths, with the setting sun painting a gold glaze on their faces.

Overseer Nick Bergen appeared from the direction of his cottage. He walked toward Tom with a bounce in his step, as if eager for his next task. His honest face and competent manner suggested that the job of driving gangs of men through fields of cotton was an intelligent trade when an intelligent man did it.

Tom took Nick aside to explain his intentions. The immigrant farmer, who shared Tom's disdain for forced labor, nodded his approval as the young inventor spoke of his plans. The men talked animatedly, smiled in mutual respect, and shook hands.

Then Tom faced the group. The mumbling in the crowd stopped as they turned their attention to the tall, trim man with the bright yellow hair.

"I called you here because I want to tell you that there's a new age coming, and things are going to be different than they were before. In the new age, each and every one of us is a master." He pointed to a few of them. "You, Henry, you're a master. And you, Violet, you're a master." He swept his hands across the crowd. "*All* of you are masters."

The slaves looked at one another, baffled. Had their master gone mad?

"In the new age, we're all masters of only one person, and that person is ourselves."

Tom paced before the group. Behind him, the big house and the gangly oaks with their swaying moss were like the background of a painting in which the artist would create a world to his liking. Could Tom do the same?

"Because each of you is master of yourself, you're all different from one another. You shouldn't all have to wear the same clothes or eat the same food or live in the same kind of cabin or have the same things in your house. You should have what you want as individual, separate people. And you should decide for yourselves. It shouldn't come from me. You should all wear the clothing you want, eat the food you want, grow whatever you want in your gardens, and for goodness' sake, marry whoever you want. Those decisions should be *yours* to make. That's what it means to be master of yourself."

More than one hundred pairs of eyes followed him as he paced. Separate from the throng that were sitting, three people were standing near him like allies: Solo, Jerome, and Nick.

"Now, if you were really masters of yourselves, you could choose the type of work you want to do and be paid for it. You could decide whether you want to work for me, or work for someone else, or save your money and buy a farm or a shop of your own and work for yourselves. That's not possible because the new age hasn't arrived yet. Right now, we're glued together, you and me, on this farm. We can't change that, but we can still get around it some.

"For instance, we see that a task that you need to do in a day, if you put your mind to it, can actually be completed in less than a day, sometimes in much less than a day when you really work hard. Jerome did an experiment, and he discovered this."

Tom saw Jerome smile at the mention of his name.

"I want to apply this experiment to *all* of you. I want to take a day's task for each of you and make a rule that when you finish it and finish it properly, you've done your work for the day and you're through. Then you can have the rest of the day to yourselves. You can relax or socialize or work for yourselves. I want to be sure all of the tasks we assign are reasonable, so you can complete them and still have time to spare.

"Maybe in your free time, you'll want to grow your own vegetables or raise your own hogs or chickens or do wood carvings or weave baskets, and then sell your products in town. We have some of that going on now, but with the new system, we can have more of it. Maybe some of you will want to start your own business like Jerome did with his chocolate squares."

Jerome's smile broadened with pride.

"You see, Jerome pretty much is his own master. Do you know why?"

The group silently waited for the answer.

"Because he has the same thing any master has, the thing that makes him a master, and that's his *intelligence*." Tom looked at the silent figures watching him, wondering if they understood. "None of you needs any other master than that. You have inside you the one thing that makes you master of yourself."

The sun glowed on Solo, who listened intently.

"In the new age, you'll get to use your intelligence." The breeze sent strands of Tom's blond hair dancing in the air like a lively fire. "And right now, we can adopt new ways to start us on that path."

His audience remained still. Perhaps from habit or distrust, or simply from bewilderment, their faces revealed nothing to their master.

"Here's how these new ways will work. You'll get cocoa beans for completing your tasks. And we'll open a plantation store with food, clothing, and other things you need and want to have. Then you can use your beans to buy whatever you want in that store. The more work you do, the more beans you get, and the more you can buy. If you prefer to have time off, you can buy that too with your beans. Later on, I think we can convert your beans into real money. Then you can go to town, if you want to, and buy things we don't keep in our store."

Tom glanced at Nick, who smiled in agreement with the plan.

"Cocoa beans are the key to the new way. Cocoa beans mean that I no longer can take your work for nothing. I have to pay you for it. Cocoa beans also mean that you no longer can avoid your work and get the same provisions you would if you had done it properly. Cocoa beans mean I can't take advantage of you and you can't take advantage of me. And they mean you can spend your earnings as you please, not as I determine. You control the beans you get and how you spend them. That's how you start to become masters of yourselves."

Tom turned to the young teacher, whom he had heard expressing a similar theme in her lessons. In their odd way of relating to each other, in which the boundaries of master and slave had blurred, he shot a questioning glance at her as if to ask how he was doing, and she shot back a nod of approval.

"Like a carpenter or a gardener needs tools, a person who's master of himself needs tools too. And an important tool that you need is *education*. I'll supply that to you, if you want it. I think you all know by now that we started a little school here, which is our own special secret."

Like explorers on a new terrain who were encountering an unfamiliar life form, the group studied him cautiously.

"I'll pay your teacher in cocoa beans for every class she holds."

He politely bowed his head to Solo, and she returned the courtesy.

"Does anyone want to say something?" Everyone remained quiet. What were they thinking? he wondered. "Are there any questions?" There were none. Tom waited in the awkward silence.

Then Solo stepped forward. "May I try?" she asked.

"Go ahead."

"I'm speaking to the students in my class." Like a birdcall that could be heard over long distances, Solo's voice resonated. "You sure do a lot of talking during your lessons. Too much!" Some of them grinned. "Let's hear from you now. . . . Come on." She waited. No one stood up.

Jerome stepped forward to employ his own manner of calling for volunteers. He pointed to his apprentice. "You. Get up!"

Brook, a hardworking young man whom Jerome had drafted from tending the kitchen garden to cooking, obligingly rose to his feet, his face part fearful, part smiling. "Mr. Tom, when I's a master o' myself, kin I go inta town a lot, like Jerome do?"

"If you do your work here, and if you're law-abiding when you're in town, why not go whenever you want to, like Jerome does? I'll sign the passes." Tom smiled. "You see, here's the thing that interests me. I need to produce the cotton crop, so I need your jobs to be done. But outside of that, who am I to regulate your lives, to arrange your affairs for you, to restrict your own inclinations? That's all your business. When you're masters of yourselves, that sets *me* free too."

Brook sat back down on the grass; he looked incredulous as he tried to absorb a message that was as simple as it was unbelievable in that time and place.

Another man stood up tentatively. It was someone who had recently joined Solo's class. "Mr. Tom, I hear there's slave musicians who play fo' massas' parties on their plantations." The speaker was part of a talented slave trio that played banjo, drums, and mandolin at social gatherings of the slaves on the plantation. "Can me, Frank, an' Boone hire ourselfs out fo' playin' at them parties?"

"Why, yes. I can post a notice in town that I have for hire a trio of musicians."

The questioner smiled with pride at the last word being applied to him.

"You can keep what you make from any jobs you get. If you need to buy new instruments or supplies, that comes out of your earnings as the cost of doing business. Being masters of yourselves mean you keep the rewards, but you also pay the costs."

The speaker's hesitation had changed to eagerness. He reached out to tap the shoulder of one of the other musicians, sitting near him. "You hear?" he said. His friend smiled, looking interested.

"And if you want to be invited back, you'll bring your *manners* along with your music to those plantations," Solo added sternly. The speaker nodded respectfully to his teacher as he sat down.

The sun had vanished behind the trees. In the deepening blue of twilight, a lone figure stood up at the back of the group. It was a field hand who had mustered the courage to speak.

"Sir, kin us maybe has our own plots to plant a little cotton? There be bare land a-sittin' out there, sir." He pointed in the direction of a stretch of uncultivated land still remaining on the property.

"What do you think, Nick?" Tom turned to his overseer.

The obliging Nick nodded his head. "Can be done."

The questioner looked stunned by the consideration his idea was getting.

In his deep German accent, Nick added: "Those of you who want to take more work, I assign plot that you cultivate for yourself. I arrange for field hands who want own plot to work together in same gang, so you can go fast and finish task early to take advantage of new opportunity."

Tom added, "Just plant a good crop for me, and you can have your own plot and keep the money you make from it."

A ripple of excitement stirred through the crowd. After a lifetime of servitude, their spirit had not been killed, Tom thought. Lying dormant and now being jostled to awaken was the remarkable sleeping giant of personal enterprise.

Tom had a further thought: "And you can use your profits to buy materials to build additions on your cabins."

This possibility—beyond their wildest dreams—caused an outburst, and the slaves chatted among themselves until Jerome hushed them so that the meeting could continue.

From the middle of the group, someone rose to speak. It was a shy woman who worked in the fields. Tom and the others strained to hear her timid voice. "I likes to ask iffen I kin go to them classes goin' on in the big house."

Tom looked at Solo to respond. The teacher nodded to acknowledge the would-be student. "Who else wants to take classes? Stand up so I can see you."

Solo's sinewy body and wild hair looked primal, while her voice, with its proper diction and grammar, was pure intelligence. She waited, but no one else rose to join the lone woman standing.

"If you want to be the master of your own music, and the master of your own cotton, and the master of your own comings and goings, you first need to be the master of your own *thinking*. That's what learning does for you. It teaches you how to think for yourself. And it gives you *knowledge,* so you can take care of yourself. Now, how many of you want to take classes? Stand up."

Two others rose to join the woman standing. There was what seemed like a long pause, and Tom wondered if any more would rise. Then four more joined them. Then there were ten. Like spring bulbs growing strong enough to break through the surface, twenty standing slaves soon sprouted across the field.

With the help of his cane, a gray-haired man with bad knees struggled to rise. Two teenage slaves standing nearby assisted so that he could stand with them to request an education.

Some of the ones who were standing reached down to prod their friends and family to join them. More figures rose to stand like silhouettes against the twilight-blue sky. Soon, so many were giving their silent standing ovation to learning that the ones still sitting seemed out of place, so they stood too. Many looked hopeful, others looked scared, and some looked cynical. But in the end, they *all* stood up to be counted.

Tom looked astonished.

Solo looked energized. She spoke to Tom in the optimistic tone of someone eager for a new challenge and already analyzing how to tackle it. "It can be done. I can move the house servants' classes to the early morning, then teach the field hands in sessions in the late afternoon and evening."

Tom nodded. Then he assured the group, "We'll hold classes for everyone who wants to learn." Silently, he resolved to build them a new, hidden classroom to keep secret what was becoming a formal school. "We'll work out a plan for everything we discussed tonight."

He turned to Solo. "It appears you'll be getting a lot of cocoa beans."

She flashed one of her rare smiles, and the moment seemed to him more like daybreak than dusk.

\* \* \* \* \*

A few hours later, the candles were extinguished in the cabins, and the slaves had retired for the night. With the stars shining like medals pinned on the clear sky, and the night creatures giving the woods its symphony, there were only three lights still glowing at Indigo Springs.

Jerome's light was burning in the kitchen behind the big house. The man who ran Tom's kitchen, supervised various servants, and operated his own chocolate business frequently worked at night. Especially after he had been away from the plantation during the day, he made up missed chores, prepared chocolate squares for customers, or read from his primer long after the others had gone to sleep. That night, after Tom's talk to the slaves, Jerome was in the kitchen, but this time he was thinking about his future.

Solo's light was burning in the library. She spent many nights in the room with the dusty volumes that were her cherished companions. They were the sages that took her on journeys through history, the explorers that showed her the people and places beyond her sight, and the poets that invited her into their fantasies. That night she was reading a book of short stories to select one to present to her class.

The third light was Tom's. It burned in the workshop on the hill. That night he had felt an eagerness to continue his work that he hadn't experienced since the time of the murder. After the day's revelations at the Crossroads, he felt strangely free of the guilt that had shadowed him since Barnwell's death. After his evening talk with the slaves, he also felt free of any allegiance to the precepts of farming imposed on him by his father, Barnwell, and the others. With the new work system at Indigo Springs, he would run *his* farm *his* way.

With his dejection gone, he had felt almost lightheaded entering his workshop for the first time in three months. Regardless of whether Sheriff Duran's new suspect in Baton Rouge, Ladybug, would lead to the recovery of his invention, he was now ready to move on with his work, building a new prototype if he must.

He glanced over the shelves and worktable of the orderly cabin that looked like a machine shop. Everything was as he had left it. There were the notebooks recording his experiments and ideas, the texts on mechanics frayed from heavy use, and the numerous articles on the latest advances in machine power. There was the first gas-powered motor he had ever made: a mere flywheel, a belt, and a fuel reservoir on a wood board.

There were extra parts remaining from his tractor's assembly: a few valves left over from the ones he had painstakingly adapted from a steam engine for use in his engine block, a scrap from a steam engine's exhaust pipe that he had adapted to form his cylinders, and two pistons made of iron. There was a crankshaft made in a plant in Baton Rouge that he had used to fabricate various components of his device to his specifications.

On his worktable he saw the experiment with electricity that he had been conducting before leaving for his trip. He needed a better ignition system. What was the best way to deliver a spark to ignite the gasoline and start the engine? He was trying to find out. He sat down and began working on the experiment as if he had just left it yesterday. . . .

After a while, Jerome extinguished his light in the kitchen; his white hat could be seen moving in the darkness as he walked back to his cabin.

Solo fell asleep reading in the library; her light remained on, its reflections bouncing off the red-brown tangle of hair that covered the desk.

The big house looked peaceful in the darkness, with its mossy oak branches brushing the roof and its one soft light visible beyond the closed drapery in the library.

Suddenly a stranger appeared, breaking the serenity of the night. He rode up to the big house on horseback, carrying a burning torch. He stopped directly outside the lighted room.

The trespasser was a man who had been chastised, humiliated, fired, and cast out like a vagabond that day. His sister had verbally boxed his ears in front of the others. Then a man had taken his life and twisted it like the neck of a chicken. That man was behind the curtain in the room he now faced. He had hated men like that his entire life, men who had book learning, who had money, who spoke fancy, who flaunted their silly manners, who thumbed their noses at him and made him feel small. That day everybody thought he'd been beaten. But he hadn't, he thought, sneering, his breath reeking of alcohol.

Before tonight, the hatred he had always felt for men like Tom was something he had to hold in check. There was always somebody around that stopped him from expressing his most urgent impulses—first there was his mother, then his sister, then Miss Polly. That day, after the others had left their meeting, his sister hovered over him like an angry hen. He couldn't even whack a few of the worthless slaves. That would've made him feel better, stronger, on top of things again. That would've calmed him like a tonic. He tried another remedy, this one from a bottle. But that didn't stop the rage building inside him, ready to explode. In fact, it stoked the fury he couldn't contain and wanted so much to let loose.

That night he needed another cure. They wanted him to be beaten, to stay beaten, and to just swallow it. Well, tonight they'd know he was no patsy. Tonight he'd get respect. Tonight he'd do what he was itching to do. Tonight the bastard behind that curtain who dared to smash him would get *his*.

He leaned over the gallery and with a sweep of his arm tossed the lighted torch inside the open window. Then he whirled his horse around and galloped down the road.

The torch landed on the floor where it caught on the drapes. Soon the flames rose to the windowsill. The breeze blew the sparks against a bookcase. There the growing menace found a feast to devour in the books. With a crackling that was merely a whisper, insufficient yet to announce its fearful presence, the blaze proceeded unchecked in its voracious path to strike, to spread, to engulf everything. Within moments, it transformed the learned words of centuries into a raging wall of flames—while the young teacher slept.

# CHAPTER 25

On that clear night, with the moonlight blinking between the trees, Tom finished his experiment, closed his workshop, and headed home on his horse. As he was turning onto the path up to the big house, he nearly collided with a man on horseback careening down the road. Tom's horse reared, almost throwing him. In a flash of moonlight, he saw a face of pure hatred: Markham! The overseer galloped away, leaving a dust storm and the stench of alcohol behind him.

Suddenly, Tom saw smoke billowing from the direction of the big house and heard a woman scream. He dug his heels into the horse and raced up the road. The only person in the house at that hour would be its other resident, who slept in the tutor's room and lived in the library: *Solo!*

He reached the end of the road and gasped. His house was a fireball blazing in the gray night, with flames shooting out the library windows and smoke clouds funneling into the sky. The blinding flames, the choking fumes, and the desperate screams of a trapped woman catapulted him into action.

He leaped off his horse and jumped onto the gallery. Then he pushed open the front door. He ran down the smoke-filled hallway to the library door, where red flames curled like serpents' tongues around the frame, daring him to approach. His blond hair turned a sooty gray, his eyes burned with smoke, and his face smarted from the intensifying heat by the time he reached the door. A molten beam fell, barely missing him as he rushed into the inferno.

Inside the library the fire raged. The furniture burned, and scorched ceiling beams caved inward, threatening to collapse. At the far end of the room he saw the source of the screams. Solo, half hidden by the smoke and half spotlighted by the flames, was trapped. Behind her, the windows were blocked by white sheets of burning drapery. Bookcases to the sides of her were aflame, as was the desk in front. Encircled with hellfire, she looked like a woman being burned at the stake. She tried to grab a clear edge of the desk to push it out of her way, but the crackling fire quickly spread to her spot and her hands reflexively shot away from the sting of the heat. Tom veered clear of a shaking chandelier to approach her.

"Tom! Tom!" she exclaimed, choking, searching for an opening in the flames to reach him.

"Look out!" he shouted, pointing to her side, where a bookcase came crashing down. She moved away from it in time. The burning books tumbled out, turning the words of centuries into dozens of little torches spilling onto the carpet, igniting new fires along the floor. Tom saw her small figure trapped behind the growing wall of flames closing in on her.

He moved back toward the door, where he found a table still untouched by fire, draped with a tablecloth, with a lamp and flower vase sitting unharmed on top. In one swift pull, he grabbed the tablecloth, sending the lamp and vase crashing to the floor, adding to the commotion. He returned to Solo and used the bunched cloth to smother the fire on a corner of the desk. Then he gripped the heavy piece with the cloth and flipped it over. It crashed against the wall, making a temporary pathway free of flames under it. Solo ran through the clear patch of floor into his arms. They rushed to the door, racing against flames that were spreading across the ceiling in the same direction. The flames prevailed, and the door frame collapsed in front of them. Their exit was now blocked.

Tom looked around, frantically wondering what to do next. There were no windows clear of the flames. He saw he could reach the stone fireplace, and rushed toward it. Coughing, choking, trying to keep his bearings in the thickening smoke, he grabbed an andiron and smashed it repeatedly against a wall. He made a hole, then kicked it out, widening it to give them passage into the hallway.

"Watch out!" She gasped, pointing to the ceiling.

Fire-eaten ceiling beams gave way and fell near them. He covered her head with his arms. The chandelier came crashing down, shattering across the floor, sending glass shards flying into the mix of smoke, flames, and heat. A ceiling beam grazed Solo's shoulder, setting her sleeve on fire. Tom knocked the beam away, then hit Solo's sleeve repeatedly with his hand to choke the flames. He picked her up and pushed her through the opening in the wall; then he leaped out after her. The two of them raced down the hallway. Weakened by the effects of the fire and smoke, choking and staggering, she fell. He picked her up and carried her to the back door of the house.

In the heavy smoke, they met a man who was charging in.

"Get out! Get out, Jerome! We're okay," Tom ordered.

Seeing that the home's residents were headed for safety, Jerome turned and exited with them. He ran to the plantation bell to summon the other slaves.

Tom rolled over on the ground with Solo, stifling the patches of smoldering flames on the two of them. He was on top of her when they stopped rolling. His eyes searched her smoke-covered dress, her hair entangled with debris, and the surface burns on her arms. "Are you okay?" He stroked her hair and stared into her eyes, waiting for reassurance.

"Yes." With her arms around his neck, and with her brilliant eyes and white teeth the only shining spots on a face covered with soot, she smiled at him.

He slid his arms around her waist, buried his face in her neck, and held her close. Feeling her supple body, he sighed in immense relief from the still-vivid image of her caught in the flames and the dread that he would lose her. He raised his head, and their eyes locked for a moment.

She began coughing. He picked her up and carried her away from the smoke, putting her down on the grass near the pond.

They caught sight of the wiry figure of Jerome. He had summoned the slaves, along with the store of lightweight leather buckets kept in the tanner's shed specifically for use in a fire. Jerome was forming a bucket brigade. Tom and Solo saw him lining up men from the pond to the house to haul a stream of buckets onto the fire. Jerome was also forming another line, of women and boys next to the men, to pass the empty pails from the house back to the pond for refilling.

Tom's eyes, two blue beacons on a smoke-covered face, watched intently the procedure Jerome was organizing to save the house.

Solo read his thoughts. "Go. I'm all right," she assured him.

He observed her condition. Her voice was weak and hoarse, she coughed intermittently, and she had a few superficial burns. She needed to rest and clear her lungs of smoke, he figured, but otherwise she looked unscathed. "You'll be okay?"

"Go!"

"Stay out of the smoke and rest." In a flash, he was gone.

Battling his own coughing, he joined the growing group of slaves by the house.

Like the captain of a distressed ship, soaked to the waist in water, with a shirt still unbuttoned in his haste to respond to the emergency, Jerome moved about from the pond to the house, until everything was set. Then he positioned himself last in the line to receive the buckets, and he directed the water onto the flames. As he threw bucket after bucket on the fire, he continued to monitor the human assembly line and give orders to new slaves arriving. He summoned one: "Git more buckets. Git every last one o' them— outta the stable, outta the barn, outta the well house, outta the kitchen. Go!"

He summoned another one: "Git lanterns; we need light here. Go!" He turned to another slave: "Git—" Just then Tom approached, and Jerome abruptly stopped speaking, deferring to his master. "Oh, 'scuse me, sir."

"You're doing fine, Jerome. Continue."

Jerome looked curiously at Tom, then smiled and resumed. "Git the ladder from the stable. Go git it, quick!"

Soon, more buckets appeared for the brigade and lanterns dotted the landscape. The ladder came, and Tom climbed up to douse the flames on the roof. Jerome forked off part of the brigade to supply Tom.

Hearing the bell and seeing the smoke, Nick and the field hands came running. They brought another stack of fire buckets from their area. Nick organized his slaves into a second brigade and joined Jerome and Tom at the house.

* * * * *

The prodigious efforts of the people of Indigo Springs proved fruitful. Before long, the flames were extinguished, and the smoke clouds drifted away from the house. The relentless rumble of the advancing flames and the frenzied sounds of the people fighting it were now still. The library was significantly damaged, but the rest of the house was saved.

Despite Tom's admonition to stay clear of the smoke, Solo joined him and the others to peer at the damage. The library was a disaster of fallen planks, smoldering debris, a partially caved-in ceiling, blackened carpeting, and singed furniture. Books charred to varying degrees were scattered everywhere. Those items that had escaped the fire were covered with soot. Everything was doused with water.

The slaves from the brigades approached. Soaked from standing in the pond and exhausted from hauling the buckets, they silently took in the scene. Tom had never seen the slaves push themselves with so much drive. He stood with the charred remains of the library behind him and the bedraggled, muddied slaves before him, and he smiled at their victory.

"I've never seen a finer bucket brigade anywhere," he told them. "I've never seen a finer bunch of firefighters than right here."

The slaves stood before him, some without shirts or shoes in their haste to come and help. Their bodies looked spent, but their spirits seemed lifted by his words and their deed; they looked as proud as if they were wearing the imposing uniforms and shiny hats of a true fire regiment.

"This house is still standing thanks to the extraordinary efforts of all of you." He looked at the group with heartfelt gratitude. They seemed to sense it and smiled in response. "Jerome, I think some rum is in order."

That brought a wild cheer from the slaves.

"Yes, sir!" Jerome, ever full of energy, charged ahead toward the liquor storeroom with a platoon of thirsty slaves following him.

One of Solo's students brought a bowl of water with rags to wash the burns on her teacher's arms. Sitting on the grass, Solo accepted treatment, trying not to flinch from the sting. Tom walked over and bent down to observe the lean figure. She was covered with soot, but what he saw were the flashing eyes and the hints of glowing skin and glossy hair beneath the grimy surface, and he realized that from their first encounter, at the height of her wretchedness, he had always seen her inner luster.

"How do you feel?"

"Tom . . ." She had forgotten the *Mister.* "I feel . . . happy . . . really happy . . . to still be here." Her words were spoken simply, without the trimming of a smile, but her lingering glance at him held gratitude for his rescue of her.

Both of their voices were softened with affection. In the aftermath of an event that had torn down walls in the house, he wondered if it had also torn down walls in the places where their feelings lived.

Nearby, students from Solo's class were coming out of the house with books. They had found ones with only minor damage, which they carried gingerly, like sacred texts. They gently patted some of the books with rags to dry them from the water damage. They were gathering a collection of saved books on a clean blanket.

Tom walked toward them, and Solo followed.

"These will dry, Mr. Tom. They'll be good agin," said Tom's butler.

"We can save these," said the gardener, pointing to a little stack.

"Remember this one, Miss Solo?" The weaver held up a slightly charred volume. "This has a chapter you read to us."

Solo nodded, smiling.

As the butler and the gardener were about to go back into the house, Tom stepped in front of them. "What are you doing? You can't go in there."

"But Mr. Tom," said the butler, "what if the ceilin' falls down? Then the books will be done for."

"If the ceiling falls down, then *you'll* be done for!" He raised his voice so everyone would hear his admonition. "No one can go in the house until it cools down and we can assess the damage. Right now, it's too dangerous."

"But, sir, our primers are still in there—" the weaver protested.

"We'll buy more, and we'll rebuild the library, which is now your classroom. We'll build a bigger and better library." He smiled. *And we'll build it to contain a secret underground room where I can hide your class*, he added to himself.

Solo stepped forward. Her students looked at her with affection. She said between coughing, her voice still hoarse, with Tom holding her arm for support: "There are a few hours left before dawn. Have a little rum; then go back to your cabins and get some sleep." Battling her weakness from the ordeal, she raised her voice in triumph. "You all get a perfect grade in firefighting!"

She smiled fondly at her students as they left to join the others at the storeroom.

Tom's hand lingered on Solo's arm. "When we started the classes, I asked you to make them care about something." He pointed to the books on the blanket. "You have."

She smiled with satisfaction.

While the slaves were having their drink, Jerome had slipped away, leaving his apprentice in charge. Now the chef, who had changed into clean, dry clothing, walked over to Tom and Solo. He carried a sack, which he put down by his side; then he bent down to remove a few items among articles of clothing.

Tom's eyes absorbed the purposeful gait and the items in Jerome's hand. He looked with astonishment at his slave, anticipating what he was about to say.

"Mr. Tom, I wants to—" He glanced at his teacher, whose eyebrows raised at his grammar. "I mean, I *want* to give these back."

Jerome placed in Tom's hands a watch, an ivory comb, a scarf pin, and a few other small valuables from the big house that had made their way into Jerome's possession prior to his reform.

Tom accepted the objects, placing them in his pocket, with his eyes still fixed on Jerome for what was coming next.

Jerome reached into the sack for another item. "Here's your mama's book, sir."

Tom took the housekeeping journal that Jerome had used to prepare many recipes; he placed it on the grass next to them. The slave seemed hesitant, as if the words to come were harder to find.

"What's going on, Jerome?" Tom asked kindly, knowing the answer.

"Sir, it's about our *deal*. Remember that?"

"I do."

"You always said it still stands. Does it?"

"Yes."

"I'm ready now, sir. I'm ready! I been sellin' pans o' my chocolate squares to the captain o' the Cincinnati steamer. You remember him?"

"I do."

"Well, the captain, he says Jerome has a job anytime to bake them chocolate squares on his ship, with your pass, sir."

"And did you talk to him about the . . . rest . . . of the deal?"

"Yes sir, and he says it still on with him."

"And the money, Jerome?"

"I have enough, sir, and then some. I done good with my bizness here."

"I see." Tom smiled.

"The captain, he's goin' through with the deal. I'm supposed to be on the ship in the mornin'."

Solo's eyes slid back and forth from one speaker to the next, and her quick mind grasped what was occurring.

"I arranged this before the fire, sir. I was gonna tell you tonight. But with the meetin' you had with the slaves, then after it, I couldn't find you. . . . You weren't around the big house."

"It's all right, Jerome."

"Then come the fire, and, well, I don't wanna leave now, but if I back out with the captain twice, he maybe not give me 'nother shot."

"I think you already did your part here. You saved the house, Jerome."

The slave reached into his sack again. Amid his clothing he found a paper and pencil. "If you write the pass for Jerome to work on the captain's ship, he takes me." He held out the items to his master.

Tom hesitated. He couldn't seem to raise his hands to take the objects from Jerome.

"Sir, I trained Brook real good for you. He kin keep the kitchen, and he knows the system for givin' out the cocoa beans. And I showed him how to make the chocolate squares for you."

"Brook does a good job. I'm not worried about that."

"Then . . . sir?"

It was Tom's turn to falter at words. "Are you . . . sure, Jerome?"

"Like you say, the new time's a-comin'. *My* time's a-comin'. That's how I feel."

"What about the snake with two heads? You said you dreamed of that snake, and that the head facing north was scarier."

"Funny thing, sir. Now when I dream 'bout goin' north, I don't see that snake no more."

"I do," said Tom.

"That snake, I don't fret about her no more."

"But I fret about her." Tom realized that it had been easier to let Jerome go when he hadn't cared about him.

"Gee, Mr. Tom, you ain't worryin' 'bout ole Jerome, now, are you?"

"If you stay here, you can come and go as you please. You can have . . . *leeway.*"

Jerome smiled and shook his head. "'Taint the same, sir."

"But I can protect you here. You can have *security.*"

"'Tain't the same, sir." His voice held affection for Tom's concern and a resolve of his own. "I want what I saw in that book Miss Solo showed us."

He turned to his teacher, who nodded in understanding.

"That shop there in Paris, with the winder full o' pastries—I want a shop like that. I want what free folks call a *deed.*"

Tom also nodded in understanding.

"I want a family too, an' a little house for my family. I don't see no snake no more, sir. I see a shop with my name on it! Clear as I see *Jerome's Squares,* I see *Jerome's Shop."* The yearning in his voice seemed to say that he saw *Jerome's life.*

"I understand, Jerome. I really do. But I want to know that *you* understand too. You might escape the marshals and bounty hunters because I won't report you, but do you realize there are still dangers?" Tom saw the snake vividly, the vicious, hissing monster that could bite with deadly venom. "There are laws working against you, and there are kidnappers who'll try to capture you and bring you back to the South to sell—"

"They ain't gonna git me, sir." Jerome smiled confidently.

"What about the . . . safe house?"

"I know the address, sir. That I do." He recited it for Tom.

"You *must* get to that address! That's the key!"

"I will. Jerome will git there sure as yer standin' here, sir!"

Tom sighed in resignation. He had to face what was inevitable . . . and right. He forced a note of optimism into his tone. "Above all, make your hosts some chocolate squares."

Jerome laughed.

"Before, sir, when you made yer deal with Jerome, when I was worth nuthin', we didn't discuss a price." When the law had allowed manumission in prior years, it was common for a slave to save money from extra jobs and buy his freedom from his master. "Do I need to pay you to buy myself, now that Jerome is worth somethin'?"

Tom grinned. "Forget it."

"Why's that?"

"Because we're *both* worth something."

Tom took the paper and pencil from Jerome, wrote the pass, and gave it to him.

Handling it carefully, like the deed to his future, Jerome folded the pass and placed it in his pocket. "Thank you," he whispered.

"Take a horse. You can leave it at the livery."

Jerome nodded.

"And take this." Tom gave him the housekeeping book with his mother's recipes.

Jerome was speechless.

"I'm sure they'll need some good cooking in Cincinnati." He looked at Jerome solemnly. "I want you to have it. It was our family heirloom; now it can be yours."

"Why . . . why, thank you." Jerome took the book that was now passed down to him and his future family, and he placed it with the utmost care at the top of the sack. It rested next to his chef's hat, folded lengthwise at the pleats and jutting out of the bag. Then he turned to Solo.

Always practical, the teacher faced him. "Finish your schooling. You'll need a class in bookkeeping to run your shop."

Jerome smiled. "Yes, Miss Solo."

"And write to us!"

"I will."

Impulsively, she removed Mrs. Edmunton's journal from the sack. "And, please—" her voice broke, "*please* keep the book right here!" She slipped the volume inside Jerome's shirt, like a plate of armor over his chest.

The meaning of the gesture was obvious—and chilling—to the three of them. The two slaves stared at each other in a moment of naked, abject terror that Tom, as a free man, could only observe on their faces but never fully grasp.

Solo sighed and bowed her head as if she regretted the act, yet she was unable to shake off the fear that had provoked it.

Jerome spoke reassuringly. "I'll keep that in mind, if I meet trouble. But right now, I reckon I'll git to the docks jus' fine with Mr. Tom's pass." He cocked his head in search of her troubled eyes—she was staring at the ground—and he smiled. "That be okay with you?"

Slowly, Solo looked up and returned his smile. "Okay." The moment had passed.

He removed the book from his shirt.

"I *want* you to go, Jerome." Her voice was steady now, and it held hope. "I want you to fly north like the hummingbirds. Fly north and spend your summer there as they do." Her eyes glided out to the fields and to the mystery and promise beyond them. "Think of it, Jerome!" Her glance returned to the chef she had crowned with a toque. "You'll get to make your own recipes for your own life!" The longing in her voice was palpable.

In a display she had up to then reserved only for the horses, she raised her arms and placed them around Jerome's neck. With the fondness of siblings, they embraced.

Then Jerome turned to Tom.

The inventor wondered if there were something he could do to help. Should he offer Jerome a weapon? But if the steamship captain discovered the unthinkable—a slave with a gun—would he renege on the deal? Tom pondered the matter. Could he offer Jerome something more powerful than a weapon? Could he offer a kind of mental weapon to bolster the man's first steps to freedom?

"Jerome, you plunged into the plantation cooking with real vigor. And you mastered it with real skill. You know what that means?"

"What, sir?"

"It means you have a talent and you made a choice to pursue it. It means you found a line of work that interests you and makes you happy. A lot of free people never find that, but *you* did."

Jerome listened, attentive to every word.

"And you invented a way to prompt the slaves to work better for my benefit and theirs—and, I might add, for your benefit too, as their agent." Jerome smiled. "And you organized the fire brigade that saved the house tonight. You know what that means?"

"What, sir?"

"It means you're resourceful, and you're a good leader of people."

Jerome nodded thoughtfully, as if he were realizing for the first time things about himself that neither he nor anyone else—except the speaker—had ever observed.

"And you created a new recipe, a brand-new confection that everybody wants, and you found a way to sell it and make money from it. Do you know what that means?"

"What, sir?"

"It means you're an innovator and a businessman."

Jerome seemed to marvel at the notion. "I reckon it does."

"Do you know what *all* of that means?"

"What, sir?"

"It means that you belong to the new age, Jerome. And *it* belongs to *you*."

Jerome swallowed hard, as if ingesting the words like a tonic to fortify him for the journey ahead.

He reached into his pocket and gave his set of keys to Tom, who put them in his pocket.

The men looked at each other in a silent salute. The blue eyes and brown ones, so different in color, seemed to share a common vision. Tom held out his hand. Jerome didn't looked surprised at the gesture that was rare between masters and slaves. Jerome's hand met Tom's in a viselike grip, with all the feeling the two men held for each other contained in it. Then Tom pulled him closer. With the lingering affection of two brothers parting, they embraced.

Then Jerome picked up his belongings, beamed a final, confident smile at Tom and Solo, and walked away, a man in pursuit of a deed—to a shop and to a life.

# CHAPTER 26

The night's emergency had distorted Tom's sense of time. Standing in front of his family home, with lanterns spread like embers among the charred debris, he glanced at his pocket watch. On what had already been the longest night of his life, he was surprised to realize that it was only three in the morning, and daybreak was still a few hours away. It also seemed as if days had passed since Sheriff Duran's meeting at the Crossroads, yet it had occurred only twelve hours earlier.

On the other hand, the past three months had seemed like one prolonged night of anguish. It was that long ago that his invention had been stolen, yet he felt its loss as acutely as if it were yesterday.

His mind paused on the invention to which all of his thoughts eventually led. It could be only a day or two more before he would learn something about its whereabouts from Ladybug, the slave from the Crossroads, if Duran could find her in Baton Rouge, and if she weren't . . . silenced . . . before she had a chance to talk.

Tom was impatient to report the fire so that the sheriff could send deputies out to find Markham without delay. Since Duran would surely wait until morning to begin what was a long trip, Tom thought, he could get a note to the lawman before he left for Baton Rouge. That way the search for the man who almost killed Solo could begin in the sheriff's absence.

Tom walked behind the big house and into the kitchen to look for writing materials that Jerome kept there to do his class exercises. He found them and composed a note to the sheriff reporting Markham's arson. Then he sent a trusted servant to town to deliver it.

As he walked back to the front of the house, he noticed that the human voices dominating that frantic night had now vanished, returning the outdoors to the sounds of the nocturnal critters. Most of the slaves had gone back to bed.

He saw the most precious item saved from the fire still at the scene. Solo was gathering the rescued books into a hand-pulled wagon to take into a cabin for safekeeping.

He also saw the indomitable Nick clearing debris from the gallery himself after sending the field hands back to their cabins to rest before the day's work. As he was about to tell Nick to go to bed, Tom spotted a carriage coming up the road.

"Mr. Tom!" The driver stopped the carriage in front of him.

"Hello, Lance." Tom recognized Charlotte Barnwell's driver from Ruby Manor.

"Miz Charlotte and Miz Rachel sen' me." The man stared agape at the burned house. "Oh, Lord in paradise!" he said, shaken by the sight.

"Go on, Lance."

"The ladies, they sees smoke a-comin' from yer direction. They smells smoke. They afeared there's fire here, sir. They wonderin' if you okay. They say fer you to come back wid me, sir, if you got fire here, and bring 'long anybody hurt an' needin' Nurse Bina."

Ruby Manor, a larger plantation, had a cottage that served as a sick house, where a doctor-trained slave treated common ailments of the Barnwells and their slaves.

"The missus, she given me this fer you." Lance reached into his vest pocket and produced a note.

The inventor unfolded the paper and moved toward a lantern to read it.

> *Dear Tom,*
>
> *Rachel and I fear this note will find you in peril. We saw smoke filling the sky from the direction of Indigo Springs, and we suspect you've suffered a fire. If you or any of your slaves have been injured, please come here so that our nurse can minister to all of you.*
>
> *I was taken aback by the threatening words uttered to me and you this past afternoon, and I greatly fear that the man who pronounced them is the culprit behind the fire. I worry that this madman is loose and might set his sights next on Ruby Manor to exact his wild revenge.*
>
> *Tom, please come, so you can tell us what happened. And if my suspicions prove true, we need you to protect us from that vile man. Please stay with us, at least through this frightful night. Rachel implores you, as do I.*
>
> *God willing, you have escaped harm.*

The letter was signed by Charlotte Barnwell. Tom thought he should alert her and Rachel to Markham's culpability, just in case the madman, in the throes of alcohol, decided to pay a visit to Ruby Manor and include Charlotte in his vengeance, as she feared. If he had any sense, Tom figured, the man would be racing out of town after his crime, but it was precisely sound judgment that he lacked, so his potential to cause more harm couldn't be ruled out. Tom relished the thought of being there to exact justice if Markham did ride in to Ruby Manor that night. His fists clenched as a cauldron of anger boiled inside him for the man who nearly killed . . .

He looked at Solo. The burns and bruises on her arms, as well as his own skin injuries, needed careful cleaning and bandaging. Maybe Bina had a salve or emollient to soothe their burns as well.

He glanced at the house. It reeked of smoke and was uninhabitable. He needed to prevail on Charlotte that night, just as she needed to prevail on him.

While the carriage driver waited for a reply, Tom told Nick about the letter.

"You can do nothing inside till she cools," Nick said of the big house. "If something come up, I send for you." Ruby Manor was only a mile away. "Go. I watch everything."

The hardworking German with the direct gaze and decisive manner inspired confidence. Tom told him of Jerome's signed pass to work on the steamship. That way his overseer, the only other free person on the plantation, wouldn't unwittingly report Jerome as a runaway. Then he gave Jerome's keys to Nick to hold while he went to Ruby Manor.

\* \* \* \* \*

"There are neighbors close by who have a nurse that can treat your burns, and I need to warn them of a mutual enemy we have who set the fire," Tom explained to Solo. "Besides, you wouldn't mind getting cleaned up and resting a little, now, would you?" She looked uneasy. "We'll come back first thing in the morning."

Solo went along in the carriage reluctantly. Unlike the other slaves, she showed no inclination to go to town, visit other plantations, or otherwise venture outside of Indigo Springs. Through her books, she traveled the world, but she seemed to want nothing to do with the local town or its people. She was an outcast, he thought, an educated woman, a voracious reader, and a talented teacher who was trapped in the dying age. If she harbored a hostility toward the society that held her captive, could he blame her? He couldn't predict her reactions. He knew only that he didn't want to provoke her . . . feral . . . side, which he had sampled in their first encounters. He told her nothing about the Barnwells and didn't intend to stay beyond the morning.

\* \* \* \* \*

White columns and scattered lanterns shone in the darkness as the carriage trotted toward the Olympian home that Wiley Barnwell had built twenty years earlier for his wife. Also visible in the night were countless small reddish puffs, swaying in the breeze; come morning, they would appear in their full red bloom as the trademark roses that encircled Ruby Manor, completing the extravagant gift of a loving husband to his young bride.

Charlotte Barnwell appeared at the entrance to greet the carriage. With her red hair loose and tumbling, she still possessed the youthful beauty of Wiley's bride. Rachel followed her, with the same long red hair and trim form. In the night, the two women in pastel dressing gowns looked like sisters.

As the carriage pulled up to the house and the two passengers came into the light, the women gasped.

"Is that you, Tom?" Rachel called. "My God! You look burnt to a cinder." She turned to a servant who had accompanied her outside. "Roderick, fetch Bina."

Tom jumped down from the carriage and helped Solo out. The two young women stared at each other. Rachel looked as pristine as a fairy-tale princess in her pink silk gown with a V neck exposing the delicate lace frill of a nightgown beneath. Solo, in her smoke-covered slave's frock, with torn sleeves and unkempt hair that had been exposed to fire, dirt, and mud, resembled a vagabond. Rachel looked at her aghast. Solo responded with a look of suspicion, as if she too were making a less-than-favorable appraisal.

Tom bowed his head to the Barnwells in greeting. "Ladies, as you surmised, there indeed was a fire tonight at my house. The two of us were caught in it, and we would be much obliged to rest here and have a chance to clean up and change clothes."

Bina, a corpulent slave in her forties with a motherly manner, arrived from the sick house. Her steps quickened at the sight of the bedraggled arrivals, suggesting she took her job as a healer seriously. While Tom spoke to his two hostesses, Bina smiled kindly at Solo and drew her aside to examined her burns by a lantern's light.

"Are you all right, Tom?" Charlotte inquired.

"Yes."

"You read my note?"

"I did."

"And?" Charlotte's manner was cordial but cool as if Tom's stinging words to her and the others the preceding afternoon were lingering unpleasantly in her mind.

"I'm sorry to say your suspicions were correct."

"It was him!"

"I saw him; he was drunk and galloping away from my house just after the fire started."

"My God! I knew I shouldn't have listened to you! I didn't want to fire him—*you* did!" Charlotte said accusingly. "I hope you shot him!"

"I'm afraid he got away, but I reported him to the sheriff."

"What if he comes here, Tom Edmunton?" Rachel's question sounded like a scolding. "What are we to do then?"

"He's probably in hiding and passed out from drink by now."

"Maybe not. If he's drunk, who knows what he'll do?" Charlotte's face paled with worry.

"Well, I'm glad that you at least had the consideration to come here to protect us tonight." Rachel seemed to have forgotten about Tom's and his companion's injuries. "We'll post servants outside to warn us if anyone rides up." She turned to Charlotte. "Will that make you feel better, Mama?"

"Nothing will make me feel better until that madman is caught . . . and until we have some peace from our recent horrors." She looked pointedly at Tom.

"In the meantime, this woman needs care." Tom pointed to Solo.

Rachel suddenly remembered the vagabond. "Oh. Bina, come here."

The nurse joined the group, along with Solo. "Be sure to take care of her burns. And Mr. Edmunton's too."

"Yes, ma'am," said Bina.

"Tom, you can stay in Papa's room," Rachel continued. She looked at her mother, who nodded her approval; then she turned to the nurse. "Bina, put the girl up in the sick house."

"Wait," said Tom. "You can't do that."

"What do you mean?" asked Rachel.

"There could be *sick* people inside."

"Of course there are sick people. That's why it's called a sick house."

"You could have people in there with a fever, a contagion of some kind."

"There's only one case of fever, and it's only suspected. We're watching it—"

"Absolutely not!" said Tom, alarmed.

"How very rude of you to order me around at my own house!" Rachel remarked.

"Either she stays here"—he pointed to the big house—"or we both leave now."

Rachel's eyes darted suspiciously from Tom to Solo. "What is she to you, anyway?"

He stared irritably at her. With his nerves worn thin from the wickedness of Markham's deed and his fierce battle with the blaze, he had lost all urge to be pleasant.

"Tom Edmunton, what's that slave to you?" Rachel demanded.

"Frankly, it's none of your business." He took Solo's arm and guided her back to the carriage. "Lance, take us back."

"Tom, really now!" Rachel rushed up to him. The voluminous folds of her dressing gown rubbed against his dirty clothing. Her hands covered a shirt that had been white but was now as dark gray as his tattered vest. Her eyes looked up at him alluringly, as from a time past. "You can't leave us, Tom! Why, whatever would we do if that horrible man came here?"

"Call Nash." He pushed loose of her.

Like a storm-scuffed cat whose body was disheveled, Solo observed the two of them with piercing eyes and drew her own conclusions.

"I declare!" said Charlotte. "Your daddy, the colonel, must be twistin' in his grave with the outrageous things you say, and with the disrespectful way you talk and try to bully us around!"

Tom looked at the two of them with contempt. Then he turned to Solo. "Let's go." He was ready to assist her into the carriage when Rachel again entreated him.

"All right! All right, have it your way. I won't argue with your crazy notions about . . . things." She sneered at Solo, then fixed a smile to her face and a lighter tone to her voice. "Bina, take the girl to my wardrobe room." She turned to the male servant. "Roderick, take Mr. Edmunton to my father's room. You and Bina are to see to it that they get lots of soap and water for washing . . . scrubbing, I should say." She looked disdainfully at the two people who had barely escaped a scorching death. "And get them fresh clothing."

She turned to Bina. "She's not to touch *anything* in my wardrobe room. Give her a blanket to sleep on the floor." To Solo she added, her face pleasant but her eyes resentful: "Is that understood?"

Solo didn't reply. Tom recognized the feral look gripping her features, the same look she had displayed on their first encounter, right before she had socked him.

He quickly whisked her off with Bina toward the house. "Go. I'll check on you later," he whispered reassuringly.

"And Bina," Rachel called after them, "don't let her traipse through the house like a wounded dog. Take her up the back stairs."

Solo looked daggers at her.

Rachel turned to the coachman. "Lance, you're to stay out here all night and guard the front entrance. Get Rex to watch the back. If anyone comes up to the house, wake us fast!"

Then she looked at the man who was so difficult to manage. She brushed her gown and hands to shake off the soot from her contact with him, as if ridding herself of his feel.

"There, now, that should take care of everything." She smiled.

Her feigned cheerfulness reminded Tom of her acting roles on the Philadelphia stage at a time that had become distorted in his mind, for it seemed like centuries ago.

\* \* \* \* \*

Just before daybreak, the second-floor hallway was dark and the Barnwell household was finally asleep. Behind one of the doors, Tom stood before the mirrored panels of an armoire, looking at himself. His tanned face and blond hair had been restored to their proper coloring. He wore the bulky shirt, pants, and vest of the man who had betrayed him, garments that ill fit his body and his sentiments. Nevertheless, he was glad to be cleaned up and wearing fresh clothes, with his burns washed and bandaged. Now that his physical condition was improved, his attention turned to the room of the man who had been the distinguished leader of the town.

Tom could almost sense the presence of the deceased senator in the chamber. A dresser displayed Barnwell's comb and pocket watch. A half-open desk drawer still held a gun in a holster with Barnwell's initials. A suit was draped over a chair, with a top hat on the seat and leather boots alongside, as if waiting for the senator to step into them.

Tom glanced at the items on the walnut secretary that was Barnwell's desk. It provided a glimpse at the different facets of its proprietor. Tom thought of the faces of a stone that had the potential to be a prized gem. If the stone were cut properly, it could produce a diamond, but if it were cut improperly, the gem's brilliance would be lost and mere rhinestones would result. How had Wiley Barnwell's life been cut? Tom tried to appraise the man's various facets.

In its cubbyholes, the desk held the agricultural journals and almanac of the intelligent farmer who had raised a prodigious crop and taught Tom the business of cotton growing. On the shelf above the desktop, Tom saw a copy of the Louisiana statutes and its slave code, laws that Barnwell as senator had helped to pass and strengthen, preserving the privilege of a dying age.

Wiley Barnwell was a farmer and businessman who harnessed nature on a grand scale. As a farmer, he took the raw offerings of climate and soil to produce a commodity of great value, and as a businessman he traded his product on the world markets and amassed a fortune. Few could accomplish that, Tom had to acknowledge, giving his mentor his due. But Barnwell was also a politician of pull and a slaveholder, a man who sought control over others. In that sense Barnwell harnessed people, forcing them to do his bidding against their own choice and benefit. Barnwell possessed some of the luster of the new age as well as the flaws of the dying age.

Could he have become a great farmer and made his fortune with free workers? Tom thought enough of his mentor to believe he could, and he thought enough of the human spirit to believe Barnwell would have done better with willing hands.

But Barnwell hadn't gone that route. Instead, the luster had been scraped off his character. It wasn't the mastery of farming and trade that had corrupted him, Tom thought, but the other mastery he had sought. Tom sighed in sadness at the stone with the bad cut that destroyed what might perhaps have been a rare gem.

The inventor was too restless to sleep or to stay in the eerie room. The reason was that the presence of someone else in the house was even more palpable to him. With the threat of an attack by Markham vanishing with the coming dawn, his attention felt free to wander. He left the chamber, closing the door behind him on the conflicting faces of Wiley Barnwell. Then he walked down the quiet hallway to the room at the end, the home of the legendary wardrobe of Rachel Barnwell.

Tom remembered the time when he had seen Rachel in her wardrobe room. She had been reclining on a daybed, relaxing for a moment in between measurements and fittings. She looked like the subject in a painting of a princess in her toilette, with a hoop-skirted dress form and a full-length mirror near her. The background added to the palatial setting, with French doors opening to a gallery, and beyond it the stunning perimeter of roses and the winding road up to the estate.

He recalled the two massive armoires with dresses made of fine silks, satins, velvets, cottons, and lace from New England and European mills. Rachel had outfits for horseback riding, carriage jaunts, recreational hunting, serving tea, afternoon entertaining, reading, and visiting, as well as gowns for evening wear. Accessories of every kind—shoes, bonnets, gloves, jewelry, shawls, jackets—overflowed from the armoires and dressers to fill etageres that other people used to display fine china.

He had seen Rachel in her wardrobe room just before twilight, which seemed fitting, since it was the . . . inducement . . . that had ended their life together in Philadelphia. Now, he wondered what the room would look like at daybreak with another woman.

He saw lamplight shining underneath the door and a shadow of someone moving. He knocked. The movement inside stopped, but his knock went unanswered. The door creaked as he let himself in and creaked again when he closed it behind him.

The bronze beauty that was Solo turned to stare at him. She was standing before the mirror, its oval rim of gold leaf framing her. The slave's frock given to her had been tossed over a chair. Instead she was wearing one of Rachel's gowns, a stunning crimson evening dress cascading in tiers from her tiny waist to a six-foot circle of crinoline at the floor. The small bandages on her arms were overshadowed by the splendor of her gown and the proud way she wore it.

Tom stopped to gaze at the alluringly feminine side of her that he had never seen. The off-the-shoulder gown had a plunging neckline. Her bare shoulders and the tops of her breasts were covered with a little black cape of translucent Spanish lace tied with a bow at the neck. The lace sparkled with red garnets to match the dress, with the small gemstones sewn into the fabric, transforming the cape into jewelry and the jewels into apparel. Her hair was swept off her face by an ornament, but defiant of any further containment, the tresses made their tumbling descent down her back like a latticework of soft tendrils behind a rare orchid. The serene, imperial look of her gown contrasted sharply with her unsmiling mouth, gaunt cheekbones, and piercing feline eyes. She looked at once like a princess and a tigress. Tom was astonished at how remarkably well the formal dress blended with the raw honesty of features that needed no refinement.

She remained poised and silent, making no effort to explain her astonishing behavior in flagrant disregard of Rachel's order not to touch anything.

Tom walked toward her. As he crossed the room, her eyes widened in fear. He walked closer still. She reached down under puffs of crinoline to grab an item strapped to her calf. He recognized the object that looked incongruous in the hands of one so regally dressed: his hunting knife. She had apparently carried it with her through the fire, and now she aimed it at a threat perhaps more menacing to her.

As he walked directly in front of her, she pointed the knife at his throat, but her eyes seemed to be looking past him at a disturbing image of their own. The terror on her face, he sensed, came from a wound burned on her memory, a wound that was still acutely painful when disturbed. The sight of her trembling in fear brought out a tenderness in him that he didn't know he possessed. Gently he stroked her hair, traced the smooth curves of her face, and wrapped his arms around her waist, with his hands lingering on every touch of her.

She clutched the knife tighter, gripping it with two hands, the point just inches from his throat.

He drew her against him. The cool blade of the knife now pressed flat against his neck. All she had to do was turn it so that the point . . . Would she kiss him or kill him? He placed his bet. He tightened his arms around her and kissed her softly.

She was caught between an old fear and a new pleasure. She pushed against his chest, yet she could not resist letting her head fall back in surrender. She abandoned her resolve, answering his desire with her own awakening need. He pressed his mouth harder against hers. Soon he felt her arms drop limply at her sides. Then he heard the knife fall to the floor. He wrapped her arms around his neck, where they soon tightened, pulling him closer.

He thought he should feel guilty for picking the most inappropriate of places, but the setting served only to intensify his excitement.

As they discovered the exciting feel of each other, he lifted the ornament off her hair, and a thicket of wild curls tumbled onto her shoulders. He untied the garnet cape, and it fell to the floor. His hands traced the enticing landscape that was Solo—the tiny circle of her waist, the hills and valleys of her back, the taut tracts of her arms. He buried his face in a luscious mix of warm flesh and tousled hair. His mouth found her neck, then her shoulders. He swept back the voluminous tresses to chart the smooth curves of her breasts.

The sensitive creature under Rachel's gown responded. Casting aside the grim past, she closed her eyes and opened her mouth to the exciting present.

He tasted Rachel's lip rouge on Solo's mouth. He breathed Rachel's perfume pulsing from Solo's skin. He saw Rachel's—

Suddenly, his hands stopped; his gaze froze; his head shot up abruptly. He saw, perched above Solo's heart, the same image on her bronze flesh that he had seen on Rachel's ivory skin. He saw—reddish, beguiling, and heart-shaped—the little birthmark.

He gasped in utter incredulity.

"Ladybug?"

# CHAPTER 27

Solo and Tom broke away from each other in astonishment.

"How do you know that name?" Her voice trembled. "And what exactly do you know?"

"I know you saw my invention at the Crossroads Plantation."

"*Your* invention?"

"Yes!"

"You mean *you're* the man I've been trying to find?"

"And *you're* the woman they're trying to—" He couldn't utter the unthinkable word. He glared at her, stunned by the implications suddenly pounding his mind, all of them dire. He ran his fingers over the birthmark in disbelief. "My God, *Ladybug*!"

She reached for the cape and tied it around her shoulders to cover the telltale mark.

"It's too late for that." His mind whirled, trying to fathom the new situation. "You're Ladybug. That birthmark identifies you!" He grabbed her arms. "Listen to me! There are people looking for you who want to do you *harm*." His mind flashed before him a determined sheriff who wanted her arrested, furious planters who wanted her hanged, and mortified women who'd stop at nothing to prevent a family scandal.

She stood before him, incredulous. "You're saying that *you* invented the machine I saw in a shed on the most . . . horrible . . . day of my life?"

"That would be my tractor. You took it, didn't you? Where is it?"

"It's safe."

He closed his eyes, quietly thrilled by her news.

"It's by the old factory just north of Polly Barnwell's plantation."

"I looked there. It wasn't in the factory, and it wasn't along the road that served it."

She smiled at his bewilderment. "Where I put it isn't accessible by any road."

"Oh?"

"There are pulleys there that I played with as a child. I used them to hoist your tractor where you might not have thought of."

He remembered the knowledge of pulleys she had displayed in her attempts to free her horse from under the fallen tree. He took her by the arms, smiling at an intelligence that had outsmarted him. "You . . . *you* saved my tractor?"

In a fleeting rush of pleasure splashed in a sea of grief, she whispered excitedly: "I should have known the inventor would be you!"

He led her to the daybed. As they sat and he held her hands, he was already putting the story together.

"So you were Polly's slave, from the Crossroads Plantation."

"Yes."

"The slave Wiley Barnwell sold on the day of her funeral."

She bristled. "Yes, to Fred Fowler."

"Then you ran away from Fowler. That must've been when I found you after the storm with your horse trapped."

"Yes. After you freed my horse, I got further north. But the slave patrol caught up with me. They brought me back to town, to that despicable beast, Fowler. That was when I saw you again, when he was about to take me away. If you hadn't . . . intervened . . . either Fowler or I—or *both* of us—would be dead by now."

He nodded, believing it. His body tensed in rage, remembering the man's brutality as he struck her, hung a noose around her neck, and tried to pull out her tooth.

The torture of her ordeal softened his voice. "Then there's the matter of what . . . happened . . . to Barnwell."

Her face locked into an unreadable stare.

"Listen, Ladybug"—he felt awkward addressing her by a name other than the one he had given her—"you're in *grave danger*. I want to help you, but you have to trust me and tell me *everything*."

"Why would you help me? After you hung Senator Barnwell's portrait in your home? That night, when I overheard you talking to the artist, I realized you not only knew the senator, but you *loved* him. You swore his death would be avenged! When you smashed your glass, in *fury* at his . . . his . . ." She couldn't say the word that indicted her. "I knew I could *never* tell you about me!" She breathed deeply, forcing herself to remain calm. "But now that it's out, I have to set you straight on something, and *you* can trust *me* on this: The senator was no friend of yours."

"I know that now. Believe me, I have no allegiance to him over you, or to . . . anyone . . . over you."

She paused to absorb what was said and unsaid.

He looked at her in earnest. "Now that you know who *I* am, you have to tell me who *you* are. Why don't you start with your real name? I mean, Ladybug is a nickname, isn't it?"

"It's the only name I ever had. Miss Polly said that someone gave me to her when I was an infant. I was wrapped in a basket of flowers, she told me. I guess she wanted me to think I started out in a special way, so I might feel better about my condition, because after that, my life wasn't nearly as pretty." She spoke with a tinge of sadness. "Miss Polly said there was a critter on the petals that was scarlet red with black spots, a *ladybug*. So she called me that."

"Who gave you to Polly?"

"She never said."

He listened, filing the information in his mind.

"As I grew up, the name seemed to suit me. When I was a child, I'd pretend I was wearing a beautiful gown when it was only a homespun frock, and I'd pretend I was dancing at a ball when I was only in the barn, or I'd pretend I was getting out of a fancy carriage when it was only a hay wagon. The other slaves laughed at me. They said, 'Look at Ladybug! She thinks she's a lady, but she's only a bug.'" Wistfully, she looked at herself in Rachel's gown. "I guess I'm still pretending."

His face showed compassion.

"When I was a child, Miss Polly taught me to read and write. I devoured all of her books and magazines and any other printed material I could find. Reading was the only thing I loved to do. It gave me a lot of material for playacting." She smiled. "I tried to do what the people I read about did. I made believe I was serving tea and sipped it with all the manners of the gentry. I talked to imaginary companions about a new book I'd read, or a city I'd say I visited, or a new play I supposedly saw in New Orleans. I'd describe in detail how the stage looked, how the orchestra sounded. . . . Miss Polly would lose her patience and say, 'Dear girl, you carry on so!' But I kept on doing it."

"So Polly raised you?"

She nodded. "Miss Polly was kind to all of us, but especially to me. I was her servant, although I sensed I was also like the child she never had."

"Do you know who your mother and father are?"

"No. When I was little, I sometimes asked, but Miss Polly just repeated the story of the basket and said nothing more. Actually, I never much cared." She spoke with a feline-like emotional detachment from people that seemed a long-standing trait, but her eyes lingered on him as though her indifference could encounter an exception.

"Do you have any siblings, any . . . sister . . . that you know about?"

"No."

"Did you know Wiley Barnwell?"

"Occasionally he came to visit Miss Polly. I knew he was a senator and her brother-in-law. He always treated me coldly, as if he were angry at me. I never knew why. I avoided him whenever I could."

"Did he ever bring his family?"

"No."

"Do you recognize the women in this house?"

"I never saw them before. Why do you ask?"

"We'll talk about that later. Right now, the sheriff is our main concern. He found out about you yesterday afternoon at a meeting we had. Just when he ran out of suspects, your name came up. He learned that you knew about the invention and that you were sold to Fowler. He's going to Baton Rouge to see Fowler and question you. When Fowler tells him that you ran away and were unaccounted for on the night of the murder, that'll intensify the sheriff's suspicions. And when Fowler tells him that he later found you and sold you in Greenbriar, that'll bring the sheriff right back here—to arrest you for Barnwell's death."

She covered her face with her hands and suffered quietly. He felt helpless to console her on a matter whose gravity couldn't be diminished.

He glanced at the French doors, where the light of dawn was filtering in through the drapery. "The sheriff could be leaving for Baton Rouge now and be back here before nightfall. We don't have much time." He squeezed her shoulders urgently. "You have to tell me *everything*—about you, Barnwell, and my invention."

She bowed her head in anguish, then raised it in resolve. Too tense to sit, she propped herself up on the cushioned arm of the daybed and faced him. He looked up at her, waiting to hear the events of the night that had uprooted his life and hers, and that had, oddly, brought them together. Poised and dressed as she was, she looked too dainty and elegant to have lived through the gruesome events she began to relate.

"On the morning of Miss Polly's funeral, Senator Barnwell rode up to the Crossroads. I hid in a cabin to stay out of his sight, as I always did. From where I was hiding I watched him hauling something very curious, which he put in the old carriage house. When he went inside the big house, I went to take a look at what he had brought."

A hint of excitement colored her voice as she described her discovery. "I learned about machines when I was a child. I used to play in the old deserted factory." She smiled, reminiscing. "I often slipped away and went there to look at the remnants of the machinery, the tools, the waterwheel."

"Why would you want to go there?"

"It was pretty much the only contact I had with anything outside of Miss Polly's plantation. I was Ladybug, a little critter that couldn't fly far and had to keep from getting smashed. But when I played at the factory, I felt somehow . . . powerful . . . when I moved boulders and fallen trees around with the pulleys and when I saw how things worked. Why, I could even start the waterwheel! I read all the papers, diagrams, and books that were left behind. I understood the machines and was amazed by them."

"I see," he said, recognizing an interest that he understood well.

"So when I saw the invention the senator brought in, I was curious. You see, nothing exciting ever happened at the Crossroads. I served Miss Polly tea, I stoked her fire, I read to her, I fetched her shawl, I arranged her clothes. But there was a whole world out there that had nothing at all to do with Miss Polly. And on the day of her funeral the senator brought something here from *outside*."

She pronounced the last word as if it were *heaven*.

"I slipped into the old carriage house and studied the device. I traced the tubes and rods and chambers to figure out what they did. I found papers in a compartment. There were diagrams showing how to start the motor and run it, and drawings that showed it doing farm work, and amazing calculations of how the machine could do more work than a whole field of men. I studied everything.

"In one of Miss Polly's magazines, I remembered once reading an article called 'The Horseless Age.' It described a search that was going on for a new kind of motor, a little engine that could operate small vehicles. I realized I was looking at one of those new inventions of the horseless age. I was looking at the *future*."

He studied the face that livened with intellectual curiosity.

"If this machine meant that slaves wouldn't be needed any longer for farming, if machines could do the work faster and better, then that could . . . change things . . . I thought. I climbed into the driver's seat and pretended that I, Ladybug, was plowing a field faster than a whole gang of prime hands!" She smiled. "I even thought of slipping away during the funeral and going back there to start the engine when nobody was around, just to hear how it sounded, but the papers said to expect loud noises that scared horses and people, so I figured I'd better not cause a commotion."

"You were wise."

"Of course, I wasn't around long enough to attend the funeral."

He heard pain creeping into her voice.

"As I sat there on the machine, I heard two men's voices outside. They were coming toward the shed. I had forgotten danger, and there was no time to get away! I slid off the seat and hid inside the old coach that was there."

Her eyes stared ahead as she relived the disturbing events of a life-changing day.

"Senator Barnwell walked in with Bret Markham, Miss Polly's overseer. They closed the door behind them, as if they were having a secret meeting.

The senator described the device to Markham and offered him a lot of money to—I couldn't believe my ears—to *smash* it. He said it had to be done that night because the inventor would be taking it away the next morning. The senator never mentioned you by name. He said only that a crazed inventor, a demon among them, had wild plans to destroy their lives with that machine."

Tom felt his anger rise.

"I was shocked," she continued. "Why would the senator do that? What was he . . . afraid . . . of? As I hid there in the coach and listened to him that morning, I realized that I was *right* to dislike him. And, you know, he made it sound as though he were saving the world. He said, 'Providence has placed the device in my hands for this one night.' " She spoke pompously, imitating him. " 'Yes, fate has chosen *me* to save us from the Satan in our midst who created this monster and must be stopped before he destroys himself and the rest of us.' "

Her eyes narrowed in contempt as she recalled the incident.

"He was a thief and a destroyer, but he pretended he was a saint. He was going to smash someone's work and future and make it sound noble. Well, that made me mad!"

Tom nodded as he listened to the only person he had heard speak the truth about Barnwell. He wondered about people like the senator who pose as benefactors while doing evil deeds.

"Markham was much cruder and more honest about what he was doing." She imitated the overseer: "He said, 'If folks won't need no more lackeys in their fields with this here contraption, then they won't need me supervisin' them none neither.' So he was happy to destroy the invention. Besides, Barnwell offered to pay him, and he grabbed the chance like a dog grabs a bone. The senator told Markham to make it look like the slaves were up to mischief and stole the invention. Markham was happy to do that; he even volunteered to line up the slaves and whip every one of them for the imagined crime. He said they needed whipping anyway, and this was as good an excuse as any. I huddled there in the coach, loathing the two of them. Maybe I was just a ladybug, I thought, but a ladybug could fly and dance on flower petals, while those two could only wade in the mud."

Tom listened intently, picturing the scene she painted and the paradoxes it implied, with the town's most distinguished citizen and its least wallowing together in the mud, and with someone else—the ultimate outcast of all—the only one to recognize the glory of his invention. Who did the dying age destroy more completely, he wondered, its subjects or its rulers?

"Barnwell gave Markham money and promised more when the job was finished. Then the senator walked toward the window. He seemed to want to be sure that no one saw him give Markham a purse. He was so close to me that I could hear him breathing. Then the worst possible thing happened. He saw a patch of my dress and discovered me there in the coach!"

The drama of the moment was apparent on her face.

"The senator was furious! He dragged me out of the coach. Markham told him I was lazy and given to daydreaming. I was glad for that excuse, because I didn't want the senator to know that I understood the invention and I didn't want him to smash it."

Involuntarily, Tom's eyes swept over her. She seemed too distraught to notice.

"He ordered Markham to whip me, then he left. Markham always carried a whip, so he took it out. He said, 'This'll teach you yer place!' With Miss Polly no longer there to protect me, he used that whip with great glee. He knew that I—a *slave*—thought he was depraved, and he knew it was true. I don't know whether he was more angry at himself for being what he was or at me for seeing it, but he was merciless. As that horrible whip hit my back, he taunted me. He said, 'This'll teach you to look down yer snooty nose at me!' "

Her cheeks reddened and her forehead glistened with perspiration, as if she could still feel the lashes. She paused to blot her face with a handkerchief she found in the dress pocket.

"After the lashes, I staggered out of the carriage house. My dress was untied and hanging off my shoulder. I leaned against a statue, shaking from the pain. I pulled my hair up to catch a cool breeze on my skin. I noticed a man, a stranger who was coming for the funeral. He approached me. He saw my birthmark and was curious about it. He wanted to look at it close up. This was so odd. No one had ever mentioned the birthmark before. He frightened me, so I quickly tied my dress and ran away! I rushed into the kitchen and up the ladder to the cook's loft. The cook helped me; she wiped away the blood on my back and gave me a clean frock.

"The next thing I knew, Senator Barnwell came looking for me. He grabbed me and threw me into a wagon. I was afraid, so I resisted. He locked my hands and feet in irons and dragged me away. He took me to Stoner's Saloon at the docks. I knew what that meant."

Her voice broke. She slid down off the arm of the daybed into Tom's arms.

"Why would he have me beaten—I mean, why would he damage the goods—if he intended to sell me? He seemed to have a sudden change of heart about keeping me. I don't know why."

"I do." Tom thought of Nash and the telltale birthmark he discovered. "I'll explain that to you later."

"Barnwell sold me to a disgusting man who was in the saloon, Fred Fowler. To my great misfortune, he took a liking to me. Fowler was here from Baton Rouge. He was a gambler, and I think he was here to collect money someone owed him on a bet. My one day with him started and ended the same way . . ."—she dropped her head—"with . . . rape."

She buried her face in Tom's chest, her voice reduced to a whisper. His arms tightened around her as he imagined himself beating Fowler to a pulp.

"To my horror, Fowler said he didn't have a wife to object to me! I couldn't bear to think of what my life would be like with him!"

"So that skunk Barnwell didn't sell you to a nice family after all!"

"Is that what he told people?"

Tom stared introspectively out the window, making other connections about the man who had condemned the woman before him to a life of unspeakable cruelty. "Now I know why nobody cried for him when he died. No slaves, no friends, not even his family. They knew him. Everybody knew him. They wouldn't admit it, but deep inside, they knew he wasn't worth any tears." Then Tom turned back to her, waiting to hear the rest.

"Of all my childhood imaginings, there was one role, above all others, that I playacted in my mind over and over. And that was how I would escape. Now, on that desperate day when I was sold, Fred Fowler brought to a head all of my yearnings to make that dream real. He took me up the bluff to Greenbriar, where he rented a room for the night, a 'purtier' room than at the docks, for *us*, he said. My gosh, I was horrified. It was like his wedding night! Later, as I sat there in his room, with him drunk and passed out on the bed, I knew *this* was my chance."

The painful recollections pulled her features into a silent cry.

"I felt so desperate that horrible day. Miss Polly's protection was gone. Barnwell was cruel. Fowler was intolerable. I summoned my courage and made my plan."

Her features flashed before him the tumult of her feelings on that dreadful night. Her mouth tensed in fear of her plight, yet her eyes held the hope of breaking free.

With her identity revealed and the fear of Tom's discovering her past now gone, her manner toward him was changing. He was amazed at the transformation in a face that had been unreadable to one that now flashed at him a range of emotions. He felt as if a door had opened to a secret place he wanted to enter.

"And your plan was . . . ?"

"Miss Polly had taken me to Natchez several times to visit her cousin there. Once, the road we took was flooded, so our coachman tried a less-traveled route, which passed through an old Indian trail by Manning Creek. I memorized the route and imagined that I would one day use it to run away. I figured that if I crossed the state line into Mississippi, that might slow down anyone trying to catch me."

Tom nodded. Greenbriar was less than twenty miles from the Mississippi border, and Natchez was the first major port city beyond that. With its interacting population of whites, free people of color, and slaves, Natchez was a place where a clever runaway might slip by unnoticed for a time.

"What were you going to do when you reached Natchez?"

"I was Ladybug. I was going to do what I had always done, only this time for real."

A grin slowly formed on Tom's face as he realized what was coming.

"I was going to get the cosmetics and outfit I needed to pose as a white woman, then buy a ticket on a steamer headed to the North. With my hair cut short and pulled under a bonnet, and with gloves and boots on, no part of me needed to show but my face. With my English features and a little ivory face powder like Miss Polly's, which I had already sampled to see the effect, I thought I'd have a chance. I was going to play the role of a lady, while being just a bug."

He smiled at her characterization, at the many paradoxes of the dying age, and at the question raised in his own mind: If a burning desire to hold the deed to one's life and to break free of society's paper claims was the measure, then of the women around him, who was the true *lady*?

"I had a stash of money from things I had produced on my own and sold in town over the years. And I had a knife from Miss Polly's kitchen that I had hidden with the money. I rehearsed a story that I'd use on the steamer about who I was and where I came from. I was going to feign illness and stay in my cabin as much as possible, but when I had to converse with others, I was going to use my best manners, my best speech, my familiarity with Natchez and its people from Miss Polly and her cousin, and my knowledge of places and culture from my readings."

He grinned at her daring, and then his smile vanished as he thought of the part of her tale still to come. "What happened next?"

She moved back, away from the reach of his arms, and straightened her shoulders, bracing for an unpleasant task and determined to get through it.

"I got Fowler's horse from the stable near his lodging. He had me bring the horse in earlier, so the sleepy stableboy didn't question me when I took it. I also grabbed a long rope that I could use as a harness, because I was going to a place where something else was in danger. It deserved to live too, and I had a plan for that to happen."

He realized that the courage he had mistakenly attributed to Barnwell for defending his device actually belonged to the woman facing him.

She continued, her voice solemn.

"I went back to the Crossroads. I dug up the knife and money I had hidden. Then I went to the carriage house and looked inside the window. In the moonlight, I could see the invention was still there. You see, Markham drank. I knew his habits; everybody knew them. He was still at his cottage drinking. I had a chance to take the invention away before he could destroy it. I opened the door, careful not to make a sound.

"I discovered the top wasn't on the engine. It had been on that morning! I wondered how long it would be before I could locate the inventor to let him know where his machine was. I thought of the dirt that could get into the engine when I moved it. I thought of the rain and leaves washing down on the new motor and the animals that could nest in it if I didn't put the cover back on. I struggled with the weight of it, and it slipped out of my hands. It made a loud clang, and I hoped to heaven that no one was around to hear it.

"Moments later, a lantern shined in the shed and exposed me. I saw the senator at the door. He must've heard the noise. With Miss Polly gone and the funeral over, I didn't expect anyone to be staying in the big house, so I was shocked to see him. I never wanted to . . . meet up . . . with him, but only to get my things and take the invention.

"The senator put down his lantern. He lunged at me and smacked me. I stumbled and fell. He pulled me up by my hair and smacked me again. He told me if I made a sound, he'd beat me to a pulp. He said I had no business there, and I was going back to Fowler. I told him Fowler raped me, but he said he didn't care. He smacked me again and told me to shut up; I was going back, and if I resisted, he would cut off the tips of my fingers, one by one, until I stopped fighting him."

Tom had heard of mutilations like that used to punish slaves, but only on rare occasions and only by unusually cruel masters. Now he learned that the town's most distinguished citizen had no compunction about resorting to that brutality.

Ladybug continued. "I begged him not to take me back to Fowler. My defiance riled him, and he tore at me again. He didn't see the knife, which I had tied to my leg. As he came at me, I pulled it out and plunged it into his chest. He made the most horrible groan I ever heard, then he fell."

She covered her face and composed herself.

"I needed to have the knife, so I pulled it out. I could feel it tearing his flesh." She closed her eyes in revulsion. "I tried to stay clear of the . . . blood. I wiped the knife on his robe and quickly finished what I was doing. Before I got there, I had made a primitive collar and harness for the horse with the rope. I thought it would hold because I was planning to go only a short distance to the factory with the invention. So I swung out the rods on the side of the machine that were there for pulling it, tied them to the rope ends, and hauled the device away."

He listened, stone-faced.

"I knew the old road feeding the factory, so I took the tractor along it to stay out of sight. Once I got to the North, I would find out who the inventor was and write to tell him where I put his device. Surely he'd run a notice in a local newspaper, looking for information about his machine. Or a news article would mention his name in a report about the Barnwell . . . death. I would find a way to learn the inventor's name and address, I hoped.

"When I got to the factory, I found the old block-and-tackle from my childhood. I think the factory workers used it to move machinery around.

When I saw it, I remembered how it pleased me to lift large objects much heavier than myself, how it gave me the only sense of power I ever had. I figured I could use it to hide the invention. So I got the pulley system to the road on the ridge above the factory, where I had left the invention; then I dragged it up the hill and fastened it to a sturdy tree trunk. I hitched one end to the invention and the other to the horse, and I was able to pull the device up the hill. When I finished, I hid the pulleys in the brush up there."

She sat in a mound of red silk and black lace. He smiled at the notion of the slight figure before him hauling his tractor up the slope.

"The storm that came at dawn I think washed away any tracks I might've left on the hill. And since runaways and slaves fish in the stream and take shelter in the factory, I figured that any dust I disturbed wouldn't arouse attention. I left your invention alongside an area of tall shrubs at the top of the hill, so I think it's inconspicuous and safe."

"I see," he said simply. His solemn tone said he was profoundly grateful.

"I was heading north in the storm when a violent flash of lightning struck a tree near me. It was frightful! My horse bucked and threw me; then he got pinned under the tree. I was frantic. I still had the rope with me that I had used to haul the invention, so I tried to free the horse with it. I wasn't strong enough, and the rope was about to break. I felt I'd rather crawl under the tree and die there with the horse than go back to Fowler. It was the most wretched moment of my life. That's when you came along and freed my horse."

She bowed her head. "I'm afraid I was a bit unkind to you."

"You socked me in the face."

"I wasn't human any longer. I had no kindness left in me."

"You were kind to the horse."

She laughed for an instant. The little puff of air and sweet tone that was her laughter was like a new music that could easily become his favorite song.

Then she whispered grimly. "I was dead inside. I felt nothing that could qualify me as human. I felt no remorse for the man I killed, and I felt nothing but hatred for the man who whipped me, the man who assaulted me, and any other man too!"

"But you wanted to find the inventor. You liked him, didn't you?"

Again, the little laugh. But quickly it vanished, and she continued her tale.

"After you freed my horse, I continued north. My progress was slow, with trails flooded and a bridge down after the storm. I was at Manning Creek when the slave patrol and their bloodhound caught up with me. They snatched me off my horse. I struggled to get away. My leg rubbed against the horse's back as they pulled me off, and the knife that was tied to my calf came loose and fell into the brush. The men didn't notice it as they carried me away. But they did find the money in my pocket, and they took it.

"They rode back south a ways and hunted without success for another runaway, and then they camped for the night. It was the next day when they brought me back to Greenbriar, where Fowler was waiting for them. That's when you saw us and stopped him and you brought me to Indigo Springs."

He nodded, already figuring out the rest of the story but wanting to hear it from her.

She looked at him with the gratitude she had not yet expressed. "After you . . . saved my life, Indigo Springs became my sanctuary. I felt safe there, safe with you . . . freer than I'd ever felt before. But I was afraid to leave the plantation. I stayed clear of town, fearing I might see Markham there. If the senator sold me in the morning and was killed that very night, even Markham could put that together.

"I couldn't tell you who I was and where I came from. For all I knew, there was already a hunt out for me."

Tom nodded, following her tale.

"I was frantic to see a newspaper, but you didn't bring any home. The agricultural weeklies you read didn't carry news, so I couldn't learn about the murder case and discover the inventor's name. But I thought maybe he would post a notice in the agricultural paper about his lost device, since it's a farm machine. That was why I kept taking your journals to read the advertisements. And you were there with me in person all the time!" She shook her head in disbelief. "I should have known the inventor was you. I mean, you speak about a new age. Your device is part of that, isn't it?"

"Yes."

"There was no indication you were an inventor. I didn't see any books an inventor would read or journals he'd keep or experiments he'd do."

"They're all there in the shed on top of the hill. That's my workshop."

"Oh!" She smiled at the interesting discovery.

"After the invention went missing, I didn't go in there, so it's been boarded and locked the whole time you've been at Indigo Springs."

"Now I understand."

"Tell me about the unsigned letter that I received about the knife."

"When you unveiled Senator Barnwell's portrait, you said his murderer would hang *the next day*. I was horrified! I wrote the letter and made it look as if a stranger left it overnight. I didn't want an innocent person to die." She sighed. "Since the sheriff's looking for *me* now, I guess I was successful."

"You were," he said to the woman with a conscience.

She sighed and said nothing more.

"So, is that it? Anything more to tell?"

"Only that I love the school we started."

He smiled as she named what they both felt. He stood up and curled a hand around her arm, helping her to rise.

"Now I have a question for you." He tucked a finger under her chin and lifted her face up to his. "Why did you rescue my invention?"

She looked away introspectively, and her voice quivered with longing. "I always hoped my life would be . . . special. I always thought, 'Shouldn't there be more to my days than fanning Miss Polly or fetching her glasses or pouring her tea? Shouldn't there be something *I* choose? Can't I just once do something more important than puffing Miss Polly's pillow?' In the shed that day, the senator said fate had put him there to destroy the invention. 'Well, maybe fate put me there too,' I thought. I, Ladybug, could do something to *change* fate and make it go the way *I* wanted it to. I could save the new invention of the *horseless age.*"

She leaned back, looking up at him. His hands curled around her waist. The molten terror he had seen in her eyes in the past when he was close had now drained away. He had seen the horror of her fear and the intensity of her anger. But this time she looked unafraid, her eyes filled with a different kind of fire.

"You're the only person around here who saw the promise of my invention and wanted it to succeed," he whispered. "Ladybug, you're part of the new age . . ."

She brightened as if he'd said she was the most beautiful woman in the world.

". . . and you're part of me too."

He resisted the maddening urge to draw her closer. Instead he broke away, with his desire yielding to worry.

"Look, we need to get out of here now! Fowler and I never exchanged names, but he called me *Yankee*. Now, everybody calls me that. So when the sheriff gets to Baton Rouge and Fowler relates how he sold you to a man in Greenbriar who talks like a Yankee, the sheriff will instantly know it was me. He'll come back, go to my place, learn I'm here at Ruby Manor with a slave that fits your description, and he'll come riding up that road." He pointed to the French doors, in the direction of the winding path they had taken to Ruby Manor. "But we won't be here. We'll be long gone!"

He rushed out to the gallery and leaned over the railing. "Lance," he whispered to the slave Rachel had posted outside to be on the lookout for Markham, "saddle two horses for me, right now! Bring them around the back."

He came inside to find Ladybug shaking her head. "But you're innocent. You can't come with me. I have to leave here *alone.*"

"I'm not abandoning you to get caught!"

"Then I'll turn myself in."

"You don't know how angry—how *terrified*—these people are over what you've done! You won't get justice. You'll get *hanged!*"

Her eyes closed in terror at the thought. "But you mustn't get involved. You can explain what happened, and how you didn't know who I was, which is the truth. If you try to protect me, after I did the . . . unthinkable . . . then you'll . . . you'll be . . . hanged . . . too! You mustn't protect me!"

"Oh, no? You watch me!"

He glanced at a clock in the room and ran his hands through his hair, thinking, planning. "I need to reach the bank and get access to my funds. Then we'll get out of the South. You'll travel with me as my slave. If we get out of town before the sheriff comes back, no one will stop us."

"But—"

"No buts."

They stood facing each other. This time it was she who drew closer. Her hair tumbled down her back as she raised her head to the man who had saved her from a storm, a brute, and a fire and who now seemed determined to expand that list. She stroked his face, then wrapped her arms around his neck. Her open mouth warmed his lips, giving him a taste of the spirit stirring in defiance of her painful scars and her resolve to despise all men.

He stood still, savoring the feel of her own desire and will driving their kiss.

Slowly, as if reluctant to lose contact, she slid her arms off his body and stepped back. "Okay," she whispered. "But it's very important to me to go past the factory, so I can point out to you where I hid your invention."

"It's on the way to town, and it'll keep us off the main road." He moved toward the door. "I'll grab Barnwell's coat. And I'll take the gun I saw in his room. He won't be needing it now."

"I'll put on the frock." She pointed to the slave's dress that she had tossed aside.

"It would attract less attention," he quipped, trying to ease the tension of the dangers still ahead. "I'll be back for you in a minute. We'll leave quietly, while everyone's asleep."

He was about to open the door, then turned back to her, jolted by the thought of a telltale mark and her mysterious relationship to someone else who had that same mark and was in that house.

"The sooner we get out of here, the better!" he whispered. "And we mustn't let anyone see us!"

As he opened the door, his hand stopped in mid-motion. There in the hall facing him were Charlotte and Rachel.

# CHAPTER 28

From the half-open door, Tom was the only one visible inside. He stood there staring in astonishment at the two women whose flustered faces were nearly as red as their hair.

"Lord in heaven!" Charlotte gasped. "Consorting with a *slave*! In my house! Is that what you're doing?"

Tom offered no denial.

She stammered in disbelief. "You . . . you . . . scoundrel to end all scoundrels!"

"Merciful God! How can you insult me like this?" Rachel scowled.

"Why aren't you sleeping, instead of checking up on me?" Tom asked her simply.

"Your arrogance knows no limit! It's *your* fault I couldn't sleep. You've been drifting away for so long that I went to your room to learn your intentions once and for all," Rachel said petulantly. "I thought maybe we could . . . reconcile . . . our differences." She looked at him expectantly. He looked unmoved. "When you weren't there, I called Mother. And now we find this . . . this . . . outrage!"

"We're breaking all ties with you, Mr. Edmunton!" Charlotte planted her hands on her hips, the strength in her clenched fists contrasting with the frailty of the lace nightgown sleeves puffing out under her robe. "You've insulted us with your vulgarity! You can be sure I won't be needing you any longer to run the Crossroads."

"Nash is most eager to help us, Mama. We'll accept his offer and be rid of this beast!"

"I agree!" Charlotte jabbed a finger in Tom's face. "And I forbid you to call on my daughter *ever again*."

"I understand completely. So if you'll excuse us, we'll leave."

Standing firmly in the doorway, blocking his exit, the women clearly were not finished.

"When your father died, we opened our hearts to you, and what did we get?" charged Charlotte.

The frill of Rachel's negligee in the V slice of her robe billowed like a sail in the angry wind of her breath. "You dishonor me with a *slave*? A dumb, miserable, wretched *slave*?"

"I see you're eager for us to leave, so we'll oblige you right now." Tom tried to enter the hallway and close the door behind him to give the unseen occupant a chance to change.

Rachel eyed him suspiciously. "What are you hiding?" Suddenly, she swung the door wide open—and gasped. There was the creature she despised, wearing her best evening dress, quietly observing the uproar.

"Good Lord Almighty!" Rachel stormed into the room. "My gown! And my . . . my . . . *garnet* cape! That cape's worth three times what *you* are. Take it off, wench!" She reached for the cape.

Ladybug moved away. "I'll take it off without your help!"

Tom saw the feral look he had come to dread creep over Ladybug's face. He was about to intervene between the two adversaries when Charlotte grabbed him, shook him by the arms, then beat her fists against his chest, her voice hissing like a kettle that had finally reached its boiling point. "I've had it with your invention, your arrogance, your insolence, the misfortune you've brought upon our family, and now this disgrace, this dishonor!" She clutched his shirt. "I'll *not* have a scandal! I won't! I won't!"

"You needn't have one. We'll leave *now*." Tom tried to break free of the furious fists.

"I'm *respected* in this town, something you neither know nor care anything about. I have my standing to keep!" She had the crazed glare of someone obsessed with a matter beyond all reason.

While he tried to subdue Charlotte, the young women pushed each other around the room. Quickly they were entangled, hitting each other, losing their balance, falling into the French doors and swinging them open into the gallery, and landing on the floor. Red and brown hair flew wildly as their heads snapped, their fists flew, and their nails scratched. First Ladybug rolled on top, her voluminous hooped crinoline and pantalets exposed in the fray while she slapped Rachel with her left hand and then her right. Then Rachel was on top, her dressing gown tearing at the underarms with the brawling swings she took at Ladybug. Neither woman seemed to notice her immodest condition or care. They pulled each others' hair, hurling insults all the while.

"You wicked wench!" shrilled Rachel.

"You bully!"

"Take those clothes off!"

"I'll *never* take them off now!"

Then came a hoarse whisper that struck a deeper chord. "Stay away from Tom, you bitch!" Rachel demanded.

"He doesn't want you."

"You're a slave and a slut. You'll be whipped and you'll obey!"

"He still won't want you."

Tom freed himself from Charlotte's attacks and tried to break up the girls. He pushed his way past soft lace and hard fists, perfumed skin and venomous words, silky arms and flying elbows. While he controlled his strength in an effort not to hurt them, they intensified theirs in the grip of their fury. They looked like two hissing cats overwhelming a larger canine that could fight a battle with its own kind but was disarmed by the wiry little combatants who scratched, clawed, and jabbed.

Charlotte grabbed a poker from the fireplace and struck him on the back, the arms, and the chest with it, screaming, "I'll not have any scandal. I'll not lose my reputation!" until he had to extricate himself from the girls to disarm the raging mother.

He looked astonished. Her fears seemed too extreme for a guest's misbehavior in her home.

As the young women tumbled, the cape was pulled this way and that, but it remained on Ladybug's shoulders. Then Rachel straddled Ladybug and loosened the cape's bow. Ladybug threw her off and tried to stand. Rachel pulled her down and reached for the cape. Ladybug blocked her. Finally at an impasse, the combatants sat back on their haunches, facing each other.

"I'll tear those clothes off you and burn them! They must *never* touch me after touching you."

"They look better on me. You're fat!"

In one quick tug, Rachel pulled the cape off Ladybug's shoulders.

Ladybug grabbed the V-shaped panels of Rachel's robe and pulled the fabric off her shoulders, along with her nightgown. "There, how do *you* like it when someone pulls at *your*—" Her voice suddenly choked.

Rachel's hand fell limp, and the prized cape she had so ardently sought slipped indifferently through her fingers to the floor as she stared at the wild creature in her evening gown. Visible between strands of hair, Rachel saw the mark above Ladybug's breast.

Ladybug, frozen, stared at the same marking on Rachel.

The morning sun was streaming in through the open French doors. It shone like a spotlight on the girls' incredulous faces . . . and on the birthmark above each of their hearts.

At first, Charlotte didn't realize what had occurred. Tom held onto the poker he had wrestled from her, but he was gaping at the girls. She followed his glance. Ladybug's back was to her as she saw Rachel's clothing torn. The attack on her daughter inflamed her.

She bent down to Ladybug and shook her by the shoulders. "Why, you little vixen, you'll get *fifty* stripes—" Then Charlotte caught sight of the little mark on Ladybug. Her hands flew off the girl's body as from a surface too hot to touch. Startled, she smothered her gasp with her hands.

Like mirror images, Ladybug and Rachel faced each other. They slowly rose to their feet, each open-mouthed, with bruised face, tumbling hair, and disbelieving eyes. Each touched her own birthmark and eyed the other's.

Tom sighed in resignation of that which now had to be faced. He identified her adversaries to Ladybug: "This is Rachel Barnwell, the senator's daughter, and Mrs. Barnwell, his widow." To Rachel and Charlotte, he said simply, "Meet Ladybug."

Seeing the two young women together, the resemblance he hadn't identified before seemed uncanny: the tapered nose, the sculpted lips, the petite form.

Bewildered, Ladybug looked down at her own birthmark, then her eyes slowly traveled to Rachel's. She glanced at Tom. "Is this passed down?"

"No, never!" cried Rachel. She turned to Charlotte. "Oh, Mama, this is terrible!" She embraced the woman who was still too shocked to speak. Then in a flash she turned back to Ladybug. "You killed my father!"

Ladybug shot back, "Whoever killed your father gave him just what he deserved."

Tom wedged himself between them. "Rachel, your father sold Ladybug to a vicious man, Fred Fowler, who assaulted her."

"And how exactly do *you* fit into that picture? What are *you* doing with *her*?"

"I was in town when Fowler was there torturing her. I bought her to stop the cruelty. I didn't discover till a little while ago who she really was."

Rachel bristled. "Hmm. I wonder how you made your discovery."

Tom shook her by the arms. "The cruelty I couldn't bear to watch and had to stop was of your father's making."

"She'll hang, regardless!" said Rachel. "Won't she, Mama?"

Charlotte didn't reply. She looked distant and disturbed, in the throes of a vivid memory.

"Mama, are you all right?"

"Wiley . . . Wiley . . . what did you do?" Charlotte spoke in the dazed manner of a sleepwalker.

Ladybug looked curiously at Rachel. "If the senator was your father," she said, her curiosity turning to revulsion, "does that mean he was also . . . *my*—"

"No! He's nothing to you. I'm nothing to you!"

"I wonder . . ." Ladybug stepped away, toward the French doors opening onto the gallery. She looked out, absorbed in her own recollection, whispering to herself. "I was left with Miss Polly in the basket of flowers . . . with the scarlet ladybug. . . ."

Charlotte was glassy-eyed, disturbed by something in the past.

Rachel placed her hand on her mother's arm. "Mama, are you feeling all right?"

Charlotte absently patted Rachel's hand while she stared at the strange new person in their lives. Then her face looked alarmed. "Wiley, don't! Don't!"

"See what you've done?" Rachel said to Ladybug. "You've upset my mother. She's in shock because you're trying to ruin us with lies, all lies! You murderess!"

Deep in reflection, Ladybug didn't reply. As her eyes were pulled outside the French doors, her attention was pulled out of the scene and into the distant past. "Miss Polly said the *flowers* were red too. Yes! I remember, there was a scarlet ladybug with black spots on the scarlet flowers in the basket. . . ."

"Goodness, Tom, you've gone and spoiled everything we could've had!" cried Rachel. "Tom?"

He wasn't listening to her. Ladybug's recollections had captured his attention. He walked toward the disheveled figure in the gown, trying to hear her over Rachel's raving and Charlotte's rambling.

"Miss Polly said the flowers had no stems . . . just the blossoms were in the basket. . . . Miss Polly said I looked so tiny and fragile among all those blossoms."

A few tears dropped softly from Charlotte's unblinking eyes. "Wiley, what did you do?"

Rachel vigorously tapped her mother's hands. "Now, Mama, snap out of it!"

Then the young redhead walked close to Tom. She pressed against him, clutching his shirt, her robe and negligee slipping off her shoulders.

"You know, we've suffered enough already, thanks to your invention and the tragedy it caused. Now you come here with this girl to bring shame to us. Don't you see, this whole matter will ruin Mother? Look at her. She's in shock. Everyone looks up to her. She'll never be able to show her face again in town. And what about me? I have a standing to maintain too."

He quietly studied her.

"What if my father had an . . . indiscretion . . . years ago? Why stir up ancient ashes to make Mother ill and bring us disgrace?"

Distracted by another voice, Tom slowly took her arms off his chest and turned back to Ladybug.

"Why would someone snip off the stems?" Ladybug asked herself aloud.

Tom's brows arched sharply, anticipating the direction of her thoughts.

"Unless there were *thorns* on the stems . . . if the flowers were . . . roses . . . like those." The girl from the basket pointed curiously to the perimeter of blossoms outside, which the morning sun now captured in its full crimson glory.

Charlotte whispered to herself. "Oh, Lord, we were . . . so . . . young. . . ."

Ladybug's finger stood suspended in space, pointing at the roses beyond the gallery. "Who would wrap an infant in flowers? I always thought it would be a . . . woman." She suddenly looked astonished. Her body pivoted so that her finger was now pointing inside the room. At Charlotte.

Her look of astonishment turned to certainty. She lunged at Charlotte. Her formal attire proved no excuse for manners and femininity, with her elbows high, her eyes ruthless, and her furious tangle of hair flying through the air and blocking the view of her prey to anything but her urgent presence.

"Stop! Stop! Leave me alone!" Charlotte looked like the hapless victim of an attack by a wildcat. "You mustn't! Stop!" She tried to throw off the headstrong creature, but Ladybug was tenacious.

Rachel rushed to stop the assault on her mother, but she was halted by Tom's powerful arms thrown around her.

Ladybug tugged at Charlotte's robe and the nightgown beneath it, pulling the fine silk garments down to expose the older woman's ivory shoulders and the skin above her breasts.

Then everyone froze: Rachel stopped fighting. Tom's arms loosened their grip on her. Ladybug halted her attack. And Charlotte broke off her screams. She and Ladybug stood staring at each other.

The ever-modest Charlotte, she of the high-collared dresses and the obsessive concern for propriety, possessed skin that was still as smooth and lovely as that of the young women now gaping at her.

Another feature of hers also matched that of the two others, one that still looked as exotic and beguiling on her as it did on them. It was the little heart-shaped birthmark.

# CHAPTER 29

Mortified, Charlotte closed her eyes. When she opened them again, she was staring at the person from whom she had hidden for nineteen years. Her face softened to show a tinge of regret, even of motherly caring. The sadness in her eyes met the coldness in Ladybug's. Charlotte took a step toward her, but Ladybug moved away.

Then the mother turned to face the other daughter from whom she had hidden the truth.

Rachel was aghast. A hoarse whisper replaced her voice. "Mama! How can this be?"

Charlotte spoke with resignation, almost relieved at no longer having to hold the lid on a powder keg. "I couldn't explain, not even to you, dear. When you were two years old and your . . . when *she* was born"—she gestured to Ladybug—"I saw on her the same mark that *we* had. It was scarcely the size of a pinhead on her newborn skin, but it was there from the beginning. After that, I wore high-necked clothing and applied powders to conceal the mark, even around you, Rachel. And I used a doctor outside of town, in Mortonville," she said, naming a nearby village to the east. "I was discreet, so no one would discover my secret marking and ever link me to . . . her."

The person to whom she pointed stared at her with contempt.

"Your father and Aunt Polly knew about her," Charlotte added. "And also my midwife, who died a few years later. I couldn't let anyone else know. Not even you, Rachel."

"*This means I was born free!*" Ladybug almost sang the words like a hymn. According to the law, children of mixed race were pronounced slave or free depending on the status of their mothers.

247

"You're a free person *of color* at best. That's *not* the same thing." Rachel corrected her.

Free people of color were caught in the corridor between the two great halls of slavery and freedom, and they shifted nearer to one or the other depending on local laws and the men who interpreted them.

The three women had not moved to cover their exposed birthmarks: Ladybug in a plunging gown, and the Barnwells, who were either too stunned to pull their night clothes up over their shoulders or no longer cared because the truth was now out.

"The tombstone!" Tom suddenly recalled. "At the Crossroads burial grounds, there's the grave of Leanna Barnwell, the stillborn child of Charlotte and Wiley, who was two years younger than Rachel." He shot a questioning glance at Ladybug.

"I've seen that grave," she said.

"That's *you*. You're Leanna Barnwell." He turned to Charlotte. "People would've known you were expecting a child. You had to account for that. So you went through a mock burial, didn't you? Who could suspect there was no body inside a cast-iron casket supposed to contain a lightweight infant? That casket's empty, isn't it?"

"It was filled with straw," Charlotte admitted.

"That's why you declined to join Rachel when she put flowers at Leanna's grave after Polly's funeral. You knew there was no child buried there."

"Yes."

"Rachel, this is *Sis*." Tom gestured to Ladybug. "This is the sister you always wanted to have, the sister you yearned for and made your imaginary companion through childhood. You wished she were alive. Well, she *is*. She's *Ladybug*."

"No! Never!" Rachel screamed. "She can't be my sister. Mama, if this unspeakable scandal gets out, I'm *ruined*. I might as well be *dead!* How could you do this to me?"

Ladybug looked as unhappy with her newfound relatives as they were with her.

"Of course, Leanna wasn't the stillborn child of *Wiley* but the very-much-alive child of another man." Tom's eyes sparked as more circuits connected in his mind. "That was why the senator was in a hurry to sell Ladybug on the morning of the funeral, with Polly's body hardly cold. He wanted her out of there before you arrived, didn't he, Mrs. Barnwell?"

"Wiley talked of selling her. He worried about my seeing her after all these years and what I might do." She looked solicitously at Ladybug, as if she could ease her own guilt with a sign of her daughter's forgiveness. "You know, one can never completely stop the beating of a mother's heart."

248

"You needn't keep such a weak thing beating on my account, Mrs. Barnwell." Ladybug spoke with the detachment of a judge hearing a case about someone else's mother.

Tom continued. "So when Nash noticed the birthmark on Ladybug, that cinched the matter for your husband. It pushed him over the edge to do what he was tempted to do anyway."

"I'm sure."

"At the funeral, when I heard the senator tell you that he took care of *more* than he had expected to do that morning, I wondered what he meant. You knew what he meant, didn't you, Mrs. Barnwell? You knew that he had disposed of your daughter. Isn't that so?"

"Yes." Charlotte lowered her head guiltily. Then, as if a mother's shame were battling with a wife's supposed duty, with the latter winning for the moment, she raised her head more boldly. "Wiley didn't discuss the matter with me. He didn't consult me, but why would he? It was his right to do what he did."

"It was his right to sell your daughter—born a *free* woman—to a cruel man who abused her?"

Charlotte looked dismayed. Tom had a pesky way of unsettling her conscience. "Polly treated her well, and I can't help what Wiley did. But she couldn't *ever* be free. That was *always* out of the question."

"Only because you couldn't admit to being her mother."

"How could I admit to such a thing, Tom? Do you think Wiley could hold political office after such a scandal? Do you think I could be received in a single household here? Do you think Rachel could grow up here and find a husband? It would've destroyed our lives."

"So instead you destroyed *her* life."

"You're heartless, you are! The colonel's son, and you have no pity!"

"So that's why you never visited Polly. It was always Polly who visited you, wasn't it, Mrs. Barnwell?"

Charlotte looked away evasively.

"You said the air at the Crossroads didn't agree with you, but what didn't agree with you was having to come face-to-face with the daughter you abandoned to slavery," Tom charged. "By your laws, she was born free. You condemned her to bondage!"

"I let her *live*! I saved her from Wiley! Do you realize what a *feat* that was?"

Ladybug, who had stepped away from the others, detaching physically and emotionally from her newly discovered family, now approached her mother. "I'd like to know, if you'll tell me, who is my father?"

"A wonderful man!" A glow appeared on Charlotte's face. "You remind me so much of him, with those flashing eyes . . . and the spirit!"

Charlotte glanced out the window and off in the distance, reminiscing about someone who brought a smile to her lips. The worry lines seemed to vanish from her face as she suddenly looked younger and more vibrant. "He was a slave child who was my age, living on my father's plantation. We played together as children; we were inseparable, actually. I secretly taught him to read and write, and I brought him books he liked to read, especially ones about building and architecture. He drew sketches of beautiful palaces and placed me in them. He was so playful and made me laugh! When he was old enough for a man's labor, he became my father's carpenter, and when I married Wiley, he came with me to the Barnwell household."

She sighed with contentment at her recollection.

"Every loving sentiment that the town thought Wiley felt toward me really came from Leanna's father. He adored me. He built this house for me. The plans and the majesty of it were his idea. He made it a joy for me to live in," she said fondly. "He was more than a carpenter. In another place and time, he would've been an architect. He took so much care in picking just the right site for Ruby Manor and designing all the rooms to suit me. He placed my music parlor where I'd have beautiful vistas and my bedroom where I'd have cool breezes. Wiley just approved the plans and paid the expenses. He didn't dwell on me the way Leanna's father did."

Charlotte pointed out the window to the brilliant red streak along the grounds outside.

"And it was Leanna's father who created the border of roses to surround me with my favorite flower. He went to great lengths to get the heartiest stocks with the most vibrant color and fragrance, and he supervised every detail of the planting . . . all for me. By the time I moved in, the roses were already blooming. In years to come, the little bushes grew to the massive display you see today. I awake every morning to the sight and fragrance of those stunning blossoms because he planned everything that way."

She put her hands up over her heart.

"He was the prime mover of this manor . . . and of my affections. Ruby Manor wasn't a testament to Wiley's love, as the town thought. It was a testament to another man's love for me, a romantic man who always kept my pleasure and comfort foremost in his mind." She sighed wistfully. "That was Daniel."

"Daniel?" Tom said. "That name means something. . . ."

The daughters turned to him as he pondered the matter. Charlotte offered no help.

"I know!" he said. "When I looked back in Polly's plantation journals to find a record of Ladybug's birth, I didn't find any mention of her, but right about that same time Polly noted that some of her slaves went to Ruby Manor to attend the . . . funeral"—he looked incredulous—"of a slave named *Daniel* who had . . . *drowned*."

The last word gave Charlotte a start. Tom and Ladybug looked at each other grimly, forming the same conclusion.

"Daniel's death wasn't an accident, was it, Mrs. Barnwell?"

Charlotte's fearful eyes met Tom's probing ones.

"Your husband drowned him, didn't he?"

Rachel looked dismayed. Charlotte looked grieved. Ladybug and Tom looked repulsed. But none of them looked surprised at the charge against Barnwell.

"Dear God, Tom, you don't understand." Charlotte's reproach had the tone of a plea for mercy. "You have this wild devotion to your ideals, and you're oblivious to how things really are! It makes you cruel!"

"I'm cruel for mentioning it, but your husband wasn't cruel for doing it? For drowning your lover? That was the price Daniel paid for Ladybug, wasn't it?"

Charlotte wept softly, covering her face with her hands, as if the pain was fresh and piercing.

"I saved the child!" she whispered, composing herself. "It wasn't Daniel's fault. I provoked him. Back then I had *passion*. It's funny, because now I can't even remember what that felt like. But then, oh, I had an overwhelming passion . . . for romance, for a man who cherished me, for *him, Daniel*. I provoked him . . . and that led to his . . ." The agony on her face was evidence that she too had paid a price.

"Daniel was everything Wiley was not. Daniel was full of life, whereas Wiley was cold and aloof. Daniel looked at me in a way that Wiley never did, as if I were the sun rising in his world. He was so gentle, affectionate, and caring. Wiley was none of those things. Wiley ignored me. He showed so little affection. You see, Wiley didn't love people. Instead, he . . . controlled them. He wanted a wife to host his parties, to look beautiful on his arm, and to say the right things to suit his political ambitions. My father pushed me into the marriage. Wiley was a successful planter and a budding town leader— everything *my father* wanted! But Daniel was what *I* wanted. I was young and spirited. So I did the only daring thing I've ever done in my life. And I was unbelievably happy in Daniel's arms!"

Ladybug listened intently to the story of the love that had conceived her.

"It didn't last long. I was terrified and broke it up. I didn't think my trysts with Daniel had led to anything. Then when Leanna was born, it was obvious I was wrong. Polly was with me when I gave birth. Wiley walked in on us. He took one look at Leanna in my arms, and he knew who the father was. The way Daniel and I looked at each other, even a dull man like Wiley could sense the sparks between us that he himself was incapable of feeling.

"I tried to explain to Wiley how lonely I was, how ignored I felt, how attracted I was to someone else. Is that so bad, to be attracted? I told him it was completely my fault. But he would have none of it! He told himself I was forced. And in his mind, that justified *anything*. He stormed out and . . . the next day the slaves found Daniel's body."

251

Charlotte wiped away a tear.

"When Wiley left to go after Daniel, I knew he would come back for Leanna. I had the midwife go out and pick the roses. I told her no stems, no thorns, just the softest blossoms. I wanted a basketful of them. She brought me the flowers as I lay in bed with you in my arms," she said, looking at Ladybug as she spoke. "I wrapped you in the roses your father had so lovingly planted for me. And I gave you to Polly. She agreed to raise you; she loved you from the start." Charlotte smiled at the image of the bundle in her arms. "You were such a sweet baby. You made no sound. You seemed to like lying in your perfumed blanket of flowers. That was how Polly sneaked you out into her coach.

"When Wiley came back, I mustered all my courage, a *mother's* courage, and I told him the baby was with Polly and I would *not* let him have her. It was the first and only time I ever stood up to Wiley. I was prepared for a fierce fight, which I was willing to wage for you," she said to Ladybug. She seemed to want credit for her act from a daughter whose face was unreadable. "Wiley backed down. He didn't go after you." She turned to the others. "But he made me swear never to go to Polly's home to see the baby. And Polly was never to bring her here. I swore."

Charlotte's eyes returned to Ladybug. "As the years passed, Polly would whisper to me about how beautiful and smart you were. I thought of how Daniel would have adored you!" She smiled at the stunning beauty who was her daughter. "You would have been his little princess."

The girl nodded, her contempt softened by the story of her parents' love.

"So I arranged for your care as best I could. Then I spent my life with Wiley." She looked at the others, her smile vanishing. "If only you knew how unbearable he was after Leanna's birth! I tried to atone, but there was nothing I could do." She turned to her other daughter. "So I tried to ensure that *your* life would be better than mine, Rachel. I tried to subdue *your* wayward ways. Oh, yes, you were spirited too. That's why I had to get you back here from Philadelphia, from your dangerous fascination with a suitor who I feared was quick on passion but slow on a marriage proposal." She glanced disapprovingly at Tom, then turned back to Rachel. "And your work in the theater? My God, that had to end! I wouldn't allow you to become as headstrong as I was."

At the mention of Philadelphia, Rachel and Tom looked at each other, with a heated resentment on her face and only a detached sadness on his.

"Thank goodness, I rescued you, Rachel. But you still managed to defy me with your daring dresses that revealed the birthmark. I see now that it was that telltale little mark that got us into trouble after all! It's like a branding, a way for fate to punish me for trying to change something more powerful than myself, something that mustn't be throttled, something that destroys its foes."

"What's that, Mrs. Barnwell?" asked Tom.

"The soul of the South."

Charlotte's eyes took on that glassy look again, as if she was once more slipping away from reality and into a dream-like state.

"All I got for my efforts to redeem myself was Wiley's scorn. My devilish deed constantly lived in his reproachful eyes. It wasn't just Daniel and Leanna who were punished. I was too, because I dared to reach for . . . what . . . couldn't . . . be." Her story ended with a shudder and a bent head.

As everyone digested the tale, the only sound was Charlotte's weeping.

Tom was the first to speak, his voice softened by her pain. "Mrs. Barnwell, it seems so sad that you spent your life with a man you didn't love. Before you married, you could have run away to the North with Daniel. Back then the laws were more lax, and Daniel would have had a good chance of escaping recapture by your father. With his carpenter's trade, you two could have lived well. You could have found a tolerant community and made a life together with the man you really loved. Wouldn't you have been a lot happier then?"

"Oh, my, yes! But of course, that wasn't possible."

"But *you* weren't a slave. What stopped you? It wasn't a bullet or a chain or a whip."

"Condemnation. Being disowned by your family, rejected by your friends, and shunned by the whole town! That's *worse* than a bullet. Can't you understand that?"

"You mean, it was just the *displeasure* inside someone's mind that stopped you from living the life you wanted? Just someone's ignorant, unkind feelings toward you? Isn't that all it really amounts to, Mrs. Barnwell, this soul of the South that scares you so?"

"You make it sound so bland. Public scandal is real and frightening!"

"You were *free*, but you let your life be controlled by others. You stifled your own spirit and will, the way a . . . *slave* . . . has to do."

Rachel intervened. "Stop it! Stop it, Tom!"

"You pretend to have this grand existence," Tom said, glancing at the stately room, "while inside, you're . . . chained." He whispered, more to himself than to the others, "Who's the *real* slave?"

Rachel shot an angry finger at his face. "You keep throwing your haughty contempt for our lives at us." She taunted him, though he looked unmoved by her accusations. "I thought you'd be a man like my father. But you'll *never* be the man he was. My father was respected and admired wherever he went. But what are you? An outcast and a slave-lover." The jabbing finger moved toward her sister, who stared at her in quiet contempt. "You're carrying on with *her*? You chose *her* over *me*? I've never been so humiliated and degraded in my life!"

"You threw away our life together in Philly. For what? You sold our happiness for a life of dresses and parties, and you didn't care at whose expense they came. Now you bathe in your father's false claims to glory and you carry out the life he carved out for you. Do you think that's attractive to me?"

"You threw away a life we could've had together here at home to cast your lot with our enemies."

"Are *science* and *progress* the enemies you detest with such vigor?"

Tom caught a glimpse of Ladybug staring at him. In one breathless hour they had discovered a trove of information about each other that they hadn't uncovered in their previous three months together. He paused to dwell on the face of the woman who understood how he felt.

Then he turned back to Rachel. "The glow you had in Philly—the spirit and the innocence—are gone. The only lust you have now is for malice. When you let others smother your own inclinations, then who's the slave and who's the master?"

"You bastard!" Rachel was livid.

She snapped her arm back to strike him, but Ladybug caught it and forced it down. "Don't touch him!"

The sisters sneered at each other. Their mother watched in silence.

Tom observed the complex mix of emotions coloring Charlotte's face when she looked at Ladybug. He sensed sadness, regret . . . a latent affection. Could he reach her? Was it too late? He grabbed her arms and made a fervent plea. "Mrs. Barnwell, you have an extraordinary chance here to save your forgotten daughter. You have a chance to do something that Daniel would've desperately wanted you to do—and what I believe *you* really want to do too."

"Whatever would that be?"

"It's in your power to throw the sheriff off Ladybug's track. She had no intention of harming your husband, and she didn't commit murder!"

The sympathy on Charlotte's face gave Tom hope.

"When the sheriff gets to Baton Rouge, Fowler will tell him that he sold Wiley Barnwell's slave to a man in Greenbriar who talks like a Yankee. That will set the sheriff on my trail. He'll return to town and go to Indigo Springs. There he'll find out that I came here, and that I took with me a slave who matches Ladybug's description. So the sheriff will be coming *here*. Probably before nightfall. He'll come to arrest your daughter for an action she can explain and justify, but she won't get a fair hearing to clear herself."

"What would you have me do, Tom?" asked Charlotte.

"You can stall the sheriff and buy time while Ladybug escapes. You can tell him we went east to Mortonville. You can say we were treated by your nurse last night, but today we saw that our burns from the fire had worsened. So you sent us to Mortonville to see the doctor there, who's your personal

254

physician and trusted friend. After that, you can tell the sheriff, I was planning to return to Indigo Springs."

The women listened as Tom formulated his plan.

"You can say that I didn't appear to know the slave with me was Ladybug, or the man I bought her from was Fowler. You can act surprised when the sheriff tells you that. You can tell him I mentioned buying the slave when she was mistreated by a stranger that I encountered in Greenbriar. It'll confirm what Fowler told the sheriff—that he didn't get my name or give me his or the girl's—so Duran won't question it. You can emphasize that you don't believe we're running away, so if the sheriff will simply go back to Indigo Springs and wait for me, I'll show up with the girl. You can be a real good actress, Mrs. Barnwell, just like Rachel. Won't you play this one great role for Leanna?" He searched Charlotte's eyes for a sign of self-assertion. "You can either feed her to the wolves of this town or you can throw the sheriff off her track while I help her escape. *Choose*, Mrs. Barnwell."

"Well . . . I . . . Oh, my!" Charlotte looked frightened. "Rachel, dear, oh, what should I do?" she said helplessly. She lifted her arms, trying to reach out to Rachel, but Tom blocked her.

Ladybug walked to her mother. "I never willfully harmed anyone in my life, Mrs. Barnwell. I never attacked anyone who didn't attack me first. I just want a chance to leave here. It's what I've yearned for my whole life. Whenever I saw your husband in past years at the Crossroads, he always made it clear that he detested me. On the day of Polly's funeral, he knowingly sold me to a monster. Your husband wasn't very kind to me, or to you, Mrs. Barnwell."

"How about it?" Tom added. "In the name of the man you loved and your daughter who wants to live. You gave up your own happiness. Now will you let Leanna try for hers?"

"Oh, my, my, *my!*" Having to make a crucial choice paralyzed Charlotte.

Tom pressed her. "Mrs. Barnwell, you're out of your husband's grasp now. You can think and act on your own. For once, you can be master of yourself!"

"No, she can't!" said Rachel. Three sets of eyes turned to her. "Mama, if that bastard child is ever linked to you, this town will crucify us both! She's wanted for murder. What if you *did* help her escape, and she got captured anyway? She'll try to get a real trial like free folks do. She'll show the birthmark and insist she's *your* daughter!"

"Lord have mercy!" Charlotte gasped.

"I'll be ruined, Mama. Do you want to save one daughter by destroying the other?"

"This is ghastly, just ghastly!" Charlotte wrenched her hair as if she were going mad.

Tom stared bitterly at Rachel, who had now become his formidable competitor in a contest for a prize named Charlotte.

Then he dug his fingers into Charlotte's arms, his voice as rough as his hands. "If you won't help your daughter escape because it's right, then help her because it'll avoid a trial and a scandal for you!"

Charlotte's body went limp in Tom's grip; it seemed as weak and spent as her will.

"Rachel's right. If Ladybug is caught, she'll have to prove she's a free woman—your daughter—to get a better shake at justice. That means you'll be ordered by the court to show your birthmark, and Leanna's grave site will be dug up to show there's no one buried there. You'll have a scandal that'll rock this old town, Mrs. Barnwell. You'll be exposed as Ladybug's mother. You'll be disgraced. You'll never be able to show your face in public again!" Tom was merciless.

"Good Lord! Whatever will I do!" Charlotte trembled. "There'll be a trial! And a *scandal*—"

"Not if we think like Papa, there won't be." Everyone turned to Rachel, whose voice was rich with malice.

Tom had always thought Rachel resembled her mother. But at that moment he recognized in her shrewd voice and calculating smile something that was pure Wiley Barnwell.

"The murderess could be . . . taken care of . . . before any court hears the case. If Nash helps us on that score, Mama, he might be rewarded," she said coyly, "with a blushing bride and with the Crossroads as a wedding present."

"Are you crazy?" Tom was taken aback, for Rachel made her proposal with coldhearted calculation.

"If we're unable to . . . take care of . . . the matter beforehand," Rachel continued, " then the case of a slave murdering a senator will be heard by a tribunal of Papa's friends. Her story about the birthmark will never come out. It'll be a case of a slave killing a master and nothing more. Open and shut." Rachel strutted around the room like a queen addressing her court. "Why Tom, you look like a wounded puppy. What do you think politics is for, if not to . . . *massage* the law from time to time?"

"Your father's friends can't massage Sheriff Duran. Ladybug's real identity will come out," Tom insisted.

Rachel didn't seem worried. "We'll go abroad, Mama and me. You see, Mama hasn't been feeling well lately. The ordeal over my father's death has weakened her. So she and I simply won't be available when the case is tried. Papa's lawyer will argue that Ladybug made up the story, and the judge will order the tribunal to proceed."

"Ladybug can show *proof* of her ties to you and your mother by comparing her birthmark to yours," said Tom.

"Not if Mother and I aren't here to make the comparison." Rachel pulled her clothing back up over her shoulders, then did the same to her mother's, hiding the little markings that had caused such a ruckus. She said coyly, "What birthmark?"

"The empty casket will be dug up."

"Will it? On the grounds of lies from a desperate slave? Papa's attorney will stop it."

"You can't stop Duran. He'll pursue justice."

Rachel laughed like a card player who held all the aces. "Didn't I speak plain enough for you, Tom? The judges and slave owners that will hear the case are our friends. Why, Mama, remember the times we've had Judge Jackson and Judge Holland and their families here for dinner?" she asked cunningly. "That silly sheriff—why, I reckon he can be run out of office too."

"Do you realize what you're saying?" Tom was incredulous. "You want to sabotage the law—to make it *kill* for you, in order to soothe your vengeful feelings. Is that the kind of person you've become?" Tom looked at the woman who was now a stranger to him. "Don't you see that your father could have been killed in an act of self-defense?"

"All the evidence points to this creature as the only remaining suspect. A slave killing a master is *never* self-defense. No circumstance could ever excuse it. Do you think there'll be any planter on that tribunal who won't feel the same way?" Rachel's smile mocked him. "Do you think the verdict on the wench is going to be anything but guilty? . . . Not to mention the verdict on anyone who tries to help her flee."

"You have to do the right thing. Not for *her* sake, but for yours." He looked at her grimly. "You're crossing a line, Rachel—"

"Really?" She laughed derisively.

"There'll be nothing left of you if you have your sister *killed* for nothing more than to satisfy your own jealousy and malice."

She waved her hand contemptuously. "Why, Tom, sometimes your . . . purity . . . amazes me."

"You can't get away with your evil scheme. You can't treat the law as if it were your personal plaything, to twist and turn to suit *your* ends while it destroys other people's lives. You can't hold yourself above the law."

"Oh no? What do you think politics is for?" Her eyes were sinister. "Why do you think Papa spent so much time planting his seeds in that field? So we could be treated just like anybody else?"

Her remark left Tom speechless. Suddenly, he understood the nature of something that had disturbed him since his return to Greenbriar, something that was never captured in the untroubled painting of itself that Greenbriar presented to the world. Beneath the calm waters on the canvas, he felt the town's undertow, the pernicious current that swallowed so many victims: the forced shutdown of a factory, the uncontested assault of a helpless woman on the town's main street, the laws against contrary ideas and practices, the school he had to keep a secret, the schemes to sabotage his invention, and above all, the many whom the town, like a reckless mother, had abandoned to bondage. It was people like Wiley Barnwell who sought to control the town's current, to drive it this way or that to suit their purposes, and to drown anything that got in their way. But how did they get away with this? Now, he realized the answer. They had to snare the *law*, to pull it away from the clear stream of justice and into the murky swamp of power. Rachel understood and approved of this abduction and was now joining the ranks of people like her father.

Tom glanced at the slender figure in the ballroom gown with the untamable hair of a huntress. He would *not* let the town's current carry her away.

He turned to the disoriented mother to make a final plea. "Mrs. Barnwell, this is your chance to assert your own will. Rachel lives in your home and off your money, so you have the upper hand. You can shut Rachel up. You can threaten to cut her off. You can show her *you're* calling the shots. Tell her you insist on stalling the sheriff and giving your other daughter a chance to escape. To atone for Daniel's death and his daughter's bondage, you have to act now. You have to stand up to Rachel!"

Charlotte looked as if something had snapped in her mind to disengage her from a reality she could not handle. Her face took on a distant, detached look. "Wiley protected us," she said dreamily. "Wiley always made our choices. He knew what to do."

"I'll take care of you now, Mama," said Rachel soothingly. "I'll take Papa's place."

"Yes, dear. You do what your daddy would have done. You take care of us now, dear."

The woman who had lost her will conceded to the daughter who had lost her character.

"You just let me handle this. Papa's gone, but you're not to worry. I'll take care of everything now."

"All right," said Charlotte pleasantly. She glanced at Ladybug as if she no longer recognized her.

Ladybug quietly looked on, witnessing the final collapse of the two women who formed her family.

Tom turned to her. "We'd better go," he said sadly to the daughter who was being abandoned for a second time.

She nodded.

Just as Ladybug's eyes lingered for a moment in sadness, disappointment, and final farewell on the woman who was her mother, Tom caught sight of something outside the French doors. He tried not to react, but Rachel, who was watching him and who knew every nuance of his face, sensed something was amiss. She followed his glance . . . and smiled.

Through breaks in the oak trees, Tom noticed a man coming up the winding path toward the mansion, a man whose perseverance surprised him, a man who had not slept the previous night but who instead had set out on a lengthy trip following his meeting at the Crossroads. With ruthless persistence in carrying out his duty, this man had no doubt already been to Baton Rouge and Indigo Springs and was now here to arrest Ladybug. Riding up the hill and just minutes away from arriving, accompanied by a deputy, was Sheriff Robert Duran.

# CHAPTER 30

"Why, that looks like the sheriff, Mama!" Gleefully, Rachel pointed outside. She hurried toward the door. "I'll tell him we've got the murderess!"

"Oh no, you won't!" Tom caught Rachel in mid-stride.

With one hand he lifted her up by the waist; with the other, he covered her mouth. She kicked furiously and tried to bite him, but he held her fast as Ladybug grabbed a few fabric scraps lying in a basket, then gagged her sister and helped Tom tie her feet and hands.

Charlotte, still dazed, put up little fight as Tom and Ladybug dispatched of her in the same fashion. Tom dropped each of the bundles inside an armoire and closed its doors while Ladybug undid a few fasteners and peeled off her gown, hoop, and petticoat in one motion. In a corset and pantalets, she jumped over the small mountain of fabric at her feet and threw on the slave's frock.

Tom whispered an instruction in her ear.

She nodded and said pointedly, facing the closed armoires with the women inside: "I know a way to Natchez that'll keep us off the main road."

"Shh! Let's go," said Tom.

Ladybug slid her knife back in its strap on her leg and hastened out of the room, with Tom closing the door behind them.

He grabbed the gun and holster from the senator's desk, and they headed down to the first floor just as two house servants were arriving to begin the day's work.

A morning breeze brushed their faces as the two fugitives shot out the back door and onto the horses that had been brought there for them.

\* \* \* \* \*

Tom and Ladybug were concealed by trees and shrubs along the back roads to Bayou Redbird . . . until they came near the factory. The road on the ridge midway up the hillside made the fugitives more visible. On one side of them was the drop to Cutter's Creek, its stream racing toward the port town where the bayou met the great Mississippi. On the other side was the steep climb to the top of the hill, with its intermittent thickets of foliage and fields of clover. Tom eyed the openness of their new surroundings warily, eager to get past this leg of their trip.

He had traveled this road before, in the opposite direction, when he was leaving the murder scene at the Crossroads Plantation and heading north to Ruby Manor. Then, he had wanted to avenge the death of the man he thought had fought to save his invention from a thief. Now, he was riding alongside the thief and killer, and his all-consuming goal was to help her escape.

Along the way he had constantly looked back, but he saw no sign of the sheriff. Surely the Barnwell women had been discovered and set free, and surely they had told the sheriff what they overheard when tied up in the armoires—Ladybug's comment that she and Tom were headed north to Natchez. Could the sheriff have fallen for the ruse and gone in the wrong direction?

Up ahead the inventor saw the turnoff to the switchback he had taken down to the factory. They were close to town! Would they reach the docks without a snag? Could he dare hope that he and his precious companion would soon be out of danger?

He turned to her, impatient to complete the nerve-racking trip, his anxiety increasing with the openness of the new stretch of road. "Let's go faster!"

Just when they needed to make haste, Ladybug got off her horse.

He looked at her in disbelief. She was standing on the road, ten feet behind him. "What are you doing? We can't stop now!"

She had stopped at the edge of a line of shrubbery and the beginning of a field of clover going up the hill. "This is where I hauled your invention, over this clover to the top of the hill. It's sitting by those trees and shrubs up there." She pointed. "I want to take you to it."

"We don't have time! I'll tell Nick where it is, and he'll ship it to us. We have to move fast now!"

"For the past three months I wanted to get the inventor to the invention. Now that I've done that, I have to leave you here with the tractor and go on *alone*."

He stared at her incredulously. Slowly, he dismounted and faced her. "What's this all about?"

"I once read a newspaper story about a free man who helped a slave escape. He got *ten years* in prison! You'll get worse, because I'm wanted for . . . murder. I can't do that to you, Tom."

He studied the figure on the road, her mouth unsmiling, her gaze direct, her feet firmly planted. Everything about her said she was adamant.

"Listen to me, Ladybug. Every bad thing that's happened to you, from being whipped by Markham to being sold to Fowler to battling with Barnwell—it all happened because of my invention. You risked your life to save it. If there were no other reason, obligation alone would demand that I help you."

"I free you of that obligation."

"I don't want to be freed of it."

"I don't want to live knowing I saved the invention but destroyed the inventor."

"Look, I *choose* to do this. I *want* to do it. We'll talk about that later. But right now, we've got to get out of here!"

He walked toward her, wanting to grab her shoulders and shake some sense into her, then plunk her back on the horse. Suddenly, she grabbed her knife and pointed it at him.

"Put that away." He grinned, walking into the knife.

In a flash, she flicked her wrists so that the blade was pointing directly at her heart. "Stay back!" she warned.

His face froze and his legs stopped in sudden paralysis.

Her hands were steady on the knife and her voice was even, the signs of a deliberate, rather than impulsive, act. "Tom, I wanted to go this route not only to show you where I hid the invention but also to leave you here with it . . ."—her voice was sad but resolute—". . . and to say . . . goodbye."

"*Goodbye?* We've barely said hello."

"If you leave town aiding a murderer and a slave, you'll *never* be able to return. If you come back, you'll be arrested. Good grief, Tom, you could be *hanged*. If you leave here with me now, you'll lose *everything*: your plantation, your bank, your whole life. I can't do that to you. I *won't* do it." The knife blade caught the morning sun and glistened menacingly close to her heart, highlighting her words.

"Don't you think I knew all of what you just said *before* I started this ride with you? I don't intend to come back, not ever. I want to start a new life in the North . . . with *you*."

"That's impossible! You can't even think of that!" She shook her head decisively. "Who would accept you?"

"Would *you?*"

She was stunned by the question.

When she didn't answer, he persisted. "If we were in another place and time, free of everybody's rules, and we could do as we please, then would you . . . say yes?"

All of her fervent wishes for something important to happen in her life seemed to coalesce in her face and voice as she replied. "If we lived in another place and time, in a world where the people who stand in the way, thwarting my dreams like monolithic stone figures, immovable and heartless . . . if we lived in a world free of them, my answer would be yes." Her face softened and her smile caressed him. "*Yes*, Tom."

"But we *can* be free of them, as soon as we get out of here. We're already acting free. In case you haven't noticed, I'm proposing and you're accepting." He looked tenderly at her and nervously at the countryside around them. "Now, if that's settled, we can't linger here! It's too dangerous!"

It apparently wasn't settled. The knife still pointed at her heart. "What you're saying can't be done."

"The whole world isn't Greenbriar, you know." The softness that the subject brought to his face vanished when he saw her hands stiffen around the blade of the knife. The earnest look in her eyes frightened him.

"Tom, my answer was yes for another place and time. For this place and time, it's no! If you help me escape, it'll destroy your life *here*. If you stick with me in the North, it'll destroy your life *there*. I can't let any of that happen!"

"But I *won't* be destroyed! And you won't be either. *Giving up* is what'll destroy us!"

"Every person will shun you. Every door will be closed to you. You'll be ruined."

"There will be places that accept us. And even if there aren't, why would we care? No one can stop us from living as we please. Now's the chance for *both* of us to break free and be masters of ourselves."

"You'll have parties and social gatherings to go to. You'll have business to do, customers to meet, people to deal with, events to attend, entertaining to do in your life. You couldn't have *any* of that with me. If you go any further with me, the risk, the harm, the danger, and the loss will all be yours."

"The *happiness* will be mine too."

His words floated to her in the morning breeze. She stood facing him on the road, her hair swaying in the wind in tempo with the shrubs on the hillside behind her. "But Tom—"

"I'm not leaving you, Ladybug. You're the only one who saw the glory that I saw in my invention. You're the only one who wants to dream new dreams, the only one who isn't blinded by pictures that others paint of the world."

Her dark eyes were filled with desire and fear. She looked as if she wanted simultaneously to run into his arms and to run away. Both urges seemed to be vying within her as she swayed uneasily, her voice now faltering. "But . . . Tom . . ."

"Your mother betrayed the man she loved, and she betrayed herself too. She accepted the world others made for her and spent her life with someone who wasn't her real choice and who didn't make her happy. Is that what you want *me* to do? To betray the person who's *my* choice . . . because I'm afraid to stand up to others and follow my own will?"

She stared at him, speechless.

"I'm not going to betray my choice. . . . Are *you*?" he asked.

Her arms lost some of their tautness, and her fists eased their grip on the knife.

"Well, Ladybug? Do we get to finish what we started this morning?"

He flashed a radiant, lusty smile of supreme self-confidence, like a young David who could slay any Goliath. His proud face and dogged hope slayed her fears. Slowly, the anguish lost its grip on her face and she smiled.

In surrender to what they both wanted, the knife dropped to her side. He rushed up to her and seized the weapon. He crushed her body against him and kissed her hungrily.

She whispered in his arms: "When I punched you the first time we met, I had to do it. Not because I hated you, but because you looked at me then the same way you do now. And I wanted you to look at me like that . . . I wanted you to. . . . From the start . . . I . . . wanted . . . you." He tasted a sweet, warm mouth that found his with a passion that matched his own.

Suddenly, he pushed away. He whirled around and stepped protectively in front of her. He thought he'd heard something. In the same instant Ladybug also reacted; the shrubs rustled behind him as she dove into them.

He reached for his gun. But it was too late.

Up ahead, at the top of the switchback, a man on horseback appeared, his gun already aimed and cocked.

"Drop it!" said Sheriff Duran.

# CHAPTER 31

"You heard me. Drop it!" Duran ordered.

Tom dropped his gun.

"The knife too."

Tom complied.

"Get up here, Jeff, fast!" The sheriff called to his deputy, who was just coming into view up the switchback. "Get the girl! She jumped into the bushes behind him."

"Don't shoot her!" Tom yelled. "She's unarmed!"

In a flash, the deputy dismounted from his horse.

"Sheriff, please!" Tom pressed.

"Jeff, restraint . . . if possible," said the sheriff as the deputy disappeared into the brush on the hillside.

Duran rode up to Tom, dismounted, and picked up the weapons, all the while aiming his gun at the inventor. The two men faced each other on the road while the shrubs on the hillside swayed helter-skelter in the deputy's search. The sheriff waited hopefully—and Tom waited grimly—for the result.

"When the Barnwell women told me you were helping the girl escape, I reckoned you'd head south to your bank. So when they told me you let it slip that you're going north, even if it came from the girl, I'm not buying it. I figured you wouldn't be that careless. I didn't underestimate you, as you apparently did me."

"It seems I've been outwitted," Tom conceded. "But how'd you know I'd take this road?"

"I didn't. You see, I didn't want to take the *wrong* road and miss you, and I didn't want to take the *right* road and risk you seeing me and slipping away. So instead I took a flatboat."

"I see." Tom nodded in acknowledgment of the man's keen intelligence. Like other plantations with water access, Ruby Manor had flatboats on hand to float cotton downstream to the steamship docks. These boats were ample for carrying horses as well.

"The current was brisk, so I reckoned I'd get down the creek to Redbird before you did, then wait for you to arrive." The distance by boat was shorter than by land. "But then you surprised me when I spotted you and the girl on this ridge."

Tom filled in the rest. "So you kept your boat close to the shore, out of our view, then you docked at the factory and came up the switchback."

"Too bad you didn't work that out sooner."

"You're good at your job, Sheriff. I assume that job is to serve the cause of justice. That's why I have things to tell you that I'm sure the Barnwell women left out, since they serve a different cause."

"After you attacked them and imprisoned them in their closets, I'm sure they weren't feeling up to par."

"Did the women tell you that Rachel and Ladybug are sisters?"

"Haven't we all figured out that the girl traces back to the senator?"

"But she doesn't. Rachel and Ladybug have the same *mother*, Charlotte Barnwell."

"Are you *serious?*"

"Did the women leave that out of their report to you? Charlotte, Rachel, and Ladybug *all* have the same birthmark over their hearts."

Tom knew that the revelation about Greenbriar's grande dame, the one woman beyond reproach, stunned the sheriff—as it would everyone else in town.

"After I fired Bret Markham, he set a torch to my house."

"The Barnwell women told me."

"I sent a note to you reporting it, but you had already left for Baton Rouge and were on your way back by then, weren't you?"

"Like you said, I'm good at my job."

"The possibility that Markham could retaliate against the Barnwells, along with our injuries from the fire, brought me to Ruby Manor with a slave I bought three months ago. After I got there, I found out her real identity. The birthmarks on her and the Barnwell women—and the truth about their relationship—came out this morning at Ruby Manor, and I was a witness."

Tom proceeded to tell him about Charlotte's lover who built Ruby Manor, Leanna's birth, the empty casket, the enraged Wiley Barnwell drowning Leanna's father despite Charlotte's admission that it was she who started the affair. The inventor described how Charlotte's child was reared in slavery by Polly and renamed Ladybug, and how he came to buy her from Fowler without knowing the seller's or slave's identity until a few hours ago. He related how Ladybug was whipped by Markham, chased by Nash, sold by Barnwell, and raped by Fowler.

Tom paused for a response from the man whose eyes drilled through him like two intense beacons. The sheriff simply waited to hear the rest, so Tom continued.

"If you see the birthmarks of the three women, as I have, their relationship will be obvious. If you dig up the casket of Leanna Barnwell, you'll find it empty. And if you read Polly's note in her plantation journal nineteen years ago about the funeral for Ruby Manor's carpenter-slave, Daniel, I think you'll find that it occurred immediately after the birth date marked on Leanna's fake tombstone. If you can speak to Charlotte before Rachel manages to dominate her completely, you might get her to admit all of this, as she did to me and Ladybug. She's terrified of a public scandal, but if you talk to her in private, you might be able to capture these facts from what's left of her sanity."

The sheriff remained stone-faced.

"So you see, Sheriff, Ladybug was born *free* as the child of a white woman. But she was abandoned to slavery by her mother. She was sold to a brute by Wiley Barnwell, the finest, most upstanding citizen of your town, who also murdered her father. What happened to her has everything to do with servitude, abuse, and cruelty and nothing at all to do with murder. You know, self-defense isn't a crime."

The sheriff continued to stare at Tom without blinking.

"Now, if you're good at your work, Sheriff, which you are, and if your job is to serve justice, which I think you pride yourself on, then tell me this: Will Charlotte ever be tried for abandoning her daughter to slavery? Will Fowler ever be tried for raping her? Was Wiley Barnwell ever tried for drowning Ladybug's father, Daniel? Where has justice been for Ladybug's whole life?"

"What happened the night of the murder?" The sheriff proceeded on his own track. "Fowler says she took his horse and went missing. That gives her the opportunity. Barnwell's mistreatment of her provides the motive."

"Duran, I swear to you, that can all be explained. She's not a murderer. But her mother and sister will *never* let the truth be made public about her birth and status as a free woman, so she can't step forward to tell her story and ever hope to be treated fairly. You *must* know that Barnwell's political friends will come to Charlotte and Rachel's aid. All the power Barnwell had amassed will come to bear to dispose of this defenseless girl, just as he disposed of her father."

Tom closed his eyes painfully at the thought of Ladybug in the town's grip.

"In the name of justice, Duran, you can't deliver her to an angry mob, or to a mock slave tribunal where Barnwell's friends will sentence her to hang."

"I'd have to be *dead* before any mob would get her from my custody. As for a trial, far as I'm concerned, everything will be done to get her one. That would hold with me whether she was free or not."

Tom believed him. He wondered how many others felt as he and Duran did but were silenced by a small elite trying desperately to prop up an empire built on a fault line and ready to split wide open under their feet.

"Even if she got a trial, tell me, Duran, when the jury is put together from a population outnumbered eight to one by a people it's enslaving, and when it lives in constant fear of a rebellion, and when the defendant is accused of doing the very thing they dread the most—*how* can they be impartial? I believe *you* would be, but you're not one of them."

The adversaries looked at each other with a grudging respect.

"In the name of justice, you *must* let her go and let me help her!"

"Tom, it's not for me—or you—to decide her guilt or innocence. That's for the court. And it's not for me to justify myself to you, so you should know what an exception I'm making to try to give you . . . hope."

Tom felt certain that Duran knew the matter was deeply personal to him.

"I intend to ferret out the evidence you claim exists, like the birthmarks and the empty casket, to establish the suspect's status at birth; then I'll get her all the legal protections I can. I want justice, and I'll get justice," Duran said earnestly.

"You'll get her *killed* with your well-intentioned—but doomed—quest for justice in this case."

"I'm afraid you have no say in the matter, Tom."

"Look, Duran, Rachel is consumed with resentment toward her sister, and she's determined to thwart your efforts. She's going to claim her mother is ill and take her for a lengthy trip abroad to recuperate, so you'll get nowhere trying to reveal their birthmarks. Ladybug will be summarily tried as a slave and *hanged*, with the help of the Barnwells' attorney, the judges, and the planters on the tribunal—all of whom are their personal friends. I don't think you'd want it on your conscience that you delivered a defenseless young woman to a system rigged against her."

"I have grounds to arrest her, and I will. I have grounds to arrest you too, which you've foolishly given me!" A crack seemed to be forming in the sheriff's marble countenance. He scolded Tom like a concerned older brother.

"Your face tells me you don't want to arrest me, and perhaps not her either. Shouldn't you examine an inkling that might be telling you there are extenuating circumstances involved here?"

The sheriff shook his head with more vigor than was necessary to deny Tom's notion, as if he were trying to shake off his own misgivings. "My only inkling is to enforce the law and carry out justice."

"But in this case, the law *doesn't* carry out justice. It serves a different master. By enforcing the law, you'll be sabotaging justice and delivering an innocent to the hangman. You'll never be able to claim you're a man of justice again."

The sheriff's hand stiffened around his gun. "You have a choice, Tom. You can cooperate and coax the girl to give herself up—I think she'll come out if she hears you urge her—or when we find her, it might not be pretty. Either way, I'm running you both in. You have no choice about that."

"*You're* the one who has a choice, Duran. If you bring Ladybug in to face the rage, fear, and prejudice of this town, you'll need to replace that figure you pin so proudly over your heart." Tom pointed to the sheriff's badge.

Duran involuntarily glanced down at the emblem of the blindfolded goddess of justice on the silver badge he kept so carefully shined.

"You're at a crossroads, Sheriff. You have to choose between justice and a corrupt law. And Ladybug's life hangs in the balance."

With one hand, the sheriff kept his gun aimed at Tom; with the other, he reached up for a pair of handcuffs strapped to his saddle. "I serve justice and enforce the law, which are one and the same thing."

"What if they're *not* the same thing at all? Which one do you choose?"

"Enough! Shut up, Tom!"

"If you take us in, you'll have to exchange your badge for one with a figure that took off her blindfold to wink at power and tip her scales to the politically connected. Which do you want to serve—a goddess or a whore?"

As the sheriff was unstrapping the handcuffs, he looked rattled by Tom's words. He hesitated in mid-motion. His face looked like a battlefield for his emotions; his brows were furrowed in doubt and his lips pursed in resolve. Then he breathed deeply and made his choice. He completed the motion and grabbed the cuffs. The man who had been ready to hang his own uncle now looked at Tom with the same unflinching eyes. "Mr. Edmunton, you're under arrest for aiding and abetting a fugitive from justice."

The sheriff raised his voice and called into the bushes. "Jeff! Jeff, come out here."

Soon the deputy appeared from the hillside and walked toward the sheriff. "I can't find her yet, but I reckon she didn't stray far. For one thing, *he's* here, and he's her ticket out." The deputy pointed to Tom. "And I didn't hear no rustlin', so by the time I got in there, she coulda tucked herself in some good hidin' spot close by."

The sheriff gave him the handcuffs. "Bind him up and tie him to a tree. Then go back in and look some more. I'll search with you. Move fast!"

Tom stood in the road by the spot where Ladybug had stopped. Her riderless horse next to him was a grim reminder that she might not be coming back.

"Hands behind your back," ordered the sheriff.

Tom complied.

The sheriff got back on his mount, his gun still pointing at Tom, while he spoke to his deputy. "I'll scale the hill and look up there on horseback." He moved a few paces up the clover field, impatient to climb the hill as soon as the inventor was bound. "Hurry up, Jeff."

The deputy clicked the handcuffs open and was about to place them on Tom's wrists.

The inventor's head dropped, his face no longer visible. He stood disconsolately waiting to be shackled.

Then suddenly in the distance, Tom heard a sound he knew well. His head shot up and his heart pounded with hope.

A rumble rocked the tranquil air like thunder. It vibrated the ground under the men. Then a barrage of sputtering and clanging assaulted the air, the likes of which neither the lawmen nor the horses had ever heard. The lawmen gasped in astonishment and the horses shrieked as an unknown menace suddenly came toward them.

The horse that Tom had been riding ran away. The deputy's steed took off after it. As Jeff tried to stop it, the frightened animal knocked the manacles out of his hand and sprinted away. The distracted deputy chased after his horse.

The sheriff's horse bucked and threw him. Before it too fled, the animal stomped the ground a few times in high agitation, while Duran twisted and turned, struggling to avoid being trampled by panicked hooves.

Tom was the only calm figure in the scramble. At the start of the commotion, he grabbed the reins of Ladybug's horse next to him, held its nose down firmly, and turned the animal around to spare it the scene that jolted its brethren.

Then he looked up the hill at the cause of the bedlam. He saw—coming over the top and rolling down the clover field and heading directly at the men and their animals—his tractor. Sitting in the driver's seat, her expression tinged with fear but wild with exhilaration, was Ladybug.

# CHAPTER 32

Tom's face held the immense relief of a father reunited with a lost child. As the tractor jaunted down the hill, its cheerful bounce and loud clangs made it look to him like a toddler taking its first steps. The new age flashed before him in a split-second rush of excitement.

But his thrill instantly turned to fear. The prototype tractor carrying its stunning driver was going too fast . . . and it *had no brake.*

He watched in mounting horror as the tractor careened down, swerving from side to side because Ladybug was unaccustomed to the steering wheel and prey to a device that wasn't built to handle steep hills or sudden turns. By driving directly downhill toward the lawmen, Ladybug caught them off guard and saved Tom and herself from capture. Now Tom would have to guide her in driving the device, for if she couldn't keep the tractor stable and make the turn onto the road on the ridge, she could tumble down to the creek and be—

The sheriff's steed had run away, following the other two horses and the deputy chasing after them. Duran was left wheezing and pale, his body weakened, his legs unsteady. He looked as if he had taken a hoof to the abdomen and gotten the wind knocked out of him. He rose, faltered a few steps, lost his balance, and fell again.

With the lawmen foiled, Ladybug instinctively tried changing direction to traverse the hill instead of plunging straight down. She was moving away from Tom, who quickly mounted the horse he had held onto firmly during the commotion. He moved along the road they had been taking to town, to meet her as she descended. He shouted directions to her, trying to guide her through the perils of a terrain that he himself had never experienced with the tractor.

He worked feverishly to get Ladybug onto the flat road along the ridge. Once on level ground, they could safely bring the tractor to a stop, get her onto his horse, and escape before the lawmen could resume their pursuit. That was his plan. But the tractor was not obliging.

She obeyed the instructions he fired at her, steering this way and that, avoiding a boulder, a hollow, and a sharp step down off the hill. In a spot with a gentler slope, she maneuvered onto the flat road. He sighed in relief. She had managed to avoid the drop to the creek.

But because the tractor was built high off the ground for working unplowed fields, it tended to be unstable. The bounce down from the hill to the road jerked it off balance. It teetered to one side on two wheels. The jolt threw Ladybug out of her seat. Her hair blew wildly and her legs slipped out the side. She was about to be thrown under the vehicle and run over by the rear wheels.

"Grab the column under the steering wheel!" Tom yelled.

She managed to swing an arm around the sturdy column. Then she struggled to pull herself back onto the seat.

Tom watched in horror as his benign invention was fast becoming a death trap. He tried to get alongside Ladybug so he could pull her onto the safety of his horse, but when he came close to the device, the animal rebelled. It neighed and reared, insisting on keeping its distance from the blaring motor that was spewing exhaust fumes and intermittently backfiring. Tom had to fight with the animal simply to remain behind her.

Just as Ladybug was trying to hoist herself back on and regain control of the steering wheel, the tractor came to the fork in the road.

"Steer to the right. Don't go down the switchback!" Tom shouted.

The vehicle was drifting to the left.

"Stay right, on the flat road. Stay right! Right!"

It was too late. Before she could change direction, the tractor had swayed onto the jagged switchback with its steep descent and hairpin turns toward the factory and creek.

He needed to slow her down. But what happened next did just the opposite. He heard the gears slip into neutral. Without them engaged and limiting the speed, the tractor began accelerating dangerously.

He agonized. She needed to get the engine back into gear to slow it down. But shifting gears on the downhill acceleration was risky because any abrupt decrease in speed could catapult her off. Which of the three forward gears would he pick to slow her down without jolting the device? As these thoughts tumbled on their own wild, split-second ride through his mind, he decided.

"You need to shift into intermediate gear to slow down." He had to yell to overcome the engine sounds and their distance apart, yet he tried to quell his panic at the situation by filling his voice with confidence. "Take the turn first. About a full turn of the wheel."

He stared with a scientist's intensity and a lover's worry as she maneuvered her first turn. The wheels squealed with the strain, but she made it—barely—on two of them. She would have to slow down before the next turn, or the increasing acceleration would make the maneuver impossible.

"Grab the lever under the steering wheel on the right. Push it away from you halfway. . . . With your right foot, depress the clutch pedal all the way to the floor. . . ." He rapidly fired instructions, taking a second between each one to let her execute the moves. "Grab the gear shift, the big stick on your left. Pull it all the way out to the left, then move it backward. . . ."

Her face was intent as she listened, watched the road, and glanced down to find the controls.

"Now ease your foot off the clutch. Easy now!"

He heard the gear engage and saw the vehicle slow down without jarring. "Good!"

The next turn went more smoothly, with Ladybug taking it on all four wheels. "Very good!" he said encouragingly.

She waved a hand to him in victory when a bump in the road took all four wheels off the ground. No sooner did she steady the tractor after that bump than it became airborne again over another one. The wheels of the wobbling vehicle found the ground as her next turn approached.

He continued to direct her. She was handling every obstacle the road put before her. If she could make it to the bottom of the switchback, then they could slow the device to a halt, get her on his horse, and race to town. That was his hope. But quickly it was doused.

Tom glanced behind him to see a new terror. The sheriff and deputy were back on their horses and racing down the switchback.

When Ladybug finished her next turn, she glanced back and saw them too. "Tom!" she screamed. She held the wheel with a white-knuckled grip.

"I see them. Just keep driving." He tried to sound calm as he rapidly searched his mind for a new plan.

He couldn't wait for Ladybug to get to the bottom of the switchback. By then, their pursuers would overtake them. He would have to snare her *now*. Once again, he tried the horse. He snapped his whip and dug his heels into the animal to get it to overtake the invention. But the reluctant beast reared its refusal, and Tom struggled to avoid being thrown.

If he could get out in front of the invention, so the horse wouldn't see the tractor or hear the full power of its blasts, then, he thought, he could slow down and maneuver next to her.

He jerked the horse off the switchback and onto the hillside. He glanced back to see the sheriff and deputy gaining on them. "I'll meet you further down," he told Ladybug.

His new route alongside the switchback was a shortcut down the hill through the brush. He whizzed through the uneven ground with the horse's hooves slipping on the dusty terrain. He saw Ladybug swerve to avoid an outcrop at the next turn. He heard the ominous sound of metal scraping against rock and saw a large bolt fly into the air. It was one of the bolts that fastened the gasoline tank to the tractor. The tank had rubbed against the rock and was now dangling and about to fall off. Its cap had loosened. He saw a spark—

Without a moment to spare, he drove his horse over a dead tree, circled around shrubs and rocks, then jumped back onto the switchback with the horse now ahead of the device and, as he had hoped, less disturbed by it. Tom slowed down and eased alongside of Ladybug, his arm outstretched to give her a hand.

"Jump!" he ordered.

She had apparently not seen the spark from her seat. Strong-willed and protective of the device that she had gone to great lengths to rescue, she hesitated. "Can we save it, Tom? Can we?"

The sheriff and his deputy appeared behind them, close enough for Tom to see the implacable look on Duran's face. The lawman yelled: "Halt now! Stop that thing!"

Duran fired a warning shot into the sky.

Tom grabbed Ladybug roughly by the arm and yanked her out of the seat. "Hurry! It's gonna explode—"

Just then another spark flashed, this one larger and more menacing. It caught her eyes, and she gasped in terror.

The sheriff bellowed behind them, his voice reaching its lowest possible range. "Stop, Tom, or we'll shoot!"

Ladybug, now galvanized, leaped onto the horse, straddled the animal behind Tom, and hung on for her life.

The lawmen's guns were cocked and aimed. Duran yelled to his deputy: "Shoot!"

With one violent kick, Tom hit the gasoline tank. It spun into the air as his horse streaked away.

The cap flew off the tank and the gasoline fumes instantly met the engine's hot air in a torrid dance. Behind the fugitives, the tractor exploded with the force of a cannon, shaking the earth and thundering through the air. The blast sent the lawmen hurling off the road, with their gunshots flying astray. Tom glanced back to see the tractor in a fireball of flames and behind it a gruesome mass of hooves, tails, and animal torsos amid twisted arms and legs on human bodies—all tumbling toward the creek. He heard the men cry out in pain. They were alive, but they looked too injured to continue their pursuit. He figured they'd be stuck there for a while before a passing flatboat came along and aided them.

Tom raced the horse toward town, with Ladybug behind him. On their first ride together, she had rigorously avoided touching him. On this one, she moved her body and legs flush against him, wrapped her arms tightly around his waist, and pressed the side of her face affectionately against his back as one would clutch a rare treasure.

She glanced back at the explosion with profound sadness. "Tom, your invention! It's gone! . . . It's because of *me* that it's destroyed."

"*You* didn't destroy it." He thought of the instability in the design, the lack of brakes, the slippage of the gears, the loss of control down the hill, the placement of the gasoline tank. He sighed. There was a lot more work to be done. In a final farewell, he painfully looked back at the heap of metal charring in the blaze on the road. His voice heavy with disappointment, he said, "It's not ready for the new age yet." Then he turned to her, and couldn't help but smile with newfound hope. "But *we* are!"

She cocked her head to gaze into his eyes. "Yes, *we are!*"

A change had come over her, he noticed. The explosive shocks rocking their lives that day had shattered the wall that hid her from the world and from him. Her eyes squinted in the sunlight, like someone coming out of a long confinement to experience a cloudless summer day. She smiled at him with the fearless joy that only freedom can bring.

A change had come over him too. After his painful disillusionments with his fellow planters, his mentor, and the woman he once loved—people blind to the new age who had tried to destroy him and his work—he had finally found his beautiful defender and like spirit. He squeezed the arms wrapped tightly around his waist and looked eagerly to the road ahead.

As the two fugitives headed toward their future, they laughed—in relief, in triumph, in celebration of the great promise of their lives. They laughed until the sun-soaked air around them echoed with the sound of their joy.

# EPILOGUE

Tom and Ladybug escaped from the South and began their lives anew. They married. They concealed their identities, stayed abroad for a spell, and when they thought it was safe, finally settled in Philadelphia, choosing a community known for its tolerance and strong abolitionist sentiments.

Through furtive letters and newspaper clippings from the only person in Greenbriar who knew Tom's whereabouts—his overseer, Nick—the inventor kept tabs on events there that affected his and Ladybug's lives.

He learned that after the explosion a flatboat had come along to rescue the sheriff and deputy. The lawmen survived, although they sustained lacerations and broken bones. Fresh from having his broken leg set, the sheriff hobbled to his office on crutches, wasting no time in resuming his work on the Barnwell murder case. But he soon encountered obstacles. When he sought to exhume Leanna Barnwell's casket to investigate Tom's claim about Ladybug's true identity and free-person status, the judge, a friend of the Barnwells, denied his request. When the sheriff tried to have Mrs. Barnwell examined to determine if there was a connection between a birthmark she allegedly possessed and the one seen on his suspect, he found that Charlotte had abruptly left town with her daughter on a long journey abroad and was therefore unavailable for any inspection.

Then two pseudonymous articles appeared in the local newspapers. One charged that Sheriff Robert Duran had acted suspiciously in a recent burglary case in which the stolen goods were never recovered. The other article, through nefarious assertions and unnamed sources, claimed that Duran had actually recovered the stolen goods and kept them for himself. There were rumors that the charges against Duran stemmed from the pen of Rachel's new fiancé, Nash Nottingham, whom she had placed in charge of the

Crossroads Plantation during her voyage. When she later returned home, Nash received the prize of her hand, along with the Crossroads as a wedding present from her mother, a reward he seemed happy to claim with the currency of his self-respect.

Then came the new local statute proposed by an official who was another friend of the Barnwells. It required that a free person of color accused of a crime receive the same legal treatment as a slave, with no exceptions. The reason such a statute would be introduced, the arguments against it, and a review of whether it was even compatible with the state's criminal code were matters that no one raised, debated, or cared to know.

Then came the day when Sheriff Robert Duran vanished without a trace. He left a simple note on his desk announcing his resignation, and next to it, his badge with Lady Justice. He had not polished the silver badge of late, so the figure on it had become tarnished. That day the file on the Barnwell murder case, including all notes on the current suspect the sheriff was pursuing and the man aiding her, vanished with him. Amid the disarray caused by the sheriff's vacancy and the missing records, as well as by the rapidly escalating tensions on the eve of the war with the North, the case was pushed to the sidelines—to Rachel Barnwell's disappointment.

When the Barnwell women returned from their trip, a meek and melancholy Charlotte accepted, and perhaps even welcomed, the loss of urgency about the case. But she was overshadowed by her daughter, who prodded the officials, insisting that her father's killer be caught. However, Rachel too hesitated after receiving an anonymous letter that threatened to make public her mother's extramarital affair and secret daughter if she continued pursuing the case. Rachel knew, but couldn't prove, that the letter came from the man who had disappeared from the town and from her life but who still eerily watched her moves, like a phantom that could strike unexpectedly, then vaporize again. With the success of his escape, which thwarted her plan for her sister, she knew she was taking a chance in trying to outwit him. In the end, her fear of scandal overrode the desire to see her sister captured and hanged, no matter how satisfying the latter would have been. She dropped the matter, and the case went cold.

With the aid of an attorney, Tom sold his bank and plantation, dissolving all of his ties to Greenbriar and Bayou Redbird. Nick and his brothers purchased Indigo Springs. They were able to afford the plantation because Tom, refusing to trade in human beings, placed no price on the slaves but only on the land, which lowered the cost substantially. In return, Nick agreed to implement the new work system that Tom had outlined with the bondsmen before his departure, giving them greater freedom and personal reward for their labor.

Nick also kept the plantation's school running. As a replacement for its dedicated founder and first teacher, he hired a fine instructor with the courage to accept a noble assignment in disregard of a cruel and unjust law: Kate Markham.

From a story in a Greenbriar newspaper that Nick sent him, Tom learned the fate of her brother, Bret. Once free from the moral admonitions of his employer, Polly Barnwell, and of his sister, Kate, and further emboldened by his success at arson, Bret Markham crossed the line into a life of crime. His new occupation provided an outlet for his escalating resentment for anyone who had achieved more than he had and who was therefore, in his eyes, responsible for his misfortunes. From the news story, Tom learned that Markham had fled to Mississippi, where he staged a series of burglaries, always targeting the homes of the rich. During one of them, he was fatally shot. The man who lived by violence died by it too.

Years later, Tom heard from someone else. Through Nick, the inventor received a letter sent to him at Indigo Springs. It came from a man who had promised to write but who had apparently postponed doing so until he had overcome the struggles and hardships brought on by his escape and by the great war that soon followed. He waited until his misfortune was past and success was his new condition. The writer included a photograph of himself standing in front of a store in Cincinnati that looked remarkably similar to a shop in Paris, the one from the book in Tom's plantation library that the writer's teacher had shown him. Tom and Ladybug cheered wildly at the picture of a smiling man in a tall chef's hat standing under a sign that read "Jerome's Pastries." Tom wasn't surprised that Jerome's sharp wits and indomitable will had prevailed in his battle with the two-headed snake he'd once feared.

Imbued with the spirit of the new age, Tom and Ladybug created their own new existence. After the war, they returned to the endeavors they yearned to pursue. Their lives, their work, and their love for each other ignited their days with the bright spark of happiness.

They opened a school where Ladybug taught children of all races and honed the real motor of the new age: the free, inquiring minds of the young. She taught her students the mental skills needed to become masters of themselves, preparing them to be independent, self-reliant, and ready to flourish in the industry, progress, and freedom of a new age.

Tom continued his work as an inventor and opened a manufacturing plant that designed and fabricated machines of every kind for the growing industrial age. He kept a laboratory where he developed innovations for machines and devices that played an important role in the burgeoning industrial sector, and he accumulated many patents. His passion was always the small motor vehicle for farming and transportation with the revolutionary engine that would power the modern age. He continued his work on the new device and made many contributions toward its development. However, he came to realized that the tractor was still in its infancy. Its incredible complexities would require a few more decades of work and the efforts of other inventors as well. Eventually, it did indeed change the world and amass fortunes for those involved with its launch and wide-scale use, as Tom had foreseen.

As the Civil War ended the scourge of slavery and the modern age began, Tom and Ladybug stood at the crossroads of history. They witnessed the spectacular era of man's intellect unleashed, of his ability to grasp science, to realize the immense practical applications of its principles, and to create breathtaking industries. They saw a new age of power, not of man harnessing other men but of man harnessing the great potential of nature through science to vastly improve human life. They saw a peaceful, prosperous world of commerce emerge, with abundant food and a growing array of innovative products readily available on a grand scale. They saw man at his finest: passionate, creative, brilliant, and free. And they saw his great mental gifts and productive capacity bestow on the world an unimaginable progress.

But Tom and Ladybug also began to see ominous signs of the old age creeping in. Although the immense evil of slavery had been eradicated, the forces driving the old era stubbornly persisted. Those forces, they realized, hadn't originated in the Old South, nor would they die with it. Since humans had first appeared, those forces had ruled. Now they were eager to gain a footing in a new world that had for a time risen above them. And there were troubling signs that they would succeed.

Man had made himself wings to fly across the heavens, but like Icarus of the old legend, he came too close to the sun, daring to roam in the province of the gods. Icarus had soared exultantly up and up, paying no heed to any limits on his flight, and then the gods had melted his wings and dropped him into the sea.

Like Icarus, the people of the new age soon found the grand sphere of their flight shrinking. More and more, new masters and overseers emerged to pull them down. The rulers and subjects took on different forms, but the struggle remained the same as it had always been. The men of the new age saw the fierce independence of their will, the sweeping range of their actions, and the abundant fruits of their efforts slip into the hands of new overlords.

The new players, Tom realized, were remarkably similar to the characters he thought he had left behind in the dying age.

He saw the new Nash Nottinghams, who wanted to expend no effort but merely to tap into the efforts of others to support their life of comfort. Indolence, incompetence, and privilege were not just the province of the old aristocracy, Tom observed, but the goal of a fresh crop of Nashes of various social and economic groups. These modern Nashes were all those who were trying to get someone else to pay for their particular needs, and this time finding a virtually unlimited new revenue stream in the public till.

Tom saw the new Ted Coopers, whose pragmatic goals superseded any concern for moral standards in their dealings with others. The new Coopers didn't have plantations that used forced labor, but they had other businesses, causes, and interests for which they sought special privileges that they couldn't obtain through free commerce and voluntary interactions. As the original Cooper did before them, they tried to elect politicians like Wiley Barnwell in order to enact laws and regulations that favored them, to the detriment of others. Political pull replaced free trade and competition as their enterprise.

Tom saw the new Wiley Barnwells emerge, the leaders who tried to put the friendly face of goodness on the baseness of ruling others. These new Barnwells didn't seek to control slaves in order to obtain their labor but instead sought to control citizens in order to obtain their political allegiance. They lured people away from the glory of being masters of themselves with the great opiate of security. They painted a sparkling new age of unprecedented opportunity as a house of horrors, fraught with peril, where men were helpless if guided by their own intelligence and efforts. Tom heard the new Barnwells sounding just like the old senator from Greenbriar when they declared that their power over their subjects sprang from noble intentions, that it was for the citizens' own good, that their charges were the little people who couldn't care for themselves and needed leaders to look after them. Tom saw these modern masters revel in their newfound positions of power and nurture at all costs the dependence of others that they were creating.

Tom saw the new Bret Markhams arise in the modern world, men who had no interest in cultivating their minds but who wanted to make their mark on the world through fists, whips, and guns. Instead of beating slaves in a field, he saw these new Markhams become leaders of nations, introducing violence on a grand scale, with the worst of mankind ruling the best, with the men who burn libraries ruling those who read and write the books that fill them.

Tom saw too the more sophisticated versions of Markham, who would never view themselves as related to such an unsavory creature as the old overseer, yet they were filled with the same resentment and envy toward those who had achieved more than they had. These new Markhams spent their time not on plantations scorning their employers but in intellectual circles scorning the producers. Tom heard them using high-sounding words, but what he saw was Markham's old sneer when they attacked and denigrated the productive and successful. These new Markhams didn't find it necessary to burn the houses of those they envied; instead, they only had to take the possessions out of them to give away to those who didn't earn them. While Markham the overseer made no higher claims for his urges to cut the rich down to size, the refined Markhams hailed their similar desires as a new form of justice.

Tom saw the new Charlotte and Rachel Barnwells also emerge in the modern age. They gathered in the press, at political parties, in literary circles, and at the universities. They were the new elite who didn't question the people in power but accepted and backed them in order to enjoy the benefits and prestige of being part of the favored class.

Tom saw that the representatives of the dying age knew how to use a powerful weapon to give them a stronghold. While the men who conquered nature created the machinery of industry, the men who conquered other men grabbed the machinery of the state. Their weapon was the law. Tom saw a whole slew of new acts, edicts, and rulings crop up. These laws were aimed not at curbing criminality but at curbing productivity. The new statutes clipped the wings of man so that he could no longer surge into the sky to pursue his dream of daring but instead had to seek the permission of new masters before every flight. Tom saw the rule of law seized from the hands of Lady Justice and pulled into the folds of the power brokers.

As Tom saw all the old types that had plagued man in the past now vying for control of the modern world, he knew that the dying age would not go down easily. He, as well as Ladybug, who thought as he did, came to realize: Not only was the tractor in its infancy but man too was in his infancy.

They saw that the forces of the dying age had survived all epochs of man. But the current age, they knew, was unprecedented. Man the infant was fast becoming a toddler, taking his first steps and discovering the early morning country road of freedom. Tom and Ladybug knew that mankind would not reach maturity until the day when people fully grasped the notion that had impelled the two of them in their own struggles, the notion that everyone must be a master of himself.

When men understand that their greatest gift is their intelligence, that their glory is to use it, that their own will is their trusted guide to chart their course, that their labors are theirs to choose, that the fruits of them are theirs to keep, and that surrendering this immense power to the rule of others is beneath the dignity of man—that is when the new age will soar to heights unimaginable.

That is when Icarus will fly into the vast, cloudless sky, and he will once again dare to reach the sun. But this time his wings will hold strong.

# IF YOU ENJOYED THIS BOOK

Please help sell it by giving it a short review at www.Amazon.com.

And enjoy a copy of Gen LaGreca's other acclaimed novel
**Noble Vision**
available in ebook, paperback, and hardcover editions.

# ABOUT THE AUTHOR

Genevieve (Gen) LaGreca is a Chicago writer whose first novel, *Noble Vision*, won a *ForeWord* magazine Book of the Year Award and was a finalist in the *Writer's Digest* International Book Awards—two of the most prestigious national literary honors in independent publishing.

Aside from fiction, Gen also writes social commentary. Her articles have appeared in the *Orange County Register*, *Daily Caller*, *Real Clear Markets*, *Gainesville Sun*, *Mises Daily*, and other publications. She has been a lively guest, discussing her writing on talk-radio programs.

Why does she like writing fiction? "Ever since I read *Gone With the Wind* at age 13, I've been enthralled by sweeping novels that capture a historic moment in an unforgettable way," Gen explains. "I want to tell stories of unusual people doing unusual things, stories with something vitally important to say, and stories that inspire us to reach for our highest dreams—through the spellbinding magic of fiction."

Gen is currently working on a third novel, and she has completed the screenplay adaptation of *Noble Vision*. For more information, see www.wingedvictorypress.com.

You may contact Gen at glagreca@wingedvictorypress.com.